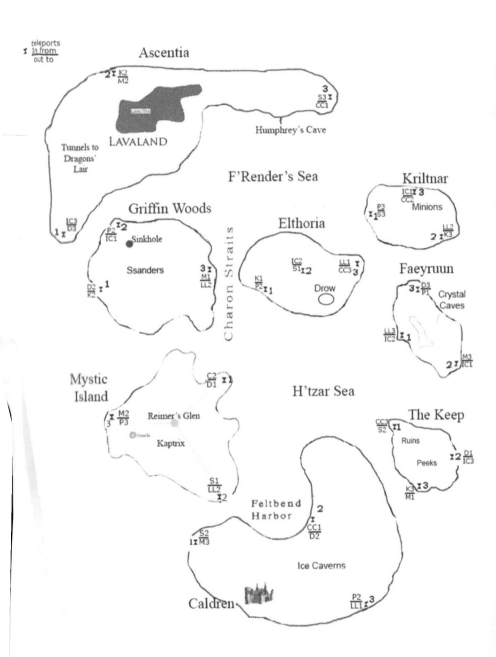

A J. & J. ADVENTURE

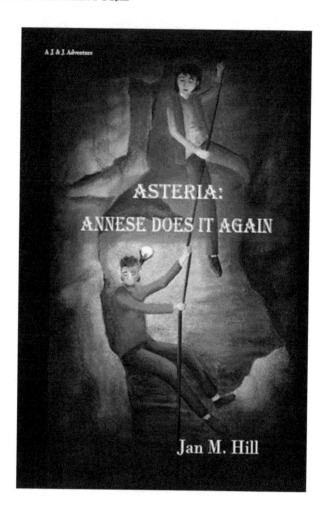

By Jan M. Hill
2021

Cover Art by Katie Cuthbert

NOTE

While Whidbey Island, Washington, is indeed a real and beautiful place, the locales and caves of this novel are not. Any references to real people or places is strictly coincidental.

DEDICATION

This book is dedicated to my son Tyler, whose curiosity and kind heart belong everywhere. Thank you for being my backboard and stress breaker. I forever appreciated your ability to make me laugh, and your willingness to work through the battle scenes with me.

THANKS

My heartfelt thanks go out to my children and their friends for continually challenging me to write more quests and adventures. See you at the D&D table, guys!

And to Christian, James, Rosemary, Maddie, Kylan, and Liam for being my Beta readers and trailer voices. Your input has been invaluable!

TABLE OF CONTENTS

PROLOG

Jugene sighed as he stared at the blank crystal ball on the table. His tired gray eyes just wanted to close. The position of the ex-prince's personal wizard was definitely taking a toll on him. Still, he would do his best.

He pulled the leather from his hair, letting the long, matted, brown hair drop down his back. What he'd give for a bath! He glanced around. Nothing but rock and some furniture. They had taken refuge in the caves. He didn't even know what the weather was outside.

Life for the last... how many months?... had gone downhill fast. They had gone from a life of luxury to a life of hiding. The caves were cold, especially at night. Food was scarce. They often raided the palace's store hold for supplies, especially for Mikkel's life elixir. He heaved a sigh as a sound came from behind him.

The tall, thin man with graying black hair dropped another supply sack on the ground. His glare didn't help Jugene's mood. He rose to help Mikkel put the supplies away.

"Here's all I could get," he grumbled. "We're going to have to figure another way in there. The guards are catching on."

Jugene simply nodded. Of course, it would be up to him to figure out a way past the guards.

"Any luck?" the man asked.

"I'm sorry, your highness," the young wizard replied in a sad voice. "There is nothing."

"Why not? Where could they have disappeared to? You've been searching for months!" the man began angrily. Patience was not his forte.

"Did you not read the prophecy?" Jugene replied patiently. "The boys are not from here. I don't know where they are. I cannot scry into their domain if I don't know where they came from. We can only wait and hope they return!"

"I don't care if you have to scower the universe!" Mikkel yelled at him. "Find them!"

"Your highness, they're just a couple of boys!" Jugene tried. "There are other..."

"Those *boys* killed my father! Those *boys* destroyed my future! I will get them if it is the last thing I do!" Mikkel ground out, waving a finger in front of Jugene's face. "Find them!" He stormed out of the room.

Jugene sighed. "Yes, highness," he replied sadly and returned to his seat at the table to stare blankly into an empty crystal ball.

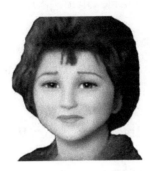

1 – THE PROOF

ANNESE

Annese let the back-screen door slam behind her as she came out into the bright morning sun. Her chores done; she could go play. Thinking about whom she'd call on, she wandered out front and stopped. There was a strange boy sitting on the neighbor's steps. His sandy hair was shaggy and a mess. He wore a black t-shirt and dusty jeans. Annese looked at the sad face resting in his hands, elbows on his knees. He just stared at the steps at his feet.

Annese huffed. She marched herself over next to the boy on the steps and crossed her arms.

"Who are you, and why are you on Jordon's steps?" she demanded. The boy looked up startled.

"Huh?" he asked, confused. The petite, thin, black girl with short, tight curls stood authoritatively next to him. Her dark brown eyes stared holes into him, yet she looked like she'd fall over if he blew hard. Her yellow t-shirt with the teddy bear on it made her skin look darker than it really was. Dark blue, jean cut-offs stuck out from underneath.

"Who are you, and why are you on Jordon's steps?" Annese asked again, looking for all the world as if she had the right to know.

"I'm Tyler. Who are you?"

"I'm Annese. I live next door. What're you doin' sitting here?"

Tyler shrugged. "Sitting."

Annese rolled her eyes. "Why?"

"'Cause Aunt Jean said I should go play."

"Aunt Jean?" Annese asked curiously. Her face scowled.

"Yea. My aunt and uncle live here." His body sagged and his voice became solemn. "Well, I guess I do now, too."

"Oh!" Annese threw her hands up with dawning realization. "You're Jordon's cousin! He said you were coming to live with them."

"Yea," Tyler replied flatly and went back to staring at the stairs.

"How come?"

"How come what?"

"How come you came to live with the Hallsteads?"

"My parents went out of the country for a few years." He paused. "Again."

"Again! You mean they've done it before?"

Tyler shrugged. "They do. They're archaeologists for some high and mighty research university in New York. The university got the grant they wanted, so my parents are off to South America to find some long-lost city." Tyler's voice indicated he really didn't like his parents' career. "So, this time my sister and I got dumped on Aunt Jean and Uncle Mike."

"Dumped?"

"We stay with a different relative every time they go away. 'You're too young to be hanging around a dig site!'" he imitated his mother's high-pitched voice. "Just once I wish she'd be my mother instead of an archaeologist."

Annese felt sorry for the boy. She didn't remember going from family to family before the Blackhursts adopted her, but it must've been lonely - never knowing who wants you and who doesn't. She assumed that was how Tyler was feeling.

"I think you'll like living here. We all have a good time together." Annese tried to be encouraging.

"We all?" Tyler asked, still confused.

"Yea! See, my mom and your aunt are best friends, so we do lots of stuff together. And on Saturday mornings, my dad and your uncle go golfing together." Annese paused and thought for a second. "Though, they don't take any golf clubs, so I don't know how much golfing they do. Anyway, my brother Niko and D.J. are best friends, and my brother Jeremy and Jordon are best friends. So, I guess you and I can be best friends. How old's your sister?"

"Ari's five."

"Perfect! She and my sister Tasha can be best friends, too! They're the same age."

"You're really into this 'best friends' thing, aren't you?" Tyler remarked.

"Well, you got any other friends around here?" Annese asked knowingly.

Tyler slumped guiltily. "No."

"See? And school doesn't start for another two months. How old are you?"

"Ten."

"Really? Me, too! We'll be in the same class!"

Tyler looked skeptical. "Don't be so sure."

"Why not?" Annese asked.

"We could get different teachers."

Annese laughed. "Naw! We'll have Mrs. Cramer. She's the one who teaches the fifth-grade class." Tyler scowled uncertainly at her which made Annese laugh harder. "We have so few kids in Corinth that there's only one elementary school. It has one class of each grade through eighth. After that, we go to Oak Harbor for high school," she explained.

Tyler swallowed. "Oh. So, like, everybody knows everybody?" He already didn't like being the new kid.

"Not always. There's three colleges on the island. Professors and students come and go all the time. With the changes in them, there's always new kids at school." Annese tried to encourage Tyler. "Have you gotten around much?"

"Kind of," Tyler returned to staring at the ground. He didn't realize Annese was talking about the island. "Once my dad took me to Egypt. They hired him to dig out some smaller pyramid. My tutor showed me around the main cities of the area."

"Wow! You had your own tutor?" Annese seemed impressed.

"She was more of a babysitter." Tyler's voice was disappointed, then softened. "But she had some ins in places. We went to a museum that had the real mummies on display. She got us back to the workrooms. I was allowed to touch a real mummy, only they weren't sure which one it was. From what the scientists told me; I think it might have been the handmaiden to Tutankhamen's wife."

"No way! Wait! Wife? Wasn't he the guy that was still a kid when he was Pharaoh?"

"Yep. He got married at twelve years old. Shame he was dead by the time he was 16. His wife was younger than he was."

Annese shivered as she sat on the stairs next to Tyler. "That's awful! That means we'd be getting married in two years!!"

"Only if you were Pharaoh. That trip wasn't all that bad. I learned a lot about hieroglyphics and how languages formed that year. And the year they took me down to Central America to explore a Mayan temple was pretty cool, too. The artwork and the rituals they held were pretty sweet."

"You know what kind of rituals were held in a Mayan temple?" Annese sounded skeptical. She moved to the stairs next to Tyler.

"Oh, yea. There were all kinds. From standard worship right down to human sacrifice. There's murals all over the walls, though, they weren't in very good condition."

"What else have you seen?" Annese began to search her mind of things she'd seen over her short ten years. Nothing. She lived a very boring life compared to Tyler.

"There's the gigantic heads from the Aztecs," Tyler thought of the few places he'd been allowed to accompany his parents.

"Boy, your parents get all over, don't they?" Annese seemed impressed.

"They do. I don't." His voice got depressed again. "It's pretty rare when I get to go with them."

"What else have they done?"

"I suppose the most interesting one to me was when Dad got called to the Serbian mountains to explore a cave that supposedly held a real dragon. He said the remains were frozen, but showed all the signs of either a dragon or a dinosaur. He was able to help get the body out of the ice and make the initial records, but they had to call in a medical team to do the testing on the body."

"I didn't know there were real dragons here," Annese scowled. "How come we don't hear about it in history?"

Tyler shrugged. "I don't know. I'm not real fond of history."

Annese huffed in amusement. "Coulda fooled me," Annese teased.

"What did you mean 'here'?"

Annese suddenly realized her blunder. "Here, um, you know, this world." She cringed again.

"What other world is there?" Tyler chuckled.

"Worlds...you know," she pointed to the sky. "There's tons of them in the solar system."

"In the universe, but what's that got to do with dragons?"

"Where else have you been?"

Tyler shrugged. "A few other places. What's around here to explore?"

OK. So, Tyler was into exploring things. This might prove a problem. "We have the sea lion caves on the northwest side, but you can't go into them. The tours go by them and you can see them laying on the rocks. We have Indian tribes across the bay that give tours now and again. The ocean holds lots of things. There's scuba diving along the south side. Then there's the caves at Deception Pass," she tried hard to think. "Just about every class goes to see the Stalactites in the caves. Most of us can recite the information from memory, we've been there so many times."

"My dad showed me caves with old Incan artwork in them."

"That must have been cool!"

"It was ok. I found the ancient pottery more interesting. I can decipher the language on them."

"Cannot!"

"Can, too!"

"Scientists can't even do that!" Annese accused. "They just guess!"

"Well, I can! And it's better than some dumb old caves!" he challenged.

"Well, Jordon, Jeremy, and I went to another world in one."

"One what?" Tyler asked.

"One cave!"

"Did not!"

"Did, too! It was so cool! Eight islands, gigantic birds, and funny people. Oh, and they really do magic there!"

"Yea, right!" Tyler retorted. "You've got some imagination!"

"You don't believe me?" Annese sounded hurt.

"You can't get to another world by going into a cave," Tyler argued logically.

"I did!"

"You didn't!"

"I did!" Annese got indignant. He was calling her a liar.

"Did not!"

"Fine! I'll prove it! You got a bike?"

"Yea, in the garage. So what?"

"Let's go! I'll prove to you I can get to another world!"

"You can't! Wait. What do I tell my aunt?"

"Hmmm. I know. I can show you the area on our way. Just tell her I'm going to show you around the island."

Annese followed him inside the house. They walked down the hall into the kitchen.

"Aunt Jean?" Tyler called.

"Downstairs!" came the reply.

The two ran downstairs and found Jean Hallstead in the laundry room. Her short body was half into the dryer pulling clothes out of it and stuffing them into a basket. The washer was filling with water for another load. Several baskets of folded laundry were about the floor.

"Aunt Jean, is it ok if I go with Annese? She said she'd show me the island."

Mrs. Hallstead smiled at Annese. "That would be a wonderful idea! Why don't I make you guys some lunch? You can eat on the beach."

"That'd be great!" Annese smiled. "I'm gonna run and tell my mom."

"You do that. Come on, Tyler. Let's get some things ready."

In a short time, Annese and Tyler were riding around the island, backpacks filled with food, sun block, towels, and just stuff! Annese began with the areas Tyler might find interesting. They had fun at one of the beaches, saw the school, played at the park, then headed around toward Deception Pass.

"The caves are up here. Come on. I've got proof! Not just some stories!"

Annese led the way up the footpath to the waiting area for the caves as Tyler sighed with a small shake of his head and followed. The footpath opened onto a gravel lot. On the far side were some picnic tables on a grassy patch under a pavilion. A small group was waiting for the tour to begin. Tyler watched Annese as she looked around while they locked their bikes to the bike rack. She went over to the lone tour stand and slid a dollar into the window.

"Two, please," she requested.

Two blue tickets came back towards her. She smiled at the older woman behind the glass, then led Tyler over to the tables.

"Tickets?" Tyler asked skeptically. She needs tickets to get to another world? Sure.

"Stay in the back," she whispered. "And stay close to me."

"Why?"

"You'll see."

It was a short wait before the tour guide, a young man in his early 20s, greeted everyone and gave them the safety instructions before he led them down the narrow path to the first cave. Annese kept back, making sure she was the last one in line. As the crowd moved into the first cave, she grabbed Tyler's shirt and pulled him along the outside wall.

"What're...."

Annese's hand covered his mouth. "Shhh! You'll give us away!" she hissed. She listened to the voice of the tour guide giving the tourists the history of the caves. Nodding, she began the journey down the path.

"We have to hurry. They're only in there for fifteen minutes. We need to be out of sight by then."

Annese led Tyler quickly along the path, using signals to hurry him along. She led him right past the second cave.

"Where're you going?" Tyler asked, following behind.

"This way!"

"But there's a blockade!"

"I know. We need to go to the bottom of the path. Hurry! If we're seen, we're in big trouble!"

The two ducked under the blockade, then slipped and slid down the gravelly, washed out path, and ran past the cave called Bundee's Grave. Tyler looked at the caved-in entry curiously, wondering what in the world happened there. Annese didn't slow down until they were under the cover of the trees at the bottom. Just in time! They could hear the echo of the tour guide's voice as he led the tourists from the first cave down to the second.

"Whew! That was close! Come on!" she heaved.

"You're nuts! How are we gonna get back?" Tyler waved his hand behind him.

"We will. Don't worry. Come on!"

Annese pulled a flashlight out of her backpack as they turned into Docker's Cave. The bright beam cut through the darkness of the cave. Still, it was difficult to see.

"You always carry a flashlight with you?"

"Ever since our first time here, yes. I decided I'd never get caught in the dark again. Now shush!"

"Why?" he asked, following her into the cave. Annese pointed the light beam at the ceiling. Tyler followed the beam to see bumps of blackish-brown hung from the rock face. "So? Why be quiet around some rocks?"

"They aren't rocks," Annese whispered. "They're bats!"

Tyler's eyes went wide as he looked back at her. "Bats? Like in vampires?"

"No. They're just brown bats. They eat mosquitoes and flies and stuff, but there's hundreds of them. I purposely learned about them after my last trip through here."

"Oh," Tyler whispered.

"Come on." Annese led Tyler down the path to the back of the cave. She searched the walls with the flashlight.

"What are you looking for?"

"Our names," she replied. "We scratched them into the wall so we'd know where the door was."

"Door?"

"To the other world. Asteria. Trust me."

"Su-re!" Tyler was still skeptical, but he didn't want to leave her there. What if she got hurt?

After a bit of looking, Annese found the etchings in the rock. Smiling, she took 12 steps to the left. She gleamed at Tyler, then sighed.

"Come on!" she grabbed his hand and tugged him over to her. "It's easy. Just walk through the wall."

"Right!"

"Watch." Annese took a few steps forward and disappeared into the wall.

"Annese!" Tyler cried startled.

Annese stepped back into the dark cave, grabbed Tyler's hand, and pulled him through the portal.

Tyler stumbled and blinked. The soft glow from the ore in the rock face lit the cavern. He stared around him in awe.

"Sweet!" he muttered.

"Yea. Isn't it? This way! We're not done!" She began up the tunnel to the ocean cliffs.

"Wow!" Tyler exclaimed in amazement. From the opening in a shear rock cliffside, they looked out over clear blue water. Seven other islands peeked out of the ocean waves. Bright sunshine bounced off gleaming or wet objects. "This is lit! You weren't kidding, were you?"

"You can say that again! This way! They'll be up here." Annese darted up the stone stairs to her left.

"Who'll be up here?" Tyler asked, following her.

"The giant birds! That's our ride to the palace."

"The palace?"

"Yea, but it's ok. We're friends with the king."

"But...whoa!" Tyler came up short at the sight on the top of the cliffs. Almost two dozen huge brown and white birds the size of a large semi-tractor trailer sat on various nests staring at them. A few squawked, hurting Tyler's ears. Annese giggled at his reaction.

"Oh, look!" Annese sang. She approached one nest with three little heads poking out from under their mother. "She's got babies!"

Annese oohed and ahhed at the baby birds that were nearly as big as she was. The mother, however, squawked loudly at her. Annese jumped back so suddenly she fell on her rump. Tyler chuckled to himself.

"Okay. So how are these...um...birds supposed to get us anywhere?"

"They carry you!" Annese replied excitedly. She approached a gigantic bird and pushed it. "Come on!" she grunted. "Let's go! I wanna go to the palace."

The bird didn't budge. Annese pushed harder.

"You could help me, ya know!" Annese called over her shoulder.

"I don't think she wants to be bothered." Tyler looked up at the huge bird glaring at Annese.

At last, the bird squawked and leaped into the air. The sight was astounding. The majestic wing span brought the bird soaring into the sky. Sun bounced off the gleam of its feathers as it rose high on the breeze. With graceful beauty, the bird swirled around and headed back.

Annese and Tyler stood slack-jawed, watching. Tyler didn't start to panic until he realized the bird was diving straight for them, claws extended.

"Umm.... umm.... run!"

Annese grabbed his shirt. "Stand still! It's o.k.!"

In a swift swoop, the Rho'taak captured one in each claw. Annese's joyful cries echoed as the bird took off over the ledge. Tyler screamed, clutching at the bird's leg.

"Isn't this great!" Annese exclaimed. "Relax! He won't drop us!"

"Yea, right!" Tyler seemed skeptical.

Annese looked around and scowled. "Hey!" She hit the bird's leg. "You're going the wrong way! The castle's that way!"

The bird ignored her. Swirling high around an island full of high green trees, Annese continued to argue with the bird. At length, the bird swooped down towards the trees! Tyler screamed!

Suddenly, the claws opened. Both children dropped with a holler, bumping to a sudden stop. Their "landing pad" was made of sticks, leaves, feathers, and fur. The sides were nearly as high as they were tall. The smell of rotten eggs permeated the air.

"Where are we?" Tyler asked fearfully.

"I have no idea," Annese replied. She stood on tip-toes, trying to look over the edge. "It looks like some kind of nest."

"I'd bet that's a good guess."

"It would be a very good guess," a soft, demure voice came from behind them. "And what have we here?"

The two looked at each other with wide eyes. Slowly, they turned towards the voice. They swallowed hard as they looked up into almond-shaped black eyes. The large golden head with a shining black beak was held back regally. The thick layer of feathers below its head formed a mane around its neck. Its chest was mottled with golden brown and white feathers, coming down to large, thick, yellow claws. The back was split, moving from the majestic eagle to form hindquarters covered in yellowish-brown fur that reminded the children of a lion. A long, slender tail wrapped around its legs with the thick, black hair at the end draped in front.

The creature bowed. "My lady. Kind sir," it greeted with a glint of amusement in its eyes. "What brings you to my humble home?"

"Um... we... she..," Tyler stammered.

"Well,... um... see... um... the bird," Annese stumbled.

The creature laughed heartily, obviously finding the children's reaction amusing. Two others flew down from the canopy and joined her on the tree.

"Well, I'll be!" the one on the right remarked. "Mortals!"

"Strange mortals," the one on the left expressed in disdain. "Just eat them and get it over with."

"Not much meat," the right one sneered as she eyed the children up and down. "We could have them as an appetizer!"

"Ladies!" the first one interrupted. "Enough!" She turned back to the two cowering children. "Now, how is it you are here?"

"I... I was tr... trying t... t... to g... g... get that b... b... big bird t... t... to... take us... t... t... to the castle," Annese stuttered fearfully.

"Ah," the creature nodded. "The Rho'taak are no longer controlled by sorcerers at the castle, young one.

Apparently, the bird felt you needed looking after, so he or she brought you here."

"Could you take us to the castle?" Annese asked hopefully.

"What!" the left companion shrieked. The right one simply gasped.

"Certainly not! Griffins are not for cargo!" the large beast sounded indignantly.

"Perhaps the Centaus..." the one on the right began.

"Very good idea," the first one nodded.

"We will carry you to the meadow below. In the forests, there you will find the Centaus. Perhaps they would be willing to carry you to the castle."

"Centaus?" Tyler asked, confused.

"Correct," the griffin replied.

"What are the Centaus?" he asked. "I've never heard of them."

The three griffons sighed. "The Centaus are the people who live in the forest," the one on the left remarked.

"Weren't you listening?" the one on the right asked.

The first griffin sighed again. "Ophelia, if you are through harassing our guests, please fetch the basket!" The griffon on the right nodded and flew off.

"It's really quite simple, dears," the griffin on the left began. "Ophelia will bring a basket here. It's the one we used to gather food in. You two will climb into it, then Rosemerta and I will fly it down to the meadow where you'll climb out."

"Wait a moment," Tyler began. "If two of you can fly us down to the meadow, why can't you fly us to the castle?"

"As I explained before," Rosemerta, the first griffin, replied. "Griffins do not carry cargo!" She puffed up her feathers.

"Oh, in the name of Svarog, Rosemerta! Give the boy a straight answer!" the other one said.

"Carry along, then, Tristan," Rosemerta replied, turning her head away.

"Griffins do not have the strength to carry things long distances. It will normally take us many trips to gather enough food for several days. Of course, we'll be taking you *down* to the meadow. It would be much more difficult to bring you *up from* the meadow."

Tyler nodded his understanding. "Gravity."

"Gravi-what, dear?" Tristan asked.

"Gravity. It's the force from the center of the earth that keeps things from floating off into space," Tyler explained.

The two griffins exchanged a pitying look, then turned back to the children.

"Whatever you say, dear," Tristan conceded.

Ophelia returned with a large, empty, woven basket of dried vines and placed it in the middle of the nest. "Your chariot," she said to Rosemerta.

"Thank you, Ophelia," the first griffin responded. "Climb in, dears."

"How?" Annese asked.

Tyler examined the sides of the basket. He used the outside weaves to start climbing.

"It's like climbing a fence," he told her. "Stick your foot on the outer edges and climb."

Annese set her jaw and began to climb up. It wasn't as easy as Tyler made it look. She nearly slipped off at the top when Tyler reached over and grabbed her wrists. She was thankful he helped pull her into the basket.

With a nod from Rosemerta, the griffins flew up. The basket teetered precariously as the griffins glided down to the ground.

"For goodness sakes! Sit still!" Tristan exclaimed as the two griffins tried to keep control. Finally, the basket bumped the ground. The griffins landed next to them. A few yards away loomed a thick forest.

"Now," Rosemerta said firmly. "Follow that path there until it splits. Stay to your right, and you'll find the Centaus."

"Thank you," Tyler replied with a sigh of relief.

The two children watched the griffins fly off with the basket until they disappeared into the trees.

"Glad that's over," Tyler mumbled. "I thought we were going to get eaten."

Annese sighed. "Me, too. Thank goodness Rosemerta has a conscience."

They turned to look at the forest looming ahead. Tall, thick trees with a heavy canopy overhead peered out at them. It seemed comfortable in the shade, but they couldn't see into the forest too far. The path disappeared from view after a few yards.

"What do you think?" Tyler asked.

"I don't know," Annese swallowed nervously.

"What do these centaus look like?"

"I don't know."

"But you've been here before."

"Not here here! I was at the palace." She didn't dare tell him she was a statue for most of that time. She took a deep, calming breath. "You got a better idea?"

"No."

"Then in we go!"

Proceeding carefully, the children followed the faint path. The surrounding woods echoed with the sounds of animals. Silence lay heavily around them, however, as they entered each new area. They felt like a multitude of eyes were watching their every move. Occasionally, light filtering through holes in the tree canopy dispersed the darkness.

The sound of a branch snapping made them both stop. Slowly, they looked down at the ground. No branches beneath their feet. They glanced about. The trees and bushes seemed undisturbed. The deafening silence gave off an eerie feeling. Annese looked warily at Tyler.

"Was that you?" Tyler whispered.

"No. You?" Annese replied hopefully.

"No."

They continued on slowly, looking around as they went. Nothing moved. Nothing unusual in sight. Only trees, grass, leaves, and brush. Sure enough, another rustle in a nearby brush caught their attention. Both sets of eyes looked at the thick green bushes.

Annese wet her lips when Tyler put a finger to his mouth and slowly tip-toed towards the bush. He waited quietly until the bush wiggled again. Quickly, he pushed through the bush to see what was on the other side.

"Hi!" A round, tanned face with long, chestnut hair and dark brown eyes looked up suddenly.

Tyler tumbled backwards with a scream. Annese ran to help him up.

"What is it?" she asked worriedly.

"It's a... it's a... it's a..." Tyler stammered, staring at the bushes.

The bushes parted. An impish, round face peered out. Her brown hair was a mass of unruly curls. Her eyes were wide with concern under long, dark lashes. "Are you alright?" she asked.

Annese looked up with a start. She met eyes with the face looking through the bushes. "Huh?"

"Is he alright?" the face asked again.

"I'm fine," Tyler grumbled. He pushed himself up and brushed off his jeans. "You startled me, that's all."

"Why are you back there?" Annese asked.

"I... was following you," she replied shyly.

"Why?" Tyler scowled suspiciously. "Why not just come walk with us?"

"Because..." The child squirmed a bit. "My father said mortals don't like us."

"Mortals?" Tyler questioned, looking at Annese. It was the second time he'd heard the reference.

"People," she explained.

"Well, he was wrong."

"Oh." The girl seemed uncertain.

"So, you want to walk with us?" Tyler offered.

The child perked up. "Sure!" she replied excitedly. "It'll be right there. Stand back!"

"You were scared by a girl?" Annese teased as they backed up.

"I told you," Tyler said crossly. "I wasn't expecting her."

Their eyes widened and their jaws dropped as four hooves attached to a chestnut pony's body came flying over the bushes. A long brown tail fluttered behind on the breeze. Instead of a horse's neck and head, a girl's torso, head, and arms emerged from the shoulders of the front legs. Her brown hair was down to her shoulders. She wore a green midriff just under her arms that covered her to the waist.

The girl glanced at a scratch on her shoulder with a scowl. "Nasty tree! It shouldn't have put that branch in my way!"

"You're... you're... a horse?" Annese exclaimed.

Tyler elbowed her in the ribs. "No!" Tyler rebuked her. "She's a... a... what's the name? Centaur! She's a centaur!"

The girl giggled. "No! I'm a centaus!" She turned to show two small, brown wings on her back. "Centaurs don't have wings." Her elfin face scrunched. "Actually, there aren't any centaurs anymore."

"What? Why?" Annese recovered from her surprise.

"Hmm, let's see if I remember the story. Oh, yea! A long, long time ago, the centaurs were dying out. There were only a few left and no children had been born for centuries. One of the women got an idea. She traveled to a land where the Pegasii lived. They would come trade with us, but they weren't part of Asteria. Shortly after she came back, she had a baby – a little girl. She was real pretty, but she had wings. Soon, more centaur women traveled to the Pegasii land and came back to have babies. Before long there were lots of children, but each of them had wings. As the children got older, they learned to fly. After a while, the centaurs died off and the ones remaining changed the name of the race to Centaus to combine both parents." She heaved in a breath. "There. I think that's right."

"Cool!" Annese exclaimed.

"So, you wanna play?" The girl asked hopefully.

"Sure!" Tyler and Annese replied brightening.

"There's a real fun meadow over this way! Come on!"

"I'm Tyler," the boy introduced. "And this is Annese. What's your name?"

"Odessa," the girl replied leading the way. "You're the first mortals I've seen around here. How come you're here?"

Tyler and Annese explained what happened with the Rho'taak and how they ended up in the griffins' nest. They explained the griffins' refusal to carry them to the palace, but that they sent them to find the Centaus for help.

"We'll ask my dad! He's big and strong. I'm sure he'll take you!" Odessa said proudly.

They broke out of the forest into a large, secluded meadow. Bright yellow, pink, and purple flowers poked out of long, green grass. Tiny insects buzzed between the flowers and the trees. The far side of the field dropped; into what Annese couldn't tell. The woods encircled the rest like a protective wall. Odessa quickly turned and tagged Tyler.

"You're it!" she giggled and hopped off to one side.

Tyler turned to Annese quickly and barely touched her shoulder as she tried to dodge him. "You're it! No tag backs!" he cried and took off running.

For the next while, the sounds of children's laughter rang off the trees. Carefree and delightful, the children forgot about differences and time. They played, explored, and shared stories.

The beating of wings broke the peaceful atmosphere, and a sharp screech rent the air. The children, sitting on the far side of the meadow looking for clover, looked up into the sky with surprise and horror. Closing in quickly were the sharp, outstretched talons of a strange half-woman/half-bird creature. The golden claws gleamed like razors in the sunlight. Red, yellow, and brown feathers covered her body. Long black hair flew backwards between huge black wings. White fangs showed from an open mouth as bloodthirsty red eyes glared at her target.

"Run!" Odessa cried, rising. "Into the trees!"

Before any of the children could move, an arrow shot the creature out of the sky. The three watched the large creature gasp in surprise and tumble to the ground. It shuttered once, then lay still in a crumpled heap.

An intimidating male Centaus flew towards them from the meadow entry. His coloring was similar to Odessa's. The exception was in his hair, beard, and tail; they were black to Odessa's brown. Two large, silver wings flowed all the way down to the back of his haunches. He landed nearby and walked to them regally.

"Odessa!" he snapped, obviously annoyed.

Odessa shrank down a little. "Hi, Father," she greeted meekly. "These are my new friends, Tyler and Annese." She sounded like she hoped to change the subject.

The large male looked them over and nodded. He turned his attention back to his daughter.

"What have I told you about playing in this meadow?"

Odessa looked down guiltily. "Don't," she replied weakly.

"Young lady, you had better have a *very* good explanation for your disobedience," he said with strained patience.

"Well, um... I... m... met Tyler and Annese in the woods, and... well..."

"O-des-sa!" he warned.

"O-k!" she shouted and stamped a front hoof. "We wanted to play, and this is the best field for playing, so I brought them here. We were only playing!"

"You were only a harpy's target for her next meal!" he pointed at the now dead harpy on the ground. "You know this is where the harpy's like to hunt. Not only did you disobey, but you put three lives in danger!" He was clearly angry now. "You are to return home and remain there until I return. As for you two, I suggest you continue on your way!"

"Actually," Tyler began uneasily, "We were on our way to find you."

"Me?" the man asked suspiciously.

"Well, not you *exactly*," Annese put in.

"The griffins thought you could help us," Tyler explained.

"Oh, really," the Centaus said suspiciously.

"See, we need to get to the palace..." Annese began.

"Enough! Go with Odessa. We will discuss your problem when I return," Odessa's father said abruptly.

"But..." Annese began.

Odessa nudged her friend. She cocked her head, her face giving Annese a warning look. The three friends got to their feet and began across the open field.

"We're sorry we got you in trouble," Tyler said.

"It was my fault," Odessa replied. "I brought you here." Annese saw Odessa look back to see her father hoisting the dead carcass onto his back. She'd worn that exact expression many times.

Below their feet, dirt and grass began to slide. Annese lost her footing, reaching to Tyler to steady herself. Suddenly, the ground opened up beneath them. A trap. Annese and Odessa fell, sliding down the vast tunnel with a united scream. Tyler grasped for the grass, but losing his grip, fell down into the rough hole after the girls.

"Ahh!" he hollered.

MAUSELITH

Mauselith dropped the harpy and pulled his bow and arrow to the front. He scanned the sky quickly, looking for another harpy attack. He turned towards the sound of the children's screams with fear. A large, round sinkhole shown in the center of the field. He spotted it in time to see Tyler disappear down the hole.

"Odessa!" he hollered worriedly. Pouring on speed, he galloped to the hole. He couldn't see the bottom, but could hear the fading echo of the children's cries. "O-des-sa!"

2 – RETURN TO ASTERIA

JEREMY

Jeremy picked up the phone and ducked into his room. It was still early, and his chores finished—*finally*! Now to get out of the house before his mother found something else for him to do. He dialed the number and packed impatiently. One ring. Two rings.

"Hello?"

"Hi, Mrs. H. Is Jordon there?"

"Just a minute, Jay." He could hear the smile in her voice.

A few moments later, Jordon picked up the phone. "Hey, what's up?"

"Are you done?"

"Not yet. I have to finish folding towels."

"Well, hurry up! We need to go."

"Go where?"

"Asteria. I think they want us."

Jordon paused. "What makes you think so?"

"I had a dream about them last night."

"Me, too!"

"And this morning, the globe on my staff was glowing."

"I thought you said it didn't work here?"

"It didn't! No matter which spell I used, I couldn't get it to work, but it was glowing today."

"O.K. I'll hurry. Pack a lunch. I'll meet you in the garage."

"Bring your stuff!"

"What do I tell my mom?"

"Um. Tell her we're going exploring. It's not a lie."

Jordon chuckled. "True. O.K. I'll be there soon."

JORDON

Jordon finished quickly, threw some lunch in a bag, and ran up to his room. He threw some supplies from Asteria into his backpack, setting *Sharijol*, his sword, diagonally across the back. He opened the bottom drawer of his dresser, dug under his jeans, and pulled out his breeches and tunic Dracaina had made him. He'd have to stop and see them on this trip. His clothes were getting a bit tight. He stuffed the clothes in his backpack, then added the vest. He threw his lunch on top, tied the bag, and ran downstairs.

"Mom, Jeremy and I are going exploring," he yelled downstairs.

"Are your chores done?"

"Yes."

"O.K. Take the trash out with you, please. Be careful."

"We will. Wait! Where's Tyler?"

"Annese took him for a tour of the island."

Great! That meant both Tyler *and* Annese would be out of their hair today! What luck! His little cousin had been dogging him ever since he got there yesterday. And Annese, of course, followed them anywhere she could. Well, these were two less things to worry about today.

With that thought in mind, he ran to the garage, grasped his bike, and headed to Jeremy's garage. Jeremy was ready and waiting.

"Took you long enough!" he greeted with a grin. He pushed up the kickstand on his bike.

"I went as fast as I could. There's a lot of laundry in our house. It's almost as bad as your house!" They both laughed as they coasted down the driveway.

"Did you bring your stuff?"

"Yea. I figured we could change in the cave."

"Me, too," Jeremy chuckled. The two of them thought so much alike.

"I brought my camera, too. I figured if we had pictures of people and stuff, people might believe us... if we ever get to tell anyone."

"Great idea! I hadn't thought of that."

JEREMY

Jeremy raced Jordon past their usual haunts as fast as they could go. They pushed their bikes up the hill to the gravel yard where the tours of the stalactite caves started.

Looking around, Jeremy realized a few problems. First problem was at the bike rack.

"Isn't that Neesie's bike?" Jordon asked, staring at the pink two-wheeler with the purple streamers hanging from the handlebars.

Jeremy examined the bike cautiously. "Could be. But I doubt she's the only girl on the island with a bike like that. Mr. Sanders' Bike Shop downtown had at least 30 of them when we got it."

"You're right. I'm being paranoid. 'Sides, she's giving Tyler a tour of the island."

"Sweet. It'll keep her from following us!" He started following Jordon to the ticket booth.

Jeremy turned briefly to look over his shoulder at the bike again. He had this nagging feeling in his chest. Would she? Nah! He was being silly.

Their next problem was how to get to the path. The assembly area consisted of a large yard covered in gravel, a ticket booth, and several picnic tables sitting under a large shelter. A small group of people were already gathered under the canopy. The old lady behind the counter was eyeing them suspiciously.

"You got a buck?" Jeremy asked.

"Maybe," Jordon pulled out his wallet. "Yea. Here, but I hate paying for something we're not even gonna see."

"Me, too, but I don't know of any other way down."

"Me, either."

Jeremy went over to the ticket booth. He slid the dollar under the glass window. "Two, please," he asked.

"Interesting walking stick," the lady remarked about the staff slung over his shoulders as she slid two tickets back to him.

Jay glanced at it. "Yea, it is," he smiled. "A friend of mine gave it to me. Great for hiking."

He moved away from the window quickly and joined Jordon under the canopy. He glanced back at the ticket booth. A family with three little kids was there buying tickets.

"What's wrong?" Jordon asked, leading the way to the tables in the back.

"The lady made a comment about my staff."

"So? My mom said she really liked it."

"Yea. I guess. Is Donny still doing the tours?"

"Don't know. He should be up soon."

As if on cue, a tall, dark-haired young man in his early twenties led a group up from the caves below. He had a baby face with sparkling green eyes. His shoulders showed of years of swim meets. His voice carried over the murmurs of the crowd that had just finished their tour.

"You can learn more about the formation of stalactites and stalagmites from your local library. If you haven't been there yet, be sure to take a trip on Mystic Ocean Tours to visit the sea lion caves.

"Thank you for coming. Have a great day!"

"Yep," Jordon smirked. "Donny's still giving the tours."

"This'll be easy."

As the crowd thinned, the young man approached the next group at the pavilion.

"Good morning, ladies and gentlemen. Welcome to the Caves of Deception Pass," he began. He launched into a well-rehearsed litany of the history of the caves, then explained the safety rules. "Now, if you'll follow me, please, we'll begin the tour."

As the small group gathered behind Donny, Jordon and Jeremy stayed put. They followed behind the last family, leaving a good gap between them. As the last of the group entered the first cave, the two boys shot down the path.

Knowing speed was of the essence, they ducked under the red and white barricade. The washed-out path was no easier to manipulate than it had been the last time. Jeremy nearly slid off the path, landing on his rump to stop the slide off the edge.

"Come on! We've only got three more minutes!" Jordon urged, grasping Jeremy's pack to stabilize him.

"I'm going! I'm going!"

"Quick! I hear Donny's voice coming from the cave!" Jordon urged.

"He's gotten faster," Jeremy remarked as he dodged behind the brush covering the path.

"You say the same thing over and over again, and you'd get faster, too," Jordon replied. He nearly barreled into Jeremy as he dove for cover.

The boys leaned against the mountain, trying to catch their breath. With hearts pounding, they listened as Donny continued his informative monologue. They both breathed a sigh of relief. No one had seen them, and the apparent dust in the air hadn't keyed Donny off to anything unusual. Jordon cocked his head towards their destination. Jeremy nodded and continued down the path. They passed Bundee's Grave silently, then moved down into Docker's Cave.

Jeremy shivered slightly from the chill of being underground as they grasped their flashlights. Following the tunnel down to the cul-de-sac was the easy part. Not disturbing the bats was a little more difficult. After that, it didn't take long to find the inscriptions on the wall.

The two boys glanced at each other with excitement. They dropped their packs and began stripping off their clothes. In a matter of moments, the boys had changed into what they called their "Asteria clothes".

"We can leave these here," Jordon said, balling up his clothes and pushing them into a corner. "Nobody comes in here."

"And it'll make the pack lighter," Jeremy nodded. He added his modern threads to Jordon's.

Once set, they heaved a sigh, paced off the distance from the names to the entry, and entered Asteria. The soft glow of the rock face was a welcome sight. The fresh ocean air still permeated the cavern.

"I wonder how things have been going," Jeremy mused.

"Well, it's been, what, almost three months since we've been here?"

"Yea, about that; but don't forget we were here for a week!"

"O.K., so figure it's been almost 90 days." Jordon began calculating.

"That's 90 weeks!" Jeremy exclaimed wide-eyed. "That's over a year and a half!"

"Wow! It didn't seem that long. Time does fly, doesn't it?"

The wind caressed their hair as they looked out over the familiar site of the eight islands. Above, the Rho'taak glided on the air currents with grace.

"I still get the creeps looking at them," Jeremy remarked dryly.

"Yea. Me, too. Come on. We still need to figure out how to let them know we're here."

Jeremy followed Jordon as he climbed the steps to the aerie. A few dozen eyes watched them at the top. They, in turn, stared at the collection of Rho'taak nesting on the flat top of the mountain.

"So!" Jordon said nervously. "This is how it was supposed to look, huh?"

"Hmmm. So, um, you wanna try and walk through to Ascentia?" Jeremy asked, looking at the spaces between nests.

"Can't hurt to try. Weapons ready?" Jordon pulled Sharijol out of his pack.

"Ready," Jeremy replied. He pulled the staff from behind him and gripped it firmly.

Slowly, the boys made their way between nests. Other than being watched with a few squawks, the trek was uneventful. The stretch to the mountains was wide open now. The snow on the mountain peaks twinkled in the sunlight like the tiny lights on a Christmas tree.

"Look!" Jeremy pointed towards the mountains.

"Things must be good," Jordon smiled. "The dragons never hunted during the day." They watched as four or five dragons flew about the mountain peaks.

One suddenly broke off from the others, speeding straight for them. The green scales glinted as it soared towards them. The dragon, small by dragon standards, circled over them, then landed a few yards ahead of them.

"Master Jeremy! Master Jordon! Thou art back!"

"Catlara?" Jeremy asked surprised. The dragon had been little bigger than he the last time they saw her.

"Thou remembers!"

The boys ran up and hugged the young dragon they had befriended on their previous visit. Catlara nudged both of them lovingly.

"Look at you!" Jordon cried. "You're flying!"

"I am still a little shaky."

"Has your breath weapon come in yet?" Jeremy asked excitedly.

"Tis starting to. Yesterday I twas able to throw acid a short distance," Catlara answered proudly.

"Way to go!" the boys cried, slapping hands with each other.

"So why hast thou returned?" the dragon asked.

"We're not exactly sure," Jordon began.

"My staff was glowing, and we both had dreams of Asteria, so we thought we'd come see what's going on," Jeremy explained.

"Can you take us to Thaurlonian?" He was eager to see their friend and ruler of the dragons.

Catlara's face clouded a moment as her head hung low. "Father tis no longer with us."

"What?" Jordon exclaimed in shock.

"Why?" Jeremy's expression mirrored his friend's.

"Father's ascension hast come to pass. Oh, twas a glorious sight! He twas weak and worn. Never recovered completely from the battles at Caldren, but his body began to glow. One by one, he issued a blessing on each of us, naming mine elder brother Aristopole as his successor. Twas then his body began to dissolve into tiny, bright stars until it was a huge ball of light; then he floated straight up through the ceiling. It twas magnificent!" Catlara paused, looking up. Slowly, her head came down until it hung again. A tear dropped to the ground. "Still, I miss him terribly."

"It's gonna be ok." Jeremy placed a comforting hand on Catlara's neck.

"Yea," Jordon said, choking up himself. "My mom says that even though people die, or in this case ascend, they don't really leave us. They can look down from heaven and see what's going on."

"Yea," Jeremy tried to console his friend. "And my mom said that even though they're not here, we can still tell them things, and they'll hear it."

"Tis true?" Catlara asked hopefully.

"That's what she says," Jeremy encouraged.

"Who knows," Jordon comforted, "Maybe dragons have found a way to communicate between worlds."

"I knowest not," Catlara replied thoughtfully.

"Whatever happens," Jeremy tried. "Just remember that Thaurlonian was always proud of you."

"And he loved you, too," Jordon nodded.

"Thank thee," Catlara smiled at both of them mistily.

A large blue dragon came flying near. "Catlara! What art thou doing?" he ordered.

"Look!" Catlara called more cheerfully than she must have felt. "Tis Masters Jordon and Jeremy!"

The dragon flew closer, peering at the boys. He circled once and touched down next to Catlara.

"Well, I'll be! Far thought that we shouldst e'er see thee again!" Metiblee said. "What art thou doing here?"

The boys once again explained what happened.

"Hey, wait! Let's get a picture! Jay, stand between them!" Jordon quickly lined up the shot and took the picture.

"Here!" Jeremy reached for the camera. "You get in there. We're a team, after all." Jeremy peered into the camera. "Smile!"

"I do not understand what a small box has to do with smiling," Metiblee remarked curiously.

Jordon pressed a few buttons and showed the dragon the picture on the viewscreen on the back. "See. It takes an image of us and keeps it inside. Later, when I get home, I can make it larger and put it on paper so I can see it again and again." Both dragons seemed amazed by the tiny box with their image in it.

"We'd better get going," Jeremy said quietly. "There's got to be a reason we were called."

"Then we had best get thee to the palace. Up you go, young masters!" Metiblee instructed. He laid on the ground for them. "Come along, Catlara. The fly will help strengthen thy wings."

"Oh, boy!"

Jeremy followed Jordon up on Metiblee's back, just in front of his wings. Excitement coursed through his veins at the realization of a dragon ride.

"Hold on!" Metiblee called.

"To what?" Jordon teased with a laugh.

Walking to the edge, Metiblee jumped off the ledge, wings spread to catch the wind. Higher and higher they soared until you could see almost everywhere. Catlara followed right behind her instructor.

"Oh, yea!" Jordon shouted.

"Woo-hoo!" Jeremy echoed.

"Like it?" Metiblee asked, amused.

"This is great!" Jeremy cried.

"Greater than great!"

The two dragons chuckled as they flew overhead.

"Look!" Jordon pointed. "There's Kriltnar!"

"Is that Elthoria?" Jeremy asked.

"Yes," Metiblee replied.

"Faeyruun," Jordon's voice died a little. Jeremy's heart grew heavy as he remembered Teesha.

"There! The Keep!" Jeremy pointed.

"Sic!"

"Palace straight ahead," Catlara announced.

From where they were, the castle looked like a Lego toy on a hillside with the ocean waves rolling in the background. It grew, of course, as the four drew closer. Up high in the sky, they could see people about the palace scurrying about anxiously. Some just pointed at the dragons. Others huddled together.

The people grew as well as the dragons circled lower over the castle. They scattered along the catwalks. The clear dome on top of the palace glinted in the sun, reflecting the grand sight of the dragons descending. A tall, gray-haired man in green robes stepped out on the roof.

Walking to the edge, Metiblee jumped off the ledge, wings spread to catch the wind. Higher and higher they soared until you could see almost everywhere. Catlara followed right behind her instructor.

"Oh, yea!" Jordon shouted.

"Woo-hoo!" Jeremy echoed.

"Like it?" Metiblee asked, amused.

"This is great!" Jeremy cried.

"Greater than great!"

The two dragons chuckled as they flew overhead.

"Look!" Jordon pointed. "There's Kriltnar!"

"Is that Elthoria?" Jeremy asked.

"Yes," Metiblee replied.

"Faeyruun," Jordon's voice died a little. Jeremy's heart grew heavy as he remembered Teesha.

"There! The Keep!" Jeremy pointed.

"Sic!"

"Palace straight ahead," Catlara announced.

From where they were, the castle looked like a Lego toy on a hillside with the ocean waves rolling in the background. It grew, of course, as the four drew closer. Up high in the sky, they could see people about the palace scurrying about anxiously. Some just pointed at the dragons. Others huddled together.

The people grew as well as the dragons circled lower over the castle. They scattered along the catwalks. The clear dome on top of the palace glinted in the sun, reflecting the awesome sight of the dragons descending. A tall, gray-haired man in green robes stepped out on the roof.

"Thrundra!" Jeremy shouted, leaning over to see. His first mentor on Asteria, the wizard had saved Jeremy from being tried and executed for damaging a sacred location. He was the one who found Jeremy's talent for magic.

"Careful, Master Jeremy!" Metiblee chided. He tilted slightly in his flight to keep Jeremy on his back.

The older man looked up with a smile and waved. He, at least, did not seem disturbed about the appearance of the dragons.

Metiblee and Catlara landed gently on the rooftop.

"Here thou art," Metiblee chuckled.

The boys slid down and hugged the dragon. "Thanks," they said, then shot off towards the wizard. "Thrundra!"

The elder man whisked the boys into a big, grandfatherly hug. He chuckled as he held them tight.

"How're my boys?" he greeted lovingly.

"Great!" Jeremy smiled.

"That ride was so lit!" Jordon exclaimed. "I'll never get tired of riding them."

"Me, either," Jeremy agreed.

"Good work, Metiblee," Thrundra greeted the dragon.

"Not I, Master. Catlara found them. We thought it best to bring them here."

"Yes, it was. Good work, Catlara. We've been awaiting their arrival. Thank you, my friends."

"See thee soon!" The dragons chimed and dropped off the edge of the palace. They nearly touched the ground before soaring up over the ocean to catch the air currents. They spun in the air as they passed over the palace. The boys cheered at the small show.

"Where's Narim and Zelmar?" Jordon asked, turning back to Thrundra. He was anxious to see his friends. Even though his friendship with Zelmar began rockily, the Krilt became a great teacher and body guard. Narim had joined the party with Jeremy, a young warrior having been assigned to keep Jeremy safe. Who knew he would become king?

Thrundra laughed at the boys' excitement. "His majesty is in conference right now, and Zelmar, of course, is standing guard. They shall be available shortly. However, Durmond is eager to see you both. Come."

The walk through the palace seemed different, Jeremy noticed. The decorations were more cheerful. The feeling was lighter. The guards in several places were still adults, but now the servants were adults as well. They were a wonderful mixture of the races, too.

"So, how have things been going?" Jordon brought Jeremy back to his surroundings. They were walking down the corridor where they had defeated Jamiss. He could hear murmurs behind the closed doors.

"Quite well. Narim has managed to smooth things over with virtually every leader in Asteria. Inter-island trading has begun, and with it, increased jobs and economy on every island. Zelmar has trained the palace guards well and is in the process of training the Kingdom Army. Dauren managed to find homes for almost all the children, either with their real families or adoptive ones. All in all, things are coming together nicely."

"So which kingdom won't cooperate?" Jeremy asked. He was expecting to hear Elthoria.

"The Centaus of Griffin Woods," Thrundra mention.

"Whoa! Stop!" Jeremy cried, coming up short.

They had walked down the corridor where Jordon and Jeremy had duped the guards with the staff. On the wall hung a tapestry depicting the scene. The boys stared at the wall.

"It's like looking at the wall in the nursery," Jordon murmured as those murals flashed across his mind.

"Why?" Jeremy asked Thrundra. He pointed at the tapestry.

"His majesty has had a monument erected at each site of your battle to reclaim Asteria. There is a mural in Thaurlonian's council room, a monument at Teesha's grave, one where you killed the dark Wight, and so forth."

"But why?" Jordon scowled. He didn't like this.

Thrundra smiled. "Narim thinks very highly of you. He wants these monuments visible to the people to inspire them to continue to strive despite the odds, just as you did. You do understand that the chances of you actually completing what we sent you out to do were miniscule, don't you?"

"It wasn't us alone," Jordon replied. "It was teamwork. Not just the five of us, but everyone else that helped. We were all a team."

"Yes," Thrundra agreed. "But the five of you had the job of infiltrating the impossible fortress. All would have been lost if you had not succeeded, and Narim wants that remembered.

"Come. Master Durmond awaits." He referenced the elderly wizard Jeremy had met early in his visit. Durmond was over 500 years old and still going strong. He was part of the original High Council when the cataclysm struck.

The remainder of the walk was silent as Jordon and Jeremy continued to follow Thrundra. They had passed several more tapestries with images from their trek through the castle when they came up against Jamiss. Jeremy felt uncomfortable with all the recollections depicting their battle. They simply did what had to be done and were lucky enough to have it work. When he exchanged an uneasy glance with Jordon, he knew his friend felt the same way.

"Um, Thrundra?" Jeremy asked nervously.

"Yes?"

"Whatever happened with Jamiss?" He remembered the stone statue he had changed the former tyrant into.

"We have moved the statue to the back garden near the other kings of the realm, both good and bad. Why?"

"Well, like, can someone bring him back? Like I did with Annese?"

Thrundra smiled understandingly. "No. He was using an anti-aging elixir to stay alive. Without it, he would die a normal death. He has been encapsulated now for over a year. The elixir would have worn off, and the body deceased by now. Even if someone got past the stone, all they would find is dust." He smiled at Jeremy.

Jeremy let out a breath he didn't know he was holding. "Ok. Good. I didn't want to have to come up against him again."

They arrived at a set of double doors. Thrundra opened one side and stepped in, ushering the boys in behind him. "Nothing to fear."

The elegant room was octagonal. Each wall depicted a different scene, some with two or more. The murals were so well done they seemed real. Each mural went from floor to ceiling.

"Sweet!" Jordon murmured, turning to see all the walls. "I want my room to look like this!"

"Is that... The Keep?" Jeremy asked, looking at one wall. "And Narim. Hey, Thrundra! You're on here! And Durmond! And Dauren!" He pointed to each face as he said their names.

"Look! There's Zelmar and Dracaina and Gralena and King Rauthdel!" Jordon cried, staring at Kriltnar. "Faeyruun!" He ran to another wall. His hand reached out shakily as he touched fairy Teesha's smiling face. His gaze grew watery as he remembered her last sparkle. Jeremy joined him.

"Look! Master Wren!" Jeremy tried to pull Jordon's attention away from their lost friend.

"The Siren," Jordon pointed out disdainfully.

"Over here! Look!" Jeremy pulled Jordon's arm. "Is this Elthoria?"

"Must be. There's Eliramond. But who's this?" Jordon pointed to a pretty young lady with long brown hair. Her spring green eyes stood out of pale, sharp features. She had an elegant look about her.

"That is Aresa, Eliramond's daughter. She is now Queen of Elthoria," Thrundra informed them, regarding the Elfin community.

"You mean...." Jeremy faltered as he looked behind him at Thrundra.

"Yes. Eliramond passed on shortly after your victory. He had sustained wounds during battle that neither cleric nor wizard could heal. He lived long enough to attend Narim's coronation and pledge Elthoria's loyalty to the King of Asteria. Aresa, though bitter about the death of her father, has been a wonderful asset in healing the wounds that separated the Elthorians from the rest of Asteria."

"Look, Jay! Thaurlonian!" Jordon tugged his friend.

"And Catlara and Landr, and lots more!"

"It's Ascentia!" Thrundra chuckled.

"Then this must be Griffon Woods," Jeremy pointed to the next mural. "That's Lady Matikata, right? Look at all the griffins!"

"Correct," Thrundra smiled. He pointed towards the bottom of the mural. "And the Centaus."

"And Mystic Island?" Jeremy asked. "With Tanis?" He referred to the seer he had met only once.

"Correct again."

"And Caldren," Jordon pointed at the last wall. "It's magnificent!"

"Why did he do this?" Jeremy asked, looking around. "It's so sick!"

"Sick?" Thrundra questioned.

Jeremy laughed. "Sick doesn't mean ill. I mean, it does, but in this case, it means good, great, impressive."

"Ah!" Thrundra chuckled over the boys' euphemisms.

"This is the new council room," an old voice announced from the long wooden table in the center. He stood from one of the high-backed, purple velvet-cushioned chairs. "Each mural reminds the council members that we are one. We stand together for the benefit of our land."

"Durmond!" Jeremy shouted.

Both boys took off at a run towards the old wizard they had missed in their excitement. They laughed with glee, wrapping him in two huge hugs.

"Ooof!" the wizard exclaimed, rocking a little as the boys wrapped their arms around him. "Darned, blasted youth!" he grumbled good-naturedly.

Thrundra laughed heartily at the scene. Durmond smiled warmly as he laid a hand on the back of each boy. A tear of joy slid down his cheek and was swallowed up by his mustache.

"It appears, my friend, that you make a wonderful grandfather after all," Thrundra teased.

"Great!" another deep voice interrupted. "But where's mine?"

Every eye looked at the tall, broad man at the door. He smiled broadly with his hands on his hips. A blue tunic with a royal symbol spread across the broad chest while a thick black belt tucked it in at the waist. His blue eyes sparkled in the tanned complexion. His boyish grin showed his pleasure at having the boys with him again.

"Narim!" the shout echoed, and the boys were off across the long room again, ready to tackle their friend.

"Wish I had their energy," Thrundra whispered to Durmond. The old wizard nodded in agreement.

Narim scooped the boys up in a massive hug. "Welcome home!" he whispered.

"All right! Come on! Move on, now!! Some of the rest of us want to say hello, too!"

"Zelmar!" Jordon scrambled out of Narim's grasp.

Zelmar pushed his way into the room, only to get assaulted by the two boys bigger than him. The krilt tried to stifle the sniffle in his nose and quickly wiped away the tears in his eyes with the bottom of his braided beard. His expression showed it thrilled him to see the boys again. His uniform was a golden red with white trim.

"Allergies," he muttered. Everyone chuckled, having had much the same reaction.

"It was really crazy," Jeremy said excitedly. "I had a dream about here."

"And I had one the same night," Jordon added.

"And when I woke up, the staff was glowing. I hadn't been able to get it to work in our world."

"So, we figured we needed to get back here for a visit anyway, so now was a good time."

"And the dragons were flying around Ascentia and picked us up to bring us here."

"That was after we sneaked past all the Rho'taak sitting on the top of the cliffs."

The men all smiled and nodded as the boys expounded on the adventure. Narim motioned towards the table.

"Let's have a seat," he offered. "Lilly will be bringing us some refreshment momentarily." Narim nodded to a woman standing by a side door that no one else had noticed.

The small group moved to sit around the long, wide table. The boys noticed the others remained standing until Narim took his place at the head of the table. His chair was slightly taller than the rest, with a crown engraved on the back's top. Several maids entered, carrying trays of drinks and food. One set out plates and utensils while others began pouring drinks and removing covers from the trays.

"Will there be anything else, Majesty?" one young lady asked. She was tall and thin with flowing brown hair. Her skin was clear and tanned from the sun. Her green eyes sparkled in a slender face as she inquired of her king.

"No, thank you, Lilly. This is wonderful."

Lilly curtsied. "Yes, sir. Saritha will stay behind to refill as necessary."

"That will be just fine."

Jeremy watched the maids each curtsey and leave the room. One, a young lady of about 15, stationed herself in a corner where she was out of the way, but could still see the table.

"Wow! The monarchy has really treated you well!" he teased his once-bodyguard.

Narim laughed and waved a hand to indicate they should begin eating. "It goes with the territory, but it drives me crazy!" he whispered. As soon as everyone was settled, he cleared his throat.

"We're really glad to see you boys again," he began, "And we have much to fill you in on."

"We already heard about Thaurlonian and Eliramond," Jeremy said solemnly.

Narim nodded. He took a breath. "Fact is, it was not a coincidence that you both had a dream and the globe glowed all in the same night. We weren't certain the efforts of our esteemed wizards were going to work, but apparently, they have. You see, we sent for you. We have a problem and figured you two were the best men for the job."

"What's up?" Jordon wanted to know. He helped himself to the food on the tray in front of him. Jeremy dug into the platter in front of him, then offered some to Thrundra, who sat next to him.

Narim smiled at Jordon's question. He had long ago gotten familiar with the boys' expressions. "Actually, it's what's down," he responded. He took a deep breath. "I'm not certain how much of our history you've been exposed to or remember, so I'll try to expound on only the pertinent information.

"At some point after Jamiss took control of the throne, he began exploring the palace. He found a special chamber deep below ground that held a special gem. Our records indicate it was a blue gem, about the size of a small child. It was held suspended by eight rays of special light in the center of the chamber. When he removed the gem from its cradle, the cataclysm occurred, splitting the land into separate islands and driving us into another dimension.

"Our records indicate the gem split and the pieces hidden somewhere below Caldren. We've tried to locate the pieces but have had no luck."

"We believe we have found the opening to an underground cavern, but no one can fit into it except the young children," Zelmar explained. "We felt they were too young and inexperienced to send down to explore the area."

"Also, the opening appears to have been blockaded from the inside."

"Hmmm," Jordon thought out loud. Jeremy could see his friend's brain at work by the expression on his face. "Couldn't you just teleport someone down there?" He remembered when Thrundra transported them to Caldren.

"We could if we knew what was there," Thrundra explained. "We have no idea how large the cavern might be. We could transport someone into a wall. That would be terrible."

"How far below the palace is this chamber?" Jeremy asked.

"Well below sea level," Durmond said quietly. "There is another problem, however."

The boys looked at the elderly wizard. He seemed tired. "Jamiss had a son, Mikkel, who also partook of the anti-aging potion his father would use. While Jamiss remains in his stone state, Mikkel and Jujene, one of Jamiss' sorcerers, have never been found."

"We believe he may be hiding in the sealed cavern below the palace," Thrundra sighed wearily.

"What about Durmond's scrying spell?" Jeremy asked. "Couldn't that tell us?"

"We have used the scrying spell, and the seers have used crystal balls, and several other devices. All they have confirmed is that Mikkel is indeed still alive. No one seems to recognize the location," Narim said quietly.

"Wait, wait!" Jordon sat back. "Let me see if I understand this. There's a giant blue crystal that's missing that you think is in a sealed off room so far below the palace that it is well below sea level."

"Correct," Zelmar replied.

"And you think Jamiss' son is holed up in there."

"Correct."

"And you guys want *us*," he pointed between himself and Jeremy, "to go down there and find them."

Thrundra smiled. "Straight and to the point. I like that."

"You've never been straight and to the point in your life!" Durmond growled.

A commotion in the hall outside the door brought Zelmar to his feet with a scowl. As he reached for it, the door burst open. A huge half-man, half-horse with large silver wings burst into the room. Three guards were trying to restrain him.

Narim rose and looked at the visitor curiously. His eyes widened with recognition. He waved the guards away.

"Mauseleth," he called the visitor by name. "Welcome. What brings you here?"

The man's dark eyes darkened even more, his agitated prancing displaying his mood. "Wonderful greeting," the Centaus growled. "Armed guards the entire way!"

"I'm sorry. I wasn't expecting you. I've been in conference." Narim motioned towards the table. He sighed. "Zelmar, put your axe away. Mauseleth is no threat."

Zelmar eyed the Centaus suspiciously but did as he was told. Slowly, he returned to his seat, yet he refused to sit down. Jeremy could tell something inside nagged at him. He never did trust others, and this one was being way too disrespectful. Zelmar remained prepared for anything.

"Would you care for some refreshment?" Narim offered. "It's a long flight from the woods."

"No—thank you," Mauseleth stiffened.

Narim nodded. "Very well. How may I help you?"

"You can tell me why you are suddenly sending children to spy on us," the Centaus demanded.

Narim scowled in confusion. "I'm sorry, Mauseleth. I don't understand. We are not using children as spies, nor anything else. Why would I need to spy on you? You cause no harm to anyone. I completely trust the Centaus."

"Then why are there two mortal children on my island claiming to need to get to the palace and playing with my daughter?" he growled.

"I know not. Thrundra?"

"Sorry, Sire," the wizard shrugged.

"Zelmar?" Again, a confused shrug.

"Excuse me," a youthful voice piped in. "Mr. Mau.."

"Mauseleth," Narim assisted.

"Yes, well, sir, could you describe the children, please?" Jeremy asked with a feeling of dread.

"A boy and a girl. About this high," he leveled his hand. "The girl had almost black, curly hair, cut short; dark skin." He motioned to his head. "She had a yellow tunic with an image of something and short blue leggings that stopped before the knee. The boy had light hair, cut short, pale skin, a black tunic. He also wore blue leggings."

The boys groaned.

"I swear I'm gonna kill her!" Jeremy growled. His head dropped into the crook of one arm as his other hand pounded the table. "I'm gonna kill her! I'm gonna kill her!"

"It's worse!" Jordon grumbled angrily. "She brought my cousin!"

"I believe we have an answer," Narim smirked at the boys. "Would you care to explain?"

"I knew that was Neesie's bike!" Jordon slammed his fist on the table.

"Apparently," Jeremy explained, "my sister Annese decided to come back to Asteria."

"And she brought my cousin Tyler with her," Jordon added.

"Yes, those were the names Odessa said," Mauseleth agreed. "Why are they on my island?"

"That's one we'll have to ask them," Jeremy replied agitated, "And the answer had better be a good one."

"I beg your pardon, Mauseleth," Narim nodded his head in a bow. "We shall retrieve the children and leave you to your forest."

"Then you had better be able to dig very far down," Mauseleth murmured.

Narim scowled. "I don't understand."

"Odessa and those children fell into a sinkhole in the Harpy Field. We've already lowered 18 lengths of rope and haven't reached them."

Narim turned wide-eyed and looked at Thrundra. He understood the problem but was at a loss for a solution.

"Eighteen lengths of rope are lower than the room we were just discussing," Thrundra thought quickly.

"I'll go down after them," Zelmar volunteered.

Mauseleth shook his head. "You are too broad. That has been my problem as well." He looked over at the boys. "But I believe they could just get through."

Jeremy and Jordon looked around suddenly. All the other eyes were on them. Both closed their eyes, sagged with resignation, and sighed.

"O-kay," Jordon agreed. "Just... give us time to get some provisions first. We hadn't planned on staying a while."

Jeremy dropped his head into his hands, elbows propped on the table. "Ya know, this big brother stuff is for the birds. All I ever do is save her hide!" he grumbled.

Mauseleth roared with laughter. He slapped his foreleg. "Best get used to that, son," he laughed. "You'll be doing that the rest of her life! I know! I'm the eldest of eight, seven of them girls!" Jeremy let out a groan that set the rest of the adults laughing again.

"Please give us a short time to outfit the boys, and we shall accompany you home," Narim requested. Mauseleth nodded.

3 – DINNER WITH THE SNAKE PEOPLE

TYLER

Three bottoms skidded across a rocky floor. Moaning and aching, the small bodies struggled to their feet, brushing off the dirt and dust that clung to them on their trip down. The air was heavy with a moist, earthy scent, making it harder to breathe.

"Is everyone ok?" Tyler asked, looking at a scrape on his elbow.

"I think I'm bleeding," Annese said. She was patting the back of her leg. "But all I see is mud."

Tyler bent down to look. He used his shirt to wipe off the scrape. He shook his head. "It's bleeding."

"So stop the bleeding!" Annese griped. As she glanced around her, she saw Odessa lying on the floor. "Odessa? You ok?"

Odessa lay curled on the ground. One leg lay out straight. She sniffled as she breathed heavily.

Annese broke away from Tyler. "Odessa?" she kneeled down next to the Centaus. "Dess, what's wrong?"

Tyler came near and noticed a large cut on Odessa's rump. He pulled off his shirt and pressed it to the cut.

"OW!" Odessa cried.

"Sorry," Tyler apologized, "but you're bleeding."

"Is it the cut?" Annese asked.

"I... I think my leg is broken," she managed to say.

"Which one?" Tyler asked. He still applied pressure to her wound.

"The one NOT curled under," Annese replied sarcastically. "Du-uh!" Annese looked at the leg. "I don't see anything."

"Here, let me look." Tyler handed her the shirt. "Go stop the bleeding. They taught us how to identify broken bones in scouts," he said.

Tyler studied Odessa's leg. It was swollen around the hock. A few scrapes.

"Hey, Neese, you still got your flashlight?" he asked.

Annese looked around. Her backpack had slipped off her shoulder on the way down. Squinting to look into the darkness, she spotted a pink strap on the ground. Quickly she ran over, picked it up, and pulled open the zipper. She felt around inside the bag and pulled out the red plastic tube. Holding her breath, she flipped the switch. A bright white light cut through the dim glow of the cavern.

"Yes!" she cried triumphantly.

"Over here. Let me see!" Tyler reached for the flashlight.

"Wha... what is that?" Odessa shied away in fear.

"It's a flashlight," Annese tried to explain. "The batteries hold electricity that makes the bulb shine."

"Huh?" Odessa was more afraid.

"It's a light stick. There's a limited amount of heat inside that makes light come out the top," Tyler explained in simpler terms.

"Will... will it hurt?" Odessa asked.

"Only if it gets flashed in your eyes," Annese reassured her friend. "It's ok."

Tyler took the flashlight from Annese and examined Odessa's leg. He ran his hand gently over the slender leg, checking the bones. He examined the swollen ankle. The hoof seemed a little scraped, but ok.

"Well, the good news is that I don't think your leg is broken. The bad news is that you're swollen in places, meaning you're pretty bruised up. It's gonna be painful to walk."

"I can't get up," Odessa whimpered. "It hurts."

"It's going to, Dess," Tyler tried to reassure her. "My legs and back hurt, too, but we've got to find a way out."

"My dad will rescue us," the Centaus replied confidently.

Tyler walked over to look at the hole they came out of. It was at least eight feet off the floor and small. The drop was shear, with the base of the wall back farther than the hole.

"I don't think so, Dess. I'm not sure how we fit down it."

"We need water," Annese stated in the quiet. "All our cuts will get infected if we don't clean them."

"I think we need to figure out where we are first."

Tyler looked around. The beam from the flashlight disappeared after a few feet. He dropped to the ground and looked around. Moss. There had to be water around here somewhere.

"Let's go look around," he suggested. The more they walked, the better Odessa's leg would feel.

"Come on, Dess," Annese encouraged. "Try to get up."

Odessa set her jaw and drew in a deep breath. She raised her hindquarters. Leaning hard on Annese, she managed to rise up onto her good leg. Slowly, she set the other one under her. Holding her breath, she tried to put weight on it. With a scream of pain, she collapsed to the floor. Annese dropped next to her. Tyler sighed audibly.

"Alright, look. You two stay here and rest. I'm going to look around."

"But...." Annese began.

"Stay here!" Tyler said firmly. "I won't go too far."

Tyler set off to his left following the wall. Swinging the beam back and forth, he noticed the pathway narrowing. The wall to his left stayed the same. The one to his right had openings every so often about the size of a door. Somewhere nearby he could hear the echo of a drip-drip-drip. Searching the ground and following the sound, Tyler found a spot where water was dripping off the ceiling. He scowled, thinking he saw something slither away as he approached.

With a shrug, he examined the small pool that had formed over a long time. Carefully, he scooped up a handful of water. He sipped to test it. It could be seawater. Cool. Clear. Crisp. Wonderful!

"Hey, Annese!" he called behind him.

"Yea?"

"Bring my water bottle from my pack. Hurry!"

It wasn't long before Annese appeared next to him. She had her water bottle as well.

"I thought we could use one to clean with and one for drinking."

"Good idea. We can come back for more, too."

As they filled the second bottle, a scream echoed from behind them. Suddenly, the scream was muffled, but tiny reverberations of a conflict went through the tunnel. A chill went up Tyler's spine.

"Odessa!" Annese hollered in alarm. The bottle slipped from her hand.

Tyler grabbed her wrist and pulled her back as he reached under the water for the bottle. He put his finger to his lips to hush her, then capped the bottle. Picking up the flashlight, they ran back to where Odessa had been.

The site was vacant. Only their packs were still there. The ground where Odessa had been showed signs of a struggle. In the distance they could hear sounds of... something. A struggle? Something moving? Who knew? Off to one side were wide, S-shaped tracks, as if several things were being dragged.

"Snakes?" Tyler examined the tracks.

"What about snakes?" Annese asked quickly, a tinge of fear in her voice.

"That's what these tracks look like." Tyler looked in the direction they went. "Come on," he grabbed his pack.

"Where?" Annese asked, pulling her pack onto her shoulders.

"To find Odessa." Tyler handed the flashlight to Annese. He took a few steps in the direction of the tracks.

"And keep that light down. We don't want to announce our arrival."

Dodging along the outer wall, the two stayed in the shadows as they followed the tracks. They remained still with the flashlight off as movements near some of the cave openings caught their attention. Moving quickly and quietly, they eventually came to an opening between walls that would have been a clearing if they were in the woods. Tyler dragged Annese behind a large rock near the outer wall.

There were no cave openings near this clearing, but black patches splotched the ground. Odessa leaned against the far wall, sniffling. Thick brown leaves tied together around her mouth gagged her. Something bound her hands and feet with vines. Between them and Odessa were the strangest snakes Tyler had ever seen throwing branches, roots, and vines into a pile. Their heads were almost human with an elongated snout. Black, forked tongues would shoot out of their mouths from time to time. The torso was human: neck, shoulders, arms, hands. From the waist down, however, the bodies became a shiny gray scale similar to a boa constrictor. The two creatures stood about as tall as an adult man, but the tails behind went several feet more. They talked back and forth with a kind of hissing language.

"We need to get Odessa," Annese whispered.

"I know. I'm trying to figure out how."

"What are they doing?"

"I think they're trying to build a fire."

"To keep 'Dessa warm? How nice!"

Tyler turned and looked at Annese in disbelief.

"What?" she asked.

"They aren't making her comfortable! The fire is for dinner! To COOK dinner."

Tyler glanced at Annese's scowling face, then watched her look at the creatures and Odessa. After a few moments, her eyes widened in horror. Tyler's hand clamped over her mouth just before she could scream.

"Shh! Do you want to give us away?" Annese shook her head. "Ok. We're going to have to act fast. I've got a pocket knife in my pocket. I can cut Odessa free, but we need a diversion."

"What kind of diversion?" she asked warily.

"There's another rock down that way about as big as this one. Go hide behind it. Call Odessa as if we're looking for her, but holler in the direction we came. When they pass you, run back here. While they're chasing your voice, I'll cut Odessa free."

Annese took in a deep breath and squared her shoulders. "I'm ready," she announced bravely.

"Go get 'em, tiger!" Tyler encouraged.

Annese dropped her pack and the flashlight, then picked her way back the way they'd come. Behind her, she could hear the crackle of a fresh fire. She had to hurry.

Tyler braced himself, closing his knife in his hand. His heart pounded in his ears as he waited impatiently. After what seemed like hours, he heard Annese's voice.

"'Des-sa! Odessa, where are you?" Annese's voice echoed off the rocky walls. "O-des-sa!"

The two creatures looked at each other and smiled. Greed and hunger filled their eyes. Quickly, they abandoned the faint fire and slithered towards Annese's voice.

"Wow! Those guys can move!" Tyler thought, grasping the flashlight. He ran across to Odessa. Shining the light down on the ground, he fell to his knees in front of her. "Shh! We're gonna get outta here."

He quickly slit the vines at her hands. "Get that gag off!" The vines on her feet took a little more work, but he finally freed both sets of legs.

"Ow!" Odessa complained, trying to stand. "It hurts."

"You'll have to hurry, or we're *all* gonna be dinner!"

A scream rent the quiet through the chambers. Odessa and Tyler snapped towards the sound.

"Annese!" Tyler whispered. He glanced at the flashlight. "Come on!"

"Where?" asked his friend. Panic was beginning to etch her voice.

"To the wall. Hurry!" Tyler helped her limp quickly towards the wall.

Tyler handed Odessa their packs. He could hear the scuffles behind him and Annese making idle threats to her captors.

"Take these and go to the other side of the clearing. Wait for us in the shadows." Odessa limped off as quickly as she could to wait for Tyler. She whimpered quietly with each step.

Tyler waited. He needed the right angle and a powerful beam to get Annese free. Peering into the dark, he could just make out the creatures in the dim light. Annese was struggling to get free from between them. One of the snakes was hissing at her.

As the snakes reached the other side of his boulder, Tyler jumped in front of the trio and in his best bear-growl shouted, "Annese, shut your eyes!" Both snakes looked at him with a start, just as he wanted. Tyler flipped the flashlight on right into their faces. Both snakes hollered in pain, covering their eyes. Tyler grabbed Annese's hand.

"Run!"

The two had about a five second head start before the snakes followed. "Come on, Dess!" Tyler called as they passed Odessa in the shadows.

The three ran as fast as possible. Other snakes came from the dark holes to investigate the commotion. Several tried to follow them. Tyler would stop every now and again and flash the light beam in their eyes. It scared many away.

"There!" Odessa pointed. "Go there!"

She pointed to three tall stalagmites in a corner. In the middle of them was a shiny white stone about three feet by three feet square. As they approached, a short, thin man with a long brown ponytail appeared. He walked off the platform, making notes on a pad of parchment.

The three ran onto the square. Tyler turned to warn the man, but no sound came out of his mouth. Instead, it hung open. What in the world...?

4 – TRICKY GETAWAY

JORDON

Mauselith landed in the open field near the hole. A large green dragon landed next to him. Jordon, Jeremy, and Thrundra slid off his back. Jeremy patted his long neck.

"Thanks, Nes," he said to the dragon.

"My pleasure, young master."

Thrundra kneeled next to the hole. Jordon looked over his shoulder. The hole opened into a slippery, dusty tunnel going almost straight down.

"The children didn't respond, you say?" Thrundra questioned.

"Nothing. Their screams just faded away," Mauselith replied, with his arms crossed over his massive chest.

"How much rope do we have?" Jordon asked.

"About thirty lengths," Thrundra replied.

"How long is a length?" he asked.

Thrundra looked at him strangely. "It's a length," Thrundra replied.

Jordon looked at Jeremy uncertainly. The expression he received mirrored his own. How long was a length? The dragon next to them cleared his throat and chuckled.

"A length, young masters, is approximately twice as long as I am from nose to the end of my tail. Does that help you?"

Jordon nodded. "Yes, it does. Thank you." Jordon walked the length of the dragon and calculated the distance, estimating Nestiel to be about seventy-five feet long. So, a length would be 150 feet or so. Thirty of them is almost 4,500 feet. A little under a mile. He glanced at the hole again.

"I fear, however, what we have may not be enough," Nestiel remarked.

"What do you mean?" Thrundra asked rising.

"If that tis a sinkhole, it would open into a cavern. The cavern wouldst be well below the floor of the oceans."

Dawning rose in Thrundra's eyes. "Are you saying there are caverns and tunnels under the island?"

"And people as well, I expect," explained the dragon. "Below Ascentia art the lava pits that providest heat for the mountains. A strange people liveth there, thriving in the smoldering air and extremely hot temperatures. Whilest I was still a young wyrmling, I got lost exploring the catacombs and managed a glimpse of them."

"Wait! Wait!" Jeremy held up his hands. "If there's another race below the islands, how come no one knows about them?"

"I believest I just informed ye about them."

Jordon looked at Thrundra. "How far down is it to the bottom of the sea?"

Thrundra shrugged. "I don't know. We have never had reason to measure it. I would imagine it depends on the location."

"Are you going after my daughter or not?" Mauseleth pranced in impatience.

Jordon looked at the hole. "We're not going to fit with our packs on."

"We can lower them down by the rope," Jeremy suggested. "It'll keep the rope taught, too."

Jordon agreed. "Sharijhol will have to go that way as well. Can we slide your staff down the back of your shirt so we can at least *see*?"

Jeremy nodded. "Good idea."

"Let's begin then," Thrundra decided, pulling a mallet and a stake from his robes. He hammered the stake into the ground as the boys pulled off their packs.

Jordon used some twine to tie Sharijol down into the pack. He twisted the small rope around the hilt, then tied it off to the grommets on the sides. He then helped Jeremy slide the staff down the back of his shirt. Good thing it was a loose shirt. They used the twine to tie the shaft to Jeremy's shoulders.

The boys tied the end of the rope around the shoulder straps of the packs in taut line hitches. They'd hold and still be easy to release. Thrundra tied off an end of the rope to the stake. They began lowering the packs, but they wouldn't go far.

"They aren't heavy enough to slide down," Jeremy remarked.

"Why don't you slide down on top of them?" Jordon suggested.

"Why don't you?" Jeremy countered.

"Because you're lighter than I am. We'll have better control lowering you than me."

"But who knows what's down there?"

"I have a flashlight in the front pocket of my pack. Once you hit bottom, take it out."

"Also, when you reach the bottom, let the rope go slack," Thrundra informed him. "If you run into trouble, tug twice. Here." Thrundra handed each boy a pair of hide gloves. "These will keep your hands from getting scraped up by the rock and the rope."

Jeremy grudgingly put the gloves on. "I'm always the guinea pig!" he grumbled.

"And you make such a cute one, too!" Jordon chided.

Jordon helped Jeremy squeeze himself into the hole, pulling more dirt away and covering his eyes. He swallowed hard as he watched his best friend shimmy down the rope about twenty feet to the packs. He heard Jeremy whisper the command, and the globe of the staff lit up.

JEREMY

Jeremy kicked the packs free of the rocky crag they were stuck on.

"O.K.," he yelled up. "Lower them some more! The path goes almost straight down!"

The rope slid past him as the packs slid out of sight. The lighting was dim and getting dimmer. Eventually, he couldn't see them at all. After another short wait, the rope stopped.

"We can't go any farther," Jeremy heard Thrundra call. "We're out of rope! I don't believe the packs hit bottom."

"You can't conjure up more rope?" Jeremy yelled up in exasperation. "And you call yourself a wizard?" He chuckled as he slid past the outcropping. Carefully, he began lowering himself between the crevices and handholds of the shaft. After several feet, his hand or a foot would lose traction from slime or loose gravel. Ten more feet, he yelled up.

"Keep talking to me! I'm not so sure I'm going to be able to hear you all the way down here!"

"How far are you?" Jordon yelled down.

"Not sure. Twenty-five or thirty feet, but I never was good at judging distances."

"What's it like?"

"Slippery. You need to watch your pressure against the walls. You can't count on the rope to keep your spot." He was moving down steadily. "I can't see the packs yet. I think I may run into them first."

"Your voice is fading."

"What?"

"Your voice is fading! I'm gonna start down so we can keep talking."

"Be careful! One wrong move, and you'll land on top of me!"

"Gotcha!"

"And watch that outcrop where the packs got stuck. It's tricky to get around."

"How will I know where it is?"

"You'll land on it!"

Jeremy was starting to feel closed in. He took several deep breaths to calm his anxiety. It was harder to see. The light from the staff was behind him, and without actually holding it, he couldn't make the glow brighter. It took a long while, but Jeremy found the packs by landing on them. Feeling his way with his foot, he managed to slide alongside them. He had a hard time maneuvering in the tight space, but he found the right pack and pulled out Jordon's flashlight. He flipped it on and peered down.

"We got a problem, Jordon!"

"What's that?" the voice came from somewhere above. A sprinkle of dirt and stones rained down on top of him.

"We're out of rope, and I still can't see bottom."

"It's dark."

"I've got your flashlight."

"O.K. Hmm. Can you get past the packs?"

"Possibly, but it'll be really tight. I could hardly move to get your flashlight."

"Why don't you go past the packs and continue down. When you've reached bottom, I'll pull the backs loose, then follow them down."

Jeremy thought for a moment. "Sounds like a plan to me. I'm off!" He still wasn't happy about going first without protection. Who knew what was down there?

He shimmied and twisted until he was past the packs. His staff scraped the wall. Dang! Hope the globe wasn't damaged. He could hear Jordon yelling their plan up the shaft to the others. He tied the flashlight to one of the laces in his tunic, then began down. He struggled to keep pressure and stay in control. The sides were getting shearer. How in the world does Jordon do this?

"Glad we went spelunking two weeks ago!" he called up.

"Me, too!"

Suddenly Jeremy's feet slid out from beneath him. His hands flew into the air as gravity plunged his body down the tunnel, sliding all the way! "Ahhhhhh!" was all he could say.

Jeremy's body skidded across the hard dirt of the cavern floor. He lay still a few moments to catch his breath. If it had been a water slide, it might have been fun. With a groan, he hoisted himself to his feet and stretched. He was sore all over. He turned towards the sinkhole when some gravel slid down. With a plop, the packs hit the ground, sending up a cloud of dust. He pulled them out of the way just in time.

THRUNDRA

Thrundra looked at Mauselith. He sighed worriedly.

"Well, that's it," he said. "It's all up to the boys now."

"And they're to get back up how?" Mauselith questioned with a scowl.

"I'm not certain. I'm going to retrieve more rope and lengthen this. Hopefully, we have sufficient to reach bottom."

"That will be difficult to know since we know not how deep it is."

"I agree."

Thrundra looked at the hole and swallowed. "I'll let you know when I hear anything."

"Likewise." Mauselith nodded stiffly and flew off. It was obvious he didn't trust this wizard, but he had no other options.

"Thou both lacketh faith in the ability of the young masters. They shall be fine," the green dragon said with a grin.

"You see more than I, Nestiel," Thrundra replied. "I fear it will be a long wait."

"A long wait, yes," the dragon replied, nodding. "Thou fearest because this time they hath not thy aide. Trust them." The dragon nudged the sorcerer.

"Thank you, my friend." Thrundra nudged him back. "Let's go see what's in the storeroom."

JORDON

"Are you O.K.?" Jordon yelled. No answer. "Jeremy?" Nothing. "Jay! Answer me!" Still no answer.

Jordon had reached the packs. He leaned against the wall of the tunnel and felt around for the loose end of the knot. He couldn't find it. He reached into his pocket, then he began cutting the rope. Good thing he had just sharpened his pocketknife a few days ago. In a short sawing motion, Jordon cut the packs free. He listened as they slid out of sight. He counted 25 seconds before he thought he heard the dull thud of the packs landing. It was still a far trek down. Taking a deep breath, Jordon closed his eyes and let go of the wall.

Jordon rubbed his elbow where he scraped the sides of the sinkhole. A moan escaped his lips as he stretched his back and coughed from the dust. He rose stiffly and tried walking out the muscles.

"Rough ride, huh?" Jeremy smirked. He leaned against the wall with his arms crossed.

"Yea! How far down are we?" Jordon asked. He reached down and pulled the packs apart.

"Couldn't tell ya," Jeremy replied, looking around. The bright beam bounced off dark walls. The ground was loose dirt and moss. The normally colorful walls were lacking the glowing stones. A thin grain covered the ground. The air was heavy with a wet, earthy smell.

"They had 4,500 feet of rope. That's nearly a mile, I think. And we're well below that," Jordon groaned as he took Sharijol out of his pack to inspect it.

"A couple of miles?" Jeremy thought out loud. "I mean, that fall was pretty far."

"Could be. Could be further than that."

"Hey, look!" Jeremy ran over to the right. "Footprints!"

Jordon stooped over to look. "And hoof prints. At least we know they're together."

"Maybe. Look." Two sets of prints went off to the left. "Looks like Tyler and Annese went that way."

"Yea, but they came back. There aren't many hoof prints. I wonder if the Centaus girl is hurt."

"What are these?" Jeremy kneeled down to examine some tracks. Jordon followed and looked over his shoulder.

The scraping S-track continued along the way. Two ran
side by side with a few straight scrapes between them.

"If I didn't know better, I'd swear they were cobra
tracks," Jordon remarked, surprised. "But they only live in
the dessert."

"And they're dragging something with them," Jeremy
pointed out.

"This is really getting weird.

"Shh! Listen!" Jeremy hushed.

The surrounding air was still. From somewhere in
the distance, there was a scraping sound, followed by a
hiss. The boys looked at each other. The sounds came
again.

"What do you think?" Jordon whispered. Jeremy
shrugged.

Another voice came from some ways away to their
left.

"Oh! Oh! Well, how do you do?" the timid voice said.
"Oh, dear! No! No! I don't think...."

Jordon picked up his pack and started towards the
voice. "Come on!" Jeremy rolled his eyes, grabbed his pack,
and followed.

"Oh, my! N-n-no!" the voice began to panic. "No! You
don't understand!"

Jordon jogged the pathway. Dark caves appeared
from time to time. Several times he would snap his
attention to the side thinking something was moving
towards them in the shadows, but when they'd shine the

flashlight towards it, whatever it was shrank back into the dark.

The main tunnel seemed to curve around forever to the right. They passed several pools of water; the incoming liquid seeping through tight gaps in the rocks overhead. Occasionally they'd pass a pile of bones or a long-dried skin.

"I'm beginning to get freaked out," Jeremy said as they passed a large skin wrapped in on itself.

"They're just snake skins," Jordon said.

"Have you noticed the *size* of those snake skins?"

"Not really. Hey! Look!"

The signs of a scuffle showed in the dusty dirt. Similar sliding marks met two footprints. The poor soul had been dragged forward, losing articles here and there.

Jordon picked up a straight stick off the ground. He turned it over in his hand under the light.

"What is it?" Jeremy asked.

"It looks like... well, a charcoal pencil,... like in art class," Jordon scowled. "But how?"

He shined the light in the direction the tracks went. Something glistened in the dirt up ahead. The boys went forward. Jeremy picked this one up.

"It's a key."

"Come on."

As they followed the path, they picked up a leather pouch with a cloth-braided cord, several small pieces of canvas, something that looked like a compass, a cloth hat, several coins, and another pencil. The trail continued for a long stretch. Several times, the boys needed to spin in the direction of oncoming hisses.

One time in particular, the boys caught a glimpse of the "enemy". A tall, thin, whitish snake with a humanoid torso stood in the beam. Its hands flew to its eyes to block out the bright beam of the flashlight. A black, forked tongue flickered out of its snake-like face to taste the air. Large, white fangs gleamed in the mouth that was open in pain. Quickly, the creature retreated into the darkness. Slowly, the boys looked at each other in wide-eyed fear.

"Come on," Jordon swallowed, glancing back at it. "Let's keep moving."

"You *do* have spare batteries, right?" Jeremy asked with concern. He fell into step beside his friend.

"One set. You *do* have another flashlight, don't you?"

"Yes, but not another set of batteries. I didn't think we'd be using them for very long."

Jordon sighed. "Me either." The trail turned. "Look! The trail is going to the right."

"Just keep goin'," Jeremy agreed uncertainly. He glanced over his shoulder to be sure they weren't being followed.

They found themselves in a long stretch between rocks about ten feet wide. The tracks disappeared into the first cave on the left of a large cul-de-sac, less than 20 feet from the intersection. A crackling sound reached their ears as the boys approached stealthily. Jordon doused the light with his hand as they leaned in to peer around the corner. The sight frightened them even more.

In a far corner was a cage made of some kind of wood. A man no taller than Annese was sitting in it, holding his head, elbows on his knees. His face was pale beneath the streaks of dirt and a growing beard of curls.

His hair looked to be a light brown. He had it pulled back into a long ponytail behind his head. His bangs were a mess and so long they were in his eyes. He wore a light tan tunic tucked into dark brown knickers. Gray knee socks covered his calf, disappearing into worn black shoes. A waist-length coat was on the ground next to him. He was muttering to himself.

In the center of the cave was a growing fire. Two large sticks on either side of the pit poked up towards the ceiling, ending in a Y shape. Three large snake creatures were standing around it arguing about something. One reached down and put more sticks on the fire. Two smaller snake creatures were on the side between the boys and the man. They seemed to be going through the contents of a large leather pouch that obviously belonged to the man.

"What're we gonna do?" Jeremy's urgent voice whispered into Jordon's ear. "We gotta get him outta there!"

"I know. I'm thinking." Jordon looked around. There wasn't much they could use, and with five of the creatures, they were more than likely to be captured. Suddenly, Jordon's eyes fell to the staff sticking out of Jeremy's shirt. His scowl slowly turned into a wide grin.

Jeremy's eyes widened in fear. "What?" he asked. "What are you thinking?"

"Your staff!" Jordon whispered excitedly.

"My staff?" Jeremy scowled confused. His eyes widened in realization. "My staff!" He flung his pack to the ground and began reaching over his shoulder to grasp the wood. "Which spell should I use? *Flesh to Stone? Holy Burst?*"

"I was thinking *Time Halt*," Jordon replied. "We don't want to kill them, just want to get the guy out."

"Excellent! Grab hold." Both boys grasped the long wooden bark of the staff. "*Vicis Subsisto!*" Jeremy whispered.

The boys peered into the cave. No one moved. Even the flames of the fire were frozen in position.

"Let's move," Jeremy urged. "This doesn't last long."

Leaving their packs in the corridor, the boys raced through the cave.

Jordon giggled as Jeremy stopped to take the leather pouch from the snake youths with an "I'll take that." He picked up the other items and trinkets off the ground and deposited them back into the pouch.

Jordon began cutting the vine holding the bars closed. The sharp knife sliced through it like butter. Throwing open the cage, Jordon tried to lift the little man. As much as he struggled, he couldn't move him.

"Got a levitation spell in that thing?" he called to Jeremy.

Jay scowled, coming near Jordon. "Yea, but why?"

"I can't move the guy! He's too heavy!"

"I only know how to do the levitation spell one way. We'll have to drag him," Jeremy announced, tying the pouch to his belt loops. "Turn him around."

It was Jordon's turn to scowl. "Are you sure about this?"

"Yep. It's how we move Nikko when he gets stubborn," Jeremy explained, entering the cage. "Good. Hook your hand under his armpit. Now pull!"

The two boys dragged the man out of the cage, past the youths, and to the entry.

"Should we get his coat?" Jordon asked.

"It may be tight."

"I'll run." Jordon darted for the cage. He reached down and grasped the coat in his hand. Luck wasn't with him today. As he passed the two youths again, the spell ended. The two snakes looked at their hands in surprise. One of the adults noticed the cage open. Another noticed Jordon running through the cave and hissed. Something green flew past Jordon and sizzled on the cave wall.

"Run!" Jordon shouted as he approached Jeremy and the little man. "Acid."

They didn't need to be told twice. Jordon watched Jeremy grasp the dazed man's arm and tugged him along. He had scooped up the straps of his pack with his staff as he passed it. The little man tripped, landing on his hands and knees. Jeremy tried to get him up again. Jordon grasped his pack as he came running up, grasped the man's other arm, and helped Jeremy tug. The three ran through the stretch of ground towards the alley.

"Run! Don't think!" Jordon instructed. "They're right behind us!"

Jeremy stumbled as he glanced over his shoulder. He caught himself and kept going as he shouted. "*Contego!*" The invisible shield from the staff encompassed the three escapees just in time. Another green glob splat across the shield and sizzled down to the floor. They darted through the rock face arch and out into the open of their first path.

"There! Behind the rocks!" Jeremy pointed right.

"No! No! This way!" the small man interjected, darting to the set of strange, stone columns opposite them. A bright white stone plate about three feet by three feet sat on the floor between the columns.

"What good is that?" Jordon asked following.

"Come! Come!" he urged.

Jordon tried to halt his forward motion when he saw the man step on the square and disappear. Unfortunately, Jeremy plowed into his back. The two boys tumbled helplessly onto the square.

MIKKEL

"Master," a hoarse voice shook the figure on the straw bed. "Master, wake up."

"What is it?" the sleepy, deep voice replied. The man shook his head. He looked around the dark, rocky cavern. It was small and lit by a single, everlasting candle on a small nightstand. His dresser faced him from the wall opposite his bed. A table with a chair sat in the corner with his books on it. A painting of Caldren's Fields hung over it on the wall. A dusty green curtain against the adjacent wall indicated the archway to another room. An old wooden box was stashed against the bottom of the bed.

"We have visitors," the hoarse voice replied.

"What are you talking about?" the figure grumbled and rolled over.

"According to the globe, the two youths, Jordon and Jeremy, are back," the hoarse voice replied.

His master sat up quickly. "What? Where?"

"They have arrived in the cavern under Griffin's Woods."

"Are you certain?"

"Absolutely, Master."

"Have they been to the castle?"

"Yes."

"Did they discuss the crystal?"

"I do not know, sir. As best I can figure out, a Centaus and a dragon brought them to a hole in a field. They went down a sinkhole in Harpy Fields."

"They'll get past the Sanders. Those dumb snakes lack intelligence. We'll have to be certain to take them out ourselves. Those stupid youths have sentenced me to exile when I should be king!"

"Easy, Master! You know how stress upsets you."

"Never mind stress!" the master yelled. "We only have so much elixir. We've been milking what we have for almost two years! There's not much left! *You* have trouble getting the ingredients! When it's gone, we'll both age faster than normal."

"I understand the ramifications, ... Master," the man responded with strained patience.

"I'll get my revenge while I'm still alive—and I'm going to take them with me!" he grinned menacingly.

5 – LIFE UNDERGROUND

ANNESE

Annese, Odessa, and Tyler stared out at this new cave in amazement. The lanes before them were lined with green grass and pretty flowers. The air here was sweet and light. A strange bright light emanated from the rock walls around them. Small birds flew about.

"Toto, we're not in Kansas anymore," Annese mumbled one of her favorite lines from a childhood movie.

"Do I see...trees?" Odessa asked.

"Um, yea," Tyler confirmed.

"Do I see...people?" Annese asked.

Sure enough, people no bigger than they were walking around in the lanes between houses. Some had baskets. Women carried babies. Men had tools in their hands. Some wore dresses, others pants. Children ran by with wooden balls or sticks or dolls. Their clothing was green, brown, or black. Most wore tunics with either short-legged trousers or skirts. All had straight brown hair in various styles. Most wore it long. The men had it pulled back into ponytails or braids. Most women wore it up in buns. Children wore pigtails, ponytails, braids, all kinds of styles, but no one wore it straight down.

Streets went off in three directions. The people built houses into the rock face on the sides. Curtains hung in the windows. Annese spotted a black and white cat sitting on a windowsill.

"Which way do we go?" Annese shrugged to Tyler's inquiry.

One of the children stopped and stared up at them. The three looked back at the little boy with shoulder-length brown hair and big, brown eyes. He wore a rumpled, dirty green shirt, and his black pants had a tear above the knee. Dirt streaked across his face as if he'd been wrestling. Tyler was about two heads taller than the boy. He stood there, staring expectantly at them.

"Um, hi," Tyler greeted the boy. The child continued to stare. Tyler exchanged glances with Annese.

"Were you climbing trees?" Annese asked. "Your pants are ripped." The boy continued to stare.

"Maybe he doesn't speak English," Tyler remarked. "¿Como estas?" he said to the boy. The boy looked back at him.

"Hammie, you're being rude!" a nearby girl scolded. The boy turned to her and stuck his tongue out. "Just you wait! I'm gonna tell Ma, then you'll be sorry!"

Annese and Odessa chuckled at the girl's come back. Tyler smiled, liking the girl already.

"Hi," he called to her.

"Hello," she said, coming over. Her features and coloring looked much like the little boy she was scolding. Unlike her brother's hair, hers was almost to her waist.

She wore it braided down her back. She wore a faded
brown jumper with an off-white, short-sleeved blouse
under it. There were sandals on her feet. She scowled at
Tyler with confusion. "You don't look like a grown-up.
Where's your whiskers?"

"Whiskers?"

"Beard," Odessa translated.

"Oh! I'm still too young," he smiled.

"How old are you?" she asked.

"Ten," he replied. He suddenly realized he was at
least a head and a half taller than she was. "How old are
you?"

The girl smiled like she'd just won a bet. "Twelve."

"Do you have a name?" he asked.

"Yes."

Tyler waited expectantly. The girl clammed up. "And
it would be....?"

"Aresta. What's yours?"

"It's nice to meet you. I'm Tyler. This is Annese, and
this is Odessa," he introduced, pointing to each of the girls.

"Where are we?" Annese asked her.

"This is the land of Kaptrix," she said calmly. "Where
are you from?"

"Well......," Tyler and Annese looked at each other
trying to figure out how to explain where he was from.

"We're from the surface," Odessa explained. "We had
a fall."

"The surface?" Hammie scowled. "Where's that?"

Annese pointed up. "See the ceiling?" she asked. The
boy nodded. "Keep going."

"And going and going and going," Tyler added softly.

"You need to see Pop-Pop Riemer," Aresta announced.

"Who's he?" Annese asked.

"He's the oldest Kaptrix there is," Aresta informed. "He keeps a record of everyone who lives here and everyone who visits."

"O.K.," Odessa nodded. "Where do we find him?"

Aresta pointed down the lane in front of them. "He lives in the center. In the middle of the forest."

"A forest? In a cavern?" Annese asked confused.

"Yes. That's the only way to find him."

The trio looked down the long, cheerful lane. It fell into shadows around a far curve. "How long does it take to get there?" Odessa asked with a hint of fear in her voice.

Aresta shrugged. "Better part of a day."

"Thanks," Tyler's voice deflated. "Come on, guys. Let's get this over with. It was nice meeting you, Aresta, Hammie."

"Bye." Aresta waved as the three passed to go down the lane. The girls waved back. She and Hammie watched them walk a little way down before turning back to the houses.

"Shouldn't you have warned them about the forest?" Hammie asked his older sister. "I mean, after all, it's dangerous."

"Nah!" Aresta smiled mischievously. "What fun would that be?"

ANNESE

Annese gazed at the community of small people. Houses grouped together, children playing, animals bouncing around. Almost every house they passed had a green lawn and pretty flowers about the grounds. Eventually, the houses gave way to a huge cavern filled with trees. The lane still had pretty flowers alongside it, but they were scattered here and there, then lane disappeared into the trees. The forest itself was quiet and cool with soothing chirps and clicks from unseen animals that gave it a comfortable, peaceful feel. They continued walking until Annese's feet hurt.

"I feel like Dorothy in Munchkinland," Annese murmured.

"Who in where?" Odessa scowled, not understanding the reference.

"It's a story," Tyler replied. "Is it my imagination or is it getting darker?" The question took Annese's attention off her aching feet.

"It does appear to be getting darker," Annese confirmed. She looked behind her to compare the light.

"I'm *sooo* hungry!" Odessa complained.

"Lunch!" Tyler brightened. "We didn't eat lunch!"

Annese smiled as well. "So, let's sit down and eat!"

Off to one side was a soft, green clearing amongst some trees. It was just on the side of the road, so the kids didn't need to worry about getting lost. Carefully, Annese joined Tyler in splitting the sandwiches, chips, drinks, and snacks between the three of them.

"I must say," Odessa remarked looking warily at the sandwich in her hand, "you people eat most strangely."

"I guess it could be strange if you aren't use to it," Annese chuckled. "But you'll love the cupcakes!"

"O.K. Sure," Odessa replied warily. She didn't appear too convinced.

"What's a matter, Tyler?" Annese asked, tilting her head back for a drink. "You're quiet."

"Something's not right," he spoke quietly. He looked around, gazed down the lane, and peered into the forest. "I can't put my finger on it, but something isn't right."

"They're just people."

"Maybe it's the strange flowers with the eyes that are making you feel funny," Odessa tried.

"Eyes?" Annese and Tyler asked together.

"Didn't you see them? They're all over. Funny, little, purple flowers with eyes where the pollen should be. There!" Odessa pointed towards the road. "There's one. It's watching us."

Sure enough, a purple flower with daisy-like petals grew close to the ground. Where the yellow center should've been was a big, brown eye. It stared at them unblinkingly.

"How....how did you see that?" Tyler questioned, a little unnerved.

"Oh, I love flowers," Odessa smiled. "Purple pansies and white daisies. The pink gladiolus are delicious!"

"You *eat* them?" Annese was incredulous.

"Sure! Flowers have lots of uses! Food, dye, medicine, decorations. Lots of stuff."

"We'd best hurry. We're gonna be hiking in the dark as it is," Annese swallowed nervously, still staring back at the flower.

Where the village was noisy, the forest had become silent. There wasn't a sound other than the crunch of their footsteps and the chirp of some cricket-like insect. Travel was slow since Odessa's leg was still hurting pretty bad. They needed to stop frequently to let her rest. The silence bore down on them as the darkness closed in. Annese pulled out her flashlight so they could see.

"It must be past sun-goes-down," Odessa murmured shakily.

"Come on, 'Dess," Tyler tried to comfort his friend. "We'll be alright."

As the night became darker, the flashlight lit less and less. Their pace began to slow even more. Their feet ached, Annese and Odessa were shivering, and their eyes hurt from strain.

"We need to stop," Annese whined.

"This looks like a good spot," Tyler suggested. He was glancing at a grassy knoll between some trees on the side of the road.

"It's heaven," Annese mumbled. She dashed to the soft grass, dropped her pack, and lay down.

"Is it safe?" Odessa looked around as she yawned. Tyler watched her settle into the soft grass.

"Dess, we've been trampling through these woods for hours. We haven't seen a single thing dangerous. It's just dark, that's all." Tyler leaned back on a tree. "We can rest a bit. Here, take my jacket." Tyler pulled his windbreaker from his pack and helped the centaus put it on.

"Alright," she sighed. After Tyler zipped the jacket up, Odessa laid down next to Annese, who was already dozing.

Tyler struggled to stay awake and keep watch as the girls slept. It was the manly thing to do. Eventually, he struggled to keep his eyes open. Was it the quiet that was getting to him? Or was it shear exhaustion? Didn't matter. Ultimately, Tyler, too, nodded off to sleep.

Something tickled his legs. He wiggled. His sheets felt gravelly. He tried to roll over. Something snuggled tighter. Must be his cat. He reached over to pet Gwen, but her fur felt odd. Tyler opened hazy eyes to find Gwen.

Grass. He could barely make out grass in the dim light of the dying flashlight. Grass? His eyes flew open as he sat up with a jolt. Grass had grown up over his feet, legs, and hips, and was beginning to cover his arms. He wrestled his hands free. Pushing on the thickly woven mat, he managed to squeeze his pocketknife from his front pocket. With a fierce jab, he plunged the blade into the grass mat next to him. He felt the grass pull back a little. He pulled back on the blade to rip a slit into the grass blanket. Tossing the flap over, he crawled out of the grass sleeping bag. He glanced over at the girls and froze.

Two large, grassy mounds lay where the girls had been. The mounds seemed to shutter as the grass visibly pushed in on them. Realizing the girls were in danger, Tyler darted over to them. Falling to his knees, he dug the blade into the grass next to one of them. He thought he heard a tiny scream. Carefully, the knife slit open the grass cocoon.

Tyler pushed his fingers into the opening and stood up, pulling the grass layer apart at the same time. He continued this pattern until Annese and Odessa were completely uncovered. He shook the girls in fear.

"Come on! Wake up!" he urged.

Odessa tossed her head as she took in a deep breath. She woke up groggily.

"What happened?" she asked, rubbing her eyes. "I feel funny."

Tyler just nodded and continued to shake Annese. "Wake up, Neesie! Wake up!" After several long, silent moments, Annese finally drew in a deep breath. She rolled to her back and opened her eyes.

"Is it morning already?" she asked.

"It almost wasn't," Tyler breathed a sigh of relief. He leaned back on his heels. "The grass is alive."

"What?" Odessa asked confused.

"Of course, grass is alive," Annese stretched. "It has to be to make nutrients to stay green."

"This isn't that kind of grass." Tyler tried to catch his breath as he explained. "While we slept, the grass grew up over us. It was trying to suffocate you. I cut you out."

The girls looked around at the folds of grass. It had already begun to cover Annese's feet again. She kicked it off.

"So that's why I couldn't breathe," Odessa murmured. "I felt like I was under water!"

"Can we get out of here?" Annese asked, scratching her arm.

"Yes," Odessa and Tyler agreed. Grasping their packs, all three moved down the road.

As they walked, Annese and Odessa kept scratching. Tiny red dots lined their arms.

"What's on my arms?" Annese asked.

"I don't know," Odessa scratched her neck, "But it's on my back and neck, too."

"Let me see," Tyler examined their arms and necks in the dim light. He used the flashlight for a better look. He pulled a white string from one of the holes in Odessa's neck.

"What is it?" Odessa asked fearfully.

"I think it's a root," Tyler inspected it closely.

"A root?" Annese asked horrified. "You mean they're growing in us?"

"I don't know."

A rustle from the bushes on one side made the kids turn. Staring at them from the trees was a huge, white insect. Large pincers surrounded a mouth of sharp teeth. Bulging, dark eyes watched from the triangular head. White antennae stood up from the top. Two legs showed from a body that disappeared into the dark woods.

"I think we got trouble," Tyler remarked lowly.

"Let's move," Annese said, starting down the road.

"Slowly," Odessa warned. "Don't move fast."

Carefully, the three moved off down the road. The creature followed slowly as if waiting. More of the long, segmented body appeared with many more legs.

"What is it?" Odessa looked over her shoulder fearfully.

"It looks like a centipede," Annese replied curiously.

"Awfully big centipede. It's almost as tall as us!" Tyler remarked, watching it.

"Maybe it just wants to be friends?" Annese suggested thoughtfully. "We could use a friend here."

Annese turned and slowly approached the gigantic insect. She put out her hand as she approached. The creature opened its pincers. Hundreds of sharp teeth showed.

"He's smiling!" Annese sang.

Annese tumbled backwards from a tug just as the creature lunged at Annese.

"Run!" Tyler shouted.

"But...." Annese began confused. Tyler grasped her wrist and pulled her along.

"He doesn't want to make friends!" Tyler puffed as they ran. "He wants you for breakfast!"

"It's following!" Odessa cried.

"It's gaining!" Tyler urged them on. "Go! Go!"

After barely outrunning the insect a few yards, a loud 'thunk' and a small thud made the kids slow down and look behind them. An axe stuck out of the crumpled creature's head. The three huddled together as they looked at the writhing creature in the dawning light from the walls. All was silent in the surrounding woods. A light rustling came from their right, then a small man stepped onto the road. He wasn't much taller than Annese. His gray beard hung below his waist from a muddy complexion. Strong, muscled arms stemmed out from under a green tunic belted in gold braid. Gray leggings led down to green shoes.

With a strong jerk, the little man pulled the axe from the insect's skull. He pulled a rag from a pocket and began cleaning the blade as he turned and slowly approached the small huddle.

"Tell me, now," he began in a strange brogue as he approached, "What in the name of Dalph's beard are two mortal children and a centaus youth doing roaming the woods of Kaptrix?"

The three children stared at the axe in the man's hand with wide eyes. Slowly, he cleaned the blade, mindful of the sharp, gleaming edge.

"Well?" The man looked up expectantly at the children. He followed their horrified gaze to the blade of his axe and let out a loud laugh. "You afraid of this?" he motioned the axe. The children backed up a few steps in unison. He laughed some more, put away the rag, and tucked the axe in his belt. "Now," he chuckled. "Where were we? Oh, yes! I asked what you were doing roaming the woods – alone no less."

"We....um....we...." Tyler stammered.

"We're...um...well..." Annese tried.

"We're lost," Odessa squeaked out. "Some....children t-told us t-t-to f-find s-s-someone n... named Riemer."

"Ah! I see. Well, then," the man stroked his bearded chin. "How 'bout we discuss this over breakfast? You feel like fried centipede?" he asked, then laughed when the children all made squeamish faces. "O.K., then. How about some eggs and fruit?" he chuckled. "This way." He started back down a small path.

"We shouldn't," Annese whispered, scratching her shoulder.

"Why?" Tyler asked.

"We're not supposed to talk to strangers."

Annese looked at Tyler's incredulous gaze. "You're kidding, right?" he asked. "That's all we've *done* is talk to strangers!"

"But what if he...you know....eats children?"

"What choice do we have?" Odessa asked. She scratched a spot behind her neck.

"Well?" the man asked watching them. "Come along! Unless, of course, you want to be centipede food."

Annese exchanged a glance at Tyler. He simply shrugged. With a sigh, she fell in line behind him as the three followed the Kaptrix. "Why do I feel like Hansel and Gretel?" she murmured.

The man led the three children down a narrow path off to one side. As they walked, the kids explained to the man how they met and how they came to Kaptrix. The tree canopy shut out most of the daylight from the cave ceiling, giving the path a dark, eerie feeling. Annese shuttered as they walked through a grove of strange, gray trees with blue-green leaves. She screamed suddenly as large, branch-like claws lifted her off the ground. Turning, the group saw the branches of a tree wrapping around Annese and hauling her high in the air as she screamed, wiggled, and kicked.

"G'nant! Put her down!" the little man ordered as he pointed to the ground. "They're here by invite!"

Slowly, the enormous tree obeyed, gently landing her on her feet. The branches rose again to a normal position after making sure Annese was steady. It shivered once, dropping a few leaves, then stood motionless. Annese jumped away from it.

"Blasted Ents," the man grumbled as he continued on. "Don't trust no one."

"You ok?" Annese heard Tyler ask. She turned and nodded, glaring over her shoulder at the offensive tree.

The pathway opened into a bright green clearing. A small, tan thatched cottage with brown shutters stood humbly in the center. Bright pink, yellow, and purple flowers grew happily in soft beds on either side of the door. The shutters revealed clean windows with crisp yellow curtains. A stream flowed behind the cottage.

A tiny, white, furry creature came barreling out of the flowers at their host's legs. It grunted, squealed, and squeaked happily as it romped and rolled along the ground.

"Hey, there, Budsy," the man chuckled and picked up the ball of fur. He put it on his shoulder as he opened the door. The creature turned around and started squeaking again. "Yes, we have visitors. The children need breakfast and a nap. Come along, youngins!"

To their surprise, the tiny cottage was larger than it looked. The living area was large, with comfortable-looking couches and chairs. A large picture window overlooked the glen. A fireplace stood off to the right with a wooden table and four chairs. A door stood in the wall to their left. A pump handle gleamed next to the wall with the door they came in. A short table with a basin and some towels stood next to it.

"Um, what is that?" Annese asked as they followed him into the cottage.

The man put the fluffy creature on the floor before moving to the fireplace. It waddled to a food dish near the hearth.

"That," he said to Annese, "is a longairit." He began stirring the embers in the fireplace.

"A what?" Annese asked with raised brows.

"A longairit. No one could figure out what they were, so they called it a 'long-haired it'. The name got slurred together to 'longairit'."

"Is he dangerous?"

"Budsy?" the man chuckled. "Naw! He's a push-over! Loves everybody! Problem is he can't tell who to stay away from and who to like."

A good fire came to life in the fireplace. The man picked up a pan from the side, leaned over, and placed it on the rocks. He pulled a bowl of eggs over to it and started making scrambled eggs.

"You youngin's might want to clean up there," he motioned towards the pump.

"How?" Odessa asked confused.

"It's a well pump," Tyler explained. "You grasp this handle here and move it up and down. Water comes out the spout, there."

"It does not!" Odessa laughed. "You're pullin' my tail!"

Tyler smiled. "Watch!" Annese grinned as Tyler pumped the handle hard. It took a few times to get the water moving. Both Annese and Odessa squealed as the water splashed at them from the bowl. Riemer and Tyler laughed at their antics.

"Wash up!" the man instructed as he moved to the far end of the room. He opened a door in the floor and pulled out a bag of cold fruit. Quickly he set the table, served up the eggs, and cut up the fruit. He filled a pitcher of water as the kids gathered around the table.

"Excuse me, sir," Tyler began.

"Yes."

"Well, um. You know our names, but, um, who are you?"

The man looked at him as he sat down. "Isn't it obvious?" The blank look on the three youthful faces said no. "I'm Riemer." He chuckled at the three surprised expressions. "Now eat up! Eggs don't stay hot long."

"Mmm! This pompnut is nice and cold!" Odessa remarked about the juicy purple fruit she was eating. The inside was a bright red. "How...."

"I built the house next to the river. So much so that one corner of the house is over the water. I have hooks where the bags hang. The cold water keeps the fruit cold and fresh. I got tired of going outside at night for water, so I built a pump."

"This is really good!" Annese commented as she bit into a crisp, orange fruit. "What is it?"

"Manhut," Riemer replied. "Now, you said someone told you to find me?"

"Um-hmm," Annese nodded, swallowing a mouthful of food. "Mmmm, juicy! Two kids."

"Aresta and Hammie," Odessa added before she bit into another pompnut. "They said you kept a record of everyone who lived here and everyone who visits. Although, they gave us the impression you were really old. I think they lied."

Riemer let out a heartfelt laugh. His hand slapped down on one knee. A startled Budsy climbed up onto the table to look at him.

"I'm quite familiar with Aresta and Hammie. They tend to exaggerate. They probably think I record them all because I know them all! I'm a rectus. I know the woods, the animals, the insects, and the people. O.K., then. You said you're lost?"

"I guess you could say that," Tyler agreed.

"What's wrong, son?" Riemer looked at Tyler's barely-touched plate. "Not hungry?"

"I'm...not feeling too good," he mumbled.

"Budsy!" Riemer nodded towards Tyler.

The little ball of fluff ran over to Tyler. He jumped up onto Tyler's shoulder. Tyler wiggled as cool paws kneaded his neck. "Yeep!" it squeaked. It tugged at his ear, peering into it. "Oooh!" Using its mouth, Budsy scaled up Tyler's hair to the top of his head. He laid down for a moment. "Um-hmm!" As he tried to peer over Tyler's forehead, he fell. "Eeeeee!" Tyler caught him quickly.

"You o.k., pal" Tyler asked him.

Budsy chirped at him, then hopped back onto the table and over to Riemer. He chipped, chirped, and hummed to him. Riemer nodded.

"Got just the thing!" Riemer responded. The man moved to a cabinet and pulled down a bottle. "Budsy says you've been bit by a neugrit."

"A what?" Tyler asked.

"A neugrit. It's a tiny spider with a powerful poison. It's not fatal, but can have some pretty painful side effects.

Here, take some of this." Riemer poured a green liquid into a small glass.

"What is it?" Tyler asked, looking skeptically at the glass.

"Antidote. This and a few hours' sleep will have you good as new!"

Annese laughed at Tyler's puckered face when he drank the liquid. "Ugh!" he groaned.

"I know what ya mean!" Riemer chuckled as he pat the boy's shoulder.

"Got anything for this?" Odessa asked, scratching her arm and shoulder again.

Riemer looked at the tiny holes in her arm. "Mmm. Where'd these come from?" he asked. He noted they were all over her back and hindquarters as well.

"Grass." Annese was scratching as well.

"Grass?"

"Down at the clearing," Tyler explained, leaning back. "We stopped for the night. When I woke up a few hours later, my legs were covered, but the grass completely covered them."

"Ah! Strangle grass. Beautiful stuff, but deadly. You girls were very lucky. Let me make you something for that."

"Eat, Tyler!" Annese ordered. "You'll need your strength!"

"Yes, Mom," Tyler replied unenthusiastically.

Annese watched as Riemer ground up a white stone into a fine powder with a mortar and pestle. He mixed some ground-up leaves and a pink liquid into it until it became a paste. He added some water until it was a thick liquid. Taking a cloth, he dabbed it all over Odessa, then Annese.

"This will take away the itch. The roots have no lasting effect without the grass itself. Any left in the holes will die, but it can be quite annoying. I'll make up more of this for you to take with you."

"Thank you," Odessa replied meekly.

"O.k. Now. Where are you children heading?" Riemer finished up with the girls.

All three children pointed towards the ceiling.

"You mean the roof?" Riemer teased.

"Higher," Annese replied.

"The rocks?"

"Higher," Odessa hinted.

"The seas?"

"Keep going," Tyler replied. He was stroking Budsy in his lap.

"I see!" Riemer stroked his beard. "You want to return to the surface."

"Well," Tyler began. "We need to get Odessa back to her home."

"In Griffin Woods?" Riemer asked. Odessa nodded.

"Then Tyler and I need to get to the palace on Caldron so the king can help us get home," Annese explained.

"No! No! No!" Riemer scowled. "Jamiss will make slaves of you! He won't take you home!"

"Jamiss isn't king anymore," Annese said softly. "He's a statue. Narim is king now."

"Narim?" Riemer scowled more. "When did this happen?"

"Almost a year ago," Odessa picked up the explanation. "King Narim is really nice. He's made a council from the leaders of each island. My father is part of the council."

"Then that means......" Riemer began thinking fast.

"The prophecy was fulfilled," Annese completed his sentence proudly. "My brother Jeremy and Tyler's cousin Jordon did it."

"No, no, children. You don't understand, do you?" Riemer looked at the three blank faces. "O.K! Come gather around the fire. Storytime!"

"Oh, boy!" Odessa jumped.

"What about the dirty dishes?" Annese asked standing.

"They'll keep. Come."

***Riemer sat in an armchair near the fireplace. The kids and Budsy gathered at his feet.

"A long time ago, nearly five hundred years, a young man named Icherod was crowned King of Asteria. It was both a happy and sad time. One month before, his mother died during the birth of a baby girl. The young princess died a few days later. The king, very distraught over the death of his wife and child, wasn't watching where he was riding his horse, and both horse and rider tumbled over a ravine and perished. So young Icherod was crowned king at the tender age of fourteen."

"Fourteen!" the children cried.

"Yes," Riemer continued. "It was a very difficult few years. One day he met a beautiful young woman named

Narika. Narika had a personality that matched her beauty. Her gentleness and kindness smoothed out Icherod's rough edges and discontent. They quickly became quite a pair. No one was surprised when they announced their intent to marry. Over the next three years the kingdom eventually welcomed a princess and a prince." Annese leaned dreamily on her arm immersed in Riemer's storytelling skills.

"The king and queen established a kingdom of trust and unity. Each race had a representative on the King's Council. The council helped to settle disputes, refine laws, and arrange trade. On an island our size, and with as many races as we had, this council was invaluable in keeping the peace."

"Island? As in one?" Odessa asked. "But Asteria is eight islands."

Riemer smiled. "I'm getting to that. At one time, Asteria was a single island in the middle of a vast ocean. We were just a day's travel to the mainland, and made up one-sixth of an archipelago of vast trade and resorts."

"An archi-what?" Annese asked.

"A group of islands," Tyler explained quickly.

"Oh."

Riemer continued. "One of the positions in King Icherod's court was that of a page. Boys or girls between the ages of nine and fourteen usually held it. One of the pages was named Jamiss. Jamiss appeared to be a nice boy – eager to please and help. His father had died of illness, so his mother had him become a page to help with expenses. As Jamiss grew, he became jealous of the power he thought Icherod had. He also had a fascination for the dark arts."

"What's that?" Annese asked.

"Sorcery," Odessa replied darkly. "Bad magic."

"That's right," Riemer smiled. "Now, Jamiss plotted and planned through his teenage years. Then one day, he began to implement his plans. As a steward, that's what older pages were called, they sent Jamiss to the rulers of the different races with messages from the king. We suspect Jamiss began changing the messages enough to cause suspicion amongst the races. When the lack of trust split the council to the point where they only argued, Jamiss organized a rebellion and over-threw the king. By this time, Jamiss didn't care who he hurt to get what he wanted.

"Icherod, having gotten word of the uprising, sent his children into hiding. It was a good thing, too, because the first thing Jamiss did was have the king and queen beheaded."

"Beheaded?" the kids asked in wide-eyed horror.

Riemer moved his thumb across his neck and nodded. "Well, you can imagine that didn't gain many of supporters. The second thing he did was disband the council. He set up his own laws and fired all but the strongest guards. He captured children to work as servants in the castle, and would make slaves out of men he captured."

"How do you capture grown men?" Annese asked.

"With the R'hotaak. It carried you, didn't it?" Annese nodded. "The R'hotaak can carry five times its own weight.

Very strong and deadly birds. Jamiss' falconer would send out the R'hotaak to capture whatever Jamiss wanted.

"Well, as time went on, small uprisings occurred. The guards would always put an end to them, but Jamiss wasn't winning any points with the populous.

"Jamiss married and had a son, but when his wife complained about the way he treated his subjects, she disappeared. Suspicion is he had her killed. He assigned an older girl to nanny the whelp. He continued to add fuel to the dissention between the races.

"But he realized something else. He was getting older. Eventually he would die, and he didn't want anyone else to have his power. He went to the other, more powerful sorcerers. They came up with a potion that, if the king would drink it every couple of days, he would live forever. Jamiss agreed.

"Well, Jamiss had set things up so well that he found himself with plenty of time on his hands. He began exploring the castle, and the castle is incredibly old!"

"How old?" Tyler asked.

"Hmm, let's see. It has to be at least five thousand years old."

"And it's still standing?" Tyler cried.

"Yep. They knew how to build things in those days. Back to the story! Jamiss explored the castle little by little. Slowly, he began checking every nook and cranny, certain there was some hidden something that would give him more power."

"What did he find?" Odessa asked.

"A crystal," Riemer replied.

"Is that all?" Annese asked disappointed.

"Not just any crystal. A giant, blue crystal, just about your size," he pointed to Annese. "It was large and oval and suspended by eight strings of light. It gleamed with great beauty. Jamiss was certain it would bring him substantial power and wealth."

"What did he do with it?" Tyler asked.

"He took it from its light nest. No sooner did the eight lights touch than a huge earthquake rocked the island. The land tossed and turned. Dark clouds filled the sky." Riemer described the cataclysm while motioning the effects. "Huge, powerful lightning streaks sizzled as they hit the land. Winds tortured the trees and the mountains; crashed branches and houses and ripped up roots. It leveled homes, rent the earth, and many people died. When it was all over, Asteria was split into eight islands and thrown far away from its sisters. Races that used to inhabit the daytime were thrown underground."

"You mean you used to live up there like me?" Odessa asked surprised.

"Yep," Riemer confirmed. "I used to live up there when I was a very young child. There was no way out, so we made our own lives down here.

"Many prophecies have come to pass, but one."

"What happened to the crystal?" Annese asked.

"The crystal shattered into pieces. Jamiss hid them somewhere. No one knows where or if they're together."

"So why were you so concerned when we told you about the king?" Annese asked.

Riemer smiled. "Because we have to get all the races to the surface before the second part of the prophecy comes to pass."

"What part is that?" Odessa asked.

"That the crystal is found and restored to its proper place."

Tyler's eyes widened with dawning. "But, wouldn't that mean that Asteria would go back together?"

Riemer smiled wider. "Very bright, young man. Not only will the island go back together, but we suspect it will return to the place in the world it belongs."

"We gotta get out of here!" Tyler said urgently, grabbing Annese's arm.

"What's your rush?" Annese shrugged him off.

"If an earthquake tore the island apart, what do you think is going to happen when that crystal goes back in the place it belongs?"

"What's the big worry?" Annese pushed off.

"Annese! If they find the crystal and put it back, we may never get home again, much less be alive!"

"This isn't good!" Odessa murmured softly. "If I'm understanding this right, another cataclysm will pull the islands together again?"

"That's the theory," Riemer agreed.

"How do we stop it?" she asked.

"Well, keep in mind it's only a theory. Of course, prophecies are known to come true. Don't know if you can stop it. Best thing would be to prepare everyone for it.

"So, which direction are you kids heading?"

The three looked at each other.

"Don't know," Odessa said. "How do you get anywhere?"

"Well, there's three cities here on Kaptrix. You came through Trent. Those little travel pads are a bit suspicious, though. We don't understand how they work. Rendifer, one of our researchers, left by one to see what would happen. He hasn't returned."

"How long's he been gone?" Annese asked.

"Seven turns of the moon."

"Wait! How can you tell when the moon's out?" Tyler asked. "You're underground!"

Riemer laughed. "Nothing gets by you, does it? The light from the stones gets brighter when the moon is overhead. When there is a new moon, it's very dark down here, like last night."

"How do you know it isn't when the sun is overhead?"

"Because the sun is overhead every day."

"How come the rocks glow?" Tyler asked.

"I don't know for sure. The Krilts could probably tell you, but they're on the surface. But that doesn't answer my question. Where are you going?"

The kids shrugged. "To the fastest way up?" Annese asked.

"Tell you what, why don't you go to the oracle? It's not far from here. Maybe she can give you a hint where to go."

"It's better than roaming," Tyler replied thoughtfully. The girls agreed.

"That settled, you three get some sleep. I doubt you slept very well last night. I'll get some provisions together for you and wake you with plenty of time to get to the oracle."

6 – LAVA AND FIRE

JEREMY

The heat that greeted them was stifling. Jeremy immediately felt his lungs tighten with his first breath. The air was so dry it hurt. The rocks and walls were such a deep red they were almost black. A strange mist seemed to linger at the ceiling. The boys had to keep blinking to keep their eyes moist.

"Where....where are we?" Jordon asked. He wiped the sweat off his forehead as he strained to look through the haze.

"Hmmm," the strange little man began. He pulled a wad of papers from his back pocket and sifted through them looking for information. Several times he had to blow out the embers beginning on the edges. He took something long from his pocket and began looking around. He started making notations on the piece of paper in front of him.

"Lavaland?" Jeremy asked, looking over the man's shoulder. "You mean, like melted rock kind of lava?"

"I believe so," the strange man responded. "Oh, but I'm so sorry. I have failed to introduce myself. I am Rendifer Pietri Fazmarten. Most people call me Fuzz. I'm a

Kaptrix," he said with a flourish. "Thank you so very much for rescuing me."

"Don't worry about it," Jeremy brushed the gratitude away. He handed Fuzz his pouch.

"Yea," Jordon mumbled dryly. "It seems to be what we do. I'm Jordon, this is my friend Jeremy. Oh, you may want this, too." He handed the coat towards Fuzz.

"It's a fine pleasure," Fuzz smiled. He took his things from the boys and placed them in various pockets. He tied the pouch to his belt. "So! Where are you going?"

"We're...," Jeremy exchanged a look with Jordon.

"Not sure," Jordon finished with a sigh.

"Where are *you* going?" Jeremy smirked.

"Wherever the pads go," Fuzz smiled. "I am graphing where the pads lead. It will be the first directional map of the islands."

"What do you mean, first map?" Jeremy asked with a scowl. "Doesn't anyone know how to get from one island to the next?"

"No, actually. You see, the pads are a bit strange. For example, we came here from the Ssanders," he pointed to another paper, "but that same pad will go out to....to...." Fuzz fumbled with his papers. "Hmmm. I don't know where it goes, but it won't go back out to Ssanders. It's very strange."

"So, each pad comes in from one land and out to another?" Jeremy clarified.

"Correct."

"So where have you been?"

"All over. It's been a very long journey. On the brighter side, I have succeeded in mapping two-thirds of the islands."

"Maybe we should copy his maps," Jeremy suggested to Jordon.

"Or stay with him," Jordon replied. "Sooner or later we'll run into the kids."

"Maybe."

"Which children are you trying to locate? As best I can tell, there are children on Kaptrix and Droward. While the Ssanders have young, they aren't very friendly, as you've seen. I haven't found any other sentient species on any of the other islands."

"It's a little harder than that," Jordon sighed.

"You see, my sister..." Jeremy jumped in.

"And my cousin..."

"Met a centaus from up above..."

"And fell down a sink hole..."

"Which led us to those snake guys...."

"And to you."

"But we don't know where they went...."

"And if what you're telling us about the pads is true...."

"It could be months before we find them; assuming they didn't fall prey to those snake things."

Fuzz looked from one boy to the other. "Perhaps. You see I believe most species of sentient beings are willing to help you – at least with what they know. Perhaps someone has seen them."

Jeremy looked around when a rumbling sound echoed across the cavern. He didn't see anything except dark rocks, a weird haze, and large red and white flowers. "What was that?"

"Don't know," Fuzz replied. He smiled brightly. "Let's find out. We may meet someone."

Jordon and Jeremy exchanged wary glances. Should they? Jordon shrugged, so Jeremy nodded. They turned and followed Fuzz away from the pad.

"What kind of flowers are these?" Jordon asked, stooping down to look at one.

The gigantic flower had six petals in the style of a daisy. They were much larger, however, and alternated colors in red and white. The center was fire orange and fashioned like a funnel down into the stem. As Jordon looked at it, the head of the flower turned from side to side.

"Sir, Be...."

A burst of flames shot out and quickly encompassed Jordon. The flames vanished quickly, leaving his lashes and hair singed. They watched a thin wisp of smoke rise as Jordon coughed.

"....careful," Fuzz finished lamely. "I'm sorry, sir. Those are flame-throwers. Apparently, they thrive in this type of environment."

"Right," Jordon agreed flatly. "Come on."

The ground was littered with stones and black rocks. The heat caused a wave in the air making it difficult to tell distances. Small oases showed up in the heat. Jeremy noticed the rocks were glowing. He reached down to pick one up. "Ow!" he released it abruptly. The small rock skittered across the floor.

Jordon looked at him questioningly. "Hot," Jay replied, examining his hand for burns.

"You ok?"

"Yea," he sighed. He stooped to look at another rock. "These rocks look like they've been split."

"By what?"

"Who knows," Jeremy replied. "But by the way they're glowing, I'm guessing they're baking."

"Let's keep going." Jordon tugged Jeremy and rushed after Fuzz. The Kaptrix just kept going, oblivious to what was going on around him.

The trek was draining. Temperatures kept rising as they walked with the air getting hotter and dryer. Jordon took a sip from his water bottle.

"We're gonna run out of water if we stay here very long," he commented, replacing the cap to his water bag.

"I know, and I doubt there's any water down here."

"I feel like I'm getting sunburn." Jordon wiped his forehead on his sleeve.

"I'm sure I'm getting blisters on my feet. Are my sneakers melting?" Jeremy picked up his foot.

"I think mine are," Jordon agreed. He glanced down at his feet.

"Look!" Fuzz's outburst turned the boys' attention to an area some sixty or so feet away. The heat filled air made it difficult to determine the distance.

The landforms had opened up to a large pit of bubbling lava. Steam wafted up towards the top of the cavern. Many large, fiery creatures were gathering rocks near it. Some came right out of the lava. They varied in size from a little over a foot to almost six feet in height.

"Am I seeing walking flames?" Jordon asked. He squinted to look through the haze.

"I think so," Jeremy replied.

"Come! Come!" Fuzz seemed pleased with himself. "Let's see if they've seen your friends."

"Um, Fuzz," Jeremy hesitated, still looking at the creatures. "I don't think that's....."

"Come! Come!" Fuzz continued forward.

The boys sighed and followed him. They exchanged knowing glances.

"Any closer and my staff is gonna catch fire," Jeremy grumbled after a few more feet.

Jordon began coughing. The steam from the lava brought a burning sulfuric stench with it. He stopped short as he looked ahead. Smaller creatures were eating the red-hot rocks from the lava pit. Two stopped and looked at the trio.

"Excuse me!"

The boys turned towards the call. Fuzz was approaching a group of large fire creatures, waving his hand to get their attention.

"Excuse me!"

"It's a miracle this guy's made it this far," Jeremy sighed.

"Get your staff ready," Jordon suggested. "I think we're gonna need it."

"Right," Jeremy agreed distastefully as he reached over his shoulder to pull it from his pack. "Ow!"

"What?" Jordon looked at his friend.

Jeremy's outstretched hand was bright red. Blisters were already forming. It throbbed painfully.

"It's too hot to handle," Jeremy said. He blew on the blisters.

"Your staff?"

Jeremy nodded. "If the wood is that hot, don't go for your sword."

"We gotta cool your hand off."

"My water bottle may help, but I don't want to waste the water."

"I got it!" Jordon reached into his pocket and pulled out a blue bandana. He wet it with his waterskin, then wrapped it around Jeremy's hand. "Better?"

Jeremy nodded. "For now."

"Whoa! Ow! Stop!"

The boys looked up to see Fuzz surrounded by fire creatures. He kept moving, but the creatures were trying to grasp him.

"Come on," Jeremy sighed as he began running towards the fray.

"Cavalry to the rescue....again!" Jordon groaned, but followed his friend.

The boys barreled through the circle, wincing from the burning creatures. They grasped Fuzz by the arms and barreled through the other side. They kept running, but more fire creatures followed them – and were gaining.

A sudden roar echoed through the cavern stopping everyone. Taloned claws swooped down and gently grasped the trio, one by one, then soared off again.

"Hold on!" a deep rumbling voice said as the distance between them and the fire creatures lengthened dramatically.

"What? Oh, my!" Fuzz exclaimed in fear.

Jordon and Jeremy looked up into scaled bellies. They both smiled wide.

"Thanks, guys!" Jeremy called up.

"Watch the rocks!" Jordon cried, lifting his feet. "It's a little shallow down here."

The flight wasn't long, but enough that they could no longer see the lava pit. The dragons put the mortals down on cooler ground, then swooped around and settled next to them.

"Thanks so much!" Jordon smiled, patting the side of a large red dragon.

"Tis a pleasure, Master Jordon," he replied. The large snout nuzzled Jordon's neck affectionately.

"You...you...you know these...these...these..." Fuzz's eyes were wide with fear as he stared from one creature to another, expecting to be eaten.

"Dragons," Jeremy finished for him. He smiled from the shoulder of the dragon he was with. "Yes, they're friends of ours. This is Ember, that one by Jordon is Methaniel, and the one next to you is Flicker."

"Thou hast a wonderful memory, Master Jeremy," Ember complimented. Her scales glistened in the heat of the cavern.

"You guys are the best!" Jeremy scratched her behind her ear. "How could I forget?"

"But what are you doing down here?" Jordon asked.

"We fire breathers enjoy a good soak in the steam created by the lava down hither. Tis too hot for the others," Methaniel explained.

"Master Jeremy, what this wrong with thy hand?" Flicker asked.

"Oh," Jeremy held up his hand wrapped in the bandana. "It got burned on my staff."

"Keep them there!" came a commanding voice.

Jordon and Jeremy scowled at each other. "Kren?" the boys asked together.

"I asked him to come," Flicker said softly. "I hope thou dost not mind."

Jeremy smiled at the young dragon. "Why would I mind? Other than the fact that I didn't think of it myself."

Fuzz kept turning around and around at the large, magnificent creatures surrounding him.

"What's wrong, Fuzz?" Jordon asked with a knowing grin.

"They're...they're...."

"Friends," Jeremy finished. "Relax."

"What species art thou?" Methaniel asked. His nose came close to Fuzz and pulled in a deep breath.

"Methaniel!" Ember blurted horrified. "How rude!"

"Well, dost thou not wish to know? He obviously tis not mortal."

"Nor elfin," Flicker added.

"Nor dost he resemble Captain Zelmar, the Krilt."

"I am a Kaptrix," Fuzz stated proudly.

"From whence dost thou hail?" Flicker asked.

"From Kaptrix, of course!"

The three dragons looked confused. "Many pardons, kind sir, but I know of no isle called Kaptrix," Methaniel said softly.

"As best we can figure," Jordon began, "the islands are known by one name above ground and another below ground."

"So, those firelings call this something other than Ascentia?" Ember asked.

"This is Lavaland," Fuzz stated factually. "It gets its name from the lava core."

"We saved him from some snake-like guys under Griffin Woods," Jeremy explained. "He's trying to map out all of the islands."

A tall, dark-haired figure approached from some rocks. His long white cloak barely missed the ground. A black jumpsuit with red sleeves and collar clung to his lean body. His boots clicked on the hardened rock beneath his feet. He was pushing up his sleeves as he approached.

"I keep forgetting how hot it gets down here."

"Kren!" the boys cried as they ran towards him. He pulled them both up into a hug.

"Hello, young masters," he greeted with a smile. "I understand we are in need of repair?"

"Jeremy," Jordon nodded towards his friend.

Kren carefully unwrapped the hand Jeremy offered. "Hmm. You did a nice job. Try to pick up a rock?"

"Tried to grasp my staff," Jeremy replied. "It was so hot it burned my hand."

"Not surprising." Kren pulled a pouch from his pocket. He carefully spread some of the cream from it over Jeremy's hand, then re-wrapped it. "Give it a few hours to cure. It should be fine after that. Here, your face is beginning to burn."

Kren treated Jeremy's face and his elbow where he had rammed the fireling. He turned his attention to Jordon and treated him as well. Finally, he examined Fuzz and treated the burns from the firelings.

"As much as I enjoy seeing you, perhaps you should come topside. This cavern is way too hot for you."

"I feel like I'm in an oven!" Jordon wiped his forehead again.

"It basically is," Kren smiled. "Though it is not as hot as a cooking fire, it will cook you through, given enough time. Come! Let's go up."

"Sorry," Jeremy replied lowly. "We can't."

"Pardon?" Kren scowled.

"We're trying to find my sister, Jordon's cousin, and a centaus girl. They fell through a sinkhole and are down here somewhere. We need to get them home."

"Then, my brave knights, I suggest you leave here quickly. If you get stuck, the passage behind those rocks will bring you up to the dragon's lair." He pointed at the passage he had come through.

"May want to make a note of that, Fuzz," Jordon suggested. "We may need it."

"Yes! Yes!" Fuzz pulled out his papers and writing utensil again. He lined up his location and made a note of the passage on the paper.

"Now, how do we get out of here?" Jeremy asked, looking over Fuzz's shoulder.

"There should be a travel pad somewhere near here," Fuzz examined his papers and pointed to a nearby area. "There is one on the other side that way, and the one down there is where we came in."

"Travel pad?" Kren asked. He peered at the papers.

"It's the way they travel between islands," Jeremy explained. "Problem is no one knows the patterns. That's what Fuzz is doing. Mapping the pads."

"Another problem is that the pads come in from one island and go out to a different one," Jordon added.

Kren scowled. "That makes it very difficult to document."

Fuzz nodded. "Indeed."

"Very well. Carry on. It was good to see you again," Kren nodded. "I'm going to cool off!"

"The pool up in the water tower shouldst be acceptable," Ember teased.

Kren looked up with an embarrassed start. "Pardon?"

Everyone laughed. It was very apparent that Kren enjoyed swimming in the pool, but he thought he was undetected. Seeing as there were no swimsuits, he'd have to do so in the buff. He moved off towards the passage indignantly as the others tried to stifle their giggles.

"We'd best get going," Jeremy suggested. Fuzz and Jordon agreed.

"Safe passage, young masters," Methaniel wished.

"Come back safely," Ember blessed.

"May Thaurlonian's spirit be with thee," Flicker added.

"Thanks, guys. We appreciate that," Jordon smiled and hugged each of the dragons.

"Hopefully, we'll see you soon," Jeremy smiled, scratching the young dragons. He straightened himself out and turned. "Which way, Fuzz?"

"I believe we should explore this leg here," Fuzz pointed towards their left.

"Lead on, Mc Duff!" Jordon instructed.

Fuzz turned and looked at him strangely. "Who is this McDuff?" he asked.

Jordon shook his head. "It's a phrase my mother uses. Actually, I don't know who McDuff is."

"Let's just go," Jeremy rolled his eyes.

The air seemed to cool slightly as they traveled away from the dragons. Nightfall set in as the light dimmed slowly. The fire flowers closed up into themselves.

"Looks like night has fallen," Jeremy remarked.

"That may explain why I am tired," Fuzz revealed.

"We're NOT spending the night in here!" Jordon said firmly.

"Yes, well,...." Fuzz began.

"There!" Jeremy cried, pointing to their right.

Barely visible between two giant rocks was a white stone embedded in the floor. It was the same shape and color as the others.

"Let's go!" Jordon said, grasping Fuzz's shoulder and directing him in that direction.

"You..." he swallowed, "Do understand that I...I....don't know where this leads. Yes?"

"Yes," Jordon agreed. "But anyplace is cooler than here."

"I wouldn't exactly say *anyplace*," Jeremy scrunched his nose.

"Je-re-my," Jordon warned.

"Touchy!" Jeremy teased. "Let's go."

Jeremy stepped onto the pad and disappeared. Jordon pushed Fuzz on the pad next, then he followed him on.

7 – JAWS OF DEATH

TYLER

Tyler woke groggily to a tiny lick on his ear. "Not now, Patches!" Tyler waved. He hit something soft. It squealed as it fell off him. Tyler looked up to see Budsy shaking himself.

"You alright, fella?" he reached for the little fluff-ball. It squeaked back at him happily.

"Morning!" Riemer smiled at him. "The girls are picking flowers in the yard. Best get up and stretch. I've got some stuff for ya here on the table."

Tyler stretched off the sleepy stiffness as he went over to look at the table. Riemer had thought of everything. There were water skins, fruit, bread, vegetables, and what looked like cheese. Tyler grabbed his backpack from the wall and started filling it with the provisions.

"I put some lightweight blankets over there on the chair for you to take, so don't put all the food in your pack," Riemer said. "And here's an old pack of mine for Odessa. She can help carry the load."

"Thank you, Riemer. I don't know what to say." The man's generosity amazed Tyler.

"Say you'll tell every race you come across to go topside," he said sternly.

"Definitely. Um, well, not those snake dudes."

"What snake dudes? Better yet, what *is* a snake dude?"

"Dude. It's a guy. You know. A person. The platform we took here led us away from some giant snake-like people who were trying to eat us."

"Ah! No, I guess you don't have to tell them. I doubt they'd understand you anyway. They'll figure it out. How'd you kids get down here, anyway?"

"A sink hole. We slid down a long, steep hole from the fields."

"Ah. Then they have a way out. Let's get the girls and get you on the road"

Riemer and Tyler went out to the front door. The girls were gathering small bouquets of colorful flowers in the small field in front of Riemer's cottage. Riemer waved the girls in.

"The yellow flowers are really tasty!" Odessa smiled at the Kaptrix.

"I'll remember that," he smiled back at her.

"Here, Dess!" Annese ran over. She placed a wreath of flowers she'd woven on her friend's head. Odessa beamed.

Once back inside, the children split down who was carrying what. Riemer also gave them some candles, a lantern for the candles, and some flint and steel to start it with.

"These should last you a bit," he said, adding things to their packs.

With a last check and making sure the packs were balanced, the elder man led them out the door. Budsy rolled around the house, disappearing under a bush. Tyler looked around the area again as Riemer led the trio out of his house and over the river. The sparse trees quickly closed in to make a thick forest. Leaves, needles, moss, and small twigs littered the floor.

"I'll take you as far as the path," he heard Riemer instructing. "Once there, you'll need to move fast. Don't stop for anything!"

"Why?" Odessa asked.

"Because the creatures of this forest are extremely hungry. You three will make a fine meal! If you keep moving, you'll be fine. The path will take you to a small village, Arcurat. Ask around for Sujitt. He'll be able to help you. Tell him I sent you. You'll like his place. O.K?" The kids nodded.

"Mr. Riemer?"

"Yes, Tyler?"

"Is there any way up to the surface from here?"

Riemer sighed. "We've never found one on Kaptrix. Hopefully, Fuzz will return with more information."

"So, how will your people survive another cataclysm?" Odessa asked worriedly.

"We'll have to find a way up there. Air gets down here, so there has to be a way."

Tyler looked around. There was plenty of green vegetation down here. Based on the food cycle of plants and people, Tyler bet the air down here was from the vegetation, which thrived on the Carbon Dioxide the people put off. The light from the rock facing could be sufficient for the chlorophyll in the plants to produce food. He'd really need to research it more to get a positive answer.

"It's the trees," Tyler mumbled to Annese. "They make Oxygen." Annese nodded.

The group traveled through thick trees. Riemer's axe cleared the overgrown green bushes with tiny prickly brambles. The brambles stuck to their clothes anyway. High grasses also slowed them down. After an hour of bushwhacking, Reimer brought them out to a dirt pathway. It was only wide enough for one person at a time, but it was clearly visible on the forest floor. The forest looked much like what they'd just gone through.

"Don't stray off the path, watch your backs, and don't stop for anything!" Reimer reminded them. They all nodded. He pulled the axe from his belt and looked at it. His face softened as he tenderly ran his hand over the blade. With a deep breath, he handed it off to Tyler. "Think you can handle this thing?" he asked.

Tyler swallowed. "Not as good as you can."

"Well, something is better than nothing. Just remember that any creature that isn't a Kaptrix or a longairit is dangerous. Understand? Don't let your conscience try to convince you to be merciful. These creatures won't be."

"Got it," Tyler replied, taking the axe. He was surprised how light it was. It felt cool in his hand. "Are you sure you don't need it?"

"I'll be fine. You need it more than I do. Practice using it on tree branches and bushes in your way. Get a good feel for it. Criss-cross strokes." He demonstrated the motion for Tyler. Tyler took a few swings to get the feel for it. Riemer nodded with a smile. "You learn fast. Ready?"

"Ready. Thank you."

"Yer welcome," Riemer offered. He took the belt sheath off his belt and tied it on Tyler. He laid a fatherly hand on the boy's shoulder. "Now, you three stay together – *close* together!"

"We will," Odessa assured him.

"Good luck." He waved as they started off down the path. Tyler and the girls waved back.

The path was only wide enough for a single file. The canopy overhead blocked out the light from the stone ceiling, so they used Annese's flashlight. Tyler often had to chop over-growth out of the way.

"How long is it supposed to take us?" Odessa asked with fear in her voice.

"Reimer didn't say," Tyler answered. "He just said to keep moving."

A loud screech rent the quiet. The trio jumped, quickly examining everything around them. The girls' screams echoed off the woods and through the trees. Tyler rolled his eyes. A group of high-pitched squeals echoed in reply. They sounded like pig squeals; full of fear and terror. The three looked at each other.

"Someone's in trouble," Odessa said worriedly. "We need to go help."

"Reimer said to stay on the path," Tyler remarked unconvincingly.

"Come on!" Annese sighed at him and turned to lead the way.

The trio pushed their way through the brush towards the sound. As they peered between the bushes, they gasped. There was a creature that looked like a cross between an ant and a cockroach. The bug stood about four feet high. Its brown, segmented body was longer than Tyler was tall. Beady black eyes looked out over large white mandibles. A small mouth glistened red behind them. Six skinny legs sprouted out from beneath its body, each ending in a sharp, hooked claw.

The creature was bent on dinner. Its legs hurried it quickly along the ground as a group of longairits tried to roll away. Hooked claws in front would grasp a longairit and move it to the mandibles that would move it to the mouth.

"Oh! Gross!" the girls gagged turning away.

Tyler took a deep breath to calm his stomach. "O.K.," Tyler grit his teeth. "I'm going to go around and create a distraction. You two rush in and save as many of those fluff balls as you can."

"Why are *you* going to be the distraction?" Annese opposed bravely.

"Because you two are faster and better at dealing with animals, and I have our only weapon."

"He has a point," Odessa agreed.

"O.K. Give a whistle before you go in."

"Like you're going to hear it above that?" Tyler retorted at the cacophony of terrified squeals. "Just watch!"

Tyler made his way around to the side of the little clearing. With a quick prayer and a deep breath, he broke through the brush into the area with a war cry. Just as he wanted, the creature turned its head towards him. It dropped the longairit in its claws and turned. With break-neck speed, the creature closed the gap to Tyler.

"Holy Crap!" Tyler dodged as a front claw reached for him.

The creature turned and went at him again. As it reached, Tyler swung the axe. The side of the head bounced off the leg. The leg swung, knocking Tyler to the ground. Tyler watched helplessly as the axe flew out of his hand. The creature bore down, trapping Tyler to the ground. Tyler's scream got stuck in his throat as the large mandibles spread to reveal the rows of sharp teeth in its mouth.

ANNESE

Annese and Odessa rushed in as soon as the creature turned towards Tyler. As fast as they could, the girls scooped up the small balls of fluff. Annese reached down for the one that was dropped by the creature. It let out a high-pitched scream.

"Shh! It's o.k.," Annese whispered as she cuddled the little brown and white thing that was no bigger than a golf ball. A small strip of red liquid came off in her hand. "Oh, no! You're hurt!"

"Do you see any more?" Odessa asked, six of the little things clinging to her back.

"No," Annese replied with three of her own hiding under her hair. "This one's hurt, though."

"We'll see what we can do later. Come on!"

As they turned to go, they heard a scream. Looking back, they gasped in horror. Tyler was hanging from the mandibles of the monster. Feet planted firmly on either side of its mouth prevented him from getting ingested.

"Guys! The axe!" he gasped. "Hurry! Ahhhg!"

The mandibles were pushing harder against his ribs. Annese took a step forward, but Odessa stopped her.

"Here! Take these. Four legs are faster than two."

"But your ankle..." Annese began.

"I can handle it."

Annese scooped up Odessa's riders. Odessa was off like a shot, quickly closing the gap to Tyler. Annese watched her friend with admiration and worry.

ODESSA

.Odessa leaned over as she approached the axe and picked it up without breaking stride. She curled around behind the creature and swung the axe, gouging a wicked slice into the hind section. Green blood squirted out, but she didn't stop. The creature reared up and screamed, dropping Tyler to the ground. Odessa swung at a leg, slicing it off.

"Roll, Tyler! Roll!" she yelled. Odessa placed herself between the creature and Tyler as he tried to move across the ground.

"Throw it!" Tyler yelled.

Odessa swung as a front claw came at her. She went through the exoskeleton and chopped well into the leg. As the creature screamed and pulled back, Odessa lost her footing, hanging onto the axe. She tumbled backwards onto her rump.

"Ow!" she squinted.

"The axe!" Tyler yelled, getting back on his feet.

Odessa tossed him the axe. Tyler caught it as the creature moved towards Odessa. Taking a deep breath, Tyler flung the axe into the air. Holding her breath, Odessa watched wide-eyed as the axe tumbled end over end through the air towards its target. The creature eyed them both, back and forth, trying to decide which one it wanted. A loud thump echoed off the trees as the tumbling axe landed, blade first, into the creature's head. After a stunned expression crossed its eyes, it crumbled lifeless to the ground.

Tyler dropped to his knees next to Odessa. He seemed to try to take a deep breath, but he'd stop in the middle. Tyler looked up when she moved. He smiled weakly at her worried expression.

"Thanks," he whispered.

"Come on," she urged. "We need to get out of here."

Odessa stayed near him as Tyler ground his teeth to stand. They stumbled over to the creature. Tyler cringed as he tried to reach for the axe.

"Let me," Odessa suggested. She reached out, but couldn't reach the axe. Moving onto the bug, she grasped the axe in both hands and tugged. The axe wouldn't move.

"Annese!" Odessa called.

Annese looked up from her kneeling position on the ground. She had a leaf pressed to the ball of fluff in her hands.

"What?"

"Come help!" Odessa cried. "We can't get the axe free."

"Just a minute!" she called. She carefully lifted the leaf and examined the injury again. She pressed it down again. "Almost there, buddy. Hang on!" she whispered.

"Annese, we don't have a minute!" Odessa cried. "More of these things could show up!"

"If I don't take a minute, this little guy is going to bleed to death!"

"If it squeezed him as hard as it squeezed me, he's going to die anyway!" Tyler retorted. "I think it broke my ribs!"

"Annese!" Odessa sang warningly.

ANNESE

"Just a minute!" Annese snapped. "Man, I wish I could just heal things!"

Annese startled as her hands grew warm. The creature in her hands hummed comfortably. They stayed that way for a few moments, then her hands cooled to normal as quickly as they had warmed. Looking under the leaf, Annese not only didn't see any more blood, but the gash that had been bleeding was gone. The longairit in her hands seemed to be sleeping peacefully.

With nine longairits clinging to her hair and shoulders, Annese moved quickly to Tyler.

"Here, hold this," she thrust the formerly injured longairit into his hands.

"What?" Tyler exclaimed. He looked down at the white and brown fluff ball she pushed into his hands.

Annese put one hand on each side of Tyler's ribs. "I wish I could heal Tyler!" she mumbled. Once again, her hands grew warm, but this time even warmer than before and for longer. She forced herself to keep them in contact with Tyler.

"Hey! That tickles!" Tyler squirmed.

"Hold still!" Annese ordered with a scowl.

In a few moments, Annese's hands cooled rapidly. "How's that?"

Tyler took in a deep breath and let it out again. "Cool! It doesn't hurt anymore!"

"'Dess, let me see your leg!"

"It's fine for now. We have to keep moving."

"O.K." Annese gave in with an irritated sigh.

"Here, hold this," Tyler handed back the longairit. "I'll go pull."
After several minutes of tugging, heaving, and grunting, Odessa and Tyler finally broke the axe loose. Talk about a thick skull, Tyler thought.

"Come on," Tyler jumped to the ground. "Let's get out of here before any more of these things show up. I'm not keen on becoming dinner."

Annese noticed Odessa limping across the stretch of clearing. "You hurt it again, didn't you?" she stated knowingly.

"I had to get to Tyler," Odessa cringed as she took another step. "He was in danger."

Annese placed the longairit on Odessa's back. She reached down and wrapped both hands around Odessa's leg where it was swelling. "I wish I could heal Odessa," she murmured.

Again, the now familiar warmth spread through her hands. Odessa watched curiously, her muscles relaxing with the heat. After a little time, Annese stood up.

"How that?" she asked.

Odessa smiled as she walking around in circles. "It doesn't hurt at all! How'd you learn to do that?"

"I don't know. I was holding the little guy there and wished I could heal him. All of a sudden, the heat came, and he was healed. My hands get hot, then I wait until they're cooled off."

"That may come in handy," Tyler mused. "We're definitely going to need it, especially if *we don't get out of here.*"

The three made their way back to the path and continued on their way. The still shaken longairits apparently had no desire to leave the girls. All of the longairits were very tiny; smaller than Budsy. Annese wondered if they were babies. She shuttered thinking about what probably happened to their mother.

The trek continued. They paused for a few minutes to get something to eat. Tyler insisted they eat as they walked instead of staying in one place. The girls agreed, but as they tried to move on, Odessa found a vine had wrapped itself around her hind feet.

"Help!" Odessa cried, trying to break free of the vine. It was creeping up her rear hocks.

"Move," Tyler pushed Annese aside. "Start walking before we're all caught."

He moved past Odessa to her hindquarters. With a swift plunge, the axe separated the vine into two pieces. The piece around her legs went slack, and Tyler pulled it off her.

"Go!" Tyler pushed her. "Follow Annese!"

With Annese in front and Tyler taking up the rear, the three kids continued their journey. The little light they could see was beginning to dim.

"It's getting dark. We can't keep walking without light." Annese said behind her.

"Didn't Reimer pack us some lanterns?" Odessa asked, reaching for her pack.

"I think so," Tyler said. He watched Odessa rummage through the pack. She produced a small candle.

"That's all I can find," she said dejectedly.

Tyler went through his pack and found a lantern and the flint and steel. Carefully, he placed the candle in the lantern. It took a while for him to get the right amount of sparks to light the candle because he kept missing. "Is there anything else flammable around here?" he asked.

"Couple of branches," Annese remarked, looking around. "Dead leaves."

"That'd be great if we had matches."

"What about my flashlight?"

"It'll light in front of us, but not the sides. This will light three sides for us."

"How about dry grass?" Odessa asked, looking at the ground.

"How dry?" Tyler asked.

"It's fairly brittle."

"Might work. Let's try it."

He carefully laid a handful of grass over the candle making certain it touched the wick. It took several attempts, but the grass caught fire. Blowing softly, Tyler caught the wick. The tiny flame glowed brightly off the polished metal inside the lantern.

Tyler smirked, replacing the glass cover. "This should light our way. Good thinking, Dess."

A sound on the side of the path caught his attention as he put away the flint and steel. Turning his head, Tyler found himself staring into the soulful eyes of a chimpanzee. It was shorter than he was and watched all of them carefully. Tyler handed Annese the lantern.

"Back away slowly," he murmured and motioned the girls in the direction they were traveling.

"Come on, Tyler," Annese sneered. "It's only a chimp!"

"Everything but people and longairits are a danger," Odessa quoted softly. "Isn't that what Riemer said?"

"How much harm can a chimp cause?" Annese asked.

Suddenly the chimp stood up on its hind legs. Its mouth opened wide in a screech, revealing two rows of sharp, pointed teeth. With heavy fists, it hit its chest like a gorilla.

"Run!" Tyler yelled, pushing the girls on. "Chimps don't have teeth like that either. I bet he's calling for reinforcements."

"Does everything around here have multiple rows of teeth?" Annese exclaimed in frustration as she took off running.

Tyler stumbled over rocks and sticks as they clamored down the narrow path. Behind them, he could hear more chimps yelling above the forest. He knocked into Odessa as she tripped.

"They're overhead!" Odessa cried. "They'll jump down on us!"

"Hey! I think I see something!" Annese peered through the trees as she ran.

"What?" Tyler called up.

"It looks like....roofs."

"Are we there?" Odessa asked worriedly.

"Don't know."

"Keep running!" Tyler pushed her on.

Struggling to get away from the chimps, the kids seemed to burst out of the forest into a clearing filled with small houses. The path went right down the middle of the village. Wooden houses with thatched roofs lined the path in rows. Tiny twinkles of lights shone from a few windows. The smell of food cooking wafted across the road. It was getting pretty dark. There were no lights around the roads.

"I don't see anyone, do you?" Tyler asked. He cautiously led them down the road.

"Me, either," Annese agreed. She looked alongside and behind houses. "Maybe we should walk around, see if anyone's home."

"What was the name of the guy we're supposed to ask for?" Odessa asked.

"Sujitt," Tyler replied. He saw a movement between a couple of houses, but it was only a leaf.

The kids walked slowly through the village. There was no one on the streets and no sound. Unlike the first village, there didn't seem to be anyone here. No people. No animals. Nothing.

"Could it be a trap?" Odessa whispered. The fear in her voice revealed how she was feeling.

Tyler swallowed. "Maybe."

"I don't see how," Annese said. "These houses are real. Let's knock on a door and ask someone."

Tyler prepared himself to attack as Annese marched up to one of the houses. The door was barely taller than she was. She knocked on it and waited. When there was no answer, she moved to the next door. Again, there was no answer.

Odessa tried on the other side of the row. After three houses, she sighed and returned to Tyler and Annese. "It seems like no one lives here."

Tyler looked around at the manicured lawns, the flowers, and the well-kept houses. "I don't buy that," he said more to himself. "It's too neat here to be abandoned."

"Unless they were all killed recently," Annese muttered as she looked around.

"You're a bit morbid sometimes, ya know that?" Tyler squinted at his friend.

Annese whirled around behind her at the sound of a giggle. Even looking hard, no one could see where it came from. A movement several houses down made the three turn again. Nothing.

"What gives?" Annese asked in a whisper.

"Darned if I know," Tyler replied.

"Someone's here," Odessa said softly. She moved closer to Annese and Tyler. "But who?"

Movements to their left made them look towards the path. Coming towards them around a corner was a little person wrapped in dark, hooded robes way too big for him. He or she limped as they clung tightly to the walking staff next to him. Tyler reached down and laid his hand on the axe, just in case.

The person stopped a few yards away, just on the edge of the lantern's light. The head lifted as if to look at them. It had a beard, Tyler could tell, so it was a male. He couldn't see inside the hood, however. It looked each one over carefully.

"Who are you?" he asked in a gravelly voice.

"I'm Tyler, this is Odessa, and that is Annese. Reimer sent us to find Sujitt. Could you tell us where he is?" Tyler's voice came out with much more confidence than he felt. In reality, his knees were shaking.

The man looked them up and down again. At length, he turned and began back down the path. He waved with one arm for them to follow him.

The children looked at each other. Did they go? Was it a trap? The man didn't even introduce himself.

"Whatcha think?" Odessa asked.

"He's the only person here who'll speak to us," Tyler analyzed. "I say we follow."

"Follow it is," Annese said, taking the lead. "Just keep on your toes." She giggled as the longairits peered out from under her hair.

The three followed the man back out to the main road and down several rows. They kept enough of a distance that they could run away if they had to. He turned to the left, into a clearing with only one house. It seemed bigger than the others. It reminded Tyler a lot of Reimer's house. The man had stopped at the door. He opened it and ushered the three children inside.

Tyler held the girls back as he glared at the open door. The man continued to look at them.

"What?" he asked.

"How do we know you're not trying to kill us?" he asked boldly.

The man chuckled. "Smart one, you are. No. If I was going to do that, you'd be dead already. Come along, now. It's not safe out here."

As he passed him, Tyler noticed the man look around before he followed them in and closed the door. Annese blew out the lantern as she looked around. The room was cozy with a warm fireplace. A thick rug laid on an old, wooden floor. The lanterns around the walls gave the room a cheery feeling. Three comfortable, over-stuffed chairs decorated the room with a low wooden table.

An arch decorated in vines was directly opposite the door. Annese could see a small table for four in the middle of the room. Dark curtains covered the windows. A similar rug was under the table.

An older woman came from another room. She stopped short, looking at the children. They noticed her short, stocky build and cold, black eyes. Her hair was turning gray from a dark shade of black. "Rickter! What have you brought home now?" she scolded.

Tyler giggled, but stopped when Annese elbowed him in the ribs. "Sorry. She sounds like my mother," he whispered.

"The children were in the village," the gravelly voice replied as he removed his hood. "It's getting dark. I couldn't leave them there. They are looking for Sujitt."

"Sujitt?" The woman looked at them suspiciously. "Why would you want to see Sujitt?"

"A man named Reimer from the forest sent us here to see Sujitt," Odessa replied politely. "He said he could help us get to the Oracle."

"And what need would you have of the Oracle? Hmm?" She didn't seem to believe their story.

"We need to know where to go from here to get back to the surface," Tyler explained. "Reimer thought the Oracle could tell us."

"Come! Come, children. Sit down. Relax," Rickter ushered them in with a friendly voice. "Wicken, don't just stand there looking grouse! I'm certain these children are hungry. Fetch them something to eat!"

"Humf!" the woman snorted, then she vanished into another room. "You think I'm a ruddy servant?" she muttered under her breath.

"Sujitt will be along in a while," Rickter told them softly. "He doesn't come until after dark so no one will know where the Oracle is, but we all know anyway."

Now that Rickter had removed his robes, Annese could see he was a short, thin man with graying hair and a weary face, although his gray eyes sparkled with all the youth of the world. He had a kind smile as he glanced over the children. "There's a great many things Sujitt tries to keep secret, but we know them anyway."

"How do you know them?" Tyler asked with a scowl.

Rickter chuckled. "Sujitt talks in his sleep!" the man whispered. The children all giggled over the news. "Now, tell me: what it is you seek from the Oracle."

"We need directions," Annese revealed, pulling one of the longairits off her head. "We're trying to get back to the surface, but we don't know which way to go. We can't go back the way we came, and we don't know how to get anywhere."

"I see. Well, perhaps the Oracle can tell you. Sujitt will know for sure."

"Here we are," Wicken returned with a tray. It held several bowls on it. "Stew for everyone. Take some bread, too," she instructed, placing the tray on the nearby table. "I've got some milk for the babies," she revealed. She placed two small bowls on the floor. "Eat up, all of you. That includes you, Rickter!" she barked and left the room.

"Don't mind Wickie. She's not as mean as she sounds. She's actually quite a nice lady," Rickter informed the children. "And the woman can co-ok!" he swooned with raised brows.

ODESSA

Odessa giggled at Rickter. He reminded her of her grandfather. He was always lending a gentle compliment. Similar to Rickter, her grandfather was going lightly gray as well and had a similar beard. The warm stew felt good going down, and it tasted wonderful. She closed her eyes as her mouth savored the taste that burst inside.

Wicken returned with drinks. She placed them on the table as well.

"This is wonderful," Odessa complimented her. "I've never tasted anything so good!"

Wicken looked pleased. "Thank you, dear."

"It's very good," Annese said quietly. "Thank you."

"Yes," Tyler swallowed some stew. "Thank you for your hospitality. We really appreciate it."

"Hmm," Wicken looked over the three suspiciously. "We'll see."

"Why is no one out?" Odessa asked after another mouthful of stew.

"What, dear?" Rickter asked, swallowing some stew.

"There's no one about in the village, and no one would answer our knocks."

"That's because of the Orsessas," he replied.

Tyler scowled. "What's an Orsessa?"

"Brain eaters," Rickter told him. "They come through the village in the dark. They're creatures of the night with long tentacles they use to suck out your brains. No one is out at night, and no one answers the knocks for fear of the Orsessas."

"Monsters knock on the door to get a victim?" Tyler scowled in confusion.

Rickter laughed. "Monsters? No. Orsessas are very intelligent. They use cunning trickery to get their victims."

"But you said Sujitt would be here after dark," Annese clarified. Odessa nodded.

"So I did." Rickter wiped his mouth on his sleeve. "Not to worry. He'll be here. He's quite cunning himself. Sujitt's been dodging Orsessas for years."

Odessa looked over at the longairits and smiled. "Annese, look!"

A few feet away and off to one side, the longairits had all snuggled together. The brown and white one whimpered in its sleep. They almost looked like one big fluff ball. The one that had been whimpering left the group and rolled over to Annese. It crawled up into her lap and snuggled down. It heaved a satisfied sigh and went to sleep. Odessa chuckled with the others at the brown and white spotted longairit.

"Looks like you've made a friend," Rickter smiled.

"Isn't that the one you helped?" Tyler asked. He was careful not to mention the word 'healed'.

"Yea, it is," Annese replied.

"I don't think your Mom will let you keep it," Tyler sighed.

"How do you know?" Annese scowled. "You've never met my mother!"

Tyler shrugged. "Will she?"

Annese sighed. "Probably not."

The door opened quickly. A lean figure with a dark, hooded cloak came in and shut the door tight behind him. He turned back to the rest of the living room and looked around. Rickter sat in his chair with a bowl of stew and nodded. Two children and a Centaus all leaned towards each other, looking at him in fear. He hunched over threateningly and slowly crept into the room, stopping short of the children. He glanced from one to the other.

"Boo!" he burst out.

"Ahh!" the three screamed simultaneously, scooting backwards. Startled, the longairits rolled for cover.

Rickter and the man laughed.

Wicken came rushing in to see what was going on. She found three frightened children and two laughing old men. "Oh, you!" she huffed, rushing forward. "Give me that cloak!" She whipped the cloak off his head, revealing an adult Kaptrix. "Dolt!" She smacked him across the back of his head. He flinched and rubbed his head with a grin on his face. "Scaring children! What's wrong with you? Does that make you feel like a big man? Dinner's on the table!" She pushed him towards the table.

The three children shook at the man with a broad chest in a green tunic. Powerful muscles tapered to lean hips in brown jerkins. His feet were shod in black boots. His square face twinkled in merriment. Laughter filled his dark eyes. His smile was warm and amused. Short, red, curly hair went in every direction. Tyler, at least, let out a pent-up breath.

"A party?" the man asked.

"Not quite," Rickter still laughed. "They're here to see you."

"Me?" the man looked surprised.

"Dinner first!" Wicken ordered. "You have all night for questions."

"Yes, ma'am," the man gave a brief nod and climbed over people to get his stew. He chuckled as the longairits snuck out from under and behind furniture and rolled to the protection of the kids. "Quite a family, eh?" he nodded towards them while ladling stew into a bowl.

"Are...are you...Sujitt?" Tyler asked still shaking.

The man nodded and swallowing a mouthful of stew. He made his way around to sit by Rickter. He eyed the young man curiously. The boy couldn't have been more than 10 or 11 years. "So, who's been throwing my name around?"

"Um, no one....I think," Tyler scowled, not understanding the comment. "A Kaptrix name Reimer told us to come to see you."

"He did, did he," Sujitt grinned. "And why would my old friend do that?" He took another mouthful of stew.

"He said you could take us to the Oracle," Annese replied softly.

"So we can find the way to the surface," Odessa picked up quickly.

"We fell down a sinkhole," Annese remarked.

"And we need to find a way back."

"And he thinks the King is looking for the blue gem," Tyler said.

"And another cataclysm will happen when it gets put back in place," Annese added.

"And he wants us to warn as many people as we meet along the way," Odessa said.

"So they can get to the surface, too," Tyler ended.

Sujitt had stopped eating and was looking from one child to the next as the story unfolded. He looked at Rickter, who shrugged.

"I just found them in the street," he leaned back with a grin.

"Who *are* you?" Sujitt asked the children.

"I'm Tyler, this is Annese, and this is Odessa," he explained. "We're from the surface, and we need to get back there, but no one seems to know how."

"And them?" he nodded at the longairits.

"Well, they're kinda along for the ride," Annese said slowly.

"We rescued them from a really big ant-like thing with long legs and pincers," Odessa explained.

Sujitt's and Rickter's eyes grew wide. "You outran an Anknid?" Sujitt asked in surprise.

"Well, not exactly," Tyler squirmed.

"We killed it," Odessa said softly.

"You what?" both men exclaimed together in surprise.

"Sweetheart, it takes six grown Kaptrix with sharp spears to kill an anknid. How did three children kill one?"

"Two," Annese peeped up, holding up two fingers.

"Two?" Rickter asked.

***"I was rescuing fluff balls," she said softly.

"A noble gesture," Rickter commended.

"So how did two of you kill an anknid?" Sujitt asked.

"With this?" Tyler announced. He pulled the axe out of his pack.

Sujitt sat back. "That's Reimer's axe," he whispered.

"*The* axe?" Rickter leaned forward to get a better look.

"What's so special about the axe?" Odessa asked, looking at it curiously.

"That axe belonged to his father," Sujitt explained. "It was forged by the Krilts before the cataclysm put us underground. If he gave that to you," Sujitt paused and looked reverently at Tyler, "he's not expecting to survive the return of the gem, and he has declared you his next of kin."

Tyler's eyes widened as he looked down at the axe in his hand. "But..."

"No buts," Sujitt said calmly. "That axe has seen 2000 years of fighting, defense, and hunting. It is so finely balanced that an axe thrower can hit the center of a target every time. It holds an edge so well that it rarely needs sharpening. It was specially forged for Reimer's great-grandfather for saving the Krilt king's life. It has been passed down from generation to generation. Reimer never did marry, nor did he ever have children. He obviously put a lot of thought into it and must have thought very highly of you. You may not be his blood, but you are now his heir."

"I'll get it back to him," Tyler said quietly. "I promise."

Rickter chuckled. "You don't understand, son," he said quietly. "Reimer has no intention of going up to the surface. If he handed that to you, it was to let us know he'll spread the word down here and help rescue as many as he can, but he's not expecting to live."

"But...." Tyler began sadly. He tried to subdue the tears forming in his eyes.

"Don't fret," Sujitt said with a sad smirk. "He knows what he's doing. So, you want to see the Oracle, do you?" He quickly changed the subject.

"That's what Reimer said to do," Annese said quietly. She watched Tyler as he continued to stare at the axe.

"And you expect to find your answers there?"

"Yes, sir," Odessa replied.

"Well, there's some things you should know about the oracle," Sujitt replied, wiping his mouth. "The first is that she doesn't speak in clear language. She speaks in puzzles. The second is that *if* she answers, she may not answer the question you ask, but one you are thinking. Perhaps one you haven't even realized you were asking. The third thing you need to understand is that she may well give you a quest of her own to insure your loyalty"

"We don't have time for another quest," Annese spoke up worriedly. "We need to get up to the surface and get home!"

"We'll do what we have to do," Tyler said bravely.

Sujitt looked at the three children. "All in agreement?"

"Yes," Odessa replied. "My father's going to be very angry at me anyway. I might as well have something good to tell him."

The group looked at Annese. Annese pet the longairit in her lap mechanically. She looked ready to break into tears. Her lower lip trembled.

"Annese?" Tyler asked softly.

Annese looked up at him. A tear trickled down her cheek. "It's all my fault! All I wanted to do was show you I wasn't lying. Now we're in lots of trouble."

"'Neese, it's not your fault," Tyler comforted. "I'm the one that called you a liar."

"And I'm the one who brought you to Harpy Field," Odessa said quietly. "We were all wrong. But we got into this together, and we'll get out of it together. Right?"

"Right," Tyler agreed optimistically. He held out his hand in front of the others, palm down. Odessa looked at him strangely. He nodded his head towards his hand. Odessa smiled and placed her hand on top of his. The two looked at Annese.

Annese looked from one to the other. She gave them a watery smile. "Right," she nodded, adding her hand on top.

Sujitt added his on top of theirs. "Very well. Everyone get some sleep. We go see the Oracle first thing in the morning." Sujitt looked at Rickter with a raised brow. Rickter simply nodded knowingly.

8 – NEW COMPANIONS

JORDON

Jordon and Fuzz stumbled into Jeremy as they came off the pad. Jordon drew in a deep breath. The cool, moist air was so different from the heat of Lavaland that it sent a shiver down Jordon's back. He could feel a mist in the air. He glanced around at the darkening forest. Dense woods spread out before him. Colorful flowers grew in clumps along an overgrown path. Thick vines climbed the trees, with leaves sprouting every so often.

"Gosh, that feels great!" he murmured

"Yea," Jeremy agreed absently.

"What is it?" Jordon gazed at his friend.

"Fuzz, have you ever been on this island before?" Jeremy asked.

"I... I'm not certain." Fuzz replied. The Kaptrix looked around confused. "It looks vaguely familiar."

"It's getting darker," Jordon remarked. "Maybe we should make a shelter and try to get some sleep."

"Shh. Listen," Jeremy held up his hand.

The three stood perfectly still... listening... for anything... at all. There was no noise around them. Nothing. Total silence. The only sound was a slight drip of water off in the distance.

"I don't hear anything," Fuzz said quietly.

"Me either," Jordon agreed.

"I know. How many forests have you ever been in or near where there is no sound at all?"

Jordon thought for a moment. There was always sound. Birds, squirrels, the wind. Something! "None."

"Exactly," Jeremy replied. "I learned one thing during our last trip here. Where there's no noise, there's danger lurking."

"But we still need a shelter and some sleep," Jordon remarked with a yawn. "We can set up watches."

"Alright, but keep your eyes peeled for anything."

"Ok. Fuzz, what looks comfy?" Jordon turned around. "Fuzz? Fuzz?"

"Now where'd he wander off to?" Jeremy whined exasperated. Jordon sighed and shrugged.

Jordon awoke with a start. Something snapped. Quietly, he rolled over onto his stomach and peered out of the shelter they had constructed the night before. The dimness on the walls indicated it was still night. Gentle, comforting night sounds echoed off the trees. He marveled at how they seemed so similar to when they were on the surface. Hooting owls, clicking bats, chirping crickets, and the occasional squeal of a small creature being caught for dinner. Apparently, they were the danger.

Snap! There it was again. Something was out there. He could hear a light snuffling sound around the shelter. Then nothing. Another snap. It was moving away. Whew!

It was sometime later when Jordon woke Jeremy up with a shove.

"Morning to you, too," his friend mumbled.

"Wake up!" the voice whispered softly. "We have a problem."

Jordon's words must have sunk in slowly. Jeremy propped himself on his elbow. He looked at his best friend with a questioning scowl on his face.

"What problem?" he asked softly, understanding Jordon's need for silence.

Jordon pointed to the space between them. Jeremy followed the pointing finger. A ball of black and pale gray fur about the size of a beagle was curled up between them, sound asleep. The long snout had a white blaze down it, and the tip of each paw was painted white.

"When did we get a dog?" Jeremy whispered.

Jordon shrugged. "Sometime during the night, I guess. I never heard it come in."

The small creature shook as its head popped up. It gave a wide yawn, showing sharp white teeth and a black tongue. Big, soulful, brown eyes looked up at the boys as its fluffy tail wagged tentatively.

"Isn't he cute!" Jeremy smiled, then looked thoughtful. "Or is it a she?"

"I didn't look," Jordon smirked.

"Well, I guess we've been adopted—again," Jeremy chuckled.

"Um, Jay?" Jordon began. "That may not be the best idea. I mean, I'm sure its mother is around somewhere."

Jeremy stretched, then reached for his backpack. "What mother would leave a pup in the woods?"

"One that's off looking for breakfast."

"Ok," Jeremy chuckled. He took a strip of jerky and put it down for the dog. He pulled out another one and a piece of fruit for himself. The pup sniffed at the strange strip of meat. It licked it tentatively, tasting it. After checking it out, it grasped the strip between its paws and began chewing on it.

Jordon followed suit. Knowing one strip of meat would not fill the pup, he tossed it another strip, then ate his own.

"I wonder where Fuzz ended up?" Jeremy asked.

"Not a clue." Jordon paused. "We could go back onto the pad. It won't go back to the fire bugs."

Jeremy shook his head. "No, I think we should go find Fuzz. He couldn't have gotten far. It got dark pretty fast."

"Alright. Come on. Let's get going." Carefully, the boys packed up. When it came time for their bedrolls, the pup thought they were playing. He jumped up onto them as Jordon tried to roll it up. As the blanket disappeared, he grasped the end and tugged.

"No, boy. Come on. Give it back!" Jordon chuckled. He picked the pup up and put him aside.

"What about the shelter?" Jeremy asked as they stretched to leave.

"What about it?"

"Shouldn't we take it down? You know, like we were never here?"

Jordon looked at it for a moment. "Nah. Leave it for the next poor soul who gets lost in here. Besides, it has our scent all over it."

"True. O.K."

The boys started off away from the pad. Jordon noticed the path was a thin strip of overgrown dirt. It was hard to follow, and the boys had to stop often to figure out which way it went. The woods blocked out most of the light off the walls of the cavern. The trees grew tall and thick, covered with massive canopies. As they rounded a bend, a deep growl came from the woods near them. Both boys froze.

"Did you hear that?" Jordon whispered.

"Yep."

"Yip! Yip! Yip!"

"What...?" Jordon looked towards the high-pitched sound. The strange little dog that slept with them last night was hopping up and down, yipping and snarling near the woods.

"He's following us?" Jordon asked wide-eyed.

"So much for being quiet," Jeremy sighed.

Another dog came from the woods. It was bigger than the pup, but had similar coloring. Long, sharp fangs came down over its lower jaw. The suspicious gaze in its yellow eyes observed the boys as it licked the pup.

"Let me guess," Jeremy smirked. "Mother?"

"That'd be my guess. Let's back away slowly. Maybe she'll see we mean no harm, and we can get going."

"Good idea."

Slowly, the boys backed their way down the path until they were behind some trees. They turned and started off on their way. It was getting harder and harder to see.

"Flashlights?" Jordon asked as he strained to find the path.

"Yea," Jeremy agreed. He dropped his pack and pulled his from the inside pocket. He flipped it on. The light cut through the dimness quickly. "This is going to be a long journey."

"Just remember, we're short on batteries," Jordon reminded.

"Yip!" A small fur ball bumped into Jeremy's legs. Jeremy sighed. He picked up the pup. "Looks like we got company."

Jordon looked the pup over. "He really should stay with his mother."

"I know that, and you know that, but how do you tell the puppy that?"

Jordon took the puppy and put him back on the path facing the direction his mother was in. He patted the puppy's backside, tapping him lightly towards the woods. "Go on! Mommy!" he tried. The puppy rolled over on his back and began pawing at Jordon's hands. Jordon sighed. "I give up."

"Come on. Maybe he'll go back to his mother if we just keep going."

"Maybe."

The flashlight made it a little easier to see the pathway, but caused the surrounding woods to seem even darker. Much to their dismay, the puppy stayed right with them.

"I'm getting hungry," Jordon said after they'd been traveling a few hours.

Jeremy flashed the light around them. Moss and leaves mottled the cavern floor. Other than the path, there really wasn't any place to sit down. More trees filled the beam of light.

"Nowhere to really rest. There's always the path."

"Why not?" Jordon agreed. He dropped to the ground and pealed his pack off his back. "I'll swear this thing keeps getting heavier," he grumbled.

"I know what you " Jeremy sat next to him. He rolled his shoulders to ease the cramps. "Mine, too."

The pup came up and curled into Jeremy's legs. He laid his head down on his knee and dropped off to sleep. The boys chuckled as they watched him.

"Whatcha got for lunch?" Jeremy asked.

"Hmmm, let's see," Jordon replied. He pulled out a few sticks of jerky, an apple, and a candy bar. "We have toughened beef steak, pie a la mode—without the a la mode or crust, and real food."

Jeremy laughed. "Where'd you get a chocolate bar?" He began pulling his food out of his pack.

Jordon smirked. "I stashed it in my pack from home."

"Wish I had thought of that," he laughed, biting into a jerky.

"Is it my imagination, or are these trees moving in?" Jordon shone his flashlight around.

Jeremy followed the light. "I don't think so, but we should get going anyway. It'll probably take the better part of the day just to reach the middle of the island."

"Yea. We can walk and eat at the same time."

"Here, prop the pup on my pack," Jeremy chuckled while he picked up the confused puppy. "He can sleep while we walk."

Jordon carefully settled the puppy on the top of Jeremy's pack near his shoulders. Readjusting the contents of the pack, he made a small bed sunken into the top of Jeremy's pack so the pup wouldn't fall off. "Best I can do. If he gets heavy, let me know. I'll take a turn."

"He's going to slow us down if he has to sleep so often," Jeremy started off.

"He's a puppy. They're like babies. They sleep a lot."

"Ya know," Jeremy peered over his shoulder. "If this little guy is going to come with us, he needs a name."

"Don't do it!" Jordon warned.

"Do what?"

"Get attached to him."

"Why? He's cute!"

"Yep, he is. And he's wild, not a pet."

"Couldn't prove that now," Jeremy smirked at the sleeping pup.

"I'm warning you," Jordon sang. "You give it a name, you're gonna wanna take it home, then how is Princess gonna feel? This thing will be at least twice her size, judging by those paws."

"She'll get used to him. She got use to you."

"Hey!"

"Just kidding," Jeremy laughed.

The boys walked in companionable silence. Every now and then they would stop and study the ground, trying to find footprints or scars.

"See anything?" Jeremy asked.

"No. It almost seems as if no one's been this way."

"But where'd Fuzz go? It's the only path?"

"I have no idea." He looked in the direction they were going. "Could he have bushwhacked it?"

"I doubt it. Got captured again?"

"Probable. Let's keep going."

"How about Fred?" Jeremy asked after a few minutes of silence.

Jordon stopped and looked at his friend. His puzzled face scrutinized Jeremy. Suddenly, he realized what Jeremy was talking about. "It's a dog! Not a little brother!"

"Ok. Oreo? He is black and white."

"No." They continued walking.

"We could call him Narim?"

Jordon smirked. "We already have one of those."

Jeremy sighed. "OK, Hmmm. I know! How about Monstro!"

Jordon laughed. "Sure! Here, Monstro! Here, boy!" he mimicked. "I don't think so."

"Does sound ridiculous."

"Sounds more like a Killer Whale."

"Then you pick a name!"

"Hmm. I don't know. I'm not good at these things. Right now, he looks like a Cuddles."

"No way!"

"How about Fang?" Jordon asked. "His eye teeth are showing just below his upper lip, and his mom had long ones."

"Fang," Jeremy tried. "Not bad, and he'll grow into it. Fang it is."

"Now convince him of that," Jordon laughed.

"Here, hold him, will ya?" Jeremy turned to have Jordon take the pup. "I gotta go."

"Go?" Jordon lifted the dog from Jeremy's pack. "Go where?"

"I'll be right back," Jeremy replied, heading into the woods.

"Ah! Go!" Jordon realized what Jeremy meant. He put Fang on the ground. The pup immediately began playing with some leaves there. Jordon looked around carefully. It was too quiet. "Stay close, boy."

Jeremy came out of the woods quickly. He caught up to Jordon. "O.K."

Fang looked up at Jeremy and began growling. He ran behind Jordon, peered out at Jeremy, and whimpered. Jeremy took a step back.

"What's wrong with him?" Jeremy asked.

"Don't know. Bad dream?" Jordon suggested. "Let's keep going. We need to find Fuzz."

Jordon found it odd that Fang wouldn't go near Jeremy all the while they traveled. At the same time, his normally chatty companion was pretty quiet. He kept looking around.

"What's wrong?" Jordon asked.

"Nothing," Jeremy replied.

"What are you looking for?"

"Nothing."

"Are you ok?"

"Yes."

Jordon looked at Jeremy with a scowl. Did he get hit on the head or something? Yes? Still, he looked alright.

"See any tracks?" Jordon asked.

"No."

Fang ran on ahead a few feet, looking back worriedly. Jordon and Jeremy followed the pup. As they traveled around a curve, the path split. A thin, dark path traveled to the left. The broader path continued straight. Jordon found it strange that there still was no noise in the forest. If nothing else, they should be hearing birds overhead as they did when they left the shelter that morning.

"Anything?" Jeremy asked.

Jordon bent down to examine the ground again. He tried to scrutinize it to see if there were any scuffs or footprints. Nothing. The dirt was hard as a rock. Even if someone had come by, it wouldn't show.

Fang's sudden barking and growling caught his attention. He looked up at the pup to find it facing him, looking behind at Jeremy. Before his eyes, the dog grew to almost three times its size. His barking got deeper. The fangs at his lip got longer. Thick saliva began dripping from its mouth. Its body got thicker. The dog took a stance that was ready to pounce. Jordon looked behind him. Jeremy held up his staff between both hands, ready to drop it on Jordon. Jordon dove to the side, rolling away as the staff came down with a sharp crack.

"What are you? Crazy?" he cried.

A twang echoed through the woods behind him. A dark arrow with black feathers flew into Jeremy's head. A look of shock came over his face. He dropped the staff, then fell to the ground.

"Jeremy!" Jordon cried in horror. "Jay?"

He began rushing over to Jeremy, then stopped. The body was changing. A tall, thin, rubbery-type of body lay in its place. There was no actual definition to its features. The staff turned into a stick. Jordon backed up a pace in surprise.

Running footsteps came from the direction they left behind. Jordon pulled his sword, ready for battle. Even with the dimming beam from his flashlight, it was hard to see, but he stood his ground. Fang came up right next to him, ready for anything. He kept looking toward the footsteps and then to the side woods.

"Why didn't you wait for me?" Jeremy yelled, coming around the bend breathless. "I was only gone a few minutes."

Jordon lowered Sharijol slightly. He looked at Jeremy, then back at the body on the ground. He looked down at Fang. The dog had shrunk back to its normal size and was running towards Jeremy. Jordon breathed and lowered the sword.

"I think Monstro might have been a good name for him after all," he remarked.

Jeremy reached down to pet the pup. "Why didn't you wait?"

"I thought you were done," he explained. "You came back out of the woods."

"I what? No, I didn't!"

"No. Actually, *that* came out of the woods looking like you." He pointed to the body on the path. "I swear, Jay, he looked exactly like you. Acted like you, too. Only Fang wouldn't go near him. I thought it kinda funny, but it was you; so we kept going. When I stopped to look for tracks, he tried to attack me. Fang, oh man! Fang!"

"Rescued you?"

"No, actually." Jordon began scoping the woods. "Fang grew. He began by barking at the thing. Before my eyes, he almost tripled in size and probably would've attacked if that arrow hadn't hit first."

"Arrow?" Jeremy scowled.

The boys moved back towards the body. Jeremy leaned over to examine it. There were no real features, the head was oval, there was no hair, and the blank eyes were open. It had mottled, rubbery, and featureless skin with a white tint. A thin slit served as a mouth. It wore no clothes. Other than limbs, the body didn't really have a shape. The black arrow stuck out of the side of the head at what should have been the temple, its thin shaft deep in the skull. A blue-green liquid oozed from the wound.

Jordon continued to examine the woods, waiting for something to attack. Sharijol was still in his hand, ready for anything. He could feel something watching them.

"Fuzz? Are you out there?" he called.

"Fuzz can't shoot like this," Jeremy remarked. "I doubt he could shoot his foot."

Fang sniffed at the dead body and growled.

"Easy, boy," Jeremy ruffled the pup. "It's dead. Good boy." He looked up at Jordon scanning the woods and stood. "What are you thinking?" he asked lowly.

"I think we're being watched."

"I wish it wasn't so dark down here," Jeremy commented. He tried to peer into the woods with his flashlight.

"There's no noise. That's bothering me. Been bothering me since you went into the woods to go pee."

"I don't see anything."

"Me, either."

"Ok," Jeremy yelled out. "We know you're there! Come on out!" he bluffed. "Don't make me come in after you!"

The boys heard a rustle in the woods. "Get ready," Jordon whispered. He raised Sharijol to the ready.

A thin shadow stepped out onto the path near the split. In the dim light, Jordon could barely make out the shape. Petite. Slender. Only the glint of a finely sharpened arrow tip showed a bow was sited.

Jeremy lifted his staff. "Solar lux lucis!" he whispered. A bright light flared from the ball on the end of the staff. It lit up the entire area. In the staff's light stood a young girl, about their age. She glared at them cautiously, one hand shielding her eyes. Her black ponytail accentuated her dark brown skin glinting in the light. Her body was thin and graceful. Her hunting leathers blended into the woodlands. She held a black bow tightly in her hand, a black arrow nocked and ready.

"A girl," Jeremy sighed.

"Don't let your guard down," Jordon whispered. "We aren't home."

"Who are you?" the girl questioned. Her voice had a familiar, melodious quality.

Jeremy moved forward, but the girl backed up. He lowered the power of the staff so it didn't blind her anymore. "My name is Jeremy Blackhurst. This is my friend, Jordon Hallstead. We're searching for two kids that look kinda like us—a boy and a girl. They're traveling with a Centaus girl. Have you seen them?"

The girl shook her head.

"Oh. Well, then. I guess we'll be on our way." Jeremy started down the path again. The girl backed into the trees.

Jordon lowered his sword. Something was interesting about her. "Do you have a name?" he asked.

"I am Aiyalinaya. Most people call me Aiya."

Jordon smirked. "That's pretty!" he said. "You live around here?"

The girl nodded. It was a start.

"Um, thanks for saving me. You're a very good shot."

"Shot for what?" the girl watched suspiciously.

"He means you're very good with your bow and arrow. Look, there's another person we're looking for," Jeremy tried. "A short guy with a brown jacket and brown hair? He'd have had some papers in his hands."

"I believe he was taken to my village as a prisoner. He trespassed into our territory."

"Found Fuzz," Jordon murmured lowly as he shook his head. "Guess where we're going."

"Can you take us to him?"

The girl scowled. "You wish to trespass into our territory?" she questioned their sanity.

"No," Jordon replied quickly. "However, the gentleman isn't very good at looking out for himself. We need to put him back on his way."

"Besides, if you take us to him, we wouldn't be trespassing," Jeremy reasoned.

"I am uncertain the elders of our village will allow him to leave."

"We could ask," Jordon tried with a slight smile.

The girl lowered her bow a little. "Very well, but no tricks!"

Jordon sheathed his sword. "No tricks."

Jeremy sighed. "Opacus," he mumbled. His staff went dark. He lowered it to the ground. "No tricks," he agreed.

Fang began wandering over to check on the new person. Aiya moved the arrow towards the dog.

"Fang," Jeremy called. "Come here, boy!" he called. He patted his leg. The pup quickly raced back to him. Jeremy picked him up to keep tabs on him, petting the dog roughly. "Good boy! Who's the best puppy!"

"Some puppy!" Jordon muttered. "Lead on, please, Aiya."

"Why do you have an Ortiks?" the girl asked tentatively, starting down the path.

"What's an Ortiks?" Jordon asked. He fell into step next to Aiya.

"That is. The thing you call a puppy."

"It's just a dog," Jeremy pat Fang's head.

"The Ortiks are excellent hunters," the girl informed them. "They are wild beasts that are very difficult to take down. They are not pets. Though they appear as small animals, when attacked they grow as much as 25 hands higher. They can leap long distances, pounce with precision, and their teeth can rip into anything. They do not take to bipeds."

"This one did," Jeremy smirked. "He was curled up in our bedrolls this morning, sound asleep."

"Another one met him near the woods. Apparently, she didn't mind the pup going off with us," Jordon added.

"She may be following you, keeping watch; or she may be waiting for you to die so the pup can eat fresh meat," Aiya informed.

"Cherishing thought," Jordon mumbled. But his eyes weren't on the pup; they were on the girl. He took in her movements; graceful as a dancer. Long, soft, black hair bounced as she walked. She still had not put away her bow, although she had lowered it. He noticed the high cheekbones, thin chin, lanky figure. When he looked up, his eyes returned to her head. Pointed ears? They were almost to the top of her head. Her skin coloring caused them to blend right in with the rest of her hair. "Are you an elf?" he asked.

Aiya looked indignant. "*I* am a Drelt. We do not associate with elves." She took on a quizzical expression. "What is an elf? I have heard of them, but I have never seen one."

"Well, an elf would look much like you, except with pale skin, kind of like ours. Some are more brown than tan, but they're much more pale than you are. They live on the surface."

"Oh."

"So, how far is it to your village?"

"Not too far. Just down the path."

"Do you get visitors here often?" Jordon tried to keep the conversation going. He loved her musical voice.

"Rarely. Where do you come from? I have never seen anyone like you."

"And probably never will again!" Jordon teased and wiggled his eyebrows.

"I'm gonna barf!" Jeremy muttered. "Down, Romeo!"

Aiya scowled. "Romeo? I thought you said his name was Jordon?"

The boys chuckled. "It's a reference to a play back home," Jeremy explained. "We came down from the surface. The kids we're looking for fell through a sinkhole and are roaming around down here somewhere."

"I am afraid they probably will not get far without weapons. There are many dangerous creatures in the forests."

"So we've seen," Jordon smiled, watching her, "And some beautiful ones." Jeremy rolled his eyes.

"The Doppler was not a very dangerous creature."

"Not dangerous! It was going to kill me!"

Aiya shrugged. "It must have needed a meal. They gain their victim's trust, kill it, then drink all the blood from it. The other forest creatures take care of the carcass. The ortik you are carrying, however, is much more dangerous."

"Sure, if you say so," Jeremy smirked, tousling the puppy in his arms. Fang scrambled to get down, so Jeremy set him on the ground. Happily, the pup chased after some butterflies on the side of the path.

The boys took in the small flowers that sprinkled the grass under the trees. The trees themselves seemed large and round. A feeling hit them from the trees, as if they were being watched.

"Do these trees talk?" Jordon asked.

"Talk? Since when do trees talk?" Aiya asked curiously. "Do trees talk above ground?"

"Some of them," Jeremy replied. He remembered Dauren and another apprentice talking about some talking trees at The Keep.

"Trees here do not talk. Here," Aiya pointed to the right. "We must take this path."

"Fang! Come on!" Jeremy called. A strange bark and a racing pup greeted him. Fang banged into Jeremy's legs in an effort to catch him. The trio laughed at his antics.

"Is it me, or is it getting darker?" Jeremy whispered to Jordon.

Jordon smiled as he watched Aiya walking alongside them. "Seems rather bright in here to me."

"You're getting gross, man!" Jeremy pushed Jordon's shoulder.

The thick forest parted into a sparsely treed area. Strange huts were built between trees and disguised with branches and bushes. It seemed hotter here than in the forest proper. A round clearing with a fire pit sat in the center of the village. A dead boar was spitted and cleaned and cooking over the fire. A round clay pot was also near the pit, apparently heating the liquid in it. They could hear the sounds of a waterfall close by. Strangely, there was no one around.

Aiya looked about slowly. She took a step forward towards a hut on the right. The sudden movements around them were so fast, the boys didn't know what happened first. Two men grasped Aiya by the arms. Six spears pointed at Jordon's and Jeremy's chests, points glinting in the light from overhead. The men wielding them didn't look happy.

A tall, regal woman with long black hair approached the group. If it were not for the gold armband and jewelry she wore, she'd have blended in with the forest itself. She surveyed the boys, then turned to Aiya.

Before she could speak, Fang's growls grew louder. He stood on the side of the path, glaring at the people around the boys. He had already doubled in size and was getting ready to pounce.

"Fang! No!" Jeremy called.

The men began shouting and pointing. Several spears shot off towards the dog. Fang dodged them easily and began running towards the men.

"Fang! Stop!" Jeremy ordered.

"Stop it!" Jordon tried towards the men. "He's harmless!"

Even Aiya tried to get the men to stop, but to no avail.

"We gotta do something!" Jordon cried to Jeremy.

"Got it! Hold me!" Jeremy reached behind and pulled his staff out. Lifting it high, he said, "Vicis Subsisto!" Everything around them stopped. The three spears were suspended in mid-air. Fang was in the middle of a pounce, with only his back feet on the ground. He had already quadrupled in size. Aiya's mouth was wide open, yelling to her tribesmen. The woman's hand was pointing at Fang.

"Come on," Jeremy suggested, squeezing out of the circle between two men. He took one spear out of the air and stuck in it the ground. He watched as Jordon took another one and did the same. He took the third and put it back in the hand of one man. Jeremy picked up Fang and put him under his arm. He was too big to cuddle now. "Wow! You weren't kidding about him growing, were you?"

"If what Aiya is saying is true, that's still small! Twenty-five hands is taller than a horse. I think Clydesdales get about that tall."

"Clydesdales? Those big horses with the shaggy feet?"

"Yea. We saw them on a field trip to some old-time village. The horses were pulling a plow."

"Got it. If Fang can get that big, he's gonna be a handful."

"I told you not to get attached."

"Yea, I know. Wanna rescue Aiya?"

"I guess we should."

The boys went over and pried the hands of the guards off Aiya's arms. Jordon grasped her by her waist and lifted her up. He set her back down near the fire.

"Man, she's heavier than she looks!" he grunted.

"Don't tell her that, unless, of course, you're looking for a premature death!" Jeremy chuckled.

"Right. Want to stop the time freeze now?"

"Can't. Don't know how. We just have to wait for it to wear off, which should be any moment anyway."

Right on cue, the spell ended. The tribesmen were startled to find the boys no longer near them, the dog gone, and the spears in the dirt. With Aiya missing, the guards fell into each other. Aiya seemed perplexed.

"How did I get here?" she asked.

"Later," Jordon said quietly.

Fang still snarled from Jeremy's arm. Jeremy quietly placed his hand over the dog's nose. "Enough," he said firmly. Fang looked up at Jeremy with a questioning look. "No! No bark!" Fang looked back at the men but didn't make any more noise.

"Aiya! What sorcery have you brought to our village?"

"I... I know not, Chiefess. I found these boys on the path. A Doppler was about to kill one. I killed it. The boys believe the spy is a friend of theirs."

The woman turned towards the boys. "You have trespassed into our territory. The penalty is death. How do you plead?"

Jordon's eyebrows went up. "I believe that to trespass, one would have to intentionally sneak into or wander onto your territory. We have done neither. We asked Aiya to bring us here so we may see if the traveler you have captured is our friend. He's rather small with brown hair and a brown coat. He'd have been carrying papers when you found him. He's a cartographer from Kaptrix and is trying to map out the transport stones of the underground caverns."

The Chieftess' eyes narrowed. "You would contradict *me*?"

"Never, ma'am," Jordon replied respectfully. "I was merely explaining how we understand the word 'trespass'."

"Different cultures often have different meanings for the same words. Or sometimes, they have different words for the same meanings," Jeremy tried to sound knowledgeable. "My family has seven children. Each child is from a different culture. We learn about each of the cultures to preserve each child's heritage."

"In this culture, you are not welcome. You have come onto this land uninvited," the woman snarled.

"Be careful, my chief," an old woman warned from behind her. Her clothing looked like green rags. A necklace of bones hung from her neck. She was missing some teeth. She held a wooden staff with a skull impaled on it. Two embedded bright green jewels served the skull's eyes. "The sorcery is dangerous. They must be minions of the white witch. See their eyes, round. And their ears! Not just their skin color smells of her!"

"What?" Jeremy exclaimed.

"Don't you mean the black witch? White witches are supposed to be good," Jordon added.

"Silence! Take them away! We will have a fine sacrifice at dark! And you, too!" The chieftess pointed a long, clawed finger at Aiya. "Traitors are not welcome here! You are no longer a Drelt!" she snarled.

Several tribesmen surrounded them. They held their spears threateningly. One tried to reach for Jeremy's staff, but a low growl from Fang made him pull back. Aiya stiffened her back and led the way to a small hut on the outskirts of the village.

"We gotta do something," Jordon whispered.

"I know, but not yet. We need to talk to Aiya about what's going on."

"And we need to rescue Fuzz."

"I think we're about to find him."

The guard in the lead opened the door. The ones behind pushed the prisoners into the large room roughly. The door slammed behind them. They could hear a mechanism move to secure it.

The room was pitch black. You couldn't even see the shadow of the fingers in front of your face.

"Jay," Jordon said as if signaling.

"Gotcha," Jeremy replied. "Lux Lucius," he whispered.

Light beamed from the orb on top of Jeremy's staff. It was bright enough to light the shack. They looked around at the bare room. There were no chairs or tables. Only a few bedrolls on the floor served as 'furniture'. A shadowed mass huddled in the far corner.

"Fuzz?" Jordon called. The shadow moved to look at them. "Fuzz!"

The shadow stood up and moved into the light. "Mister Jordon?" the timid voice asked.

"Yes! Where'd you go? Man, we turned around to look at the woods, and you were gone!"

"I told you. I am mapping the transport locations for the caverns. I thought I would get more distance while we still had some light. I thought you were right behind me. By the time I realized you were not, it was nearly dark. I stopped for the night, but sometime later I was taken captive by these people and accused of spying. I am supposed to be executed this evening." Fuzz's head hung as he said his last sentence.

"Aiya, surely they won't sacrifice you," Jordon turned towards her.

Aiya hung her head and nodded. "The Chieftess would be happy to be rid of me. I am forever getting into trouble with my ideas of peaceful relations with other races."

"I don't understand," Jeremy said. "We have peace with many races."

"The Drelt feel they are the only race that the Supreme Being claimed this planet for. They believe all others are an absurdity, a mockery to the Supreme Being. They feel it is their duty to rid the planet of all other races. The problem is, there are no other races down here. Sure, we have doppelers, and the white witch on the southern plain, but we are basically the only other sentient beings in the cavern. Now, two other races have come in less than a day. The Chieftess feels others are spying on us to take the forest from us."

"Jeremy, we gotta get out of here, or we're all done for," Jordon turned to his friend.

"I know. I've been thinking. We have to do it before dark, but I can't think of a way to get past the door."

"Do you have a teleport spell in that head of yours?"

"No. And your sword isn't going to get past whatever mechanism is on the other side of that door."

"How did you get us out of their hands before?" Aiya asked.

"It's a time spell. Basically, it speeds us up so fast that it seems like time is standing still. Problem is that it doesn't last long," Jeremy explained.

"I have an idea!" Aiya smiled.

"We're all ears," Jordon replied.

9 – THE ORACLE

ANNESE

"Quickly," Sujitt hurried them as he dodged into another set of bushes.

"Isn't there any other way besides crawling through bushes?" Annese complained as she rubbed another scratch.

"We can't let on where the Oracle is," Sujitt informed them.

"Rickter knows anyway," Odessa said as she pushed the green branches out of the way.

"He does, does he?" Sujitt smirked. "What makes you think he knows?"

"He says you talk in your sleep," Annese replied. She carefully stepped over another large root.

Sujitt stopped and looked at the children. Tyler and Odessa nodded in agreement. "Well. I guess that sheds a different light on things. Who else knows?"

"He didn't say. Just that they know because you talk in your sleep," Tyler recovered.

"Well, this is a surprise. He never let on. I'll have to have a word with him."

"Don't be angry," Odessa begged. "Rickter was trying very hard to honor your wishes not to tell."

"What's the big deal if anyone knows about the Oracle?" Annese asked. "I'm sure they've heard stories."

"If everyone knew where the Oracle was, they'd all be going to it for all sorts of things from what to wear to whom to declare war on. It would wear out the Oracle. No one would make their own decisions. They'd become too dependent on her; forget how to think. While the Oracle is very valuable, she's there for emergencies, not to take away people's decisions."

"Oh," Annese replied.

"Come on. Let's get going."

Sujitt led the children through more bushes to a dark green, dilapidated house with white shutters. Several low bushes grew near the walls. A dark, wooden door stood at ground level.

Tyler scowled in confusion. "The Oracle lives in a house? I thought this was a stone or something?"

"Well, the Oracle is actually below the surface many, many lengths. The stone in this house is a speaking stone. She speaks to the people through the stone. I understand there's one on the surface as well."

"How do you know the Oracle is a she?" Odessa asked.

"By her voice. It's a very feminine voice. You'll see. Come along."

Sujitt opened the door and led them in. The house was one room. It went up about twelve feet. Set into one wall was a huge, sparkling green stone. Several benches adorned the rest of the room.

"There you go," Sujitt said. "Go up to her and ask your question."

The children looked at each other. "You go," Annese said to Odessa. "You're really from this land."

"No, no! You go," Odessa said to Annese.

The two girls looked at Tyler. "You go!" Annese said. "You're older!"

"We're the same age!" Tyler frowned. "We'll all go!"

The three children approached the large stone. A soft melody filled the room, sounding like blended chimes and multiple voices. It started like a whisper and grew in intensity until you could hear it clearly. The kids looked around. Sujitt had sat on a bench and watched with amusement. He waved his hand to push them on. The trio moved closer to the stone.

"Um.., excuse us,... ma'am," Tyler began.

"Soft winds and children's voices. Speak your thoughts," the soft, musical voice surrounded. As gentle as it was, it seemed to pierce into each person in the room.

"We, um,...we need to know how to get back to the surface," Tyler stated. "Please."

The soft melody continued to fill the room. No other words came. Annese turned to look at Sujitt and shrugged. Sujitt motioned for her to turn around to the Oracle. She turned back and looked over at the others. Odessa pointed. The center of the stone glowed with a gentle twinkle. It grew brighter and brighter until the greenish glow filled the room. The voice responded, much stronger than before.

Two will follow
The three within
And another
Seeks to win.

Two exits there will fare
Fire and Lava
A crystalline Stair

Danger, too, is around
People, creatures,
One under ground.

The soft glow diminished as quickly as it arose, drifting away. The three looked at each other. Tyler turned back to Sujitt. Sujitt nodded.

"Um, thank you!" Annese called.

The three turned back to Sujitt. "I don't get it," Tyler said. "That wasn't an answer at all!"

"Wasn't it?" Sujitt asked. "It sounded like an answer to me."

"But what does it mean?"

"Fire and Lava," Odessa murmured. "Lava would mean a volcano. The only island with old volcanoes is Ascentia."

"Volcanoes usually get molten lava because they're near the core of the planet," Tyler said. "The pressure of the center core breaks through the mantle and the crust and explodes out the top if the volcano."

"Yes, but are we in the center of the planet or at the crust?" Annese asked.

Tyler and Odessa shrugged. All three looked at Sujitt with questioning eyes.

"I don't know. I've never been to the surface, nor have I been to the center," he responded.

"How do we get to Ascentia?" Odessa asked.

"I don't know," Sujitt replied. "I couldn't even tell you where Ascentia is. I've never left Kaptrix. Why don't we go back home and write this down, then you can think it over while you continue on. Besides, I'm certain Wicken has breakfast ready."

The three nodded, following Sujitt out of the hut. They murmured amongst themselves about what the Oracle said.

"The Oracle is supposed to be the wisest of all beings," Odessa said quietly. "I don't think she would give us false information."

"I was looking for directions," Tyler grumbled. "Not a riddle."

Annese looked to her left at bright magenta mushrooms. The large umbrella top was nearly as high as her waist and sat on slender, white stalks. There were five of them all growing together in a clump. "Oh, how pretty!" she cried, walking towards the waist high umbrellas.

"Annese! No!" Sujitt yelled, but it was too late.

The large mushrooms began swaying back and forth and emitting ear-piercing screams. Annese covered her ears with her hands, but she couldn't step away from the mushrooms. She crumbled to the ground in tears.

Sujitt hurried Odessa and Tyler away. He ran back, picked up Annese, and carried her away from the mushrooms. Several yards away, they could still hear the piercing screams. Sujitt put Annese down when the screams no longer had any effect on their ears.

"Are you alright?" he asked breathlessly. Annese nodded as she wiped the tears from her eyes.

"What were they?" Tyler asked.

"Verisium," Sujitt breathed heavily. "They're screaming mushrooms. Their screams are meant to incapacitate their victims. The scream will cause you to crumble, as it did to Annese. As the screams get louder, the victim goes unconscious. Death comes as the skull splits apart from the decibels of the multiple screams. The grass covers the victim who then rots into the ground providing nutrients for the mushrooms."

Tyler looked towards of the screams. "How long do they continue to scream?"

Sujitt shook his head. "Until they decide to stop. It shouldn't be too long now. Come on. Let's go home." He looked at Annese. "Are you sure you're alright?"

Annese nodded. "Thank you," she murmured. "Are you alright?"

"My ears are still ringing, but I'll be fine," he smiled and stood. "Come along, young lady." He helped her up and led the way home.

Annese took a stick from near the fire and burned the tip. Wicken had given her a piece of parchment, but they didn't have any ink. Annese used the stick and wrote on the parchment. She had to reburn the stick every couple of letters, but it worked. Carefully, she wrote down the riddle the Oracle had said to them. The three looked it over.

"Two will follow the three within," Odessa repeated. "We can assume we're the three."

"But who would follow us?" Tyler mused. "No one knows we're down here."

"Odessa's father knows," Annese replied. "Remember? He was in the field with us when we sank."

"If he was looking in our direction," Odessa said sadly. "I miss him. He'd know what to do now."

"We'll get back to him, Dess," Tyler laid a hand on her shoulder. "I promise!"

"Two could be anyone," Annese rounded them back to their discussion.

"And another seeks to win," Tyler said. "Another person?"

"Sounds like a race," Rickter remarked.

"It probably is. We have to get to the surface with everyone else before they place the blue gem in its holding place," Tyler said. "But would this other person try to lock us underground?" The two girls shrugged.

"The second paragraph seems more to the point," Odessa said. "Two exits – one being somewhere near a volcano and the other near crystal. But how do we find them?"

"The only option you have is to keep trying the discs," Sujitt said as he brought drinks into the living room.

"Discs?" Annese asked.

"You mean those odd-shaped stones in the ground?" Tyler asked.

"Yes," Sujitt replied. "There are three on Kaptrix. Creatures come and go when they land on them. No one knows, however, where they come from or where they go."

"We did it coming here," Tyler reminded the girls.

"We lucked out is what you mean," Annese scowled. "We could've been killed!"

"Jumping from place to place doesn't mean we'll be safe," Odessa brought out.

"What other choice do we have?" Tyler asked. "If we stay here, we're going to die in the next cataclysm. All the rocks above us are going to drop and crush whatever's left down here."

"Probably," Sujitt replied calmly.

"The last paragraph doesn't make sense," Annese mused. She read it over again.

"It seems like a warning," Odessa replied. "Kind of like the one Reimer gave us. You know, things we don't know are dangerous."

"You're probably right," Tyler nodded.

"Eat up, children!" Wicken placed a tray of food on the table. "You have a long journey and will need your strength." She placed a saucer of milk and some crushed fruit on the ground for the longairits.

Annese sat quietly, pondering the riddle as the others talked and ate. It didn't make sense. Two will follow? Win? What kind of race were they in? The only thing that really made sense was the last verse. She sighed, unable to make any more sense of it than they already had.

10 – THE EXECUTION

JEREMY

It was well after dark when several guards came into the prison. The four prisoners were huddled in the corner whispering. The torch the guards carried blazed off the reflectively painted walls.

"Come!" the largest guard grunted. He reached down and pulled Aiya to her feet. They tied her hands and shoved her towards the door. Another guard pulled Jordon to his feet and did the same; likewise for Fuzz and Jeremy.

"Wait!" Jeremy cried as they were being pushed out the door. "My staff!"

"You won't need your staff where you're going!" the guard grumbled.

"Would you let a warrior die without his weapons?" Jeremy challenged boldly.

There was a pause between the guards as all looked at each other guiltily. Finally, the largest one nodded. The guard returned to the room and brought out Jeremy's staff.

"How do you plan to hold it?"

"In my hands, of course!"

The fire in the center of the ring was blazing high. Four posts stood around the fire. Aiya had already explained the ceremony. They would tie them off to the posts, then light the wood under it. They would burn from their feet up and from back to front. From there, it would be up to the plan if they survived.

As predicted, the guards brought the prisoners over to the posts. Fuzz played a diversion, trying to get away as they tied them to the posts. As planned, Jeremy's fist held his staff. The shaman came over, grinning at Jeremy's staff.

"I'll take this, sorcerer. You'll not be needing it," she gleamed hungrily.

"Take it and die," Jeremy challenged angrily.

"I can take it now, or I can take it later. Either way will work," she smirked greedily.

"You know as well as I that if a staff is taken, not given, the taker is cursed and tormented the rest of their brief life," Jeremy bluffed. He hoped she'd believe him. He was counting on the superstitious nature of the time period.

The shaman hesitated and let go of the staff. "I also know that when the staff owner is dead, the staff becomes fair game. So be it. I'll await your death!" Jeremy watched the witch waddle away from the fire with a smirk. Bingo!

As the guards stood back, Jeremy cried in a loud voice. "Thaurlonian! I beseech you to come to our aid! Avenge us, great god! Take our souls unto you!" He hoped his acting would strike fear in the tribe. A guard put a gag around his mouth.

Another group of warriors came around with torches and lit the wood at their feet. Jeremy waited just a few moments, pretending to struggle with the ropes. It was getting very hot, very fast. The bottom of his pants had already begun to burn. "Visus Subsisto," he whispered. Time came to an abrupt halt. Even the flames froze in their all-consuming dance. Jeremy struggled hurriedly to get the globe of the staff to touch the ropes. Finally, he could brush it aside. "Divello," he whispered through the gag. The ropes at his wrists untied. Quickly, he bent over and untied his ankles. He ran over and untied Jordon, but leaned him up against the post. He ran over and untied Fuzz, then carried him over to Jordon.

The spell was just about to wear off. Jeremy waited until he could see the flames dance, then grabbed hold of Jordon and Fuzz. "Visus Subsisto!" he whispered again. The time stopped again, but Fuzz and Jordon were with him this time.

"Quick!" Jeremy cried. "Get Aiya!" He ran past Jordon, grasped the old shaman woman and dragged her to a stake. "Man, she needs to lose a few pounds!"

"What are you doing?" Jordon exclaimed, running past him towards Aiya.

"Getting even," Jeremy growled as he tied her to the stake. "If it weren't for her, we wouldn't be in this mess. Let's go! We still need to get Fang and our stuff out of the prison."

"But... but..." Fuzz was still looking back and forth between the frozen tribesmen and his friends.

Jeremy grabbed his shoulder. "Now!" he dragged him along. They only had a few seconds left. Jeremy grabbed

Fuzz and Jordon again. "Visus Subsisto!" Jeremy timed so that the spell would run out and begin again at the same time.

A gentle breeze blew over them. Jordon and Jeremy looked at each other strangely.

"Run, my young friends," came a familiar voice. "I will hold the spell until you are well on your way!"

The boys smiled at each other. "Thanks, Thaurlonian!" they called together.

"Lots of questions, but it'll have to wait!" Jordon yelled.

"Beware of other enemies!" came the voice on the wind.

Quickly, they got the door to the prison opened. Jeremy ran in and grabbed Fang. The three ran as quickly as they could while carrying Aiya and Fang. Fang had grown some while getting angry at being locked in the prison.

"Man, he got heavy!" Jeremy grumbled.

"Wait till he's full grown!" Jordon yelled over his shoulder.

They came to the main path through the woods, but it split into three paths. The trio looked in all directions.

"Which way?" Jordon asked. "Fuzz, do you have this mapped?"

"Partly," he said. "Give me a moment."

"We don't have a moment," Jeremy hurried him.

"If we are where I think we are, we should go left," Fuzz replied.

"Right," Jordon remarked and headed forward.

"Where are you going?" Jeremy hurried after him.

"Every decision Fuzz has made has gotten us into trouble! I'm going any way other than what he decides!"

"Then why'd you ask him!"

Jordon smirked. "'Cause I knew he'd lead us out of here—indirectly!"

Jeremy shrugged at Fuzz. Fuzz smiled sheepishly. "I do have a tendency."

Aiya began struggling on Jordon's shoulder. He let her down gently. "Looks like the spell wore off."

Jeremy giggled as Fang tried licking his face. "I think so. That means we'd better move. It won't take long for those guys to track us down."

A loud scream echoed in the woods, followed by yells and hollers. Jeremy smiled as they hurried along.

"I take it the plan worked?" Aiya asked.

"Yes, but Jeremy tied your shaman to a stake. That's what the shouting was about."

"He what?" Aiya cried in wide-eyed worry.

"By the way, Jere, what knot did you use?"

"A bowline," Jeremy giggled. "I figure it'll take them a few minutes to figure out how to untie it, but it won't harm the old witch too much."

"Aiya, we need to get to a pad to get out of here," Jordon puffed.

"Where are we?" she stopped.

Fuzz pulled out his papers. He showed her what he already had.

"The camp is here," Aiya pointed to the northern side of the cavern. "Here's where the waterfall is. There is a pad here in the middle of the caverns that is covered with bushes."

"That is not a good choice," Fuzz mentioned. "I ended up at the snake hole using that one."

"Then we definitely don't want to go there," Jeremy agreed. He could hear shouting echoing behind them.

"There should also be another one down on this edge," she pointed towards the south-eastern end. "I found you on this side, so we know there's one there."

"What's the fastest way to the second one?" Jordon asked.

"Without being tracked?" Aiya asked. Jordon nodded. "Fly?"

"Not one of our abilities," he sagged.

"Wait," Jeremy's eyes opened. "Maybe it is. We need a blanket, quick."

Jordon pulled a blanket out of Jeremy's pack. They laid it on the ground and folded in the sides so that the four could sit on it in two rows.

"Congelo Somes," Jeremy said, touching the staff to the blanket. The blanket froze solid. "It'll be a little cold, but it should work. Everybody on." He arranged everyone on the blanket. Fang curled up into his lap and dozed. "Ortus," Jeremy said and touched the staff to the blanket again. The blanket rose shakily at first, then leveled out. It kept rising until Jeremy removed the globe from its surface.

"Great, we're up. But how do we move?" Jordon asked. He peered over the edge at the ground far below him.

"Lean forward! It'll be like bobsledding," Jeremy suggested. "We have to move together, at the same time."

As the four leaned forwards, the blanket began moving towards the wall. They leaned left and began hovering over the trees and bushes of the cavern. Going forwards again, they got moving in the right direction at a decent speed. They bumped a few times before they got into sync with their leaning to go around things. Twice, Jeremy had to refreeze the blanket. The rushing air in their faces made it hard to see. Aiya often had to call out an obstacle. Finally, they put down in a clearing.

"That was fun!" Jordon grinned. "Not as much fun as riding a dragon, but fun!"

"Yea," Jeremy agreed. "We'd make a pretty good bobsled team."

"What is a bobsled?" Fuzz asked.

"It's a wooden board on.... thin rails.... that you ride down snow," Jeremy tried to explain as he put the blanket away.

"Snow?" Aiya and Fuzz asked together.

"Frozen rain?" Jordon tried. Again, the two stared back blankly.

Jeremy sighed. "It's soft white water that comes down out of the sky when the weather gets cold. It builds up on the ground like dirt, only it sticks together like heavy mud. You can slide on it."

Still confused, but having a better understanding, the two nodded slowly.

"Where to now?" Jordon looked around.

Fang began growling. He was looking into the woods. Slowly, he started growing in size. Jeremy pat his side. "Whatcha see, buddy?" he asked, looking towards the woods.

Jordon looked over on the other side. "I don't see anything."

"A small creature, perhaps?" Aiya also peered into the dark.

"I don't know," Jeremy continued to look.

Out of the darkness of the woods, a huge, red flower spread its petals in a silent scream. The inside looked like a five-mouthed monster with petals for hair. A dozen thick thorns flew at them.

"Conte.... Ow!" Jeremy hollered as one thorn stuck in his arm.

Fang snarled loudly, shaking his head. Jordon had ducked, but Fuzz, who was standing behind him, got hit in the shoulder. Aiya caught one in the chest, but her hide tunic prevented it from going further.

"Run!" she yelled. "This way!"

Quickly, the guys followed her. Jordon and Jeremy had to drag Fang away from the fight. They moved as fast as they could onto another pathway. As they cleared the attack site, they sat down. Aiya began looking through the leaves of the plants around the forest floor. She foraged with amazing speed. Jeremy sat on the edge of the path. He held his head in his hands as his elbows rested on his knees. Fuzz dropped next to him. Fang whined, then tipped over on his side.

"What's up?" Jordon kneeled next to his friend.

"I feel funny," Jeremy slurred. He could barely see Jordon. His head felt heavy and hot and pounded with a headache. A cold, clammy sweat covered his face. His skin was cold and getting colder. Jeremy lay down with a moan.

AIYA

"Jeremy! Aiya, what's happening?" Jordon asked, panic rising in his throat. Fuzz was in the same condition. Fang's fur was soaking wet when Jordon pet it.

"It's the poison," Aiya said in a panic. "Quick! Help me find the Hintona leaves."

"What do they look like?" Jordon asked, suddenly alarmed.

"They're long, thin leaves on a small plant with purple flowers. They have white and yellow stripes on the underside. Do not pick the ones with the red and yellow stripes. You'll get a rash."

"Where do I look?"

"Under the trees. They grow in the soft ground under the large trees. We need a leaf for each of them. Hurry! We don't have much time!"

Jordon ran to the other side of the path and began foraging. He looked all over, but all he could find were the red and yellow striped leaves. Suddenly, he heard Aiya call.

"Got one!" she yelled. He met her back at Jeremy and Fuzz at a run. Fuzz had already passed out, and Jeremy was delirious. She quickly stuck a leaf in Jeremy's mouth. "Chew it!"

"Eww!"

"Chew it!" Aiya ordered. "But don't swallow it!." Quickly, she smashed one leaf with a rock and pushed the crushed leaf into Fuzz's mouth. She did the same for Fang. "Keep his mouth closed," she pointed at Fuzz as she held Fang's muzzle closed. "The anti-venom needs to be absorbed by the tongue. It may take a while."

While they waited, Jordon and Aiya removed the thorns from their friends, then sat down to wait. It must have been close to an hour before anyone started moving.

"Wow! I feel like I've been hit by a truck!" Jeremy struggled to sit up. His hand went to his head.

"By a what?" Aiya looked confused.

"Never mind," Jordon smirked. "It's a long story. Just know he aches in places he didn't know could hurt." Aiya nodded.

Fuzz soon regained consciousness. He, too, complained about aching muscles. Fang whined mournfully. Jordon picked him up and cuddled him to comfort the young pup.

"You'll be alright, buddy!" he whispered.

JEREMY

"What was that thing?" Jeremy asked, holding his head.

"A Forget-me-not," Aiya replied.

"No. Forget-me-nots are tiny blue flowers that grow in clusters with a bright yellow middle. My mother has them planted in our garden." Jeremy shook his head.

"Perhaps where you are from. Here, that was a forget-me-not. They poison their victims. After they've eaten the body, an image of it appears on one of the petals. Eventually, that image gets replaced by another victim, but not for many years."

"Oooh!" Jeremy and Jordon shuddered.

"That makes you a hero," Jordon smiled at her with pride.

"No, I just remembered my lessons," Aiya replied humbly. "I'm really glad we were able to find the leaves in time. Much longer and they'd all be dead."

"Perhaps we should move on?" Fuzz suggested as he got to his feet weakly.

Jeremy pulled off his pack. He reached in and pulled out some food. "Perhaps we should eat something. It's already nighttime. We might want to just make camp here."

"Not a good idea," Aiya replied. "This area of the forest is extremely dangerous. There are other plants that may overtake us, or snakes, or cavern cleaners, or spiders, or..."

"We get the picture," Jeremy said darkly. He bit into a jerky strip and handed one to Fang.

"How far is it to the pad?" Jordon asked.

"We came a far distance. It shouldn't be too much farther. Of course, in the dark it will be much more difficult," Aiya explained.

"Not a problem." Jeremy pat his staff. "We'll have all the light we need." His head was finally beginning to clear.

"And give away our position at the same time," Jordon snickered. "Oh, well. Can't have it all."

They ate in silence, then prepared to move on. Each of them started at the hoots and screeches of the night sounds in the woods. Then everything went silent.

A small fireball came out of nowhere and hit the tree they were under. Glowing embers scattered around them. The tree caught fire. Jordon ducked and pulled Sharijol free of its sheath. Fang began to growl and grow again. Both peered into the darkness.

"Congelo somes," Jeremy pointed at the tree. Thick ice covered the tree leaves. It slowly melted into water, putting out the fire. "Solar lux lucis"

A bright light shone from the staff, lighting everything in a 10-foot radius.

"That's not helping!" Jordon cried, closing his eyes. "Can't see anything!"

"Od," Jeremy said. The chamber fell into darkness again. The entire group strained to see anything moving. Fang settled and returned to normal size. Another ball came towards them. Jordon swung, slicing it in two. The spell went out.

A thud echoed in the distance, followed by a cry of pain. Nothing more came. All was eerily silent. "Back away—slowly," Jeremy suggested. "Let's get some distance." He tapped his leg to call Fang. The young Ortiks bounded happily towards him.

"What happened?" Aiya whispered.

"Don't know. We'd best keep moving," Jordon murmured lowly.

Keeping their ears peeled, the group continued forward towards the teleport pad. While no other attacks came and the woodland sounds returned, Jordon still couldn't shake the feeling of being followed. It was only a short time later when Jordon broke the tense silence.

"I'm sorry," Jordon said solemnly to Aiya.

"For?"

"For getting you in trouble with your tribe."

Aiya shook her head. "I've been in trouble with my tribe since I could walk. I don't think like a Drelt. I don't act like a Drelt." She hung her head. "I can't even hunt like a Drelt."

"But not all Drelt think and feel the same way," came a deep baritone voice.

The group whirled about towards the voice. Sharijol came out with a swish while the globe of Jeremy's staff glittered with magic, awaiting a command. A tall, thin, broad shadow stood near a tree along the path. A glint of metal shone at his hip. Fang toddled over unassumingly to check out the stranger.

"Lux Lucis," Jeremy whispered. A glow shone from the globe of his staff, lighting the figure near the tree. Even in the light, it was difficult to make out his features.

"Kenyer?" Aiya asked softly.

"Aye," he acknowledged, then stepped into the light.

"How'd you find me?" she asked in fear.

"It wasn't too hard -- for anyone who knows you. I figured the first thing the foreigners would want would be to get away, so it was only a matter of checking the funny stones. When you didn't arrive at the one near the holt, I figured it would be this one."

"How did you figure this one and not the other one?" Jeremy asked suspiciously.

"Because you came into the village from that direction, meaning you were going the other way to start with." Kenyer reached down to pat the ortiks. "Impressive. You've tamed him well."

"He tamed himself," Jeremy replied. "What are you going to do now?"

"I came to bring Aiya these." He held up a bow, a quiver of arrows, and a pack.

"Is that all?" It surprised Jeremy how protective of Aiya he felt.

Kenyer looked at the ground. "The chief has declared that anyone who sides with you is to be put to death. Most of the village is cowering in fear. Natrina sustained some severe burns. Nice trick, by the way. I never did like that old bat!" Jeremy and Jordon snickered. "There are a handful of us out looking for you. We figured we'd need to start a new village."

Aiya shook her head. "That will only incite a war."

"No one said the village need be here," Kenyer said. He looked at the boys. "I take it you wish to return to your homes?"

"Yes," Jordon replied.

"May we accompany you? Perhaps we can find a place to begin a new village along the way."

Jeremy looked at Jordon. He shrugged. "I'm sure Thrundra could find a place for them to build a village; maybe by the seers. Or we might convince Narim to integrate them with Eliramond's people. There's enough forest there."

Jordon nodded. "Sure," he said to Kenyer. "But we'll have to wait for the rest of your group."

Kenyer smiled. "Won't be long." He turned towards the forest and stood still.

"What's he doing?" Jordon whispered to Aiya.

"He's calling to the others. Only problem is that it will give away our position to the rest of the village."

"They aren't far away," Kenyer said. "They'll be here long before the villagers can get into action. Remember?

They're afraid. Your disappearing act has them convinced that god you called on actually helped you."

Jeremy and Jordon exchanged a knowing glance with a sly smile, but then looked away feigning ignorance. Three other people arriving cut their quiet exchange short.

"This is Jadara," Kenyer introduced, pointing to a tall, thin, young woman. She was more slender than Aiya, with a petite face. Her green eyes stood out against her dark skin. Her hair blended into the night. "This is Soma," he pointed to a burlier Drelt. The man had short, dark hair and dark eyes. Other than the shine of the light on his skin, you'd never know he was there. His broad shoulders led down to a broad chest that was more like a muscled barrel. The six-pack of his abdomen disappeared into his breeches. A sword was sheathed at his waist. "And this is Du'kai," Kenyer introduced a young man who might have just come out of his teens. The youth was a little smaller than the others and much thinner. His bright blue eyes gave away his position in the group. His arms showed strength, but he clearly hadn't broadened yet. "He's the baby of the group."

The seeming youth growled at Kenyer angrily. Kenyer patted the boy's shoulder. "Relax, will ya? If I thought of you as a baby, you'd still be home with mother."

"Du'kai is an excellent tracker," Aiya added in defense of her friend. "Thank you all for defending me."

Jadara shrugged. "What are friends for?"

"Right," Jordon said. "Well, these friends had better get a move on before the rest of the village gets here. Lead on, Aiya."

Fang yawned as he trudged after Jeremy with a whine. Jeremy smiled and picked up the tired pup.

The small group began down the trail again. They hadn't gone far before an arrow flew past, then another.

"We've been found!" Soma growled. "Move it!"

Jeremy pushed everyone up front and handed Fang to Fuzz. "Keep him with you, don't leave the group, and keep running!"

"What about you?" the Kaptrix asked. He grasped the pup.

"Go!" Jeremy ordered.

"I'm here," Jordon remarked.

"Contego!" Jeremy cried as he ran. "Let's keep them coming towards us as long as possible. Watch the others, but keep back a few feet. The enemy will think they're gaining on us."

They ran almost a mile before they heard the cry. "It's here!" Aiya's voice echoed. "Hurry!" A volley of arrows flew towards them, but bounced off the invisible shield. Unfortunately, Jeremy had to continually recast the spell.

"Wish Keesha were here," Jordon murmured, looking back into the darkness.

"Wish harder. The spell just ended again." Jeremy cried, pouring on speed. "And I'm out of energy."

"Ah!" Jordon cried as an arrow stuck in his left shoulder.

Out of nowhere, Kenyer appeared. He grasped Jordon around the waist and hoisted him over his shoulder. "Go! Go! Go!" he cried at Jeremy as another volley of arrows hit the ground around them.

MIKKEL

The wizard limped to his chair. An arrow with green feathers stuck out from the rear of his thigh. Another arrow was firmly embedded in his shoulder. His breathing was getting more difficult. Blood sopped his clothing.

Mikkel reached over with a rag and pulled the arrow from his shoulder first. He added pressure to the wound until the bleeding stopped. He repeated the procedure with the one in the back of the man's leg.

"You're going to need to take time to heal," he groused at the wizard. "I take it you missed."

"The youth are very good at batting-ball, and the Drelt are excellent hunters in the dark," came the anguished reply.

Mikkel nodded. "We'll try again. Right now, get into a healing trance. You'll need your strength for tomorrow."

The sorcerer nodded. "I have a plan."

11 – BATTLE IN THE OASIS

TYLER

The change of scenery startled Tyler as they alighted off the transporter pad. The lush greens and browns of the Kaptrix changed drastically to faded pastels floating about a field of bubbles. Beautiful crystal globes surrounded them on all sides. Each crystal ball sat on a stalk. Some of them low like flowers. Others were high, like tall shrubs. A thin path led forward, barely wide enough for one of them. The glittery orbs changed colors as if someone were taking several covered flashlights and moved them around. Crystal leaves were hanging around the globes. Some crystals were shaped like diamonds. While it was beautiful, one thing made it an eerie situation. There was no sound at all.

"This is strange," Odessa's awed voice echoed, "but so beautiful."

He watched Annese look down into one globe. A soft hum seemed to come from it as it began to dance around on its stalk. "Interesting."

Tyler looked at her. "Don't touch anything!" he ordered softly.

"Why?" Annese asked.

"Everything except people are dangerous," he quoted Riemer.

"Look!" Odessa pointed ahead of them.

Tyler looked in the direction she pointed. Through the forest of crystals was something green. He could barely see it.

Tentatively, the trio made their way to the clearing along the narrow path of globes and crystal leaves. Their feet tapped on the hard ground and echoed off the rock face around them. A strange hum filled the air as they passed the globes. The path finally opened into a wide, green clearing. A tumbling brook ran through the middle, then dipped out of sight. Tiny, colorful flowers dotted the grassy knoll while tall trees were scattered about, nearly touching the ceiling of the cavern. Interesting yellow and orange fruit hung from their branches.

"Mmm!" Odessa smiled. "Amatos!"

"Ah what?" Annese asked curiously.

"Amatos," Odessa repeated. "They're really good and sweet!"

She galloped over to one tree, but as she reached for one, a little blue animal flew past her. Turning quickly, Odessa tried to spot it. She looked around curiously. It was nowhere to be seen.

"Where'd it go?" Odessa asked.

"Where'd what go?" Tyler asked, turning from examining the brook.

"That creature."

"What creature?" Annese put the longairits on the ground to explore.

"The blue one that flew past me."

"I didn't see anything," Tyler replied, looking around. "But I was looking at the brook. The water is clear and crisp, not salty. I wonder why?"

"I was watching the longairits, Odessa," Annese explained. "I'm sorry. I didn't see it either."

Another blue creature flew past Odessa as she reached for the fruit. "There!" Annese cried and pointed up into the tree.

Tyler looked up at the tree. On the lower branch stood a small, blue-furred animal. It had tiny cat-like ears, small front arms, and stronger back legs. A fluffy tail twitched behind it. From its back were shimmering blue and silver wings, almost as big as the creature itself.

"It looks like a winged squirrel," Tyler pointed out. "Only its blue instead of being gray or red or black."

"A squirrel?" Odessa asked.

"They're small creatures in our world, kinda like that one, but without wings. They like nuts and seeds."

The creature clucked and chattered at them angrily. It waved its arm towards the tree, amusing Tyler with its antics. When the kids just looked at it, the creature jumped up and down in a tirade.

"I think he's trying to tell us something," Annese scowled at the squirrel in confusion.

"I think he's saying leave him alone," Tyler observed.

"I don't know what he's saying, but he sure is angry," Odessa remarked.

"Something about the tree," Annese said.

"Let's get going. We need to figure out if anyone's here," Tyler mumbled. "Do we want to refill the water bottles?"

"Wicken gave us a bunch of water," Annese remarked absently as she gathered the longairits together again.

"I meant ours," Tyler grumbled. "Who knows when we're going to get fresh water again."

"I want some of these," Odessa smiled as she reached up and picked a fruit off the tree.

Suddenly, the branches came down and surrounded her, crushing Odessa up against the tree bark. The squirrel-like creature flew away quickly.

"Help!" Odessa cried.

"Now she wants help!" a gravely voice growled.

"Don't give it to her!" another responded.

"Hey!" Tyler cried, pulling the axe from his belt. "Let her go!"

He ran up to the tree with the axe ready. Another branch flew down and knocked him over. Annese had to duck to avoid being toppled into the brook.

"Stop! You're hurting me!" Odessa tried to push the branches off.

"Stop! You're hurting me!" a voice mimicked.

"Hey!" Odessa shouted.

"Hey!" the voice mimicked back!

Tyler stood up again with the axe. "Let her go or you'll get it!"

"Shows what you know!" the gravelly voice came again. "She violated me, and she will pay!"

"She what?" Annese asked.

"You heard," another voice, more feminine, came out angrily. "You don't just reach up and pick someone's fruit!"

"It's the trees," Annese whispered to Tyler.

"Duh!" Tyler responded, rolling his eyes, then shouted. "Ten seconds!"

The little blue creature came flying back. It flitted about the little opening in the branches around Odessa's head. It chirped questioningly in a peep, peep fashion into the branches as it dodged from opening to opening. Getting no response, it gave a mournful whistle.

"What's he doing?" Annese asked.

"I don't know," Tyler whispered back, watching. "Five seconds!" His voice bounced back off the trees.

"Peep, peep, peep," the little squirrel tried again.

Annese giggled. "I think we should call him Peeps."

"I'm more worried about Odessa!" Tyler growled the last word as he lunged forward. The axe whacked firmly on the branches in front of him, splintering the wood.

"OW!" the tree cried out. The branch swung backwards, trying to knock Tyler away, but Tyler ducked and swung again. "Ow!"

"I'll keep chopping until you let Odessa go!" he threatened.

"Tyler! Watch out!" Annese cried out.

Three other trees were now walking over towards Tyler and Odessa. Annese, with the longairits safely in their basket, ran for the outskirts of the field. Tyler twirled, axe in hand at the on-comers. Branches were twirling around.

"We need fire!" Odessa's muffled cry came to the others.

Annese quickly reached into her pack for a candle while Tyler kept the other trees at bay. As fast as she could, she lit the candle. She pulled some papers from her pack and rolled them up. Quickly she wet the bottom, then lit the top on fire. She ran the paper back to Tyler. He snatched the roll and held it at the bottom of a tree.

"Back off," he threatened, "Or I'll light this place like a torch!" Slowly the trees backed away. "Let her go!" Tyler demanded to the tree that held Odessa. The branches moved away to free Odessa from the scratchy grasp. She darted out of the hold and over to Annese at the edge of the field. Tyler knew he needed to act fast. The fire was already going out.

Tyler dropped the paper and stamped out the embers. He glared at the trees angrily. "All this over a piece of fruit! It appears you all need to learn a few lessons about sharing!"

Dodging over to Annese and Odessa, he stooped down and grabbed a few pieces of fruit that dropped and pushed them into his pockets. The trees followed.

"Run!" he cried, one of the small Peeps flying over his head.

Tyler followed the girls as they ran back down the path they came up. The trees couldn't keep up, but they had no trouble throwing. The yellow-orange fruit began flying at them.

He watched a piece of fruit fly over him and hit a globe. The explosion was deafening! In a chain reaction, globe after globe after globe exploded, sending crystalline shards flying all over. The Peep squeaked and flew up towards the ceiling. The trio dove for the ground, covering their heads.

"Don't look up!" Tyler yelled to the girls.

The explosions were loud, echoing off the cavern walls. They spread as more crystalline globes exploded. It was quite a while before all was quiet again.

Slowly, Tyler lifted his head. His ears ached from the noise. He glanced around at broken globes and bent stalks in all directions. Glass shards were all over the place, including his arms and legs. All the chaos seemed to have settled. "Is everyone ok?" he asked. He got up and brushed the shards from his jeans.

"A few pieces of shards, but nothing serious," Annese replied, getting up. "Dess?"

"The same," she replied shakily. The horse part of her shook off the loose shards. "How's the longairits?"

Annese looked down into the basket she'd been shielding. "Good. A little shaken, but fine."

"I'm sorry." Odessa hung her head. "I didn't think it would be such a big deal."

"It wasn't your fault," Tyler reassured softly, while looking around. "They just don't know how to share. Oh! Here." He reached into his pockets and pulled out half a dozen Amatos.

"What?" Odessa's surprised eyes looked at the oval fruit.

"I figured we put up a good fight and deserved a just dessert," he laughed. "Besides, they were throwing them at us. I just picked them up as I passed."

"What's that word you use? Awesome!" Odessa exclaimed, biting into the crispy fruit with a crunch.

Tyler passed one to Annese as well. Both bit into the fruit, then closed their eyes as the sweet flavor burst inside their mouths. These things were delicious! Annese began biting off small pieces and giving them to the longairits.

"Let's keep going," Tyler suggested. He looked behind him to find the tall trees had returned to the places they were when the kids arrived.

The trio continued back to the pad. The little blue creature came flying by them again. It chirped angrily at them, waving its hands and pointing to the globes and the trees. It continued to chirp and squeak as they trudged on. It finally flew off just before they reached the pad.

"Didn't seem too happy with us," Odessa said quietly. "Those poor globes."

"It's ok," Tyler replied.

"How can you say that?" Annese asked surprised. "All those beautiful globes have shattered!"

"They'll grow back," Tyler shrugged.

"What?"

"You girls have got to get more observant," he sighed. "Look!"

Tyler pointed to a globe near the pad. The stalk was smaller than the others with a bud tip on it. The tip was just beginning to open, showing a small crystalline globe inside.

"I'm not certain, but I'm willing to bet the globes carry a sensitive gas inside. As the gas builds up, the globes get bigger. Once something touches it, the globe explodes, letting off the gas, and possibly seeds. But because of how close together they're growing, it sets off a chain reaction. I'm not a hundred percent sure of that, but that's my theory," he explained.

The girls looked at each other and shrugged.

"Sounds good to me," Annese agreed.

"Me, too. Let's keep going," Odessa said. She stepped out onto the pad. Tyler and Annese followed right behind.

The area in front of them was a stone corridor. The walls were smooth as glass. Tiny sparkles twinkled from the marbled texture, kind of like a mixture of mold and dirt. There was no path leading away from the transport pad like there were on the other islands. This just seemed like a huge, dank, rocky tunnel. An odd fog filled the air. Odessa began coughing from the musty air.

12 – BETRAYAL

JEREMY

The small party stopped short as they came out of the transport pad. Huge, disintegrating, stone buildings were all over. Walls were crumbling even as they passed. Ceilings and roofs were non-existent. Piles of rubble lay strewn across old paths. Vines and plants had climbed over many of the paths and buildings. Small creatures scattered as they came into the area. Trees sprouted where living areas had once been.

"What *is* this place?" Jeremy asked in utter amazement.

"Don't know," Kenyer replied, placing Jordon on the ground. "We've got a bigger problem. Hold still." Carefully, he worked the arrow out of Jordon's shoulder. Jordon hollered as Kenyer pulled it out. "Hold on. It's out. Let's get the blood stopped." He tore a small piece off his tunic and pushed it into the wound.

"You ok?" Jeremy kneeled in front of Jordon.

"Will be.... eventually." Jordon grimaced through clenched teeth.

"Try not to use that arm much," Kenyer suggested. "It'll be sore for a few days. The bone stopped the arrow from going through."

"Too bad we don't have stitches," Jeremy remarked. He inspected the hole in Jordon's shoulder.

"What are stitches?" Soma scowled. The entire party had encircled Jordon in concern.

"They're thin pieces of string used to sew the hole shut. They help the skin heal and keep out germs."

"Germs?" Aiya raised her brows questionably.

"Things that make you sick," Jordon grit out as Jeremy paused to figure out how to explain something you can't see.

"Ah," the Drelts nodded with understanding.

"Here," Jeremy moved behind his friend. He placed the globe of his staff against the wound. "Let me try. Rememdium Pupillus Vulnus." A soft warmth spread through Jordon's shoulder. The skin closed before their eyes. "How's that?"

"Better. Still sore, though."

"It's only a cure minor injuries," Jeremy explained regretfully. "Underneath is still all torn up, but the bleeding has stopped, and the skin is closed."

Jadara pulled a small towel from her pack and handed it to Kenyer. "For padding."

"You look better. Let your pack shift over some to keep the cloth on it for a bit more for padding." Kenyer suggested as he tucked the cloth under the strap of Jordon's pack and helped him up.

"Will your villagers follow?" Jeremy asked Kenyer as he gazed at the portal.

"Not likely," Du'kai replied, following his gaze. "They think that if you land on one of those stones, you disappear for good. But they never expected something like this." He turned around in awe as he looked at the cavern. "What is it?"

"It looks like a village of some kind," Aiya said, stooping to look at a plant. "This is a flora septra."

"An old one. Careful," Soma warned. "We don't know what vegetation is poisonous."

"Yea," Jordon said slowly. "Thanks, Kenyer, Jay."

Jeremy stepped out into the pathway to check out the ruins and stopped short. The vines across the path in front of him moved out of the way. "This is weird."

High-pitched squeals rent the quiet from overhead, causing the party to look up quickly. Despite keen eyes, no one could spot where it came from.

"Was that an animal?" Jordon asked, examining the canopy overhead.

"Your guess is as good as ours," Jadara replied. "We've never seen anything like this."

"Hey, guys!" Jordon turned towards Jeremy's cry a few feet away. "Look! Stairs!"

The crumbling remains of a stone tower circled up towards the ceiling of the cavern. A set of rough-hewn stairs circled the outer wall upwards and disappeared into the canopy of the trees. The vine-covered outer wall was crumbling around them. A trickle of water flowed down some of the top stairs, forming a tiny stream over the edge and landing into a small pool underneath.

"Where does it go?" Du'kai asked. He was looking around the small pool. "It has to go somewhere."

"But it's not full yet." Jordon pointed towards the 1-inch gap between the ground and the top of the water.

"Possible it has been dripping so long it has broken down into an underground stream," Kenyer suggested.

"No offense, guys, but we *are* underground," Jeremy pointed out.

Jordon tasted the water. He made a disgusted face and spat out the spit in his mouth. "Salt water."

"Salt?" Jeremy asked confused. Jordon nodded. Jeremy began climbing the stairs.

"Jay, where ya goin'?" Jordon asked concerned.

"To look at the top and see where this goes."

"Not alone, my friend," Kenyer ran to catch up to him.

"Be careful!" Aiya called up. "It's a long way down!"

"Worse," Jeremy called back. "The higher we go, the more slick the stairs become. They're loaded with mold!"

"Mold?" Jordon asked thinking. Mold?

"What is mold?" Jadara asked.

"It's a type of plant growth that depends on dark, moist places. Kind of like mushrooms, only you can't eat it," Jordon explained. "But if the stairs are full of mold, that trickle's been going a long time."

"Do you mind if I take some time to update my maps?" Fuzz asked Jordon.

"No, go ahead," he replied, still looking up the stairs. He turned towards the Kaptrix quickly and added, "But don't wander around!" Fuzz chuckled and settled on a mossy spot to draw out the recent additions to his maps. Fuzz curled up next to him, spotting an opportunity for a nap.

The higher they went, the more slippery the stairs became. Jeremy tried to hang onto the rocks of the wall to steady himself as he climbed. It was slow going near the upper section of stairs. A thin layer of water seemed to cover most of the stairs, but the water trickled down into a drip to the pool below.

"Whoa!" Jeremy cried as he slipped on a patch of slick moss. Kenyer's muscular arm reached out to grasp him. Regaining his balance, he moved further up the stairs. "Thanks."

Kenyer nodded and followed Jeremy further up the stairs. The upper parts of the walls were all but gone. Huge vines with large green leaves and pretty, small white flowers grew as if holding the building together. They weren't more than twelve feet up when they lost sight of those on the ground. At last, they came up onto a platform. A few old stone benches were still intact. At the far end stood a deteriorated stone statue. The head was missing, the hands long gone. Still, it looked familiar to Jeremy.

"All this for a statue?" Kenyer asked.

"I've seen this statue before. I'm sure of it," Jeremy murmured with conviction. "Where? Where?" He thought and thought. He could picture it in his mind. A small wooden alcove, surrounded by stone. In his mind, the details were clearer. Rough beard, long robes, a staff in its hand. Elderly hands laid mint leaves at the base of the statue. Suddenly, his eyes snapped open wide. He remembered. "Garadain!"

"Who?" Kenyer asked.

"Garadain. He's the god of the wizards who live on the surface. I remember now! His statue is in the garden in the center square. It's the exact same statue as this one used to be."

"Ah. So, this was a wizard's tower?"

"Probably." Jeremy looked up. He was getting sprayed on. Overhead, he could see a rupture in the cavern ceiling. Water was trickling through it. Jeremy put his hand out to capture some of it. He tasted it hesitantly. Salt. "We need to get moving," he told Kenyer.

"It's just a water spout," Kenyer mentioned undisturbed.

"Yes. But above that waterspout is thousands and thousands of gallons of water. If this breaks further, this cavern is going to flood."

"I don't know what a gallon is, but that sounds very undesirable."

"Do you have gills to breathe under water?"

"No."

"Neither do I. I don't feel like drowning."

"Let's go," Kenyer agreed. He returned to the stairs to prepare for their descent.

They picked their way down carefully. The mold and moss were thicker and slicker up top. With a cry, Jeremy slipped.

"Ahhhh!" he screamed, toppling off the stairs towards the cavern floor. He braced for a hard landing. Instead, he stopped. Looking around, he wasn't sure what was going on. A tight grip wrapped around his ankles suspended him in mid-air. He looked back up towards the ceiling, expecting to find Kenyer. He found a thick vine wrapped around his ankles, holding him up instead. Slowly, he began moving towards the floor. With great gentleness, the vine deposited him on the floor, unwrapped itself from his ankles, and disappeared into the leaves above.

JORDON

Jordon's eyes bulged and his mouth opened wide as he watched Jeremy fall. They remained open in surprise as a vine from the upper walls whipped out into the open and wrapped itself around Jeremy's ankles. It held him suspended for a moment or two before slowly lowering him to the floor. Once Jeremy was safely on the ground, the vine retreated into the canopy.

"Wow!" Jadara exclaimed, watching his descent.

"Jeremy!" Kenyer cried down.

"I'm ok," Jeremy called back up. "Be careful!"

"What was that?" Jordon asked as he helped his friend to his feet.

"Don't know."

"What'd you find?" Jordon wondered.

"I found a statue of Garadain."

"Who?"

"Garadain. He's the god the wizards worship. There's a copy of the statue in the center square at The Keep; but there's something more serious. There's a fissure in the cavern ceiling that's leaking ocean water. That's where the stream is coming from. A few small stones broke free while we were up there. We need to get out of here. I don't know how long before the fissure becomes a large opening. If that happens..."

"We drown," Jordon said factually. "I got it."

"We need to go," Kenyer urged. He jumped down the last few steps.

"Let's move this way," Jordon suggested, pointing away from the pad along the wall. "There's got to be a pad somewhere else along the walls."

"That could take ages to find," Du'kai remarked.

"Fuzz, what've we got here?" Jordon asked the map-maker.

"I'm afraid I don't recognize this cavern," Fuzz responded, putting away his pencils. Jordon nodded. They were on their own.

"Any patterns to the placements?" he asked.

Fuzz once again consulted his maps. "Well," he began, "there seems to be two patterns, although, I can't guarantee their accuracy."

"Continue."

"They'll either set them up in a split pattern," he drew a Y in the dirt, "or they'll have one in the middle and two on opposite sides."

"I suggest we move to the middle. We'll be able to cover more distance, and we might luck out to find a stone there," Du'kai suggested.

"I agree," Jadara nodded. "On Drelt, we've seen that the paths lead to the pads. It might be easier bushwhacking along the paths than along the walls."

"Agreed," Jeremy put in.

"Ok. Let's go!" Jordon conceded. They needed to get moving fast.

Carefully, the group picked their way through the crumbled stones and wild growth. Chirps and twitters echoed around them. The light was getting dimmer, so Jeremy lit his staff. Occasionally, a high-pitched scream would echo.

"That sounds like a chimp," Jordon said. He studied the canopy as if he could see the creature in between the leaves and the vines.

"But there's only one," Jeremy estimated. "It could be a parrot, too. Remember the macaw we saw at school? It was pretty screechy."

"Yea. Maybe."

"I don't think it's anything to worry about. Fang is pretty mellow."

"Fang is asleep!" Jordon smirked, looking over at the pup asleep on Jeremy's backpack. Jordon yawned. "I'm pretty beat as well."

"Maybe we should stop for the night," Du'kai suggested. He tried to stifle a yawn.

"Think it's safe?" Soma asked. He glanced around nervously at their surroundings. Jordon did the same.

"We can take turns keeping watch," Aiya suggested.

"I'll take the first one," Soma volunteered. "I got to sleep this afternoon."

Kenyer stretched again. "I hate to admit it, but sleep sounds good. Do you think that water drip will hold?"

"Probably," Jeremy said. "If I'm right, that's been dripping a very long time. Generations maybe. While it's getting weaker, it would take something drastic to make it split open right away."

"One earthquake coming up!" Jordon perked up.

"That's not even funny!" Jeremy pushed Jordon's shoulder and tried to hide the grin coming to his mouth.

"Sorry," Jordon began giggling. "I'm slaphappy."

"Here's a comfortable patch of ground," Du'kai pointed to the side. "Let's bed down."

"What's up?" Jordon asked his friend. Jeremy was looking around the area as if he'd sensed something.

"Nothin'." Jeremy stooped and put Fang on the ground. "Just making sure there's nothing in the area. I don't want to get trapped again." He began laying out his blankets. It wouldn't be a long sleep, but at least they'd be warmer. Fang quickly curled up under Jeremy's blankets to stay warm.

"Don't wander, buddy," Jeremy warned the sleepy pup. "We aren't in Kansas anymore."

"Or Utah, or Washington, or Texas, or New York, or North America, for that matter," Jordon giggled.

"Go to sleep!" Jeremy laughed at his friend. Jordon was getting delirious.

"Compliance," his friend replied mechanically. The two boys broke out laughing as they remembered the quote from an old science fiction movie they had watched recently.

JEREMY

Something made Jeremy shiver. He woke up slowly. All was quiet. Still, something didn't feel right. He reached next to his head for his staff. Sleepy eyes snapped open when Jeremy's hand touched ground. His staff wasn't there. He looked next to him on the other side. Nothing.

"Looking for this?" the deep, gravelly voice asked. Soma held Jeremy's staff up over his head.

"Give that back!" Jeremy ordered in a whisper so as not to waken the others.

"I don't think so. In fact, I think I'll use it on you!"

With surprising speed, Soma swung the staff towards Jeremy's head. Jeremy rolled to the side as the staff hit the ground.

"Stop! You'll break it!" Jeremy wasn't worried about keeping his voice down any more.

A low growl came from under the blankets as Soma swung the staff again.

"What's wrong with you?" Jeremy cried, rolling back.

"Me? You're the one who came to my world! You're the one who damaged my grandmother! You're the one who disrupted everything I knew! What's wrong with you?" Soma growled as he swung the staff towards Jeremy again and again.

The ruckus woke the rest of the party. Jeremy's cries brought Jordon to his feet instantly with his sword drawn. He saw Kenyer pull his dagger from his boot as he went to Jeremy's rescue. In the meantime, Jeremy was waiting for Soma's next swing and placed himself right in its path. His hands snapped out quickly as he grasped the staff, stopping the swing. Jordon ran up behind him.

"I suggest you stop this right now," Jeremy growled angrily. "You can't hope to win this battle."

"Oh, yes, I will. I will avenge my grandmother!" Soma cried angrily.

"You don't even *like* your grandmother!" Du'kai stated loudly. "Why the sudden need to defend her?" Apparently, Soma wasn't acting rationally.

Jeremy seemed amazed as a thick, leafy vine swung down. With eyes wide in fear, Soma reached for the vine that came around his neck. It was tightening; strangling him. His eyes bulged as he struggled to breathe. Suddenly, he was being lifted into the air and swung from side to side. Fang jumped at his feet angrily, but they were just out of reach.

"Stop it!" Jadara pleaded with Jeremy.

"I'm not doing it," Jeremy replied with his free hand open. "The vine came out of the tree canopy."

"Can't you stop it?" Jordon asked. "It's going to kill him!"

"If it doesn't, I will," Kenyer growled angrily.

"What?" Aiya exclaimed.

"We all agreed before we left the village that we were in this as a team. We'd find you, move on, and start a new village. Soma was part of that pact. Killing Jordon and Jeremy were never part of the deal, especially since they were your saviors."

JORDON

Jordon moved with Jeremy towards the nearest tree and tried to find a vine similar to the one that had Soma. He kept Sharijol ready as Jeremy found a thick one and hoped it was the right one. Carefully, Jeremy laid his hand on it and concentrated. His eyes were closed, and his face scowled with concern. Slowly, Soma came back to the ground. The vine released him and returned to the canopy. Soma collapsed on the ground, barely conscious as he tried to drag in deep breaths.

Jadara and Du'kai held Fang back so he didn't kill Soma himself. The ortik had grown immense and was much stronger. They slipped a few times, but managed to hold the beast back.

Jordon patted the dog's head as he and Jeremy passed him to go to Soma. Fang seemed to settle some. Jeremy kneeled next to the Drelt while Jordon and Kenyer surrounded him. He tried to examine his neck. Soma was still having trouble gathering breath. Kenyer held his knife in the other Drelt's face. Jeremy thought for a moment, then placed the ball of the staff against Soma's neck.

"Rememdium Pupillus Vulnus," he whispered.

Instantly, Soma's breathing became easier. The Drelt pulled in huge gulps of air as he lay on the ground.

"What did you heal him for?" Jordon asked surprised.

"We never meant for anyone to die on this trip," Jeremy explained to his friend. "Soma has a valid excuse to be angry. We did set the old shaman up as a sacrifice in our place."

"She deserved it!" Jordon snapped.

"So we should be as evil as they are?" Jeremy looked strangely at his friend. "We knew they'd let her free almost immediately. A few minor burns was all she'd suffer. It would look like Thaurlonian had rescued us and punished her."

"A few burns *is* all she sustained," Kenyer confirmed, holding his dagger to Soma's chest. "The healer cured those almost instantly. She didn't suffer, but treason is another matter altogether! Give me just one good reason not to skewer you right now." Kenyer glared at his tribesman.

"It's not treason! It's revenge," Jeremy replied softly. Jordon couldn't believe Jeremy was defending this oaf.

"But revenge is not part of this pact!" Kenyer growled at Soma.

"And right now, Soma owes his life to Jeremy," Aiya said with a smirk. "My, my, my! How the leaf turns."

"Whadaya mean?" Jordon asked as Fang joined them. He had returned to his normal size.

"Our customs are quite simple," Du'kai explained. "When one saves or spares the life of another, the spared life is indebted to the savior until the reverse happens."

"I won't have him as a servant," Jeremy glared. "And right now, I don't know if I trust him as a friend."

"The curse be upon me." Soma hung his head ashamed. "We all agreed to go to another village and start over. My anger at your escape overtook me. Forgive me."

"But will it happen again?" Jordon asked suspiciously.

"I swear on Lonita I will not harm you again," Soma said softly. "I am in your debt."

"And may Lonita take your life if you are lying," Jadara replied darkly.

"I don't understand," Jeremy scowled. "Who's Lonita?"

"Lonita is our goddess," Kenyer said standing. He sheathed the dagger. "She watches over all Drelt everywhere. Just like this Garadain character is your wizards' god."

Jeremy kneeled down next to Fang to give him a hug as Jordon sheathed Sharijol. He was rewarded with happy licks on his face. "With all this action going on, I'm not tired anymore. I'll take the next watch," Jeremy volunteered.

"I think we should just keep going," Jordon stretched. "We're all pretty wired now."

"Yes," Fuzz agreed. "Good idea."

"Wired?" Kenyer asked.

"Wide awake!" Jordon explained.

"Ah!" The others also agreed to continue on for a while.

Jeremy's staff lit the area clearly. The pathway led through more ruins. Fountains, buildings, stairwells. A few large mice ran across the ground, scurrying for food. The rubble often blocked the path, forcing them to go around. A series of colors to the left caught their attention.

"Aiya, look!" Jadara called as she moved towards the garden. Jordon noticed several trees grew along the outside edge of the garden. Brightly colored flowers grew waist high. Below those, more towards the center, were more flowers, not quite as high as some others they'd seen. The three-tiered effect ended on the next layer with smaller flowers that grew close to the ground. Butterflies and small flitting birds dodged in and out of the flowers. Four tall alabaster wizards stood at the four cardinal points of a pool of water, each facing the center, and each dressed in varying types of robes. A male with a long beard held a book. A plump female with her hair in a bun held a wand.

Another rather young male had out-stretched hands. The last, a slender female with long flowing tresses, had a staff. The crumbling remains of stone benches separated the statues.

"This must have been a beautiful place once," Aiya mentioned, looking at a weathered statue. "Based on the statues, I'm guessing the garden was a resting spot." Jordon agreed.

"I think it still is," Jadara replied. She gently ran a hand over a large blue flower. The flower began to hum loudly.

"Musical flowers?" Aiya's eyes lit up. "How wonderful!" She ran over and stroked a yellow one. A different tone echoed around the statues.

Jordon chuckled from the top of the path as Jadara stroked a pink one. Leave it to girls to be amazed by flowers. A pretty harmonic tone emanated from the tall flowers. The three notes created a beautiful chord. Aiya tried a white flower. Another note blended with the others.

"Hey, guys! We'd better go," Jeremy urged. He was staring at the statues.

"Why?" Jadara smiled as she sniffed the fragrant blossoms.

Jordon followed Jeremy's gaze. Different colored pastel lights glowed from the eyes of the degrading statues around the center of the garden. The lights formed beams that merged in the center. The figure of another statue or being was forming in the middle. The sight brought his heart into his throat.

"Mayday! Mayday! Trap! Trap!" he cried.

"What?" the others asked, turning.

Another statue of an angry male wizard formed in the center of the garden. Slowly, it turned in a circle. Explosive beams shot out of its eyes towards the group. Anything it hit burst into smoke.

"Run!" Jordon cried. The group scrambled to get out of the way of the beams.

"Contego," Jeremy cried as he knocked Aiya to the ground to get out of the path of a beam.

"Ow!" Jadara cried as she tumbled to the ground.

Jordon and Kenyer each grasped an arm as they ran down and dragged her up the path. They set her down when they were sure they were out of range. Jeremy and Aiya were right behind them.

"You ok?" Jeremy asked, kneeling next to her.

Jadara held her ankle. "I think so. I think a rock hit my leg when one of those things hit the ground next to me. It just startled me, that's all."

"Let me see." Jordon reached for her ankle. He examined it carefully. "It's not bad. Just a puncture wound. Jay, can you get the first aid kit out of my pack?"

"Sure," Jeremy smirked. Ever since Jordon got his First Aid certification, he'd been carrying the kit around with him. He handed the white box to Jordon.

With gentle care, Jordon cleaned the wound and placed a band-aid on it. "All done. You're good to go."

"Why not use Jeremy's staff?" Jadara asked.

"Because Jeremy is running on very little sleep and has very little energy left for spells," Jeremy explained gently. Jadara nodded in understanding.

"Fuzz?" Jordon asked the Kaptrix. "You ok?"

The small man was patting his smoking hair where one beam skimmed it. Soma sat on the ground behind him, trying to catch his breath. "I... think so," Fuzz stuttered.

"Let me see," Jordon chuckled. He examined the man's head. "Just a hot haircut."

"What happened?" Aiya breathed hard, trying to catch her breath.

"Wasn't it obvious?" Du'kai asked her. "It was a trap! A defensive device to take attackers unawares."

"Let's keep going!" Jeremy advised, taking the lead. Fang ran happily ahead. "I'm getting a bad feeling about this cavern."

The group trudged further into the center of the island. Before long, the remains of the buildings virtually disappeared and melded into a woodland of massive trees covered in large leaves and bright green vines. Soft moss beds adorned the ground under the canopies. Brightly colored birds flew about. Small animals rummaged about in the dried leaves under the trees and brush. The change eased the tension the party was feeling.

"Hey, what's that?" Jadara pointed off into the distance.

"Funny," Kenyer remarked. "It's clear. There's no vines over there."

"Let's check it out," Jordon suggested. "It might be a mirage."

"A what?" Du'kai asked.

"A mirage. It's something that you think you're seeing, but you really aren't," Jeremy explained.

"That would make sense," Soma said. "Especially with what we've been through today."

The party stepped out onto soft green grass. A crisp pool of water was off to one side with tiny brightly colored flowers strewn about. Several tall trees stood majestically along the outside edge of the clearing. Bright, fresh fruit hung from their boughs. Tiny blue squirrel-like creatures flew about through the trees, watching the party from the branches above.

"Wow!" Aiya gasped, looking around. "Look! Food!"

"Don't!" Jordon snapped.

"Why?"

"Look!" He pointed at Fang.

Fang was nosing around the bottom of the trees. It seemed like the tree moved. He yipped as he jumped back. Taking another sniff, he growled at the tree. Slowly he began his defensive growth, growling, barking, and swatting at the tree.

Jeremy went over to the pup. "Hey," he cooed to try to calm to the pup down. "What's up, boy? It's just a tree."

"Hrmph!"

Jeremy looked up sharply. He scowled as he glanced at the tree. He didn't see anything odd, so he went back to Fang. "Come on, fella. Let's keep going! Come get a drink of water." He tried pulling on the pup. Instead, Fang launched himself at the tree. A huge lower branch swung down and swatted the dog away.

"What the...?" Jeremy fell backwards.

Fang grew larger. He got up and launched at the tree again, digging sharp claws into the soft bark. Another branch swung down, but the ortik dodged it. The tree backed up a few paces and swung again, knocking Fang to the ground. Fang rolled over the soft grass, righted himself, and launched. The blue creatures came down, flying around the dog's face to distract him.

"Stop him!" Jordon yelled, grasping for the dog, but missed.

"Can't!" Jeremy cried. "He won't listen."

Again, Fang rolled. Each time, his size increased. Each time, he put more gashes into the soft bark of the tree. Another tree came to help, also knocking the ortik off his feet.

At last, Jordon, Jeremy, and Kenyer launched on top of Fang. Each caught hold of the fur around his neck and dug in to hold him back. Fang had grown so much and so strong, he was dragging the three of them across the grass towards the trees. Jadara pulled a length of leather from her pocket and fastened it around Fang's neck. It gave them all something else to hang on to. She added to the strength, pulling him back. Aiya also caught hold of the leather and pulled. At last, they brought the pup to a halt. Fang continued to struggle to get to the tree, but couldn't move.

"Fang! Down!" Jeremy ordered over his growls. "Down, boy!"

The pup didn't heed the order. He continued to struggle. The trees didn't help. They continued to sway their branches threateningly. They seemed to be moving in together to form a circle around the group. Fang grew even more.

"Fa-ng!" Jeremy warned.

After a long struggle, the pup finally ceased his pulling, but didn't shrink to his normal size. The others collapsed down next to the pup, breathing heavily.

"We gotta get this thing trained!" Jordon heaved.

"How do you train a dog to not grow when it is his instinct?" Kenyer asked.

"I can handle the size," Jordon replied. "It's the stopping when told to."

"That's going to be a problem," Jeremy pointed out, trying to catch his breath. "He's a wild dog, remember? It's like training a wolf."

"Maybe Thrundra can do something with him."

"Who is Thrundra?" Jadara asked.

"He's a wizard friend of ours from the surface," Jordon explained.

"Hey, look!" Du'kai exclaimed, kneeling near the pond.

"What is it?" Soma asked, coming over.

"Someone has been here," the tracker declared. "And recently."

"What?" the others answered.

Jordon, Aiya, and Kenyer walked over to Du'kai while Jadara and Jeremy held on to Fang. Du'kai pointed to the impressions in the dirt around the pond. "This looks like a knee," he pointed to the semi-flat impression. "And these are hoof marks. They're all over here. This looks like a basket of some type. It's not very heavy. I don't recognize these."

"Sneakers!" Jordon exclaimed.

"Sneakers?" Jeremy's eyes lit up. "Like Annese's?"

"Possible. How big are her shoes?"

"I don't know. A six?"

"I'm in a nine, and these are about half of mine."

"These are different prints," Du'kai pointed to another set of sneaker tracks. "This individual was a little heavier. See how the impression goes just a bit deeper?"

"Wait!" Jeremy cried in realization.

"Yep. Tyler, Annese, and Odessa were here," Jordon confirmed. It was the first glimmer of hope they'd had in the entire trip. At least they now knew the three were together, and, up to this point, were alive.

"And not long ago," Du'kai remarked. "Perhaps a few hours to half a day."

"Which way did they go?" Jordon spread the search for the tracks. Du'kai, too, began following patterns to see which way they went.

"Here!" he cried. "See?"

Kenyer and Jordon joined him at the opening to a path. "Here," Du'kai pointed. "Apparently they came this way and went back this way."

"Not a great choice," Kenyer remarked dryly, looking down the path. Round globes of crystal grew in a field on both sides of the path. Some looked like they had recently been broken. Some had the glisten of new bulbs.

"What are they?" Aiya asked.

"I don't know, but I don't get a good feeling about it."

"Jay, you might want to carry Fang through here," Jordon called back.

"Sure. Tell me how to get him to shrink!" Jeremy growled.

"We have to get his mind off the trees," Jadara suggested. "He's still growling."

"I got it!" Jordon cried, dropping his pack. He rummaged around a little, pulled something out in his hand, and called Fang. "Here, Fang!" he called excitedly, waving a beef strip in his hand. "Come see what I got, buddy! Come on!"

Fang turned towards Jordon with wide eyes. He pulled loose of Jeremy and Jadara and ran towards him. He shrank down as he ran to him and sat with his bushy tail wagging and his tongue hanging out of his mouth. An eager look replaced the angry one. Jordon rewarded the pup with a beef strip. He waited for the dog to gobble it down, then gave him another.

The group laughed. "Ya know," Kenyer remarked. "I'm kind of hungry myself."

Jadara turned towards the trees. She surveyed the fruit. Carefully, she approached one and placed her hand softly on the bark. "Please, miss tree, may we have some of your lovely fruit?" she asked.

Jordon watched her strangely, but knew enough not to say anything. In his experiences in Asteria, he'd learned there were many unusual things. Who knew what a Drelt could do?

Slowly, a heavily ladened branch lowered to her height. "Thank you ever so much!" Jadara replied joyfully and began picking fruit off the bough. She handed some around, taking only a couple for each of them.

"Jadara, if you haven't guessed, is our naturalist," Kenyer smirked at his friend, taking the fruit. "Thanks, Dara."

"OK." Jordon bit into the juicy fruit. "Mmmm," he moaned in delight. "Du'kai is a tracker. Jadara is a naturalist. Aiya is an archer. What do the rest of you do?"

"I'm a bladesman actually," Kenyer replied before biting into the fruit again. "Hits the spot! Thank you, Miss Tree!" he called over his shoulder. "Delicious!" The others echoed their appreciation.

"A swordsman without a sword?" Jordon asked suspiciously.

"When we left the village, we really didn't have time to get our gear. Did you not notice we don't have traveling packs with us?"

"I noticed, but I didn't want to seem rude."

"Not a problem. It'll just be rough for a while."

"What do you do?" Jordon asked Soma as he took another bite of the delicious fruit.

Soma seemed to blush. "I cook," the Drelt replied quietly as if he were ashamed of the skill.

"Great!" the boy seemed pleased. "I'm a lousy cook! And Jeremy's not much better."

"We failed Home Ec in school," Jeremy agreed. The Drelt seemed to relax now that his skills weren't being made fun of.

"We'd best get going. The kids have a good head start on us," Jordon pointed out after they'd finished eating. "And judging by the light coming on in this chamber, I'd say morning is here."

"How do you fix the scratches that Fang caused on that tree?" Jeremy nodded towards the injured tree.

"He'll heal himself," Jadara smiled. "He's not hurt badly. Some scratches, that's all. It looks much worse to us than it is to him. Fang really didn't do all that much damage. Trees are pretty hardy."

Du'kai stood before the field of globes. He kneeled down to examine the stray, strange bulbs. "If my guess is correct, we don't want to touch these growths. Not even accidentally."

"Why?" Aiya asked, reaching for one. Soma grasped her hand to stop her.

"It will explode." Du'kai continued. "There is a gas building up inside it. See the swirls inside? My guess is that they explode anyway on their own, but these are sharp shards," he held up a shard from the ground, "that will dig in and cut. I'm guessing that because of the close proximity, one of them exploding will cause a chain reaction. I think that's what happened here."

"Oooooh!" Jordon shivered. "Nasty!"

"Exactly."

"So the kids might be hurt?" Jeremy scowled. Concern laced his features.

"Possible. OK," Jordon instructed. "Single file. Du'kai, take the lead."

"And hang on to Fang!" Fuzz reminded Jeremy. The boy nodded.

One by one the group fell into line behind Du'kai with Soma taking up the rear. Jeremy picked up Fang and held him tight. The pup squirmed to get down, but Jeremy held on firmly, reassuring the pup. Gingerly, they picked their way through the narrow path. It would take a while to get to the end.

The explosion echoed throughout the cavern. More and more of them followed. Glass shards flew all over. Jordon quickly dropped to the ground, knocking Fuzz over. He could hear the squirming pup behind him. The explosions frightened the poor pup, who quickly curled up under Jeremy whimpering. The deafening sound continued for several minutes, with the sounds of the explosions moving further away. Eventually, there was no sound at all. Carefully, Jordon raised his head to look around.

"Everyone alright?" Kenyer called from up front. Affirmatives came slowly as each person evaluated their injuries.

"Where's Soma?" Aiya inquired, looking around.

"Behind me......" Jordon remarked turning. Soma was gone. Looking around, there was no sign of the Drelt. He looked into the path behind them. Nothing. He could see all the way back to the trees, but couldn't see Soma. "Where'd he go?"

"Du'kai?" Kenyer instructed with a nod of his head.

Du'kai made his way carefully to the rear of the line. He combed the ground thoroughly, as all their footprints were there. It took a long time, but he found what he was looking for. Slowly he followed the path, then stood up confused.

"What is it?" Jordon asked.

"He vanished," Du'kai said softly.

"Vanished?" Jordon asked. "Is he a wizard?"

"No. Soma hunts small game, but is better at cooking and weaving. It's strange that he could just disappear," Kenyer contemplated.

"Something in the globes?" Jeremy asked.

"I don't know. While the gas smells funny, it doesn't seem to have an adverse effect on the rest of us. Let's keep going," Kenyer said thoughtfully.

"Soma can run," Aiya reminded her friend.

"I know," Du'kai acknowledged. "But he'd still leave prints. There's nothing. The prints stop. He's gone. I don't know how, and I don't know to where."

"If he tells the village shaman what we're doing...," Jadara said worriedly.

"They may come after us, I know," Kenyer nodded. "Therefore, I suggest we get as much distance between us and them as possible."

The group continued their trek to the transport pad quickly. Kenyer reached out and scratched the pup on his head to comfort the frightened thing.

"How is he?" Kenyer asked.

"Better than I am," Jeremy squirmed. "I think I've got some shards in my back."

"Let's wait until we find a place to stop. I'll remove them for you," Kenyer offered as he brushed the loose ones from Jeremy's shirt.

Aiya stopped at the clearing for the pad. She looked at each of the others.

"Go through," Jordon encouraged.

Aiya shook her head. "We don't know what's on the other side."

Jeremy smirked. "Only way to find out is to go through it. Right, Fuzz?"

"Correct, Mr. Jeremy. Shall I lead?" The Kaptrix seemed pleased to provide some support to their travelers.

"Lead on!" Jordon grinned. "I'm right behind you, but stop on the other side! No exploring without us!"

Fuzz blushed brightly. "Yes, sir."

MIKKEL

A dark form came into the wizard's room. He laid a plate of food on the table. "And?" he asked. "Did the Drelt do the job?"

The wizard shook his head. "He started to, but there were too many people to stop him. The ortik that has befriended the boys is also a worthy foe. Actually, I'm surprised they got through this cavern alive. There were so many traps and dangers."

"So what happened?"

"I managed keep the Drelt with them until they came to the end of the Peeks cavern. The little critters seemed amazed by them," the wizard smiled.

"I don't care about the squirrelly little brutes," he growled at the wizard. "I care about killing the boys!"

"I understand, highness. When they moved from the trees towards the transport pad, they set off the glass plants. Of course, that set off a chain reaction. It was sufficient that I lost my connection with the Drelt, so I transported him back to his village."

"Grrr! What is with these boys?" Mikkel asked rhetorically. "What is next?"

"Let me see where they have gone, and what I can manipulate. Give me some time, highness."

Mikkel nodded curtly and stalked from the room. "I'm going to take a nap."

Jujene watched his companion walk stiffly from the room. It would be only a matter of time before the future king would explode at him. Mikkel did not have the best of temperaments. Slowly, Jujene began to eat the cold food and contemplate his next move.

13 – MIKNAR TROUBLE

ANNESE

The pad emptied into a dim, dank, stone corridor. The walls were smooth as glass. Tiny sparkles twinkled from the marbled texture. The light here didn't come from the stones. It came from torches on the walls. The girls jumped when Odessa's hooves echoed.

"Wow!" Tyler exclaimed, looking around. "Where are we?"

"Don't know," Annese whispered. "This is weird. It reminds me of the dungeon of an old castle."

"It's rather strange," Odessa agreed. "No trees. No dirt. No grass. Nothing."

"I can hear noise up ahead." Tyler looked down the long corridor. "Let's check it out."

Annese cuddled the longairits closer. The corridor wasn't very wide, so the trio had to travel carefully. Each step echoed off the walls. Off in the distance, she could hear noises–bangs and murmurings.

"Do you think we're near a village?" Annese asked nervously.

"Your guess is as good as mine," Tyler replied softly. "With the way our steps are echoing, we could be coming up on just a few people."

"Hey, look!" Odessa stopped. She pointed towards the side of the corridor. A stone archway opened into another cavern.

The cavern was small, and moss covered the floor. Several ledges were built into the walls. The light was dim and the air moist. Various mushrooms grew on the ledges and the floor near the walls.

"I wonder how they do that," Tyler mused as he looked at the mushrooms.

"Do what?" Annese asked, joining Tyler and Odessa.

"It's humid in here. Feel it?"

"I do," Odessa agreed.

"But it's dry out in the corridor. How do they keep it moist in here and dry out there when there isn't a door?"

"Let's keep going," Annese suggested earnestly. "Maybe someone we meet can answer that question."

The children stopped as they turned around. Several short, mean-looking men stood near the archway. Each held a rope and an axe. Their clothing was dirty and thin, and their hair was cropped short with a closely trimmed beard.

Annese put on a smile and stepped forward. "Hello. My name is Annese. These are my friends Tyler and Odessa. We're lost. Perhaps you could help us?"

The man in the front growled with a mean smile just before the others rushed forward.

JEREMY

The duo had become a septet, one being a very unusual dog. Jeremy was getting concerned about how they'd keep them all safe. They moved into the stone corridor one by one. It twinkled in the light of Jeremy's staff. The walls were smooth and sparkling. The floor was stone. Their muffled steps echoed off the walls.

"This is strange," Kenyer remarked softly. "No trees."

"And listen," Jadara motioned him to be quiet.

"I hear... I don't know what I hear," Jeremy remarked, putting Fang down. "But it sounds like people working."

"And water," Aiya whispered. "I can hear water off in the distance."

"Fuzz?" Jordon asked

"Sorry, Mr. Jordon. I haven't been here before," the Kaptrix said, going through the papers from his pockets.

"Well, it looks like the only way Annese and Tyler could have gone is straight," Jeremy nodded towards the end of the corridor. "I suggest we check it out."

"They could have turned around and gone back through," Fuzz suggested.

"Not my cousin. Curiosity is his middle name," Jordon remarked darkly. "If there's anything to attract his attention, he'll follow it. Let's go."

They walked cautiously down the narrow corridor. A short way down, they spotted an archway on the right. The room it opened into was dim and moist. Shelves lined the walls. Jadara entered the room and looked over at the plants.

"Mushrooms," she informed them, lifting one. She sniffed at it. "Edible ones. This must be a food storage."

"Something's up," Du'kai murmured.

"What do you mean?" Jeremy inquired.

"Look at the floor. While the corridor is pure stone, the floor in here is moss; and the moss is disrupted. It looks like there was a struggle here."

"Any blood?" Jeremy asked worriedly.

"No, but there are hoof prints," he smiled, knowing they were on the right trail.

"Let's keep going," Kenyer directed. He loosened the dagger at his belt. "Be prepared for anything."

The walk down the corridor was long. Several more times they found archways similar to the mushroom room. One was vines of fruit. One held insects. One was gourds of some kind. One had a series of niches in the walls with bones and decaying clothing. Kenyer motioned for them to slow down and move to a wall. They approached the end of the corridor with stealth. It opened into an enormous cavern.

The cavern was just as smooth as the corridor. Several ornate pillars supported the ceiling. Other corridors came off the cavern. An occasional archway appeared along the walls with stone doors blocking the way. Just to their right was a slightly raised platform from the floor. Off to one side, they could spot water pouring down the wall into a pool. Canals had been dug into the ground to allow the water to move out into other areas. Someone had built stone bridges over the canals to allow access throughout.

"Aqueducts," Jeremy pointed out in a whisper.

"Krilts," Jordon murmured, pointing to a group of men in the center.

The short, stocky men were dark in appearance; different from Zelmar. Their clothing seemed worn and tattered. Their hair was dark and cropped short, unlike the long, reddish brown of Kriltnar. They wore their beards closely trimmed instead of the long, braided ones of the surface. Most of them had either an axe or a pick hanging from their belt. A few had short swords.

"Shhh. They can hear us," Kenyer whispered lowly.

"Strange," Jadara observed. "No women and no children about."

Jeremy heard the crack of a whip from one of the opposite corridors, followed by a girl's voice crying out.

"Move, you mangy horse!" ordered a rough, deep voice.

"I'm not a horse!" the girl cried back.

"Let's go, you two! You're too slow!" another voice came again.

Out of a corridor came a young Centaus girl hooked up to a halter. The halter was strapped to a rough wagon piled with colored stones. A mortal boy and girl were pushing from behind. Their feet were sliding on the smooth stone floor. Behind them walked three of the short men; one was carrying a whip. He flicked it at the Centaus again.

"Ow!" she reared.

"Move, or I'll give you what for."

"That's Tyler!" Jordon pointed to the boy.

"And that's Annese," Jeremy agreed with a scowl.

"I'd wager the half-mortal is Odessa?" Kenyer whispered. The boys nodded in agreement.

"This is unacceptable," Jadara whispered, nocking an arrow. "They've been taken captive and made into slaves in a very short period of time."

"Jordon, look!" Jeremy whispered.

"I am."

"What do you see?" Jeremy urged.

"I see the kids... pulling... a wagon. Why?"

"When have you ever seen wheels in Asteria?" Jeremy questioned.

Jordon thought for a moment. "Never," he replied.

"And look underneath the bed," Jeremy pointed. "It's a spring of some kind."

"To lift the front of the bed like a dump truck," Jordon nodded. "What do you make of it?"

"Either someone from our world has been here, or they've got something extremely advanced down here," Jeremy breathed.

"We gotta do something." Jordon scanned the cavern. "Fast." A slow, mischievous smile crossed his features. "Time halt?" Jordon smirked at Jeremy.

"Sounds good to me," Jeremy smiled in agreement.

"Wait a moment, you two," Du'kai cocked a grin. "You're not leaving me out of this."

"We need a plan," Aiya stalled. "Just releasing the children isn't going to get us out of trouble."

"Agreed," Jadara acknowledged.

"Time halt will only hold for about ten minutes," Jeremy explained. "We'll have to work fast. Anyone not touching the staff when the spell goes off isn't included. We're going to have to carry the kids."

"Ten what?" Du'kai scowled.

"A short time," Jordon supplied. "We need to get the kids out of their situation, and back to the center before the spell wears off."

"Why not just go down the corridor?" Aiya pointed to another corridor near the children.

"We don't know where it goes," Jordon informed her. "If these men are like Krilts, there are corridors all over the place. It's just a massive maze. They'll know every hallway and cavern. We stand a better chance getting out of here by having one of them as a guide."

"I'm guessing they're not too fond of strangers," Kenyer nodded towards the whipping guard.

"I'd say that's a good guess," Aiya agreed. "We can take one captive."

"That makes us no better than they are," Jeremy grimaced. "I say we demand to speak to their king. At least there we have some leverage, if we can get him to agree to give us a guide."

"Ok. But we need to stay close. If speaking to their king doesn't work, we fight our way out and take a hostage," Jordon agreed. Everyone nodded.

"Ok. Everybody grab hold of the staff," Jeremy instructed, pulling out his staff. His other hand reached down for Fang. "Vicis Subsisto."

They waited only a second before darting off across the cavern. Jeremy led the pack, jumping up onto the raised area.

"Hey, look! The entertainment is here!" a deep voice announced with a chuckle.

The group came to a screeching halt. Each one knocking into the one in front of him. Slowly, Jeremy turned towards the voice. The men in the cavern began moving towards the raised floor they were on.

"Jeremy!" Annese yelled across the chasm.

"Jordon! Help!" Tyler called. "Ow!" He scowled at the man behind him with the whip.

"Come on, you dregs! Dance!" came another voice from the front of the gathering crowd.

"We're in trouble!" Jordon whispered.

"No! Really?" Kenyer whispered back sarcastically.

"Side step?" Jeremy whispered back.

"Sure." Jordon nodded.

Taking a dancing pose, the boys side-kicked off towards the right to reach the kids.

A sharp whistle echoed around them. "Look at that! They have females! Come on, sweetheart! Shake that bootie!"

The thunk of an arrow could barely be heard. Jeremy watched the man who called out the insulting comment fall to the ground with an arrow sticking out of his forehead. Another thunk went off, and another. Each arrow hit its target.

"Wow! What a shot!" Jordon exclaimed surprised.

"Move it!" Kenyer pushed them. "Incoming! The spell didn't work."

"No kidding!" Jeremy groused back.

A deep roar of anger washed over them like a wave as all the small men in the cavern began racing towards them. More were flooding in from the connecting tunnels. One by one, Aiya and Jadara began picking them off.

"Maim! Don't kill!" Jeremy heard Kenyer yell over his shoulder. Fang was already growing. Oh, great! More chaos.

Kenyer was moving the two teens towards their targets. Several men moved in to block their way towards the kids. Kenyer pulled out his dagger, and Jordon drew Sharijol. They began circling each other back to back as they waited for the men to make the first move.

"Aim deep," Kenyer warned Jordon. "The axes have double edges and are heavier at the head than your sword. Weaken them by hitting the handle and their hands. A swing with an axe needs to be completed. You can't stop the swing in the middle like you can with a sword." Jordon nodded his understanding and waited.

Jeremy and Du'kai ducked behind a pillar.

"Got any ideas?" Jeremy asked.

"I track things, remember?" Du'kai replied with a frown. "I'm not a fighter, nor an archer. In fact, I got my bow taken away. Is that time thingy the only spell you know?"

"No," Jeremy replied, peering around the pillar. "It's just the best. I don't understand why it didn't work."

"Think of another one quick. We're a bit outnumbered."

The clang of metal echoed through the cavern as the axes and swords collided. Jeremy glanced over to see Kenyer and Jordon moving at an incredibly fast pace to stay ahead of the weapons trying to slice them. Backed behind pillars, the girls were slowly taking out one Krilt after another. Jeremy suddenly got an idea.

"Sanctum fulsi," he began. "Close your eyes!" he yelled before murmuring "de lumen!" A burst of extremely bright light burst out of Jeremy's staff. Yells of pain rang around from anyone who didn't listen to Jeremy.

"Come on!" Jeremy grabbed Du'kai and followed Kenyer and Jordon. "Girls! Fuzz! Let's go! Come on, Fang!"

JORDON

"Move!" Jordon punched Kenyer in the arm. The Krilts in front of them were still doubled over in pain.

Kenyer followed Jordon over the rows of little men. They reached the kids in just a few jumps. Kenyer easily sliced through the leather harness around Odessa with a sword he pulled off a downed Krilt.

"Um, hi, Jordon," Tyler greeted his cousin uncertainly. Annese looked gratefully over his shoulder.

"Are you alright?" Jordon asked, laying a gentle hand on his shoulder.

"I think so. A little sore."

"OK. We'll talk later." Jordon swung around to counter the little man coming up behind him. He pushed Tyler back towards the wall.

"Jeremy!" Annese hugged her brother.

"Not now. Come on!" Jeremy grabbed her hand and started down the corridor the trio had come from.

"Ortik!" Du'kai was right behind him, dragging Tyler and Odessa with him. Aiya and Jadara stopped to help Jordon, since the wall of little men they had jumped over had begun moving again.

Grumbling, Jeremy pointed his staff at an oversized Fang. "Ortus!" he said lowly. He watched as the large pup rose into the air. He moved him high enough that he was out of harm's way and couldn't attack the Krilts, either. Slowly he kept the pup in the air and coming towards him. He didn't stop until Fang was directly over him.

Jordon whirled around as the crack of a whip echoed. Kenyer flinched as the end of it caught his shoulder. He looked up with fire in his eyes. The small man with the whip grinned evilly as he swirled the whip back. He let it fly towards Kenyer again. His grin of pleasure turned into one of shock as Kenyer caught the whip in mid-air and wrapped it around his wrist. The man pulled back on the whip as Kenyer kept dragging him across the smooth floor towards him. Finally, the man's neck was even with Kenyer's sword. Jordon sidled in behind the small man.

"Call off your friends, or I'm cutting off heads," Kenyer instructed threateningly.

The man dropped the whip and ran. His escape stalled when he bumped into Jordon and Sharijol, then found himself held fast by Kenyer's hand holding onto his hair. A glint of steel gleamed as Kenyer's sword came around and laid gently on his neck.

"Call them off, or I'll add pressure," Kenyer warned. Slowly, he began to push the blade into the man's neck.

"Cut away, then," the man growled out. "Miknars hold no fear!"

"Grendal vat, brother!" a deep voice called. "I'm coming!"

"Kenyer!" Jeremy mumbled warningly from the small group, knowing the Drelt's sensitive ears could hear him.

Kenyer took advantage quickly. "Let's go!" he called to the girls. He continued to drag the little man with him as he walked backwards toward the rest of the group.

Jordon ducked and rolled out of the way. Back on his feet, he followed Kenyer towards their friends.

"Jeremy! Shield!" he called.

Bringing down the pup, Jeremy pointed his staff towards the opening of the tunnel. "Contego!" Happily, the shield held. Neither weapon, nor little man, could get through.

"The kids ok?" Kenyer asked Jeremy.

"They'll be fine in the long run. A few whip marks. Nothing we can't heal."

"Jeremy!" Annese hugged her brother. "I'm so glad you're here. I didn't know..."

Jeremy held up his hand. "Later. We gotta get out of here. That spell won't last long."

"Long enough to give us a head start," Jordon urged them down the tunnel.

"OK," Kenyer leaned over to his prisoner. "Since it's obvious we aren't welcome here, you will be our guide to get us through to the next nearest transport pad. Understand?" The man tried to nod. Kenyer assumed it was an affirmative. "Let's move. How do we get out?"

"There's no exit from here," Tyler explained. "It's just a mining tunnel. There's tons of gems down there. That's what they had us doing, because their machine broke."

"Machine?" Jeremy and Jordon asked together.

"Yea. They've got engines and gears and hydraulic drills."

"Who's working them?" Jeremy asked.

"These little men, smaller than him." Tyler pointed at the man Kenyer held prisoner.

Jeremy and Jordon looked at each other with dawning realization. "Gnomes!" Of course! It all made sense now. Gnomes were little mechanics. Very smart and very resourceful.

"Let's move away from here! We need some room between us and them," Kenyer pulled the boys from their thoughts.

"Jere, light, please," Jordon suggested as they started down the dim tunnel.

Jeremy pointed his staff back towards the opening. "Contego!" he whispered to reinforce the shield. He ran to catch up with the others. "Lux lucius," he whispered. The globe glowed lowly.

"Wait!" Annese cried. "Our backpacks, and the longairits!"

"The what?" Jordon asked.

"Small fluff balls," Tyler explained.

"Where are they?" Kenyer asked. Annese shrugged. Kenyer bent to his prisoner. "Where are their things?"

"Dunt know. Dunt care," came the gruff reply.

"Guys, we need to move!" Jeremy urged.

"We'll find them," Jordon promised, pushing Annese on down the corridor.

Jeremy and Tyler led them down the corridor as the yelling behind them became louder.

"I think the spell wore off," Jeremy puffed.

"Cast another!" Jordon suggested.

"I'm gonna run out of energy if I don't rest soon," he warned his friend.

Jeremy paused long enough to cast the spell, then hurried on. They came up short, however, when the corridor narrowed. A burly, dirty-looking Miknar stood in their way, his axe being bounced on one hand.

"Well, well, well. You brought me more workers, T'harien. Good for you!" he said evilly.

"That's my axe!" Tyler accused, looking at the red stripe around the hilt of the axe the Miknar had.

"Your axe?" Jordon scowled. "Where'd you get an axe?"

"It was a gift... from a friend," the boy's firm voice died off.

Jordon nodded and moved forward. He drew Sharijol and twirled it once in his hand. "You'll return my cousin's axe... now!" he ordered, holding out his other hand.

"Think you're that good, do you, boy?" the Miknar asked with a grin.

"Try me," Jordon whispered deceptively.

"Gareft!" the prisoner warned, but Kenyer tugged him quiet.

Gareft held out the axe slowly. Jordon reached for it. Suddenly, Gareft twisted and swung the axe towards

Jordon. Jordon dodged and blocked it with his sword. He twisted to block another move from Gareft. Both of them spun, coming to a halt with a clang of steel-on-steel, sparks flying. Turning fast, Jordon knocked the axe aside with Sharijol, reached out with his foot and tripped the small man. Gareft fell backwards as his foot went flying in front of him. Jordon hopped over him, stepping on the wrist that held the axe. He thrust Sharijol at the man's neck.

"What do you think?" Jordon asked him. "Am I that good?" He added more pressure to the man's wrist as he pressed the point of Sharijol into the man's neck just enough to be felt.

"Yield!" Gareft conceded. He let go of the axe.

Jordon motioned for Tyler to run over and pick up the axe. Quickly, the boy ran back to Annese and Odessa. Jordon stepped back, lowered his sword, and held out a hand to the man. Gareft looked at his hand for a while before reaching up to take it. Jordon helped him up to standing. "I'm Jordon Hallstead," he introduced.

"You are intruders in my home," Gareft spit at him. "I'll simply take you as slaves."

Jordon's sword came up to the Miknar's throat. "Think so?"

"I've got an idea," Du'kai smiled.

JEREMY

Jeremy watched Du'kai tightened the last knot on the rope that tied up the Miknar. He patted the man's shoulder. "That should hold you awhile. Your friends will have a tough time getting those knots out, but you can breathe, eat, and you're still alive to tell the tale. Have a nice life." Jeremy giggled at Du'kai's sarcasm.

"Let's go," Jordon urged. "Jeremy's spells should just be wearing off again."

T'harien kicked at Kenyer's legs hard. He pushed off as Kenyer was taken off guard and ran back towards the cavern.

"Get him!" Jeremy cried.

"Leave him," Jadara said. "All he can do is run back for help. Let's move out."

"You'll never get out of here alive!" Gareft growled.

Jeremy chuckled as Kenyer smiled. "Thanks," the Drelt replied. "I love a good challenge."

14 - ROCKEATERS

TYLER

The ever-growing party finally rounded a bend into another cavern. This one was a wide, open area. Stairs built into the sides went down into the layers and depths of the pit in the middle. The rat-a-tat-tat of a jackhammer sound was coming from below. A large mechanical lift was on the far side. It hummed quietly. A small, thin man about two-and-a-half feet tall was moving about it. Irons and chains clanked about his feet. His clothing was in rags as he fussed with connections and switches.

"Little men," Tyler pointed to the man. This was going to be interesting. How were they going to get the little man to cooperate?

"Anybody speak Gnomish?" Jeremy asked defeatedly. No one answered.

"I'll go," Jordon volunteered. "He doesn't seem too dangerous."

"Actually, he took a shine to Odessa," Tyler informed them. Odessa squirmed as all eyes turned to her.

"OK. Odessa, why don't you go talk to this gentleman?" Jeremy suggested. Odessa shook her head fearfully. She backed away from the group a few steps. Jeremy sighed. "You're up, Jordo. Go win another heart." Tyler snickered at Jeremy's insinuation.

"Clown!" Jordon pushed his friend, but he moved towards the gnome anyway. He grasped Aiya's hand and pulled her along as he passed.

"Me? Why?" Aiya questioned.

"You may have more in common than you know," Jordon suggested. "Besides, I'm not pretty."

Tyler watched with trepidation as Jordon approached the gnome cautiously, not wanting to scare him. "Um, excuse me?" The small gnome looked up at him, assessed his clothing, then returned to the machine he was working on to flip a switch. He turned back to Jordon and waited.

Tyler assessed the man from the distance. His black hair stuck out at odd angles. A strip of leather pulled it back. His clothes were ragged and dirty. The leather shoes on his feet had holes in the toes. Jordon had kneeled down on the ground to talk to the gnome. "I'm Jordon. Whatcha working on?" he asked.

"This is self-riser," the gnome stated. "Switch at bottom no work. I fix."

"I see. Did you build this?"

"No. Blul built."

"Blul knows about hydraulics?" Jordon asked.

"Hydra-what?"

"Air and water pressure. It makes things rise and lower."

"Yes, Blul knows."

"How do you power it?"

"Energy from rock."

Jordon looked confused. "Energy from the rocks?"

"Special rock. Yellow and black stripe."

"I don't understand."

"Course not. You mortal. Mortals no understand. This important, not about self."

Tyler got the impression that the gnome didn't understand where Jordon was confused. "Do you have a name?" his cousin asked.

"Course, I have name!"

Jordon waited. When the gnome didn't answer, he asked, "What is it?"

"Grup. Me Grup."

"The chains. You're a prisoner?" Aiya asked softly.

Grup looked down at his ankles. The chains were still there. He looked at them as if he had forgotten about them. "Grup live here," came the sad answer.

"Wouldn't you like to leave? Go back to your family?"

"Grup has no family. Blul family. And Seda, and Rexa."

"Are those others of your race?" Aiya inquired.

"Yes."

"But living here you're only serving the Miknars...." Jordon began.

"Grup! What take so long!?" came an irritated female voice.

"Questions! Always questions!" Grup threw up his hands.

Tyler looked over to another area between the three and the rocks to see a female gnome coming over. Her hair was silvery-blue down to her shoulders. Her figure was as frail as Grup's. She wore the same sort of sack-cloth rags. Her hand held a wrench. Bright blue eyes lit up at the sight of Aiya and Jordon.

"Ah! Visitors! Wonderful!"

"No wonderful!" Grup complained. "Slow down!"

"Bah!" the female balked at him. "Hello! Hello!" she climbed up a rock to see better. "Who you?" she asked.

"I'm Aiya, and this is Jordon. We're trying to find our way out. We need to find a transport pad. Do you know where we can find one?"

"Ah, yes, I do!" she smiled.

"Seda, be quiet!" Grup grumbled.

"Be quiet yourself!" she yelled back at him. "If not for you, we be home!"

Tyler exchanged an amused glance with Annese. Both children had a hard time not giggling at the antics of the two gnomes.

"Perhaps we can get you home," Jordon suggested.

"No, no, no! Home gone!" Seda shook her head sadly. "Gone in cataclysm. Must go to surface."

"That's where we're going," Jordon nodded.

The hopeful light in Seda's eyes was unmistakable. Her hands came together over her heart as she looked up at the two. "You would take Seda back to surface?"

Jordon shrugged. "Sure," he shrugged. "What's one more?"

"But we need some help. The children have lost their backpacks and their pets," Aiya mentioned.

"Seda know not backpacks. Pets, you say? What kind pets?"

"Long... longai... fluff balls," Jordon replied.

"Kitchen!" Grup spat.

"Seda get fluff balls. You wait here," the small woman instructed.

"Don't take too long," Aiya urged. "The Miknars are only a short distance behind us. I don't know how long we can hold them off."

Seda smiled. "You come with Seda. I keep you safe."

"No! No! No!" Grup stamped his foot. "Too dangerous!"

"Bah! Old biddy!" Seda grumbled at Grup. "Come, Grup! Go home!"

"No! Grup stay! Work on big mover!"

"Fine!" Seda yelled at him. She hopped down off the rock and motioned for them to follow. Jordon motioned for the others.

As Odessa passed, Grup stopped her. "Pick up all gems you find. Save. Very valuable." He handed her a glowing yellow gem and winked.

"Thank you," Odessa smiled at him. "You sure you don't want to come?"

"Miknars good to Grup. Grup fix machines, Miknars give food and clothes. We good."

"Ok."

They ducked around the large machine following Seda. Jordon stopped short when Seda bent down and ducked into a niche in the rocks. The yelling from behind them echoed off the rocks.

"Trapped," Jadara whispered.

"Like animals," Du'kai replied, looking back.

"Um, Seda?" Jordon kneeled down to peer into the hole. "We can't fit in there. And we're kinda in a hurry. The Miknars are coming–fast."

"Just a moment," Seda mumbled. "Just need to move lever. Unk. Umph. Grrrmph! Got it!" The stone slab above the little niche swung open. It was still a little low, but they could pass through without crawling. "Last one, close door!" Seda called as she led them down the hidden hallway.

Kenyer grabbed the etched handle in the stone door and pulled it closed behind him. It surprised him at how light it was. The door closed shut without a squeak and set into place without a thump. Amazing.

GRUP

The way was freed from the evil spell that kept them from pursuing their enemies. The intruders must be overtaken and must pay for the lives they took. The mob of Miknars raced down the well-known corridor and into the cavern. They skidded to a halt, looking in all the little crevices around them. Nothing.

On the lifting machine was the gnome Grup. He was tinkering with a switch. The lead Miknar went up to him.

"Alright, Grup! Where are they hiding?"

"Who?"

"You know who. Those mortals and their little friends."

Grup shook his head. "Grup see no one."

"They came through here, and there is no way out! Did they go down into the mine?"

Grup shrugged. "Grup see no one. Maybe they go down. Grup work on riser."

"You little bugger!" the Miknar grabbed the gnome's clothes. "Where are they hiding? You couldn't have missed them."

Grup looked up at the Miknar innocently. He waited for more information. Finally, the Miknar tossed him back onto the ledge he was on.

"If I find out you're lying, I'll cut you in two," the Miknar threatened. "Down the hole!" he ordered the others.

Grup watched as the mob of Miknars began climbing down into the mines. He turned back to his machine and smiled.

JORDON

Jordon questioned what they'd gotten themselves into by following the gnome. He wasn't sure she really knew where they were or where they were going. These small beings seemed to be slightly argumentative.

"Seda, where are we going?" Jadara inquired.

"Kitchen," Seda replied. "Get pets... I hope."

The tunnel was narrow, with many twists and turns. The only light came from Jeremy's staff. Other niches and tunnels spilled off in different directions. At long last Seda climbed up the rocks on the side of a wall and pointed. Above them was a grate that led into another cavern.

"Push!" Seda instructed in a whisper. She made a motion with her hands towards the grate.

Jordon stepped up onto a rock and peered into the kitchen. He could hear frantic squeals above him.

Something else, heavy, was walking around in there. The popping sound of a fire echoed off the rock face. Slowly, Jordon pushed up the grate and peered around him. He could see a large cauldron of something steaming over a fire in a rock fireplace off to one side. Several stone tables were about with jars, dishes, goblets, and other things. A large Miknar moved off into a side room.

Jordon motioned for Kenyer to help. Kenyer stepped up and helped Jordon move the grate to the side as quietly as they could.

"Get pets, come back," Seda whispered.

Kenyer gave Jordon a push up. Jordon hoisted himself up into the kitchen. He glanced around, could hear the squeals, but couldn't see anything. He leaned over the hole.

"Send up Annese," he whispered.

Before long, Annese's head came up into the kitchen. Jordon helped pull her up.

"I don't see anything. What are we looking for?" he explained.

"A basket," she whispered back. "A light brown basket with a handle."

"Like that one?" Jordon pointed to the table against the far wall.

"That's it!" she rushed forward to grasp the basket. Her hopeful face fell when she looked in it. Only the blanket was there. "They're gone!" her voice cried in distress.

Jordon listened harder. He could still hear panicked squeaks and squeals. It could easily just be mice. Slowly he moved towards the fireplace, afraid of what he was going to find. The water was boiling with mushrooms and vegetables floating on top. Jordon took the ladle hanging against the fireplace and dipped it into the water. He pulled up the ladle to examine the contents. Just vegetables. No sign of any meat. He emptied the ladle and replaced it. OK They weren't in the soup! One relief.

A symphony of terrified squeals came from the side room the Miknar went into. They could hear him grumbling and cursing at something. Something chopped into wood. A brown and white ball of fluff came rolling out of the room.

"Spot!" Annese called quietly. The ball of fluff stopped, turned, and quickly went to Annese. She scooped it up and cuddled it to her.

Jordon looked around frantically. He needed something heavy. His eyes fell to a heavy rock hammer lying on the table behind Annese. He smiled. Quickly, he retrieved the hammer and ran to hide alongside the doorway to the room. He winked at Annese.

"Yo! Where's the soup!" he growled into the doorway, then ducked.

The squeals kept coming, getting louder, as the heavy footsteps of the Miknar echoed off the walls. The unkempt cook came from the room holding a cage of fluff balls. His long, dark hair was pulled back into a ponytail. His apron was dirty and his clothing torn. His left hand was reaching into a cage.

"What are you grumbling about?" he growled.

The Miknar took three steps out of the room. His eyes fell on Annese. She simply smiled and waved. Thunk!

The heavy hammer was hard to handle, but with two hands Jordon brought it down on the back of the Miknar's head. Just enough to knock him out. The cage smacked on the floor. The longairits scattered.

Annese dropped to the floor with the basket. Spot, apparently understanding her intentions, squealed and squeaked. In amazement, Jordon watched the little fluff balls make their way over to the basket where Annese picked them up and put them back under the blanket.

"They all there?" he asked with concern.

Annese nodded. "Yep. All eight of them."

"Good. Let's get out of here before we're found out." The man he knocked out was coming to.

They lowered the basket down, then Jordon handed Annese off to Kenyer. He slid back down into the hole as an unfamiliar noise made its way into the room.

"Move it!" Jordon whispered. "Someone's coming!"

Kenyer and Jordon slid the grate back over the hole as quickly as possible. It sank back into place just as another Miknar entered the room.

"Zelt!" the man grumbled. "Zelt! What's going... oh, no! Zelt? Zelt! Come on, brother. Wake up!"

The group tiptoed back down the tunnel as they listened to whoever was up there try to wake up the cook. Jordon smirked as Seda tugged at Kenyer's pants. Kenyer chuckled and lifted her to his shoulder.

"Where to?" he whispered.

"Take next left! Go get Rexa!"

It wasn't long before they found themselves in a different cavern. Jordon had to duck, since this one was considerably lower. Seda was delighted and began gathering up possessions. She chattered with another female gnome. This one was just as frail, but had graying-blonde hair. She, too, began gathering things at a rapid pace. A male gnome came in from another tunnel. He looked similar to Seda, but much broader. Torn and ragged clothing in more places than Grup's adorned his body. He listened to the chatter and glanced over at the opening, which was too small for the party to get into. Finally, he pulled out some packs for them. Jordon heard Grup's name, and Seda replied something angrily in Gnomish.

Finally, the three gnomes came over to the archway. Seda introduced them.

"This Blul, and this Rexa."

"A pleasure," Jordon smiled.

"You take us surface?" Blul asked.

"If you'd like to go," Jordon replied.

"We go!" Blul took out a stick and began tapping on the rocks around the archway. After a moment, he put the stick back in his pocket.

"Up!" Seda said to Kenyer.

"This is going to get tricky if we need to fight," Jordon noted as Kenyer lifted the gnome.

"Give them to us," Aiya suggested. "We can...."

"No," Odessa interrupted. "Give them to me. They can ride on my back and hold on to the harness. It'll be easier for you if we need to fight. I can't fight. I don't know how. I can at least help this way."

"Blul walk," the gnome stated firmly. Jordon smiled as the small man walked nobly by.

"Rexa walk," the little, graying-blonde said and started off down the tunnel.

"Where to, Seda?" Kenyer said with a smirk as he placed her on Odessa's back.

"That way," Seda pointed in the direction the other two went.

"Do you think they'll be missed?" Annese whispered to her brother.

"That will depend on how much they do," Fuzz replied for him. "If they are the cooks, they'll be missed."

"They aren't the cooks," Jordon replied, looking in the basket at the sleeping longairits. He patted Fang's head. The ortik seemed interested in them. "But I'm sure they're more concerned with his injuries than the location of the gnomes."

"We're going to need more food," Jadara whispered to Du'kai. "We don't have any as it is."

"Seda take care," the little gnome on Odessa's back replied. "Take left," she ordered.

"No! Right!" Blul grumbled.

"Left! Blul fool! Right is center."

"Left," Rexa agreed, making the turn.

"That's what I said! Right!" Blul argued, pointing in the direction they were going. Rexa simply shook her head.

"This is gonna to be fun," Jordon heard Annese giggle. Odessa nodded with a grin.

"Yea," Jeremy scowled at his sister. "About as fun as listening to you, Jacobi, and Ana!" Jordon nudged his friend in warning.

The little gnomes led them up one tunnel and down another. Left, then right. Right, then left. The number of tunnels was amazing. It was a complete catacomb under the rocks. The tunnels finally let out into a large formation of shelves etched into walls. Stacks of bags and dried foods were piled on the shelves.

"Food," Seda pointed with a grin.

"Fill up, fellas," Kenyer said to the guys.

"Hey! My backpack!" Annese exclaimed, looking into a corner. She opened it to check inside. Any food she had wasn't there, but the blanket and candles were still there. She came out of the corner with two others—Tyler's and Odessa's.

Working furiously, Jordon and Jeremy filled up backpacks they found in the storage room and handed them off to the others. Odessa grabbed a couple of sacks of vegetables and tied them to the harness she still wore. Annese grabbed veggies for Odessa's pack and more dried fruits for the one her brother handed her. The gnomes and Fuzz put as many small things into their pockets as they could carry. Kenyer and Jadara found blankets in one corner. They gathered together back in the middle when they couldn't fit anymore.

"Well, well, well," a grating, deep voice mocked. "Did we get enough to eat?"

Jordon joined the others in turning sideways towards the arch to see one Miknar standing there with an axe in his hands. He tapped it gently in his other hand. His ruddy, broad face wore a smug expression. They were trapped.

"Isn't this cozy," he smiled evilly. "What do we have? Hmmm, let's see. We have four mortals, a horsy thingy, four dark.... whatever you are, and what? Our very own gnomes? Is this how you repay us?"

"Repay?" Blul yelled at him. "For what? Hungry? Whips? Bruise!" He pointed to his hip.

"I call the shots, pip," the Miknar yelled at him. "And the prisoners. How sweet! I get the prisoners and the traitors. This will make a wonderful dinner!"

A metal pipe came out of the side of the archway and smacked the Miknar in the back of the head. With a stunned expression, the Miknar slowly leaned forward, falling to the floor with a thud. A strange rolling machine came into view. The body was similar to a car, but much smaller. The wheels rolled soundlessly. Two large metallic arms with two-pronged claws on the ends were attached to the back and arched over the cab. The clear cockpit shield raised suddenly. Grup stood up with a smile.

"Grup change mind. Help. We go!" he smiled.

"Yay, Grup!" the gnomes exclaimed and ran for the car. They quickly climbed into the cab. "Big ones follow us!" Jordon chuckled at the gnome's ingenuity. Yep, they were going to need him.

The pathway zigged and zagged through the huge, thick stone of the island. Several times, Jordon questioned if the gnomes really knew where they were going. Still, they followed. What other choice did they have?

They had been traveling for a couple of hours without any more incidents. Jordon wanted to believe they were finally safe. Thought too soon. Out of nowhere, the ground trembled. Jordon glanced up at the ceiling as some dust rained down. The Drelts looked at each other worriedly. Kenyer urged them to pick up pace. Fang scratched at Jeremy's legs with a whine and hopped up, wanting to be carried.

"Something's wrong," Jeremy observed a few moments after picking up the pup. "He's shaking."

"Earthquake?" Jordon asked.

The ground shook again, only much more violently. Jordon stumbled. Jadara was knocked off her feet. Du'kai held the wall for stability. Tyler and Odessa grasped each other to stay on their feet. Grup stopped the machine as the pathway narrowed. He popped the cockpit and jumped out, followed by the other gnomes.

"Run!" he ordered the others urgently. "Hurry!"

"Why? What's wrong?" Fuzz questioned as he made another notation on his papers.

"Attack!" Rexa shouted, pushing the Kaptrix. "Move!"

"Attack from what?" Odessa cantered along.

"Rockeaters!" Blul urged. "Dig tunnels. Eat us!"

Jordon didn't really understand what the gnomes were talking about, but their urgency was undeniable. Something was eating through the rocks to get to them. The group ran on ahead. Jordon and Tyler picked up the gnomes and tossed them on Odessa's back for speed.

"How much farther to the transport pad?" Kenyer asked.

"Far," Seda replied, holding on to Odessa's waist.

"Keep in mind they're only two feet tall," Jordon whispered.

"Heard that!" Grup growled.

"Sorry," Jordon blushed, embarrassed.

The ground continued to tremble. Each quake became more violent inside the narrow tunnels. One quake knocked everyone off their feet. Annese screamed as an enormous boulder broke free over her head and came smashing down.

"Annese!" Jeremy cried from the floor.

Luckily, it wedged itself between the narrowing walls, leaving a gap about three feet high under it. Jordon grasped her arms and pulled her out.

"Boy, are you lucky!" he hugged the shaking girl.

"Yea. Sure." Annese stared wide-eyed at the boulder as she clutched the longairits.

"Let's go," Kenyer urged the others towards Jordon. "Crawl through." Odessa was the only one who had a problem with this.

"Centaus don't crawl," she explained.

"Lay down," Jeremy instructed as he crawled back through the space. "We'll push you through."

"Great idea!" Jadara agreed.

Odessa lay down on the hard floor. Jadara, Kenyer, and Jeremy pushed her slowly from behind, while Jordon and Du'kai pulled the harness. She complained a little as small rocks scratched her legs and underbelly, but she could dip enough to get through. The three others followed.

"Come! Come!" Blul urged.

Another quake rocked them. Jordon turned to see the passage behind them break through. Gravel was flying everywhere and bouncing off the walls towards them. A huge, furry creature broke through the wall into the passage with a growl that reverberated in the small enclosure. The party didn't need any further incentive to put as much distance between them as possible. The creature began breaking through the narrowing tunnel, starting with the boulder.

"Run!" Jordon cried.

"Grup!" Kenyer talked and ran. "Can these creatures die?"

"Yes," Grup replied, still running. "But hard."

"Rockeaters old," Seda huffed. "Hard head."

"I don't get it," Jeremy huffed.

"Rockeaters big," Blul explained as he pushed past him. His tiny legs had some good speed.

"Put it together, Jere," Jordon pushed him. "Big, old, eats rocks, hard heads."

Back behind them, the rockeater broke through the fallen boulder. It continued widening the tunnel as it chased after them. Jeremy and Aiya looked behind them. Their eyes widened with horror. The rockeater was easily five feet high at the shoulders with matted brown and gray fur. Its head was massive, reminding Jeremy of a huge Newfoundland. The jaws were thick and powerful, with a massive neck going down to broad shoulders. The teeth that showed were razor sharp and thick as spikes. The forepaws had nails that could easily rip through rubble in a second. Jordon pushed them forward as he came up on them.

"Move it!" Jeremy cried. "Here it comes!"

Kenyer stopped and ushered everyone else ahead of him. "Jordon! Come help!" he cried. "Hold it off!"

Jordon looked at the taller man as if he were crazy, but stood beside him anyway. A volley of arrows shot over them as Aiya and Jadara took up the rear.

"What did you have in mind?" Jordon asked shakily as they watched the rockeater getting closer.

"Go for the soft spots," Kenyer instructed, pulling out his short sword.

"What soft spots?" Jordon asked incredulously as he watched wave after wave of arrows bounce off the beast. "I say run!"

"Stand your ground!" Kenyer encouraged, getting ready. "Wait... Wait... Now!" the Drelt yelled and charged at the thing with the massive jaws.

Jordon shook his head at the Drelt. Crazy. With a sigh, Jordon followed Kenyer. He knew he couldn't move like the Drelt, but he'd do his best to keep the party safe, especially Aiya. An arrow flew past him and landed in the beast's paw. The creature yelped and growled.

"Hey! That's my head!" Jordon yelled behind him.

"I know where I'm aiming!" Aiya yelled back. "Just don't zig-zag."

Kenyer had already swung at the creature. In retaliation, the rockeater snapped at him. Kenyer dodged right and dug his sword in the creature's paw. Jordon swiped at the other side, giving the creature a haircut.

"Aw! Man! This thing stinks!" Jordon cried.

"Move!" Kenyer yelled at him as the huge head moved towards him.

Jordon dodged back and did a backswing with Sharijol. The sword cut through the beast's nose, causing a deep gash. Suddenly, Sharijol began to glow, slowly getting brighter. A slight hum emanated from it. The creature did a double-take. It relaxed as its eyes focused on the sword. It sat down, staring at the sword.

"What gives?" Jordon exclaimed. As he moved Sharijol, the beast's head followed it.

"It's mesmerized," Kenyer murmured, lowering his weapon. "Can you control it?"

"Beats me," Jordon replied. "Eater, down!" he tried. The beast didn't move. "OK Eater, stay!" Slowly, Jordon moved backwards. The beast followed calmly. "I don't get it," he looked at Kenyer.

"Me, either," Kenyer agreed. "But he makes a great blockade for the Miknars that are probably following him."

"Let him follow?" Jordon smirked.

"Sure, as long as he doesn't eat us."

"What about other rockeaters?" Jordon asked.

"We'll cross that bridge when we come to it," Kenyer advised, starting back towards the others. "Just don't put your sword away. I think that's what's keeping him calm."

"Ya think?" Jordon murmured sarcastically. He hoisted Sharijol over his shoulder and walked back towards the party. The beast followed calmly, eyes focused on the sword, while Sharijol hummed softly. Kenyer fell into step next to him, checking behind them often to insure the beast's cooperation.

"What...." Aiya stumbled, staring at the rockeater.

"Don't know, don't ask." Jordon turned her around. "Just keep walking."

"We need to gather our arrows," Jadara darted around the beast.

"Something about that sword you forgot to tell me?" Jeremy asked with raised brows.

"Don't ask me. We'll need to ask Zelmar when we see him again."

Calmly the party moved on towards a narrow crevice in the rock face. The gnomes happily went through, then stopped.

"Come. Come!" Grup encouraged.

"Um, we can't," Du'kai said, looking at the crevice. "It's too small. We can't fit."

"I have an idea," Jordon smirked. "Here, Grup! Take my sword. Let's see if the rockeater will follow it." The small gnome came from the crevice and reached for the heavy sword. Blul came out to help him carry it. The two disappeared into the crevice again.

The rest of the party squeezed to the sides as the rockeater followed the sword. When it couldn't get to the sword, it shook its head and growled. Opening its mouth wide, it chomped at the rock in the way.

"Yes! Go slowly, Grup! Give the guy a chance to clear the path before you move on," Jordon instructed.

"O... kay?" came the hesitant reply.

Slowly, the rockeater cleared a path big enough for the party to fit through. It finally came out into a smooth, glowing tunnel. This one had niches in the walls. Like the first tunnel they saw, there were small alcoves for growing things, burials, and storage. Grup happily gave Jordon back his sword.

"Look!" Odessa said, holding up a bow from one alcove. "There's some funny metal clothes in here, too. And some arrows!" Jeremy glanced at the excited girl.

"Armor?" Jeremy questioned, moving towards her.

"This is a Drelt bow," Jadara noted, taking it from her. "And a good one at that!"

"There are swords in here as well." Jeremy handed a dusty silver long sword to Jordon.

Jordon twirled it around his wrist. "Lightweight. Well balanced. What do you think, Kenyer?"

Kenyer handled the sword as well, twirling it and slashing the air. "I've never seen anything like this," he mused. "It needs a good sharpening, but it's much better than the one I swiped."

"I have a sharpening stone," Tyler offered. "Riemer gave it to me with the axe. Do you want to use it?"

"Maybe when we've stopped for the night," the Drelt smiled at the boy. "Right now, I think we need to keep moving."

"Do you suppose these belong to other people who have come through here?" Fuzz asked worriedly.

"That would be a good guess," Du'kai agreed. He was looking at some of the armor plates. "These are way too big for the Miknars."

"Here's another bow," Odessa said from the back of the alcove.

"'Dess, come out of there!" Jeremy called urgently. "There could be a trap in there!"

Quick as a wink, the fearful Centaus jumped out of the treasure trove in two bounds. She stared back in time to see something slither along the armor.

"I... I think something's in there," she whispered.

"Then let's leave it," Jordon advised. "Come along." He began leading the rockeater down the hall.

Odessa tried to give the bow to Aiya. "You keep it. When we stop, I'll teach you to use it," Aiya smiled at the girl. "With a little practice, you'll be an expert."

Odessa gave her a grateful smile. "No one has ever offered to teach me before, other than my father, and he says I'm still too young." A sad expression came over Odessa's features as she thought of her father.

"Come on," Tyler nudged her. "My cousin will get us home. Don't worry."

Odessa smiled bravely at her friend. "Right."

"Jordon," Jeremy called from the next cave.

"What?"

"Do you recall the picture we saw of the palace's crystal?"

"Yea, what about it?" Jordon came over to his friend. The rockeater came up right behind him.

"What do you think of this?" Jeremy emerged from the little cave carrying a blue crystal piece about the size of a bowling ball. It had clearly been shattered off something else, but was smooth on the other sides. It glimmered softly in the dim light.

"Wow!" Jordon exclaimed lowly. He examined the intricate cuts and angles of the crystal.

"It's beautiful!" Odessa whispered with wide eyes.

"I think we should bring it to Narim," Jordon suggested.

"I agree, but how do we carry it?"

"Do you still have that bag Zelmar gave us before we left?"

"I don't know. Let me look." He handed the rock to Jordon.

Jordon watched Jeremy search through his pack. Lantern, clothes, snacks, the food they'd just put in it—all of it and more came out of the pack and onto the floor. At length, he pulled a large belt pouch from the bottom. It was made of soft brown leather with a tie at the top.

"Let's see if this works," he summarized, holding it up for the crystal.

"You're going to fit a basketball in that?" Annese chided. The bag was only a third as big as the crystal.

"Maybe." Slowly Jeremy managed to get the opening around the bottom of the crystal. The bag seemed to stretch over it, then collapsed in on itself. "Wow!" Jeremy peered into the top of the bag. He could barely see the gem they had just put into it. Jordon nodded, satisfied.

"Is it really in there?" Tyler asked worriedly.

"It's there!" Jeremy nodded. "See?" He held the bag out for Tyler to look into.

"A bag of holding," Du'kai exclaimed in awe. "I've never seen one. They're incredibly rare!"

"Keep going!" Seda pushed her way through the small group.

"Right," Jeremy nodded with a chuckle. He pushed the bag into Jordon's pack, then reloaded his. They ran to catch up to the others.

The clip-clop of hooves and nails echoed off the glass-smooth floor. Behind them, the rockeater followed Jordon's sword in his strange trance. Fang had finally moved to the floor again, happily roaming ahead with the gnomes. Fuzz continued to map their progress. Time passed as they moved down the long tunnel.

TYLER

"Something's wrong," Tyler whispered to Kenyer.

"What?" Kenyer replied, immediately looking back at the rockeater. It seemed content.

"Something's wrong. This is too easy!"

"Maybe the Miknars think the rockeater did us in."

"I don't think so. They seem like the kind of guys that want to be sure the job is complete."

"You think so?" Kenyer peered up ahead. He wasn't sure the boy knew what he was talking about. Nothing was moving, and nothing seemed to be there.

"Maybe. I think we should move the gnomes to the middle of the party. They're the most defenseless."

"Stop!" Kenyer called up ahead.

The party came to a halt. Carefully, Kenyer explained their discussion. Jeremy looked up ahead and agreed.

"I've been thinking the same thing," he nodded to Tyler.

"This is the perfect setup for an ambush," Tyler defended his feeling.

"How do we know?" Aiya asked.

"We don't," Jordon devised a plan quickly. "So we prepare for it as if it is."

"We need to put the weakest ones in the middle," Kenyer explained.

Tyler watched the exchange with interest. Annese looked at Odessa and nodded. They moved to the middle of the party. After much arguing, the gnomes also moved to the middle. Fuzz moved right behind the rockeater. Jordon and Kenyer took the lead. Jadara and Aiya moved to either side of the rockeater. Jeremy and Tyler took up the rear.

"I have an idea," Tyler whispered. Every head turned to look at him. "The gnomes aren't strangers here. What if we sent one of them ahead to see what's up there?"

Kenyer shook his head. "A scout might be a great idea, but by now, every Miknar knows that the gnomes have abandoned their posts. They'll be looking for them."

"What about the fuzzballs?" Jordon asked Annese.

Annese shook her head. "They're only babies. Besides, how would we understand them if they came back with information?"

"Good point."

"Let's stay together," Kenyer suggested. "There's safety in numbers. Besides, we aren't sure whose side this beast is going to be on if it comes to a battle."

"As long as Sharijol keeps glowing, ours," Jordon replied. I hope, he thought to himself. Looking at the soft glow coming off his sword, he whispered, "Weird." Tyler nodded in agreement.

The party kept at a slow but steady pace. Tyler looked up when Kenyer finally called a halt to the party. He motioned for Du'kai to come up front.

"Look up ahead. What do you see?" he instructed.

Du'kai peered up into the darkness. "Something is moving. Looks like people. Maybe a dozen of them." Tyler strained to see, but couldn't see anything.

"Behind that," Kenyer encouraged.

"It looks like a platform. It's raised up off the floor about a forearm. There's a soft glow emanating from it, but it's dim."

"The pad?" Jordon asked.

"I think so," Kenyer mused. "But something is guarding it."

"To prevent our escape," Jadara finished. Kenyer nodded.

This was going to be an ugly battle. "I think we should leave the girls and Fuzz and the gnomes here," Jordon said thoughtfully.

"I'll stay with them," Du'kai volunteered. "I don't have a weapon, remember?"

"Jadara and Aiya can fight from a distance, but that means the rest of us have to get into the fray," Kenyer remarked.

"I can fight from the air," Tyler heard Jeremy say. "They won't be expecting attacks from the air, and they won't know how to handle it. It will serve both as an attack and a diversion."

"True," Aiya agreed. "They have axes, not arrows."

"And the ceiling is high enough that I'll be out of reach," Jeremy pointed out. Tyler's head spun with the speed the preparations were being made.

"Do it," Jordon agreed. "Just be careful of our friend here." He patted the rockeater. "And take Fang with you. He'll only get hurt down here."

"No," Odessa interrupted, petting the ortik. "Leave Fang with us. If we get attacked, he could be a protector."

"As big as he gets? That's an understatement," Jadara exclaimed. "His size alone would frighten something off."

"Just remember you have to hang on to him," Jeremy warned his sister. "He's not going to stay easily, especially if he senses we're in trouble."

"Tyler? Are you coming?"

Tyler looked up into Jordon's eyes. "Umm..."

A hand fell to Jordon's shoulder. Tyler looked up at Kenyer's understanding eyes.

"Let's leave him here to protect the girls," he suggested with a kind smile.

"We could use him," Jordon said thoughtfully.

"He's not ready," Kenyer directed Jordon away. "It's one thing to squash a bug. It's another to kill something that looks like you. If he needs to protect the girls, he'll rise to the occasion, but don't force it."

Tyler breathed a sigh of relief and nodded when Kenyer looked back and winked.

"Let's do this, people," Kenyer announced.

"Yea," Jordon agreed, smirking at his cousin. "My stomach is growling as it is. I hate to battle on an empty stomach! Everybody know what to do?"

Tyler noticed each person nod. He drew in a deep, steadying breath and nodded in agreement. Jeremy pulled the blanket from his pack and laid it on the ground. He froze it solid, got on, and levitated himself into the air up near the ceiling. He followed the others down the hallway. It was a sizeable distance away. The party split up, moving to the outer walls for safety. "Good luck," he whispered shakily as they moved out of sight.

JORDON

The moving figures at the end of the hallway stopped. They had moved into the shadows. Kenyer lifted his hand for the party to stop. He pointed toward the shadows. With each point, he held up the number of fingers for the number of Miknars there. They each nodded their understanding. They'd be outnumbered three to one. Not a good fight. Jeremy rose and found a small ledge high on the walls. The girls moved to the middle of the tunnel. Quickly, they let off a volley of arrows. Muffled screams echoed in the tunnel, indicating their target was found.

The party moved forward slowly. The arrows continued to fly into the shadows. With sudden movement, the Miknars charged the party.

"Keep your back to the wall!" Kenyer whispered loudly to Jordon.

Jeremy picked his targets carefully. "Congelo Somes," he'd whisper, then chuckled, as the Miknar was unable to move, a layer of ice covering his body. He took out a couple of others with his light spell.

To Jordon's surprise, as he swung his sword to clash with a Miknar, the rockeater reached over him and quickly devoured the man. Not what he'd wanted, but it worked. One by one, they disposed of Miknars that way.

Kenyer found himself in battle with four at one time. The girls aimed carefully at the Miknars and picked off two. Kenyer fought with ferocity. Jordon moved over to help. He swung Sharijol at one, pleased when the rockeater took the instruction. The remaining Miknars raced down the tunnel in fear. Jordon followed them, remembering they'd left the others down there. With the beast and Jordon pulling up the rear, the Miknars didn't even look at the group left behind.

"What happened?" Tyler asked wide-eyed, as he lowered his axe to watch them all run by.

"The rockeater fought on our side. When I swung at the Miknar, he picked him off," Jordon smiled. "Come on. We need to get out of here before they return with reinforcements." The group followed Jordon back down the tunnel towards the transport pad.

"That was amazing!" Jeremy cried with glee. "I wouldn't have thought it possible!"

"That was strange," Aiya remarked. "What makes a rock-eating creature eat people?"

Seda shook her head. "You no listen! Rockeater eat **everything**!"

"Ah!" the group all said together.

"Now how do we send it home?" Du'kai asked. "We can't take it with us."

"I think I know," Jordon nodded. "Let's go. Everyone go through the pad."

"Should we have something to eat first?" Odessa asked.

"Dinner would be nice," Fuzz agreed.

"No," Jordon decided. "Hopefully, we can grab a bite at the next pad. They might come back with reinforcements."

"Agreed," Kenyer nodded. "And it's getting dark. We need to find someplace to bed down for the night. I'll go through first."

"Remember, you cannot come back this way from the same pad," Fuzz reminded him. "We can only go forward."

Kenyer stepped up onto the platform and disappeared. Du'kai followed behind him. Tyler watched them go through one by one. Aiya and Jadara went next, followed by Fuzz. Annese and Odessa helped the gnomes climb up onto the platform. They followed. Jordon nodded to Jeremy.

"See ya on the other side," Jeremy whispered. "Don't be long."

"If I am, I'm done for. Go on without me." Jeremy stepped onto the platform. Tyler looked at his cousin, fear in his eyes. "Go on," Jordon instructed.

"I'll wait for you."

"Go on!" Jordon ordered. "I'll be right behind you."

"Then why can't I wait?"

"'Cause I'm gonna have just enough time to get on the pad myself. Now go!"

Tyler looked uncertainly at Jordon, but reluctantly stepped on the pad.

Jordon was the only one left. He sighed with relief now that Tyler had gone. He turned to look at the rockeater. He felt kind of funny about it: relieved and sad at the same time. The beast had come to devour him, yet it stood by him. Well, it stood by Sharijol. He wasn't sure how this was going to work. Carefully, Jordon climbed up onto the edge of the platform. He suspected he wouldn't have long. He reached out slowly and patted the beast on the nose.

"You've been a good boy," he mumbled. "Thank you. Go on home."

With a last stroke, Jordon sheathed Sharijol. The glowing sword gone, the beast shook its head. As it spotted Jordon on the platform, it growled menacingly. Not waiting to see what would happen, Jordon stepped backward onto the pad and disappeared.

JUJENE

Slowly, the wizard moved to his master's chamber. He stood at the door for what seemed like forever until the master acknowledged him.

"Is it done?" Mikkel asked from his bed.

"Not exactly, highness."

Mikkel sat up and glared at the scrawny sorcerer. "What do you mean, 'not exactly'?" he growled menacingly.

The wizard sighed. "They appear to have gotten away again."

Mikkel jumped up from the bed and stalked towards the man. "What!? How? You sent the entire Miknar empire and a rockeater after them!"

"Well, they outwitted the Miknars with the staff. Then they befriended the gnomes, who took them through the smaller tunnels. The boy's sword mesmerized the rockeater. They ended up using the rockeater to defend themselves. I had no way of knowing the rockeater would befriend them."

Mikkel's pale face was turning red with anger. The veins at his neck were sticking out, and the ones on his forehead were so large they seemed ready to burst. He let out a roar that echoed through the chamber.

"On the other side, we can get them in the next chamber. It appears to be quite clear of intrusions," Jujene suggested.

Mikkel pointed a finger at the sorcerer. He opened his mouth to say something, but nothing came out. He shook his finger, then returned to his bed angrily; kicking the trunk at the foot of the bed.

The sorcerer sighed. He returned to his room shakily and looked at his crystal ball. He needed sleep, but if he slept, he might miss a vital opportunity. He moved to the fireplace and poured another cup of energy potion. It was going to be a long night.

15 – INSIDE THE GEODE

JEREMY

Jeremy gathered his wits as Jordon bumped into him when he got off the transporter pad. Each person stood still, admiring the view in awe. Around them, millions of crystals sparkled in the light from the walls. Pastel blues, purples, pinks, whites, and greens blended together as they winked at the newcomers. The crystals were attached to every surface - the ceiling, the walls, the floor, even each other.

"Wow!" Annese exclaimed in awe.

"It's like a giant geode!" Jeremy murmured.

"It's beautiful," Jadara breathed.

"I've never seen anything like it!" Odessa stared at the colors on the wall as she turned in circles. "Look at the picture they made here!" She pointed to the wall behind the transport stone.

"Beautiful!" Aiya whispered.

"Can we take some of these?" Tyler asked, touching a crystal on the floor. "They'd be priceless!"

"Don't. Touch. Anything!" Jordon snapped at him. Tyler instantly pulled his hand back.

"Why?"

"This isn't a cave on Earth. We don't know what will set off a trap or a defense. Remember the crystal balls you walked through?"

"Oh, yea." Tyler's voice dipped as he remembered the explosion they had barely escaped.

"And the trees?"

"Yea."

"Don't take anything for granted!" Jordon scowled at his cousin. Tyler nodded.

"So, what next?" Kenyer asked.

"Dinner!" Seda announced. "Big things sit!" They all laughed, but had to agree with the gnome. Soon the rations they had procured from the Miknars were being passed around and shared.

"Hey, Fuzz," Jeremy asked between bites. "You don't happen to have this on your map, do you?" He reached a beef jerky out to Fang. The pup took it gratefully and laid down to gnaw on it.

"I'm afraid not, Master Jeremy," Fuzz said sadly. He looked around at the crystals. "I certainly would remember a place so lovely!"

"Best take some time to update your maps," Jordon suggested with a grin. "You may never be this way again."

"I'm afraid I must if I'm to complete my task," Fuzz replied, pulling out his cartography gear.

"But you won't need to," Odessa informed him, swallowing a bite of food. "The new king is going to put the

islands back together." The young Centaus became
nervous as all motion stopped and all eyes stared at her.

"Excuse me?" Aiya replied.

Tyler nodded. "Riemer, he's the old guy that rescued
us on Kaptrix, said that the next step since the new king
was in place was to return As... this place... back to where
it came from. He said that the king would be looking for the
blue crystal so he could bring the islands back together
and send it back."

Jeremy looked at Jordon with concern. Narim did
say something about a blue crystal like the one they'd
found. Is that what he wanted to do? They both would bet
Narim never thought about people living underground.
They'd have to stop him or set a different plan into action.

"What about the people who live down here?" Jadara
asked worriedly.

"That thought crossed our minds, too," Odessa
replied.

"If the king was to replace the crystal in its holding
beams," Fuzz mused aloud, "it would cause another
cataclysm. It would cause the islands to merge back
together as one. One can only assume it would send the
island back to the dimension it originally came from."

"Wait!" Jeremy shook his head and looked at Fuzz.
"You knew about this?"

"Only from childhood lessons," Fuzz shrugged.
"Every Kaptrix learns his history about our time living on
the surface. That is why our villages are fashioned so."

"So, you're trying to tell me that the Kaptrix lived on
the surface at one time?" Jordon asked, absently handing
Fang another beef stick.

"Yes. In a beautiful forest near an ocean. Others were there as well. They were seers. Mystical people, they were. No one knows what happened to them."

"They're still there," Jordon smirked at Jeremy.

"Mystic Island," Jeremy grinned back.

"Yep." Jordon looked over at Aiya. "What about you guys?" he asked. "What's your history?"

Aiya shrugged. "I was never one for history. I rarely listened to those lessons." She blushed brightly as she made the admission.

"I recall hearing something about us living on the surface once before," Jadara scowled as she struggled to remember the lesson. "But it wasn't a pleasant experience."

"We were at war with another people there. We were dark, and they were light. Both people wanted the forest for themselves," Du'kai added.

"Sounds like Elthoria to me," Jeremy sighed. "Eliramond was pretty narrow-minded." Jordon nodded in agreement.

"What about those snake guys?" Odessa shrank back. "I wouldn't want them on my island. The Harpies are nasty enough."

"And, of course, our Miknar friends would only create a war with others of their kind," Kenyer noted.

"Krilts," Jeremy murmured. "And what about the wizard ruins? I wouldn't want those destroyed."

"Big things not understand," Rexa shook her head.

"Don't understand what?" Du'kai asked, sipping some water.

"Not all creatures underground from big shaky thing. Some belong here."

"Your people?" Odessa asked.

"No, no, no!" Rexa huffed. "Gnomes from surface. Found crack to explore. Fell down, down, down! Never get back."

"Snaky things live in rocks always," Blul tried to explain. "And big wormy things."

"But others..." Annese thought. "We can't let them die with another earthquake."

"Nothing is going to happen while we're down here," Jordon announced confidently. "They're waiting for us to return. When we get back to the castle, we'll all sit down with Narim and tell him about our discoveries. After that, it's going to be up to him."

"First things first," Jeremy agreed. "First, we have to find our way back to the surface."

"I'm all for it," Kenyer agreed. "But how do we go from here? No path." He nodded towards the sea of crystals before them.

"There should be other transport pads on the island," Du'kai said quietly, gazing over the cavern. "And look. The crystals don't form around the stones."

"They do make pretty pictures behind them, though," Odessa added with a smile. She gazed up at the green and brown mountains with the sunshine coming up over the rise.

Annese saw Tyler reach out to a crystal on the wall behind him. He tried to shake it loose. Much to his dismay, it stuck fast.

"What are you doing?" she whispered, trying to keep the longairits together. They needed to get out of the basket for a bit. "Jordon said not to touch them!"

"I want to take a sample with me, but I can't get the crystal off the wall. If I had a pocketknife, I would be able to pry one off," he replied in hushed tones.

"What about your axe?"

"Too big. I'd break it."

Annese looked around as she thought. She spied her brother.

"Hey, Jeremy," Annese called over to her brother as she grasped another longairit. "Do you have a pocketknife I can use?"

"Pfft!" Tyler choked on his retort.

"Sure," Jeremy replied, reaching into his pocket. He pulled out a small pocketknife and tossed it to his sister, then returned to his conversation.

Annese caught it carefully. "Thanks," she smiled. Subtly, she slid it behind her to Tyler as she reached down for another fluff ball. "No, you don't! Stay together." Tyler pried a crystal free and just as subtly gave Annese back the pocketknife. He winked at her when she looked over her shoulder with a grin.

"Here," Odessa giggled, reaching for a longairit. "I'll help. It should be close to naptime anyway."

"I think that's the problem," Aiya giggled, bringing one back to Annese. "That's all they've done today is nap; at least, since we rescued them from the kitchen." She carefully returned the black and white ball to the basket.

"They need some food!" Odessa exclaimed, realizing the longairits were hungry. The girls watched Odessa move quickly as she pulled out some roots and vegetables they had secured from the Miknar stores. She worked with the few items she had, using Jeremy's pocketknife to chop them down into grated bits, then mixed them with water. She added some bread to thicken it and mixed it all together. Taking a small water container, she poured the liquid in the bowl and put it on the floor for the longairits. They ran to it quickly. Soon, all eight of them had eaten their fill. One by one, they climbed back into their basket.

"Good thinking," Annese smiled at her friend. She'd forgotten all about feeding the little things in the rush to get out of the Miknar territory.

JORDON

"We'd best pack up and get going." Jordon snapped his gaze up at Du'kai's suggestion. "Might be a good idea to get some distance before it gets dark."

"Distance to *where*?" Kenyer questioned.

"We go!" Grup announced, getting up and tying a small satchel to his belt. "We lead!"

"Sure," Jadara shrugged. "They're the only ones who can fit between the crystals. We'll need to pick our way through."

"This isn't going to be easy," Aiya agreed.

"At least we won't set off an explosion," Jordon replied, following the group with a murmured, "I hope." In reality, he didn't have any better ideas.

"Very good," Fuzz agreed. "That was not very nice."

"Not at all." Jeremy shook his head, then broke into a grin, thinking about it. "But what a story!"

Travel in this cave was slow and tedious. While the gnomes could easily fit between crystals, the others couldn't. Taking steps was difficult as they tried to take a path that would do the least amount of damage. Following the gnomes was no picnic, either. Many times, the crystals were as tall, if not taller, than the gnomes.

"These crystals must have been here hundreds of years," Du'kai mused, passing between some.

"Well, it's been over five hundred years since the cataclysm," Jeremy replied. "I wonder how they got here?"

"Well, some crystals form from sedimentary rock," Tyler explained. "Cavernous areas, usually spaces in limestone, get water and minerals inside. Over time, the molecular bands link together to form crystals. Other crystals form by heating and cooling, like in the case of Diamonds. The heating forms incredible pressure around the carbon. As it cools, the carbon gives way to a more formatted structure, thus creating a diamond."

"Thank you, Mr. Know-it-all," Jordon grumbled at him.

"That's not very nice," Aiya scowled at Jordon. "He was trying to answer Jeremy's question."

"So, you're saying that these crystals were formed by either water or pressure?" Du'kai asked Tyler.

"I think so. That's the usual ways crystals are formed. I'd have to get one under a microscope to examine the crystalline structure to know for sure."

"Under a what?" Du'kai scowled in confusion.

"A microscope," Tyler began. "It's a device used to magnify things so large you can see almost inside them."

"It's two pieces of curved glass and a tube," Jeremy tried to explain, "that makes things look bigger."

Jordon rolled his eyes. His cousin's smarts were going to drive him crazy.

"Unless they're made of sugar," Annese giggled, taking the conversation back to the crystals.

"That's rock candy!" Jeremy pushed his sister teasingly.

"Sorry. It's been so long since I've had sweets. I guess I'm craving it." Annese tried to make her voice sound remorseful, but she couldn't get rid of the giggle.

Jeremy smirked, reached into the pocket on the side of his pack, and pulled out the last of his candy bar. He handed it to Annese. Her eyes lit up like stars.

"Thank you!" she whispered in awe.

"Just don't tell anyone. I don't have anymore," he whispered. Jordon smirked at his best friend. As much as he complained about her, he really did care about his sister. He glanced over at Tyler and felt a small pang of guilt. Reality: he cared about Tyler, too.

Travel seemed to take forever. Stepping on the crystals hurt Jordon's feet, even through his sneakers. Carefully, they picked their way across the cavern for hours. The sparkle of the crystals made everything look the same. Several times Du'kai needed to stop and reset his mind to be certain they were going in the right direction.

"Can't we find somewhere to sleep?" Annese grumbled as she dragged behind. "My legs hurt!"

"Mine, too," Odessa agreed. "These crystals are digging into my hooves. I think I'm bleeding."

"They are kinda sharp," Tyler agreed. "And we've been on our feet all day!"

"No day," Grup trudged along. "Night."

"Exactly!" Annese whined. "It's time to go to sleep!"

"Even Fang is out," Jeremy nodded, holding the sleeping pup in his arms.

"Ken, are you thinking what I'm thinking?" Jadara whispered.

Kenyer nodded. "Yep. We're in trouble... again."

"Why is that?" Fuzz asked.

"Can't you feel it?" Kenyer asked the Kaptrix.

"Feel what?"

"The temperature is getting warmer," Aiya said absently, her elven sight gazing into the cavern ahead of them.

"So?" Jordon questioned.

"It's rising quickly," Aiya explained. "It's generally an indication of atmospheric trouble."

"We'd better find our way out of here fast then," Jordon remarked, suddenly concerned.

"But which way?" Odessa whined in exasperation.

"Come, come, big things!" Seda called. "Follow vision!"

"Vision?" the group all looked towards the gnome. Sure enough, wavering in the air was a see-through vision. The woman was pale and pretty, with a heart-shaped face and long, curly hair waving behind her. She had wings on her back coming through a pure white Victorian gown. She smiled warmly and beckoned the visitors to follow her. She didn't speak, just motioned with her hand. She continued to move backwards.

"A ghost?" Jeremy whispered to Jordon suspiciously.

Jordon shrugged. "That'd be my guess; but she doesn't seem to be in pain or anything. You know, that sad look ghosts are supposed to have."

"Maybe she's not sad."

"Should we really follow a specter?" Du'kai asked skeptically.

"She seems to know where she's going," Aiya pointed out.

"Let's try it," Kenyer suggested. "After all, none of us knows where we're going."

"I got a bad feeling about this," Jadara mumbled, falling into line. Jordon nodded in agreement.

The ghost led them for more than an hour. She would travel, then wait patiently for them to catch up. The group had a hard time keeping up with her. They were tired, and the younger ones were dragging. The crystals scratched and cut into feet and ankles. Everything looked the same. Jordon could find no landmarks to judge from. The air was getting hotter, wetter, and heavier, sapping energy and making it harder to move. It reminded Jordon of summers near the ocean—hot and sticky. And worst of all, it was getting dark. Jeremy lit his staff to shed some light for them to travel by. The gnomes just kept going and encouraging the others.

"Rest spot!" Grup called.

The ghost had stopped over a clearing. Jordon surveyed the area. It was the only flatland in view. Tyler, Annese, and Odessa instantly dropped to the ground. The gnomes gathered together with their little bags and began pulling out tattered blankets. Kenyer and Jordon took a walk around the clearing, looking for any dangers. Jordon looked over his shoulder. Jeremy, Du'kai, and the girls pulled out blankets and food. Fang was already curled up next to Tyler to continue sleeping. Eventually, everyone settled down for the night.

"I'll take first watch," Jordon said to Kenyer. "You took it last night."

"O.K.," he agreed. "Be sure to wake Du'kai for his turn."

"I will. Night."

Jordon sat on his blanket in the middle of the group. Something seemed wrong, but he just couldn't place it. The air was heavy and sticky. The ground below him was warm, as if it had been baking in a summer sun all day, and it glimmered in the dim light of Tyler's lantern. The many reflecting patterns and colors that swirled through the flat surface reminded Jordon of the crystals. The flat rock appeared to be made of the same stuff the crystals were. But why was it flat? The crystals were sharp. Every now and then he'd hear a voice.

"Get out of there!"

He looked around but couldn't see anything. The voice seemed to be off in the distance, and the ghost was gone.

A tinkling noise to one side made him turn. He watched as crystals seemed to jump up from the ground to form something. He closed his eyes, and then opened them to look again. Two columns were forming. Crystals continued to rise, fitting into places. In a short time, a torso had formed; then arms came from where shoulders would be. Jordon quickly woke Jeremy, then ran over to wake Kenyer. By the time he was done, the crystals formed a full humanoid figure, and another was starting.

"What is it?" Jeremy asked, lighting his staff.

"Outta there!" Jordon heard in the distance. He shook his head. "I don't know." He turned to Kenyer. "Did you hear that?"

"Hear what? The voice?"

"Yea."

"Yes, but I can't determine where it's coming from. Sound is echoing in the cavern."

"The crystals almost seem alive. Sort of like a swarm." Jeremy scowled. "But why build a figure? To talk to us?"

"With our current experiences," Jordon whispered, "I doubt it."

Somewhere nearby, a slight pop sounded. It echoed around them, followed by a hissing sound. The three looked around but couldn't see anything.

"Another figure is finished," Kenyer said, watching; his hand on the hilt of his sword.

"And another is starting," Jordon noted, shaking Tyler awake.

"Morning already?" Tyler grumbled. He forced his eyes open. "Can't we sleep a little more?"

"Monster. Wake up!" Jordon replied. He smirked as Tyler instantly jumped up and grasped his axe. He was learning.

The four watched as the crystals formed five figures. All at once, the five figures moved. The arms crept up to waist height. The legs lifted. The figures all looked at each other, then at the visitors. As if in sync, they all bent forward and charged the three.

"Move off into the crystals!" Jordon ordered. "Protect the others." In the meantime, he and Kenyer prepped for the attack.

JEREMY

Jeremy tripped over Aiya as he tried to move. Aiya looked up at him confused.

"Move!" Jeremy ordered urgently. He looked behind them to see one figure coming right for him.

Aiya followed his look, grabbed her bow, and ran with him. She kicked Jadara as she passed her. "Attack!" she cried.

"Don't get hit by one," Kenyer called. "Those crystals will slice you open!"

Jeremy turned around, pointed his staff at the creature and said, "Congelo Somes". The creature stopped in his tracks. Jeremy could see it trying to move. Slowly, it broke free of the spell. Jeremy's eyes widened. He didn't think that could happen.

"Sanctum fulsi de lumen," he tried as he watched Aiya's and Jadara's arrows bounce off it.

"It's a construct, Jeremy! Not an undead!" Jordon called as the bright light that should have seared the creature bounced off.

"I'm out of options," he called. "I don't know anything else!"

"Shield! Go get the girls and the gnomes together and shield them!" Jordon suggested, running past.

Jeremy ran off to find the others. Fang had woken as he approached and yawned widely. He wagged his tail happily, but suddenly realized his master's concern.

"Du'kai! Du'kai, wake up!" Jeremy shook the boy. "Wake up! Fast!"

"What is it?" Du'kai murmured, looking up.

"Wake the girls. Hurry!" he urged. "Get everyone together at the edge." He turned to gather the gnomes. "Come on, Grup! Get up!"

"Morning?" Grup stretched.

"Danger!" Jeremy pointed towards the crystalline creatures that were chasing the others. "Get over by the kids!"

Fang began growling behind him. Jeremy turned fast to see one of the crystalline creatures coming towards them. Fang was growing fast. There would be no controlling him.

"Fang, no!" Jeremy tried. The ortik continued to grow. It hunched into attack position. "No!" Jeremy ordered the pup. He moved to grasp the pup's collar, but he was nowhere fast enough.

Fang took off at a run in a direct path to intercept the creature, who was coming up on Jeremy. With a tremendous leap, Fang knocked the creature to the ground. It slid to the side with Fang on top of it and breaking apart as it hit the edge and crashed into the crystal ground. Fang leaped off and began racing after another creature.

Jeremy gathered the rest of the group together. They watched Jordon, Tyler, and Kenyer slashing at the creatures. Aiya and Jadara continued to dodge the two that were fighting with them. Their arrows did no damage to the massive creatures. Fang was heading for one. The tinkling sound behind him made Jeremy's blood run cold. The creature Fang broke apart was gathering back together.

Seda hit Grup on the shoulder. "Need boom!" she said.

"Boom?" Grup scowled, not understanding.

"Boom!" Seda repeated, moving her arms apart.

"Boom!" Blul's eyes widened with glee. He raced for his pack. Sitting on the ground, he began rummaging and mixing things in his lap. He pulled out a liquid, then put a powder in it. He rummaged more and poured a few drops of another liquid in it. He crushed something into that mixture, replaced the original stopper, and shook it up. He pulled some flexible containers from his pocket and poured a little of the mixture into each each one. As he put the contents of his pack back in, the crystalline creature stepped in front of him. Blul looked up and smiled. He picked up one container and held it up to the creature.

"For you," he offered. The creature slowly reached down and took the container. "Shake," he said, shaking his hands up and down. He stood up, picked up the other containers, and moved off towards the battles.

"Contego," Jeremy whispered, holding the staff towards the creature. He had a bad feeling about this. The slight shimmer of the area told him the shield was in place. He wondered what was so funny; the gnomes were all giggling. Annese and Odessa, realizing something was about to happen, moved closer together.

The crystalline creature looked at the container. He shook it. A slight yellow glow came over the container. He shook it again. It turned pink. He shook it again. It turned blue. He shook it again. The color turned purple, then suddenly exploded in a blinding flash of white light. The crystalline creature shattered into a rain of tiny pieces. All the other action in the chamber stopped as everyone turned to stare, except Blul. He continued running to the next golem.

The ground underneath them shook. A popping sound came from the right, followed by a hiss. Jeremy turned to see a hole formed in the ground and steam was being pushed out.

"Move!" Du'kai hollered with wide eyes. He began pushing the girls towards the crystals.

"What?" Jeremy turned to look.

Du'kai pointed to the crack in the ground that was slowly making its way towards them. "Move!" he repeated, grabbing everything he could carry.

Annese grabbed the basket and pushed it at Odessa. She helped Tyler pick up the packs and blankets. The gnomes also ran as fast as they could for possessions. They all ran for the closest crystal bank.

Grup ran towards the group carrying a blanket and a bag. He tripped on the blanket just as one of the crystalline creatures jumped in front of him. The ground below him broke into pieces, steam escaping into the air. Grup and the creature disappeared into the steam.

"Gruuuuuup!" Seda and Rexa called in horror.

"Ortis!" Jeremy cried out as another explosion rocked the cavern. The rain of crystal shards told them another creature met its match. Slowly, Grup and the creature came floating up from the steamy pit. Du'kai laid on the edge and reached out. He was just able to reach the hem of Grup's pants. With a slight tug, he moved the gnome over the bank onto the crystals. "Od" Jeremy said as he hauled the gnome to safety. The group watched the crystalline creature tumble back into the darkness as another explosion went off.

"Ofkrat!" a strange voice echoed around the cavern.

The crystalline creatures fell apart before the warriors' eyes. The war party looked around quickly, ready to attack the newcomer. Their eyes fell to an old man in rags, leaning heavily on a staff. He had gray, scraggly hair and a dirty face. His shoes were nothing more than straps and worn soles. His eyes, however, were sharp and dark.

"Solar lux lucis," Jeremy whispered to get a better look at the man. They all blinked as the light in the chamber grew.

"Who are you?" Kenyer demanded, sword ready to fight.

Jeremy watched the old man look over the injured and bleeding Drelt. His eyes moved to Aiya and Jadara. Both were heaving, bleeding from various cuts, and worn. He looked over at Jordon. The young warrior held his sword shakily and hadn't evaded injury. Cuts along his arms and torso stained his clothing. The gnome was in the best shape of them all, still clutching several of the containers. The old man started as a very large ortik sniffed his head.

"I should be asking that of you." The old man's voice was scratchy. It completed the impression of a weak, malnourished hermit. "You invade my home, go where you shouldn't, and disrupt the balance here. Your magic is dangerous."

"We didn't create them," Jordon retorted, still holding his sword aloft. "They attacked us."

"And you settle on a shelf why?" the man asked, pointing to the clearing.

"It was a clearing. We needed sleep."

"It is a thin, geologic shelf. It will break with the pressure from underneath. It will be back tomorrow, and will break tomorrow," the man said sternly.

Jeremy jumped at Tyler's voice.

"Excuse me, please," the boy interrupted. "I'm Tyler. These are my friends. Who are you?" His voice was timid and scared, but polite.

The old man looked at the voice. Something about the scared child changed the man's expression as he looked at Tyler. The old man's gaze shifted to Annese, a girl with dark skin the opposite of his, clutching a woven basket in her arms. Then shifted to Odessa, a beautiful child he probably had never seen.

"I am no one of importance to you," the old man replied quietly. "This is my home."

"This whole cavern is your home?" Odessa asked amazed.

"I live here alone. Come. I will take you to safety where you can get some sleep and bind your wounds."

Jeremy joined the others in gathering their belongings slowly. He noticed Jordon and Kenyer exchange a concerned look. Obviously, the old man knew the cavern much better than they did. Slowly, he fell in line behind all the others.

"Should we?" Jordon asked as Jeremy approached him.

"You got a better idea?" Jeremy asked. Jordon shook his head. "He's an old man. The three of us can take him if we need to, but I don't think we'll need to."

The three adventurers fell in line with the others to follow the old man.

"Are we on a path?" Odessa asked Annese

"I don't think so. Why?"

"My feet don't hurt from the crystals."

"Watch the ground as he walks," Tyler whispered.

Jeremy looked down to the ground where the old man stepped. The crystals parted and moved aside as the old man came near, clearing the ground into a smooth path. As the party moved on, the crystals all moved back into place behind Jeremy.

"Weird!" Annese whispered.

After almost an hour of travel, they came to a cave. Jeremy noticed the crystals were all over the outer walls and the arch into the cave, but once they entered the cave, there were no crystals. The walls were a smooth white stone, glowing softly. The floor was soft, almost like moss, but also white. On one side was a ledge in the wall that held jars, pots, and plates. On the opposite side was a soft-looking bed with a beat-up quilt. Someone had fashioned a chair into the wall.

"Here. Rest," the old man murmured.

"I've got bandages," Du'kai said, pulling a pile of cloth from his pocket. Jeremy borrowed a couple to wrap Fang's paws.

"Let me," Annese said to Aiya. She carefully laid her hand on the worst of Aiya's injuries and concentrated. Just like with Tyler and the longairit, her hands became warm, almost hot. Aiya sighed with the warmth. Slowly, Annese was able to help the skin close. It wasn't too long before her hands cooled. When she looked up, she was surprised to see most of Aiya's wounds had healed.

"You're a wonderful healer!" Aiya exclaimed weakly. "Why didn't you say you could heal injuries?"

Jeremy and Jordon whirled around together and stared. "You can do *what?*" they exclaimed together.

Annese smiled, embarrassed. "I can heal things. In the woods, I healed Odessa's sprained ankle, and the injured longairit, and Tyler's ribs."

"How?" Jeremy asked in confusion.

Annese just shrugged. "I don't know. It just came to me."

"Good girl," Du'kai complimented with a pat on her shoulder. "Now go help Jadara."

Jeremy went over to Kenyer. Du'kai was wrapping the bleeding wounds in cloth. The concerned look on his face made Jeremy worried. "Is he that bad?" he whispered to Du'kai.

"I don't know," the whispered reply came. "Kenyer won't tell you how badly he's hurt."

"Here. Let me try," Jeremy offered, placing the staff on Kenyer's slouched body. "Rememdium Pupillus Vulnus," he whispered. A soft yellow glow extended from the ball of the staff and enveloped Kenyer. Kenyer drew in a sharp breath. Eventually, the glow faded, leaving the Drelt alone.

"How's that?" Du'kai asked his friend. "Better?"

Kenyer nodded and smiled. "Thanks." Jeremy smiled a little and nodded in return.

"Drink, drink," Rexa ordered, bringing a cup of warm liquid over to Kenyer.

"What is it?" Ken asked.

"Gnome brew. Good health. Drink, drink! Everybody drink." She hobbled about as she poured out small amounts of the brew into tiny cups.

Kenyer accepted the brew politely. He sniffed at it and raised his brows. He looked over at Rexa, who was off handing a cup to Jordon. Glancing a hesitant look at Du'kai, Kenyer downed the brew. His eyes bulged, his mouth opened, and he let out a hoarse breath. By the looks of things, Jordon had the same reaction. The brew set his throat on fire. In a matter of seconds, however, a warmth spread throughout Kenyer's body. All the aches seemed to drift away. His muscles relaxed, and he could feel the tension seep out. He smiled as Aiya and Jadara experienced the same things.

ANNESE

Annese smiled as she worked on the soft padding of Odessa's hooves. She had watched the little gnome making the brew, and just knew it was going to have some pretty strange results. "How's that?" she asked Odessa with a grin.

Odessa, too, had been watching the reactions from the little gnome's healing brew. She giggled as she nodded. "Much better. Thanks. I'm glad I don't need any of that."

"Me, too," Annese stood up.

Du'kai sidled up to Annese. "Got enough energy left for Kenyer? Jeremy took off the edge, but he's still hurting; and I don't put much faith in the little ones' homebrew."

Annese looked over at the Drelt sitting by the wall. He had his head back and eyes closed. His face still had a slightly pained expression on it. "I think so."

"He'd really appreciate it."

Annese nodded and moved over towards him. He didn't even move as Annese laid her hands on him. As her hands warmed u, images entered her mind of injury after injury inside Kenyer's body. She focused on the ones she was being shown. After her hands had cooled, Annese looked him over. Kenyer's eyes opened a bit to look at her; a small smile creased his face. She smiled back at him.

"You are a very talented healer for one so young," he complimented. "Thank you." Annese shrugged embarrassed, but Kenyer had already fallen asleep.

TYLER

"Hey!" Tyler exclaimed, looking around. "Where's the old man?"

Those that were awake looked around the cave. The old man had vanished, and so had Blul. Tyler walked out to the archway of the alcove. He looked around the cavern, but he couldn't see anyone. Off in the distance, he could hear Blul's voice chattering away about something to do with crystals.

"They must be ok," Tyler reported to the party as he came back. "I can hear Blul chattering on and on about crystals this and crystals that."

"Shh!" Du'kai hushed, pointing to the heap on the floor.

Blankets had been pulled out. Jeremy, Jordon, and Fang were already curled up and asleep. Kenyer had Annese and Odessa laying their heads on his lap as he snoozed against the wall. The longairits were asleep in their basket next to Annese. Not far away, Fuzz, Aiya, and Jadara were sound asleep. Seda and Rexa had laid a blanket next to the Drelt girls and were curled up together. Grup laid out some blankets for himself and was getting ready to bed down.

"I guess it leaves you and me," Du'kai smirked.

"Sorry, dude! I'm not curling up with you!" Tyler teased.

Du'kai laughed heartily. "No, but you probably should get some sleep. We're going to need strength to get to the next transport. Go on. Bed down. I'll keep watch," the Drelt offered.

Tyler nodded gratefully. He moved over by Fang, who had curled up with Jeremy. He lay down next to the warm pup. Du'kai covered him with a blanket. It wasn't long before exhaustion sent him to dreamland.

MIKKEL

"You lousy excuse for a sorcerer!" Mikkel screamed at the wizard. "You still haven't gotten rid of them!"

"I'm sorry, highness," the scrawny magic user trembled. "I wasn't aware of the hermit! How was I supposed to know he was there, much less that his magic was more powerful than mine? And those stupid gnomes! They blasted my creatures to shards!"

"You had better get them," Mikkel threatened the wizard, grasping his robes around his throat. "I don't care if you have to cause a cave in and sink an island! Take them out. All of them! I will have my kingdom! Understand?"

The sorcerer sighed and tried to change the subject.

"Highness, I need to gather supplies for your medicine."

"To Hades with my medicine!" Mikkel yelled back. He threw the wizard to the ground.

"If you don't have your medicine, you will not have your kingdom. Your age will catch up with you very quickly," the wizard reminded the man, trying hard to change the subject. "Then all this would be for naught."

"Those children killed my father."

"No, highness. They turned him to stone, which prevented him from taking his medicine, and thus age caught up with his mortality, which was captured in the stone."

Mikkel glared at the wizard. "Like I said, they killed him. Now I will avenge my father and re-conquer the kingdom!"

"I will do my best, highness," the wizard replied meekly.

"Just make sure you kill them, or I'll kill you!" the former prince threatened as he left the room.

16 – CRYSTAL SCORPIONS

JEREMY

Jeremy stretched as his brain tried to bring him to consciousness. He sighed as he laid in his bedroll, eyes closed, wishing he were on a soft mattress instead of the hard cave floor. He took in a deep, cleansing breath. His eyes popped open with a start. The air was full of a sweet, mouth-watering scent. Jeremy sat up quickly and looked around. On one end of the cave, near the shelves with the dishes and stuff, sat the old man and Blul deep in conversation. In front of them was a cauldron on a bunch of red crystals. Steam was flowing from something in the cauldron.

Careful not to wake anyone, Jeremy pried himself from his sleeping position and tiptoed over to the pair. Fang looked up sleepily, then lay his head back down. The two stopped their conversation to look at him.

"Good morning, young master," the old man greeted. "Sleep well?"

"Um, yes, sir. Thank you. And you?"

The old man chuckled. "I don't require much sleep. Or is it I get too much sleep?" he mused. "Either way, I am fine. Our friend here hasn't slept at all," he pointed at Blul. "We've been having quite a discussion."

"Oh?" Jeremy looked over at Blul who shrugged.

The old man stood up and stirred the mixture in the cauldron. A burst of cinnamon scent came out of it.

"What's that?" Jeremy asked, straining to look into the pot.

The old man smiled. "It's breakfast. Hungry?" Jeremy nodded. "Good. It's just about ready."

"What is it?"

The old man shook his head. "I know you young people. You ask what it is, then turn your nose up at it just because you don't like the ingredients. Give it a try first. If you still want to know what's in it, I'll tell you."

"Yes, sir," Jeremy replied politely. A fluff of something brushed past his leg. Jeremy looked down to see the longairits brushing past to get to the warmth. Jeremy watched as they settled near the crystals. "Excuse me, how are the crystals hot?" Tyler stretched as he came over.

"Fire crystals," Blul replied. "Put two together and hot!" His hands seemed to follow his explanation.

"Blul is correct. Each crystal in the cave has a specific function. The red ones get hot when placed next to each other. A small heat, you only need two. For a large heat, like this to cook on, you need about twenty. Blul and I collected our breakfast meal and the crystals, then set out to cook. I figured you'd be hungry when you woke up."

"Yes, sir. What do the blue ones do?"

"Those clear the air. They suck up the excess steam in the cave, maintaining the atmospheric balance." ·

"And the yellow ones?"

"Simulate flowers."

"What about the green ones?"

"Those are the most important. Much like trees help with the atmosphere, the green ones help the atmosphere in the cave."

"Collect bad air, make good," Blul explained.

"Oh, I get it!" Tyler exclaimed, coming over. "They soak up the carbon dioxide and replace it with oxygen, just like green plants!" Jeremy looked at the boy tolerantly.

"How do you know so much about crystals?" Jeremy asked Blul.

The gnome sighed. "Gnome!" he said, pointing to himself as if that should explain it. When neither boy responded, the gnome went on. "Gnome build. Use crystals for energy. Make things moves."

"Ah! Now I see."

A sound from behind them made the four turn. Annese and Odessa were just waking up. Fang yawned and licked Jordon's face to wake him up. Kenyer let out a snort, making everyone else stifle a giggle.

The old man put a tin of water on the ground for the animals. The longairits quickly ran over to take a drink. Fang leaned over them carefully and drank some.

"Where'd you get water?" Jeremy asked. "I didn't see any among the crystals."

"There's a trickling waterfall an hour's journey from here. I cart it in," the old man explained. He poured a cup for the boys and one for Blul.

"Thank you," Jeremy said, taking the cup. The water was cold and crisp. It tasted good going down his throat. "I hadn't realized how thirsty I was."

"That happens, even here," the old man nodded.

"Morning," Jordon grumbled, coming up behind them. One hand was rubbing a sleepy eye. "Wanna share?" Jeremy handed his cup to Jordon. "Hey! It's empty!"

The old man joined Jeremy in a chuckle and handed a cup to Jordon. "Thank you," Jordon replied.

"Come along, Blul," the old man said to the gnome as the girls came over. "Let's get those bowls. Looks like the troops are up for breakfast."

Carefully, the old man and Blul handed out dishes of stew to the group. They even put some pieces from it down on the ground for the animals. The longairits quickly dug into theirs, but Fang whined at it. Jeremy went over to his pack and pulled out a few strips of jerky.

"Here, boy," he called the ortik. Fang happily took the strips gingerly and ate the meat.

"This is delicious!" Odessa cried as she ate.

Annese nodded. "What is it?"

"Stew," the old man replied. "I gathered up the potatoes and roots that grow near here, add some mushrooms and some spices, and simmer."

"It's wonderful," Jadara complimented.

"I don't think my mother can do better than this," Du'kai said.

"Don't let her hear you say that!" Aiya teased.

A saddened look came over Du'kai. "I don't think she ever will."

"I'm sorry, my friend," Aiya replied sadly. "I didn't mean anything..."

"I know," Du'kai forced a smile. "I'm just starting to miss home."

"We made a pact and a plan, remember?" Kenyer reminded him softly. "To go home now would mean certain death." Du'kai nodded.

Jeremy looked at the ground. He understood how they felt. This time, just like last time, he started missing home shortly after he started on the excursion. Would he ever get over that? Still, he could empathize with the Drelt.

"Alright now," the old man began, finishing his stew. "So, what is going on? We have several mortals, a Centaus, some dark elves, and some gnomes all traveling with a Kaptrix."

Jeremy looked at the man with awe. "How do you know that?"

"Just look at you all!" came the chuckling reply.

Kenyer stood up. He introduced himself and the rest of the party. "We came to help our friend Aiya and her friends when they escaped our village."

"Perhaps we should tell it from the beginning," Jordon suggested.

"Hope you're in for a loooong story," Jeremy grinned.

The boys went back and forth, telling the story from the time Mauselith came into the council room up to now. Tyler, Annese, and Odessa filled in the parts they had in the story. It took quite some time to explain everyone's part.

"Well, now. You have had quite an adventure," the old man nodded after listening to the whole thing. "And where will you go now?"

"We're trying to find a way back up to the surface," Jeremy explained.

"We know we can go back to Ascentia and climb up through the dragon tunnels," Jordon remarked, "*IF* we can find Ascentia again."

"Dragon tunnels," the old man mumbled thoughtfully. "Dragon tunnels." Finally, he shook his head. "Nope. Not a clue."

"I remember Narim talking about a tunnel under the castle, but it was too small for anyone to get through," Jordon remarked. "Something about boulders." Jeremy nodded in agreement.

"There should be a way somewhere," Kenyer muttered thoughtfully. "I can't believe the tunnels with the dragons are the only way up to the surface."

"Especially since I really don't want to meet a dragon," Jadara said with a shiver. "Deadly!" Jeremy joined Jordon and Annese chuckling.

"They're actually quite friendly," Jeremy eased his friend.

"Yea. Sure," she responded unbelievingly.

"I'm not sure which areas have tunnels to the surface." Jordon brought the conversation back on topic. "We had thirty lengths of rope to get down here and that wasn't enough," Jordon pointed out.

"No, and we slid way more than that when we let go," Jeremy added.

"That is quite a distance," the old man replied again thoughtfully.

"How far is a length?" Tyler asked.

"Well, we figured a length was approximately 150 feet long," Jeremy explained.

"So, we're about two miles underground?"

"Give or take. A mile isn't that far," Jordon pointed out to his cousin. "We walk or bike a mile back and forth to the park at home."

"Wouldn't know," Tyler retorted. "I wasn't there that long." He glared at Annese who squirmed.

"I am not certain how far a mile is," the old man said, "but judging by your descriptions, you are much farther down than that." The man sighed and held his head thinking.

"Excuse me," Odessa said meekly.

"Yes?" the old man moved his attention.

"Um, not to be rude, but you know our names, but we don't know yours."

At first, the old man just stared at her. His face softened, and he broke into a grin. "You are quite correct," he said to her.

"I'm guessing he likes it that way," Du'kai whispered to her.

"My name is... my name is... name is...," he said scowling. "I don't know what my name is. I have been down here so very long. I guess I forgot. I have traveled through all the caverns over the years, though I don't recall how. I have met with most of the inhabitants."

"How'd you get here?" Aiya asked.

"I guess the same way your people did. I got caught in the cataclysm."

"The cataclysm!" Jordon exclaimed. "But that was over 500 years ago!"

The old man nodded. "Yes, I suppose so. It would appear that the underground atmosphere on each of the islands causes aging to occur at different rates. Here, it is quite slow."

"We need to call you something!" Jordon insisted.

"Do you? I don't know," the old man replied. He scratched his beard a few times. "I don't have anything, do you?"

"Where'd you come from?" Jeremy asked.

"I suppose it is my turn for stories, hmmm?" The old man smiled as he got comfortable. "Mind you now. I'm not certain of all of this. I found this diary a while ago and read through it. I think it's mine. I'm not sure anymore.

"Apparently, I was a very young man when an uprising happened in our kingdom. Followers of the king fought with those wishing to take control of the throne. It was... how would you put it... getting very disturbing! I'm guessing we lived near the fighting because my father sent my sister and I away for an extended period. I do not know what became of my sister. I settled in a tiny village called Rumshuck on the eastern side of Faerun. Not very many people lived there, but they were well known for their manufacturing of Runiman. It is an ingredient in the Krilt ale. I set about a business of making shoes, of all things, but I learned my craft well at the hands of the man I apprenticed to.

"After a time, I came to know a young woman named …named…named…what was her name? Oh, I don't remember, but she was a beautiful maiden with dark, silky hair and equally dark eyes. Her skin was pale as the moon, and she seemed to float as she walked. She was very kind to everyone and everything. Eventually, I asked her to marry me. We wedded less than six turns of the moon after I met her.

"It wasn't long before my love and I were expecting our first child. We were quite happy about the anticipated event. However, my happiness was cut short. News quickly came that the battles were moving outward towards the islands. The castle had been overthrown, a new king had taken the throne, and those who had been faithful to the king were being, well, discarded," the old man's eyes went to Annese, Tyler, and Odessa. Their young ears should not hear what actually took place.

"With little preparation, I found a cave deep down in the earth and woods. I worked hard to adjust its structure so that my wife and I could live there without being detected. While I was working on it, the most horrendous earthquake occurred. Never had I ever had any inkling of a quake before. Trees crashed, mountains leveled, the earth opened up swallowing entire villages whole. I hid in my cave completely, expecting to be buried alive. When the shaking finally ended, I emerged from my cave to find myself here. I still don't know what caused the earthquake!

"My supplies didn't last long. I searched throughout the entire cavern to find myself alone. I found an area where roots were dangling and growing. I found the small waterfall that offered me life. But I lost my family forever. I don't even know if they lived, or if our child survived. Sometime later, as my supplies were running low, some wizards came by. They were setting up transport pads on each of the islands so that those that now lived underground who wished to travel to the other islands could get there. They were very kind in restocking my supplies.

"Since that time, I have learned to get around. As I said earlier, I have traveled to each of the islands. I have offered trade to some, and others I simply stay away from. For the most part, I sit here alone... until now. I have a large party as guests."

"We can tell you what caused the earthquake," Jeremy said gently. "The king that took over the palace was named Jamiss. He was rather evil and power hungry. He found a crystal under the palace that was held in place by eight magical beams. But he wanted the huge crystal for himself. He yanked it from its nest of light."

"When he pulled the crystal free, the earthquake happened. We call it a cataclysm," Odessa continued. "All the islands separated, and it threw Asteria into another time."

"The first time we were here, Jeremy and I defeated Jamiss," Jordon explained. "King Narim now sits on the throne."

"Is he a good king?" the old man asked warily.

"Yes, sir," Jeremy replied. "He's gathered a representative from each of the races in Asteria into a Grand Council to help advise him about what the citizens need. He's also opened up trade amongst the islands."

"There's more," Annese said softly. "The Kaptrixes think that King Narim will want to restore the crystal that caused the cataclysm. Jeremy already has one piece of it. If he does, another cataclysm will occur. It will probably destroy all the caverns down here."

"I don't understand. What's been happening up on the surface?" the old man asked.

Jordon sighed. "As Odessa said," he began, "King Narim has been working hard to bring all the factions of Asteria back together. Thaurlonian, the dragon king, has ascended. His son is now king. I believe they have worked out the issue between the Centaus and the griffins." He looked at Odessa for confirmation, but only go a shrug. "There is a total of eight islands, which I assume you know if you've traveled to each of them."

"Reimer, of the Kaptrix, thinks that replacing the crystal will create another cataclysm, returning the islands into one mass, and returning Asteria back to the dimension it belonged in," Tyler explained.

"And possibly into the time it left," the old man concluded thoughtfully.

"The crystal was the heart and soul of Asteria," Jadara explained. "Our legends tell us it held everything together. It is said that the very first king of Asteria found it in a cavern one day and had the castle built over it. The beams that held it in place were pure magic. The best wizards and sorcerers of the time spent years working many spells to decipher its purpose. As long as the crystal remained in place, Asteria would be unharmed by any natural disaster, and the main land masses would remain joined."

"Yet, no one knows where it came from," Du'kai added.

Jeremy looked at the old man for an answer. Silence prevailed through the cave for a long while as the elderly man thought about the news he had received.

Finally, Kenyer cleared his throat. "With all due respect, we thank you for your hospitality, but we really should be get back to our travels."

Everyone agreed and jumped in to help with cleanup. Annese and Odessa quickly began gathering the dishes and poured some water to clean them. Jeremy began helping the guys gather and pack their blankets and their gear. Aiya and Jadara began gathering up the longairits, which wasn't easy since they'd been playing in the center of the cave. Fang finally found the last one under a shelf in the far corner.

"Sir?" Odessa asked quietly. The old man looked up from his thoughts. "Would you like to come to the surface with us?" Jeremy whirled around as the question hung in the air in silence. No one else had thought to ask him.

The old man looked softly at Odessa. He smiled at the charming young child with bright eyes. Odessa shrank back timidly; afraid she had offended him. His eyes began to tear.

"I would love to, child," he began. "But I've lived my life. My beloved is long gone. And I would only slow you down."

"I think King Narim would love to have you stay with him," Jeremy said encouragingly.

"And we can help you get along. Besides, you've already been to all the islands," Jordon pointed out hopefully. "You could help us out."

"Are you certain?" the old man questioned their rationale. "I don't want to be a bother. I've lived alone for so long. I'm not sure how I will deal with society."

"I suggest you come along," Kenyer offered the old man. "We're not certain where we will fit in either."

"Give me a few moments to gather some things, please," the old man said with tears in his eyes. "In all my years, I've never had anyone be so kind," he laid a gnarled hand on Odessa's cheek.

The old man looked at the cave one last time. The children had helped him put things back in order. They had poured the left-over stew in strange containers to travel with. They replaced the red crystals into their individual boxes. The old man gave a few bags to Tyler.

"I noticed you were collecting these," he said to the young man. "As we go, I'll explain how to get them to grow. You think all these crystals were here when I first came? Only the red ones need to be wrapped separately. Oh, and gather as many as you can while we travel!" he whispered.

Tyler smiled gratefully as he took the bags from the old man. He carefully tucked them into his backpack. Jeremy smiled silently at the exchange, having watched it out of the corner of his eye. Tyler would be in his glory.

"If our new friend is going to travel with us, he needs a name," Du'kai smirked.

"Are you sure you didn't write your name in your diary?" Annese asked.

"Would you?" the old man asked.

"Yes. In the cover, so then if I lost it, whoever found it could returned it to me."

"Hmmm. I didn't think of that." Annese and the old man giggled together.

"How about Fred?" Tyler asked.

"Who's Fred?" Jordon scowled.

"I don't know. It was the first name I could think of."

"No. How about Merlin," Jeremy nodded. "After all, he does magic!"

"Merlin?" the old man scowled. "Who's he?"

"An old magic user of a legendary king. It's more myth than reality," Tyler explained.

"I'm not really a magic user. I know a few spells, that's it."

"Like me!" Jeremy smiled.

"What about A'par?" Kenyer suggested.

"A'par?" the group all asked together.

"It means old one in our language."

"I know!" Odessa exclaimed. "Why not just call him Grandfather? After all, he is older than all of us."

"Grandfather," Aiya tried. "I like it."

"Grandfather?" the gnomes questioned. After a heated and amusing discussion amongst themselves, they agreed.

"What do you think?" Jeremy asked their new friend.

"Grandfather," he tried out. He smiled. "It has a nice ring to it!"

"Grandfather it is!" Kenyer grinned. "So, Grandfather, where do we go?"

"Wherever you wish," the old man answered.

"You did not happen to draw a map of where each pad went, did you?" Fuzz asked hopefully.

"No, I'm sorry. I didn't," Grandfather replied regretfully. "My travels were often scattered and took a long time to find my way back here."

Fuzz nodded with a sigh and returned to his maps.

"Whatcha got, Fuzz?" Jeremy asked, kneeling next to the Kaptrix.

"I'm not certain." Fuzz turned the maps around to find the right one. "Here we are," he announced. He scowled at the page.

"Let's see," Grandfather murmured. "You say that pad takes you to Kaptrix? Then my cave would be here," he pointed, "and the pad you came in on is this one here."

"Can we get to the surface from Kaptrix?" Jadara asked.

Fuzz shook his head. "No. Only the air shafts go to the surface, but they are way too small even for our gnome friends."

"Then let's see where this other pad goes," Jeremy suggested.

"All in agreement?" Jordon asked.

"Begging your pardon, sirs," Fuzz said meekly. "I think I would prefer to go home."

"But, Fuzz? The new cataclysm?" Odessa worried.

"And how do we get along without your maps?" Jeremy asked.

"You've done fine up to now," Fuzz smiled embarrassed. "Most of our stops I did not even have recorded."

"I suggest we let the man go home, if that's what he wishes," Grandfather replied.

"Agreed," Jeremy said sadly. "We'll travel that way and make sure he gets to the transport pad ok."

"Why? There is nothing here that can hurt him," Grandfather remarked.

"And what do you call those crystal things that attacked us last night?" Du'kai asked skeptically.

"Quite right. Let us go."

"Wait!" Jordon called, dropping his pack. He rummaged around and pulled out his camera. "We can take pictures of Fuzz's maps. That should help us a little."

"Great idea!" Jeremy smiled. They laid out the maps, and Jordon snapped pictures of them while the Asterian members looked on curiously. He checked them over in the camera viewer to make sure they were clear. "Everyone get together," Jordon smirked. He waved until the group was standing close to each other, then he backed up and took a photo of the group. To ease their curiosity, he explained how the camera worked and showed them the image in the viewer. Jeremy glanced at Tyler who was trying to hide his smiled at all the oohs and aahs. Satisfied, he put the camera away with a smile. "Now we can go."

Travel was slow as Grandfather shuffled along with his staff. The group let Grandfather lead since the crystals would part for him. Interestingly, they wouldn't come back together until after the last of the party went by. Jeremy noticed Tyler picking a few along the way. The boy just shrugged at him when he realized he'd been caught. Jeremy smiled at him.

Every now and again, Tyler would pick up a crystal and show it to Grandfather, or Grandfather would point one out to the boy. The two became fairly good friends, with Grandfather extending his infinite knowledge of the crystals to Tyler and anyone else who would listen. Little outcroppings of crystals would appear from time to time, showing the crystals could form more things from nature.

Jordon and Kenyer found a good spot to stop for lunch. Grandfather pulled out some red crystals to build a 'fire' and warmed up the stew in the containers. They all shared some breads and meats along with the stew. It was a nice, relaxing meal.

"Let's not get too comfortable," Kenyer reminded them. "We've still a long way to go."

"It looks like a sea of glass," Annese murmured, looking out over the cavern. Jeremy followed her gaze. The other side was so far away they couldn't see it. It would take forever to get there. Still, the cavern sparkled with the glinting lights of the crystals.

"Looks like the lights on a Christmas tree," he offered.

"A bit," Jordon agreed.

"Come, come now," Grandfather smiled. "We'd best get going. We can still drop Fuzz off at his pad and make it to the other one before dark."

"Are you serious?" Du'kai asked unbelievably.

"Very," Grandfather chuckled. "I may walk slowly, but I know my way."

Once again, they resumed their journey.

"Begging pardon, Grandfather, sir," Fuzz interjected.

"Yes?"

"How is it that the crystals don't overtake each other? They appear to be nestled together all over the cavern, except in your cave." Jeremy found the point interesting. He hadn't noticed that fact.

"Oh, there are things here that eat the crystals. Once one has been eaten for a meal, another will grow to take its place. The cavern can only hold so many crystals. The crystal seeding that occurs when the shelf gives way can only replace so many crystals."

"How long does it take for them to grow?" Tyler asked.

"I don't know. I've never timed it."

"What determines their color?" Jordon questioned, looking at a particularly beautiful blue one.

"The seeding I suppose. I'm not certain. I just know that there is a fair balance of colors throughout the cavern." They continued to walk in silence, each person holding on to his own thoughts and questions.

FUZZ

At long last, they approached the transport stone. A beautiful array of crystals clung to the wall behind it. They had decorated themselves in a series of flowers. Greens surrounded the pad like grass. The flowers sparkled behind it. A group of yellow ones hung high on the wall as if to simulate a sun.

Fuzz looked up as the entire group turned to look at him. He moved forward timidly. He simply stared at the pad. Turning, he looked over at the party, a mixture of anticipation and sadness on his face. A strange emotion rose in his throat. Strange how this small group had become more like a family to him in such a short time. He almost didn't want to leave, but he did have responsibilities.

"Thank you all," he said through a lump in his throat. "I am certain I would have perished were it not for all of you."

"Thank you," Jeremy said, laying a hand on the Kaptrix's shoulder. "Were it not for you we would be lost forever."

"Yea," Jordon agreed. "Your maps helped us stay on track."

A warm feeling of appreciation rose in his chest. These boys were special; very special.

"It has been a pleasure meeting you," Grandfather smiled softly. "Many blessings to you and your family."

"We'll see you up on the surface," Odessa offered, with tears in her eyes.

"Yea," Tyler agreed. "We'll make sure they don't replace the crystal until you're safely up there."

"Tell Aresta and Hammie to stop sending people on wild goose chases," Annese smiled. "Although, they helped out without knowing it."

Fuzz smiled at Odessa's giggle. "I suppose. It would have been nicer if someone had warned us of the dangers first, though," she added.

Fuzz smirked. "I will personally locate the youths and give them a good talking to," he promised. "I will always remember you all."

"Have a safe trip," Aiya whispered.

"Same," Jadara agreed.

Kenyer reached into his leggings and pulled out a small dagger. "Here," he offered the Kaptrix the handle. "You may need this – just in case."

Fuzz took the dagger gingerly. "Thank you," he said in near awe. The dagger he held had a beautiful pearl hilt. The sharpness of the blade glinted almost as brightly as the crystals. "I will cherish it always."

"Don't cherish it," Du'kai smirked. "Use it, if you have to."

"I will." He carefully wrapped the dagger blade in his handkerchief and put it in his pocket. He turned back to Jordon and Jeremy. "Farewell, my friends. Safe journey."

"You, too." Jordon replied.

"Best get going," Jeremy suggested. "Saying goodbye isn't going to get any easier the longer you delay."

"Of course, you can still come with us," Annese suggested hopefully.

Fuzz smiled at the child. "Thank you, my lady," he bowed. "However, I have been gone long enough. And if the King's plans are to return Asteria to her former home, these maps won't be of any use after all."

"Certainly, they will," Grandfather reminded. "Should the caverns survive another earthquake, we'll need to know how to get around them."

"If nothing else, they can go on as part of Asteria's history," Odessa suggested. She suddenly grinned. "Children all over Asteria will learn about the caverns under their homeland and the brave Kaptrix who mapped them!" The entire group laughed as Fuzz turned bright red. "And I can say I knew him!" she brightened.

"Go on! Be safe! We'll meet up again one day," Jordon urged.

Fuzz realized he couldn't stall any further. It was obviously becoming as difficult for the others to say goodbye as it was for him. He approached the transport stone and looked at it. Fang whined in the background. With resolve, Fuzz turned towards the party and waved. As they waved back, he clenched his jaw, firmed up his face to hide his emotional struggle, and took a single step backwards onto the pad–and disappeared.

JEREMY

"I'm gonna miss the guy," Jeremy muttered sadly.

"Me, too," Jordon agreed. "It's going to be awfully dull now."

"Come along," Grandfather urged gently. "We must keep moving."

Jeremy fell in at the back of the line behind their elderly guide once again. As had been usual here, Jordon and Kenyer took up the rear. Progress seemed to take forever, but Grandfather seemed to know where he was going.

"We may make it there by nightfall," Kenyer whispered to Jordon. "We may not."

Jeremy stifled a chuckle. They would have made twice the time if Grandfather had remained behind. While he was happy to have Grandfather's experience, the man's slow pace gave Jeremy the jitters. He wasn't used to moving haltingly. Maybe the lack of attacks was making him nervous. Jeremy looked around expecting something to jump out. He spotted a few large, spider-like creatures on the ceiling in the corners, but nothing moved towards them.

After several hours, they stopped to eat. Once again, the crystals were brought out to reheat the stew. The group shared other foods as well. The longairits and Fang fell asleep almost as soon as dinner finished.

"Excuse me, Grandfather?" Annese interrupted, looking over towards the wall.

"Yes, my dear?"

"Do the crystals usually have more than one color?"

The elderly man thought a moment. "No. I've never seen a crystal with more than one color. Why do you ask?"

"Because the yellow and green crystals over by the wall have a blue tint to them." Annese pointed to a spot near the wall. Sure enough, a pale blue coloring was coming through the crystals with centers of yellow and green.

"That's odd!" Jeremy heard the old man say. Slowly, Grandfather went over to investigate. Jeremy followed. As the crystals on the ground parted, a portion of the ground glowed with a blue light. It was coming from under the surface of the floor. "Well I'll be...." Grandfather mumbled.

"Can we dig to it?" Jeremy asked, feeling the floor. Tyler and Jordon joined them.

"Possible. It's just dirt." Jordon noted.

Tyler pulled out Jeremy's pocketknife from his pocket. He opened the blade and began stabbing at the white dirt reflecting a blue glow. Little by little it pulled away from whatever was underneath. He used the blade of his axe to shovel out the dirt.

"Be careful!" Jeremy warned. "You might harm whatever is giving off the glow."

"And you might hurt yourself," Jordon remarked with a tone that indicated he clearly expected Tyler to stab himself.

"It's ok," Tyler smiled up at his cousin. "We've got a great healer with us."

"Just be careful!" Jordon grumbled.

Tyler continued around the edge of the coloring. He dug down several inches before a tiny "tink" sounded. He smiled and started using his hands. Jeremy pitched in to help. Alternating between his hands and the knife, they uncovered a large blue crystal about twice the size of a softball. Carefully, he removed it from its earthy bed.

"Wow!" Tyler held it up and brushed off the dirt.

Grandfather took in a sharp breath. "Oh, dear!"

"What?" Jeremy looked up sharply.

"This must be a piece of the Crystal of Caldren. They broke the crystal into pieces?" Grandfather's voice trembled as he said the words. "I guess the legend is reality after all."

"The bag, Jere?" Jordon instructed, taking the crystal piece from Tyler.

"It's too big to fit in with the other one," Jeremy surmised, pulling a new carry bag from his pack. "I'll have to put it in a new one.

"You mean you've found another piece?" Grandfather asked in surprise.

"Yes," Jeremy answered as he and Jordon wrestled to put the crystal into the bag. With much effort, they finally got it into the bag and secured it in Jeremy's backpack.

"What are you going to do with them?"

"Give them to King Narim," Jordon replied with a shrug.

"Oh, dear," the old man muttered.

"Why are you so worried?" Tyler asked.

"Because *if* King Narim is intent on putting the crystal back together and into its resting place, and *if* the crystal brings Asteria back to a unified island, he may be in for a shock. With the cracks and changes in the crystal, Asteria could easily end up somewhere other than where it came from."

Jeremy's eyes widened. It could end up worse than where they were. At least in this dimension they have only themselves to worry about.

"Are you sure about this?" Jeremy asked with one eye closed.

"No. I am not a crystalline expert," Grandfather sighed. "However, from what I've discovered over the years, I have no reason to believe this crystal is any different from any other crystal down here. I believe the power you spoke of emanated from a whole, unblemished crystal. With it having been broken apart, it will most likely work other than the way it was intended."

"I suggest we let King Narim worry about that," Kenyer remarked. "We're losing daylight. We can inform him of all his options when we get there."

"Quite right," Grandfather nodded. "Let's move on."

The party gathered their items, cleared up their mess, and started off for the transport pad. Fang just wanted to sleep, so Jeremy carried him. Odessa took the longairits to give Annese a break from the basket. Kenyer and Jordon took up the rear —again. They were in trouble if the attack came from the front, Jeremy thought.

Light in the cavern was dimming quickly. Still, they moved on. The slow-moving guide called back that they were almost there. Not too much farther. Jordon and Kenyer glanced at each other. Jeremy lit his staff for better lighting.

"Are you hearing something?" Jeremy heard Jordon whisper. The question pulled him from his thoughts.

"Like a clicking sound?" Kenyer asked. Jeremy watched Jordon nod. "Yes. It sounds like it's coming from behind us."

Jordon shook his head. "I don't think so. I think it's bouncing off the wall we've been following."

"Get Du'kai. He'll be able to tell," Jeremy suggested.

Jordon ran on ahead to Du'kai and went through the conversation again. Du'kai listened carefully, turning in each direction. He glanced around them as he checked for the source of the sound.

"You're right. It's coming from our right and bouncing off the wall. Good tracking. But I don't see anything moving," Du'kai confirmed.

"Let's keep our eyes peeled," Jordon suggested warily.

"Do what?" Du'kai and Kenyer questioned together.

Jeremy and Jordon laughed. "Sorry," Jordon giggled. "It means keep watching for anything."

"Oh!" the Drelt said together. They ran to catch up to the group.

"Here we are!" Grandfather announced satisfactorily.

The group stood a few yards away from the transport stone. Behind it the crystals had formed a rainbow with tiny flowers near the floor. It glistened prettily in the dim light of Jeremy's staff.

"How beautiful!" Odessa smiled. "The crystals are so talented."

"Yes, they are," the elder man smiled at her sadly. "I shall miss them."

"We can take some with us," Tyler winked.

"Yes, we can," Grandfather agreed with a conspiratorial smile at the boy. "Let's continue. It becomes harder for me to leave the longer we take."

As they approached the pad, the crystals came together quickly to form a barrier.

"What is this?" Grandfather asked in surprise. "Enough. Part!"

Behind the group, the clicking became louder. Kenyer and Jordon turned to look. From all directions came red crystals in the form of giant scorpions.

"Uh, oh!" they muttered.

"Move it, guys!" Jordon ordered, pulling Sharijol from its sheath.

"Hey, Blul! Got any more of those explody things?" Kenyer shouted, bringing his blade out into the open.

Blul laughed as he dropped his pack. "Boom! Yes! Yes!"

"Oh, no!" Grandfather's eyes widened. "Be careful! Your weapons will do no good! You will only dull your blade!"

"They're red!" Tyler cried. "They'll burn you! Watch out!"

Grandfather pushed on the crystals around the transport. They refused to move. Jeremy heard him beseech them gently, trying to coax them apart. No avail. The crystals refused to move.

Jeremy thought hard. Only one spell he knew could stop the crystal scorpions. He pointed his staff and cried "Congelo Somes!" A ball of white burst from the staff and hit one creature, freezing the crystals. Unfortunately, the heat of the red crystals quickly melted the ice. He watched the scene play out helplessly.

Jordon swung at a scorpion, catching its front claw. He must have hit it at just the right point, because the claw flew off and separated into other crystals. As he brought Shrijol up to block the stinger, the second claw slapped him down, burning through his pants. Jordon rolled aside, despite the piercing of the other crystals on the ground.

Kenyer also fought against a scorpion, not making much headway. It was a matter of figuring out which appendage was going to come at him first. As he pushed a claw away, the stinger from the tail came down on his shoulder, burning through his tunic and into his flesh.

"Ahh!" he cried as he jumped back.

Tyler went flying in with his axe. Running swiftly, he cut off the tails of the two scorpions attacking Jordon and Kenyer. Satisfied, he turned to attack another one, only to find three more facing him. His eyes widened as he prepared.

"No, no!" Blul scolded. "Come back! Boom!"

"Blul's right!" Annese yelled. "Your weapons won't stop them! They're just coming back together!"

"My shield!" Jeremy cried. "Come back into the shield!"

"Tyler, go!" Jordon ordered, pushing his cousin behind him. "Go stand by Jeremy! We'll hold them off."

"No!" Tyler scowled shakily. "I'll fight with you!"

"Don't be a fool!" Jordon argued.

"If you can be one, so can I!" his cousin challenged.

"Hurry up, Blul!" Kenyer urged as he dodged another attack.

The gnome came up near him and shook the vial. Quickly he tossed it up onto the scorpion nearby. Both he and Kenyer dove off to the side as the vial exploded. Some crystals from the scorpion rained down on top of them.

"Way to go, dude!" Jordon called, moving fast to out strike the three scorpions he was battling. Another was coming up on his left. "Now, how about one for us! We're kinda outnumbered!"

Grup ran up to Jordon and Tyler with Blul. The two began shaking vials until they started turning colors. Quickly they threw them on top of the scorpions and dove for cover. The boys also jumped back and dove to the ground, covering their heads with their arms. The explosion rocked the cavern. As Jeremy opened his eyes, the four scorpions were gone, as were many of the crystals from the ground and the ceiling. A small crater now adorned the white dirt.

"I don't know what you guys put in those things, but they are great!" Jordon smiled.

"Let's go!" Kenyer called. There were still two scorpions left, but they had stalled when they saw the destruction of the others.

The warriors ran back to the party where Grandfather was still trying to get the crystals to move. A soft hum was coming from the barrier. It became louder and louder, slowly making words.

"No go. Stay."

"You will get along just fine without me," Grandfather cooed. "I shall miss you all, but I shall return. If possible, I will come get you, but it is time I move on to be with my own people. Be strong. Be brave. Now, move aside, my lovelies."

"Best hurry," Jeremy called, slightly panicked. "My shield is about to end!"

"And they're starting to get through!" Jordon added, holding his burnt leg.

Slowly, almost sadly, the crystalline barrier fell apart. One crystal, then another, and another. Then two, and three at a time. On the other side, the scorpions backed away. One by one, they fell apart into separate crystals.

"Wow! Sentient crystals!" Tyler murmured.

"Only as a group," Grandfather whispered. "Separately, they're dumb as a tack."

"Jeremy, go through first. Raise the shield again!" Jordon pushed his friend.

Kenyer added his instructions. "Aiya and Jadara, follow him through for protection." Jeremy nodded and stepped onto the pad. The girls followed right behind him, bows nocked and ready.

JUJENE

The sorcerer approached his master slowly. How was he going to explain that they got past his scorpions and golems? And worse, they have befriended yet another person! This is not good. Not good at all. How was he going to tell his highness about these things?

Mikkel turned over in his bed and looked at the sorcerer. "What is it, Jujene? Is the job finished?"

"Actually, no, highness," the sorcerer bowed. "However, I have good news for you."

"The only good news is that those brats are dead, and I am now King of Asteria," Mikkel grumbled as he rolled back again.

"Oh. I see. Then I suppose the news that they are in the subterranean caves on Caldren is of no value. Sleep well," the sorcerer replied, and turned to leave.

"What did you say?" Mikkel twirled over and pushed up on his elbow. The blanket fell, revealing the strapping muscles that had been honed over the years by hauling and lifting rock.

"I said sleep well," the sorcerer replied over his shoulder.

"No, before that!"

"Oh. I have good news?"

"After that," Mikkel growled, getting irritated.

"Ah, that the boys are now in the caves of Caldren?"

"That's the one!" Mikkel's eyes grew wide. Slowly they gleamed with excitement. "Do you know where?"

"I do."

"At last! I can get my revenge myself! Quickly, Jujene! We must prepare. I want them to walk right into my trap!"

17 - ESCAPE

JEREMY

Jeremy shivered as he walked off the transport pad into darkness. Fang bumped into his legs as he followed Jordon through. He brightened the light from the globe on his staff and looked around as Aiya and Jadara came through behind him. Huge, dark rocks covered stood with ice everywhere he looked. The entry was a small clearing with three pathways exiting off into the unknown. Unlike the other islands, these rocks didn't let off any light.

"Why is it so cold here?" Jadara asked with a shiver.

"I don't know," Jeremy replied. "I also don't understand how there could be ice down here. The air is wet."

Grandfather, Annese, and Odessa came over next. Each had the same reaction. The gnomes followed them, moving closer to the girls for warmth.

"Is cold!" Grup complained.

"We know," Aiya replied gently.

"Where are Kenyer, Du'kai, and Jordon?" Jeremy asked.

"Apparently, the scorpions didn't want to give up. They reformed closer to the pad." Jadara explained. "They were still fighting as they backed up."

Du'kai came through the pad next. "Man, I hope it's safer over here."

"I thought you said there wasn't anything that could hurt us?" Annese asked Grandfather.

"I didn't think there was. I've never seen the crystals behave like this."

JORDON

At last, Kenyer and Jordon appeared on the stone pad. Each turned to face the party and breathed a sigh of relief. They stepped off the pad and into the group.

"Finally!" Jordon remarked, hobbling over to the group.

"Can the crystals use the transports?" Kenyer asked Grandfather. He was holding a cut on his arm.

"I don't think so. They never have before. I believe the power that gives them sentience is only in that cavern. After that, they are simply crystals that perform a function," Grandfather shrugged. "So even if they did come through, they would not be able to continue as the scorpions."

Kenyer sighed. "Good!" He looked around and did a head count. "Six, seven, eight, nine, ten, eleven, twelve, thirteen, fourteen, and Fang. All here!"

Jordon chuckled. "I never thought of doing a head count," he laughed. "My mom used to do those on class trips."

"What's a head count?" Aiya asked.

"It's when you count each person in the group to make sure you have everyone," he explained. "Like Kenyer just did."

"Ah!"

"Grandfather, why isn't there any light here?" Jeremy asked as they looked around.

"I'm not certain. It could be because it is night."

"Do all the caverns give off light?" Du'kai asked.

"No, no, no!" Blul stomped his foot. He pointed to the wall. "No light rock! See? All brown."

"That's right," Jordon snapped his fingers. "All the other caverns we've been in had streaks of blue, yellow, and pink running through the rocks. These walls are just brown; just dirt."

"Let's keep going," Grandfather suggested. "If these are simply brown, it means we are below Caldron, in the ice caverns."

"You know these caverns?" Jordon asked.

"Come here," Annese instructed him quietly. She let her hands heal his leg, then she moved to Kenyer's arm and did the same.

"Not completely," Grandfather offered. "I understand they sealed traitors or criminals down here as punishment; I think. Sounds like a good idea, doesn't it? Anyway, we may find a few unwanted items in our travels."

A single crystal-like clink echoed on the stone of the transport pad; the sound reverberating around the small area. Jordon twirled around quickly to look, Sharijol ready. The others also stared at the pad. It was a single red crystal. With a sigh of relief, he guessed the scorpions tried to follow but didn't make it. His arm flew out to the side to stop Tyler as he noticed his cousin move to go pick it up.

"What?" Tyler asked with a scowl.

"Transport pad," Jordon pointed out. "Step on it and who knows where you'll end up."

Tyler's scowl changed to dawning as he realized what he was about to do. "Right. Sorry," he sagged.

Jordon smirked. "No problem. That's what a team is for."

"I suggest we stop for the night," Aiya said to Kenyer. "We're all tired from our travel through the crystal cavern. I doubt anything will come through the pad now, and the tunnels ahead are dark and silent. We're safe here, and you, Tyler, and Jordon are worn out. Let's get some sleep while we can."

"I agree!" Odessa chimed in with a yawn.

"Tripled!" Tyler announced, moving to the middle of their location. He started pulling the red crystals from their bag and laid them out like a campfire.

"I guess it wouldn't hurt. Thanks, Annese," he smiled at the girl, then looked to Jordon for his opinion.

Jordon shrugged and nodded. "Who wants to take the first watch?" The rest of the party simply looked at each other, then looked at him. Jordon sighed and nodded. He patted his cousin on the shoulder. "Good idea."

Jordon looked over the area as the party slowly got ready for the night. Since Odessa was tired but not sleepy, Aiya and Jadara began teaching her how to use the bow they gave her. After some time, she could finally hit a large target. Annese and Jeremy went to Tyler to heal the burns they sustained while fighting the scorpions. Grandfather made a bed and dropped off to sleep. The gnomes cuddled together under some blankets for the night. Grup's light snores echoed through the clearing.

Jordon looked up as Tyler wandered over to sit with him and Jeremy. He looked worried.

"What?" Jordon watched his cousin closely.

"I'm sorry," Tyler replied as he stared at the floor.

"For?"

"Getting us all into this."

"It wasn't your fault," Jeremy replied. "As I understand it, Annese brought you here; so it's Annese's fault."

"But I followed."

"Next time, don't be in such a hurry to follow a girl on an adventure," Jordon smirked.

"I thought she was lying!" Tyler defended himself.

"Obviously not."

Tyler nodded and stared at the ground a little more. He drew in a shuttered breath. "Jordon?" he asked, with tears brimming in his eyes.

"Yea?"

"Are we ever gonna make it home?"

Jordon gave his cousin a reassuring smile. "Don't worry. We'll make it home. We may be grounded for the rest of our lives, but we'll make it home."

"Don't go sappy on us now," Jeremy nudged the boy lightly. "We aren't out of the woods yet. We still need the warrior in you. Hang tough!"

Tyler returned a watery, appreciative smile. At least the guys were giving him credit and not treating him like a baby. "Thanks," he murmured.

"Get some sleep," Jordon directed. "Tomorrow is going to be another rough day."

"How do we find our way out of here?"

"Well, if Grandfather is right, and this is Caldron, we need to search it for the opening beneath the castle," Jordon explained.

"How long's that gonna take?"

"Could be a few hours," Jeremy replied. "Could be a few days. Don't know." Jordon nodded his agreement.

"Better not be days," Jadara said quietly. "We'll run out of food."

Jordon watched Tyler's shoulders sag with despair at Jadara's comment. He sent the girl a slight glare. He knew what was going through Tyler's head. They could die in a few days. He wanted to go home *now*! Jordon had felt that way the first time he and Jeremy came to Asteria. He sighed with compassion as Tyler trudged over to Fang and set up his blankets. Fang must have sensed his cousin's distress. Tenderly, the pup moved closer to him and began licking his face. Tyler wrapped his arm around the pup's shoulder and tried to hide the small shuddering of his shoulders.

"I feel so helpless," Jordon muttered.

"Why?" Jeremy asked.

"He's scared, and I don't know how to reassure him," Jordon replied.

"No more scared than we are," Jeremy chuckled. "I'm not going to calm down until we get back to Narim."

Jordon chuckled. His friend was right. "Get some sleep." He rose and started walking the outside of the sleeping area as he kept watch for the next two hours.

DU'KAI

Du'kai volunteered for the next watch. He sat around the pile of red crystals that Tyler had set up in the middle for heat. He hummed to himself to pass time. A little more than an hour passed when he heard a thump in the distance. Another followed it, then another.

Listening carefully, he laid a hand on the ground. Something heavy was walking. He moved to another area and touched the ground as another thump sounded. It was coming this way. Tip-toeing over people, he woke Kenyer.

"Huh? Whassamatter?" Kenyer grumbled, wiping the sleep from his eyes. "Miss me already?"

"Something's wrong. Listen," Du'kai whispered.

Again, another thump sounded in the distance; then another and another. Each one was getting slightly closer to them.

"What do you think?" Du'kai asked.

"I think we've been found," Kenyer responded, getting up. He went over to wake Grandfather.

"Huh? What?" the old man looked around. "Oh, it's you."

"Listen," Du'kai instructed.

Again, a thump, then another. Again, they were just slightly closer.

"Oh, my." Grandfather reached for his throat.

"What is it?" Kenyer asked in a whisper.

"I don't know. We should gather everyone and move."

"Agreed," Du'kai nodded. "How well do you know these tunnels?" Kenyer moved to wake everyone.

"If I recall correctly, these three go out to different parts of the cavern, then come together again in the center, where there is a large clearing. Three or four other tunnels spread out from there," Grandfather explained, gathering his blankets.

"Thanks."

Quickly Kenyer woke the others and got them moving by simply saying, "Intruders. Hurry." No one needed to be told a second time.

Du'kai sat at the end of each tunnel in turn, listening. Behind him, the party rose and gathered their things, quickly preparing for departure. Aiya approached him and listened as well. She glanced at Du'kai with the question in her eyes. He shook his head. He couldn't tell where the thumps were coming from.

"We need a decision," Kenyer whispered to him. "Which way?"

"I don't know. I can't tell," he replied. "Whatever it is, it's heavy enough that the impact is spreading across the rock face. It's impossible to tell where it is."

"Left," Grandfather said.

"Are you sure?"

"No, but it is a decision."

"Yes, it is," Du'kai replied. He shrugged at his friend.

JORDON

"Jordon," Kenyer called.

Jordon hefted his backpack onto his shoulders. He looked at his friend.

"Whatcha got?" he asked.

Kenyer sighed. "Du'kai can't figure out where the intruders are," he explained. "The three tunnels lead out to different areas of the cavern and supposedly come together in the middle, at least, if Grandfather remembers correctly."

Jordon nodded and looked over at the old man. Sometimes he seemed completely lucid, and other times he couldn't remember anything. "Our options?"

"Grandfather says we should go left," Kenyer informed. "It's a decision."

"Do you have any better ideas?" Kenyer shook his head. "Left it is," Jordon sighed. "Ok, folks! Let's move out!"

Jordon set up the party two to three wide, since the tunnels weren't any wider than their halls at school. He sent Kenyer and Jeremy up front with Jadara and Aiya behind them. Their arrows will help keep Jay safe. The gnomes went behind the Drelt girls. Grup and Blul were fast enough to run in any directions. He put Annese and Odessa in the middle. He held Tyler back to walk with him, Grandfather and Du'kai in front of them. As usual, Fang stayed at Jeremy's feet. Looking over the slowly moving party, he nodded. No matter what direction the intruders came from, they were ready.

"Why keep me all the way in the back?" Tyler asked scowling. "I can handle it!"

"In case something comes up from behind," Jordon explained. "We're going to need that axe if we get ambushed."

"Ah," Tyler nodded in sudden understanding. He gave a small, grateful smile to Jordon.

Jeremy lit his staff up ahead and held it high enough that the others could see where they were going. It helped with the uneven terrain of the tunnels.

The thumps became louder, but they still couldn't see anything ahead of them. Suddenly, it seemed as if the thumps were next to them. Du'kai pointed at the wall, then made a motion to hurry along quietly. Fang whined at Jeremy's feet. Jeremy picked the pup up to prevent any further noise. Jordon and Tyler kept looking behind them. There wasn't anything there.

A sudden roar echoed through the cavern as something smashed through the walls of the tunnels. Rock rained from the top of the tunnel down onto the floor. The party ran on ahead, Jordon and Tyler helping Grandfather. Another crash came through.

"We need to run!" Du'kai urged.

"Grandfather can't," Jordon countered. His eye lit up with an idea. "Hey, Jay! What if we put Grandfather and the kids on a flying blanket? They'd be able to keep up, and we can move much faster!"

"It's not that easy to control," Jeremy shook his head.

"Then you go up with them," Kenyer suggested. "We need to move faster, or we're gonna get crushed!"

Jeremy nodded. He pulled out his blanket and froze it. He instructed Grandfather into the middle and handed him Fang. The gnomes came on as well. Annese sat up front with him and the longairits. Tyler agreed to take up the rear on the ground. Jeremy became frustrated when Odessa refused to fly, wanting to help with the fighting. The girl turned to see Aiya's smiling approval as she received some arrows. Fine.

"We'll hover above you to keep the party together," Jeremy planned. "If I can help from the air, I will." With the necessity of his staff for the blanket, Jeremy pulled out his flashlight from his pack and handed it to Annese. "Keep it pointed at the ground."

The flying blanket made travel much faster. Grandfather seemed impressed and grateful for the lift, remarking that he wished he could do such a trick. It would have made traveling the islands much faster.

Another roar shook the walls. More stones rained down on the party. Pounding shook the walls. A distance behind them, three stone golems broke through the tunnel. Jordon watched them turn towards the party and begin their trek after them. Each one of their steps was five of the ground party's.

He nodded as Jeremy's voice called down. "Incoming! Golems!"

"Golems?" Kenyer questioned.

"Giant beasts made of stone," Jordon replied worriedly. "Similar to the crystal monsters that attacked us in the last cavern. Tell Blul to make boom!"

"No!" Du'kai cried. "Cancel that!"

"What? Why?" Jordon scowled.

"Because the bombs would blow apart the rocks in the walls!" Jeremy answered for Du'kai. "We want to get rid of the golems, not bury us in rock and ice!"

"Keep going," Grandfather instructed from the air. "I think I can handle this one."

"Move, move, move!" Jordon urged the group.

GRANDFATHER

Grandfather turned to look at the golems as they rapidly caught up with the party. Each one was as high as the ceiling and as wide as the tunnel. Each made the ground shake as they got closer. The lead golem kept hitting the walls, trying to break apart the rock.

"I hope this works," Grandfather muttered, then cried as he waved his hand, "Ofkrat!"

The first golem stopped. He shook a bit, then fell apart, creating a pile of rubble in the tunnel. The second golem merely stepped over the first.

"Ofkrat!" Grandfather cried again with the same wave. The second golem fell apart slowly as well. The third golem stepped over the first two and continued pursuing the party. Again, the command echoed off the hall walls. The golem stopped and shivered. It shook off the command and resumed its pursuit. Grandfather swallowed and tried again, declaring the command a little stronger. Again, the golem stopped and shook, but it resumed its pursuit.

Jeremy took hold of Grandfather's other hand. The old man looked at him in confusion. "Now try," he suggested.

"Ofkrat!" the two cried together. The golem stopped, shook, and fell apart.

With the destruction of the golems, the party slowed down.

"How'd you know that would work?" Grandfather heard Jeremy ask.

"I didn't. I just figured that stone golems were built the same way as crystal golems, those things you were fighting in my cavern. I figured I'd try it."

"Glad it worked," Jeremy smiled.

"Agreed," Grandfather replied tiredly. He laid down on the blanket between Annese and Jeremy and soon fell asleep.

JEREMY

Jeremy looked back at the gnomes, who also were asleep. He looked over at Annese. She looked at her brother with frightened eyes. He smiled at her reassuringly. "Lean back and go to sleep," he suggested. "I'll wake you if you're needed."

Annese shook her head. Slowly, tears fell down her cheeks. "I want to go home."

"I know," Jeremy replied quietly, still following the rest of the party.

"Now!" Annese whined.

"I know," Jeremy said patiently. "But I can't take you home *now*," he mimicked her insistence. "I can only get you home as quickly as I can, and that isn't right now. Hang on a little longer."

Annese pouted as she cried to herself. She wiped her nose on her shirt and clung to the basket of longairits. She wanted to go home. She was tired of running, tired of fleeing, tired of fighting. She just wanted to go home and be safe in her bed. Jeremy understood completely.

"Don't sulk," Jeremy suggested with a smirk. "You're the one who got us into this. Be thankful I'm saving your butt—again!"

"Tyler called me a liar!" Annese raised her chin indignantly.

"You shouldn't have brought it up," he chastised gently. "It's supposed to be a *secret*, re-mem-ber?"

Her chin dipped as Annese remembered the promise she'd made after their last trip to Asteria. "Sorry," she mumbled. It was her fault. She hadn't thought things through before she opened her mouth. It was just that Tyler had so many great adventures to talk about. This was all she had that even came close. Now they were in trouble.

"Forget it," Jeremy reassured her. "Can't change the past."

"You're a great brother, ya know that?" Annese looked up at him as tears fell down her cheeks.

"Yeah. Don't go spreading that around! You'll give me a bad name." He smirked as he teased his sister. He paused a moment and took the flashlight. He waved the beam up ahead. "Hey, guys," he suddenly called down to the floor. "Something's moving up ahead."

"What size?" Kenyer called up.

"Big, but not as big as the golems."

Annese reached down and woke Grandfather. "Company," she whispered to him. She scowled as she looked forward again. "What's that clicking sound?"

"Cover the fur balls," Jeremy said, wide-eyed. "Or else they'll be something's dinner."

Large, hairy, black spiders crawled along the walls towards the party. Several were up near the ceiling, eyeing the meal coming their way. The clicking was from their mandibles knocking together as they moved.

"We could use some fire about now," Jordon called up.

"Wish I had some!" Jeremy called back with the same sing-song voice.

"Should we retreat?" Jadara asked, watching the spiders as they got closer. She nocked an arrow to be ready.

"We can't outrun them," Jeremy assessed, bringing the "carpet" down closer to the ground. "We can fight or we can smoke them out with flames, that's it."

"Light of pain?" Jordon asked.

"I can try it, but I don't think it will have an effect." He took in a deep breath. "Everyone, watch your eyes! Lux Lucis de Pena!" he commanded. The bright, searing light burst from the staff getting through even closed eyelids. The squeals of several spiders echoed around them. Some retreated, but most simply stood their ground. "Next idea?"

Grandfather surprised them when he pointed his finger at a nearby spider. "Incendia telum," he whispered. A small fireball hurled through the air, striking the spider squarely in the face. The spider squealed and dropped to the floor, writhing in pain; the hair on its face and back singed. It didn't get up again.

"Wow! What was that?" Jeremy asked.

"A small fireball. I never could master a good-sized one, but these little ones work very well. You are a magic user. Try it! Simply point your finger, or your staff, and say carefully 'incendia telum'," Grandfather instructed.

Jeremy pointed his staff at a rather enormous spider and said firmly, "Incendia telum." To his great surprise, a larger fireball than the one Grandfather sent flew from his staff and hit the spider. The same reaction occurred, with the spider falling to the ground and remaining unmoving.

"Are they dead?" Jeremy called down to Jordon.

"Appear to be," Jordon called back, not wishing to get too close to the thing.

"Sweet!" Jeremy cried.

Several spiders descended on the party. The girls began sending volleys of arrows at them, clearly hitting many. Odessa was having a bit of trouble with moving targets. Jeremy glanced down to see Aiya explaining how to estimate where the target was going and how to estimate how fast. It would take practice.

Grandfather and Jeremy continued sending spiders to their doom by throwing one mini fireball after another into the tunnel ahead. Kenyer and Jordon simply fought with their swords, cutting off limbs and heads. Tyler's axe cleared through them easily.

One particularly nasty spider dropped onto the flying blanket, throwing off the balance. It reached at the gnomes with anticipation as Jeremy struggled to get the blanket back under control. Grandfather turned and kicked it off into the wall. "Not on my watch, you won't!" he called back at it. Jeremy chuckled. Grandfather was so cool!

Another dropped in front of Annese, eagerly reaching for the basket of squealing fur balls. "Duck!" Jeremy instructed. Annese curled into a ball over the longairits while Jeremy wound up and hit the thing off the blanket with the swing of a professional baseball player. The crack of the exoskeleton echoed twice; once from being hit by the staff, and then as it splat over the wall.

It took a bit of time, but the remaining few spiders quickly retreated. Jeremy flew ahead into the tunnel to check things out. He and the blanket's occupants returned quickly.

"Looks like we're going to have to choose a different tunnel," he announced. "Not only do the spiders have a huge nest of spider webs up there, but the tunnel has caved in right behind it. We can't get through."

"Then I suppose it was very nice of those golems to cut a door for us, huh?" Du'kai smirked. The others chuckled in agreement.

KENYER

"Let's go. I'm getting tired," Kenyer grumbled, leading the way back down the tunnel. It was tough climbing over the rubble left behind by the golems, but the detour between tunnels was fairly clear and saved the party the hassle of going all the way back. It opened into a small cave. Kenyer was having difficulty keeping pace, and his vision was beginning to blur from fatigue.

"Ken, we need to rest," Aiya said, grasping the Drelt's shoulder. "We've barely had any sleep, and the children can't stay awake. We're all exhausted, you included."

"We're in danger, Aiya. We can't rest."

"We have to! How well are you going to fight as tired as you are?"

"I don't know if you've noticed, we aren't fighting things that a sword or an arrow can beat." Kenyer huffed as he looked around the dark, dank clearing. "I've never seen creatures like these."

"Neither has anyone else here," Aiya urged. "But if we're going to stay ahead, we need to rest!" Aiya turned back to the party and chuckled. "Looks like you've been usurped."

Kenyer turned to see what Aiya was looking at. Tyler, Annese, Odessa, Jordon, and Jeremy were all huddled together against a wall with Fang snuggled up in Jeremy's lap. Grandfather sat against the wall next to them, sound asleep. The gnomes were all huddled under one blanket on the opposite wall. Du'kai sat a few yards down, leaning against the wall. Only Jadara maintained guard at the opening to the other tunnel.

"All right," Kenyer moaned. "We'll rest for a few hours. Go get some sleep."

"Not this time," Jadara called over to him. "You get some sleep. Aiya and I will keep watch."

JEREMY

"I'm really getting tired of all this," Annese whined as she trudged along with her brother.

"Knock it off," Jeremy growled grumpily. Annese had been whining all morning. He could only be so patient. Jeremy glared at his sister in time to see Tyler roll his eyes.

"I want to go home!"

"We all do," Jordon replied with strained patience.

"But...."

"Come on, Annese," Aiya placed her arm around the girl's shoulder. "It'll all be over soon—I hope."

"But we've been gone so long! My mother has to be panicking by now."

"Mom will be fine," Jeremy sighed.

"How do you know?" Annese cried.

Jeremy whirled around on her. "I just know. Now shut your mouth and keep up!"

"I want my mother, too, Annese," Odessa tried to sympathize. "But we're not going to get back to them if we don't keep going."

"Jay," Jordon said quietly. "It's been a lot on her, and she is only 10." He looked over at his friend with a compassionate, questioning glance. "Can't you be a little more patient?"

"At least Tyler isn't whining his head off!" Jeremy retorted.

"No, he's whimpering and crying in his sleep," Jordon replied. "Just as bad. Try to remember the last time she was here; they locked her up in a statue. She had no concept of time. This is all new to her."

"It is very difficult being an older brother," Grandfather offered his compassion. "Especially when dealing with the emotional whirlwind that is a sister. Come. Let's keep moving."

Sighing heavily, Jeremy fell in line with the rest of the group. Annese was still getting on his nerves. He was grateful to Aiya for taking the girl.

JORDON

"I'm concerned," Jordon whispered to Kenyer as he caught up with the Drelt.

"Why?"

"We've been in this tunnel for hours, but nothing has come at us."

"Enjoy the quiet."

"It's too quiet, if you know what I mean."

"Yes, I know what you mean. Just keep your guard up and be ready for anything."

"Hey, Jeremy," Jordon heard Du'kai call his friend, "Can you brighten the light, please?"

"Sure." Jeremy brightened the light from the staff. "Why?"

Du'kai continued to stare ahead. "Because I think we've reached the end of the tunnel." He nodded ahead of them. The light from the staff, which had been bouncing off the walls, disappeared into the darkness ahead of them.

Jordon joined Jeremy and Du'kai as they made their way up to the end of the tunnel. Carefully, they looked out around the end of the walls. The tunnel opened up into a huge cavern. The rocks on the walls held a hint of the yellow rocks that emitted light. Unfortunately, it wasn't enough to see clearly. As Jeremy brightened the light some more, they saw a couple of large boulders in the middle of the cavern. The staff couldn't emit enough light to illuminate the whole cavern.

"Can anyone see anything?" Jordon asked as the others came up behind them.

"Put the light out," Jadara suggested.

"What?"

"Put it out! We see better in the dark!"

"Well, don't put out, out," Du'kai said. "Just dim it - a lot!"

Jeremy struggled to bring the light from the staff down to a candle's glow. Jordon saw the strain on Jay's face. He wasn't used to controlling the light that low. He waited as Jadara and Du'kai murmured between themselves, pointing at different areas of the cavern.

"Well?" Jordon asked.

"Can't say for sure," Du'kai replied. "There's those two big rocks in the middle."

"And four more behind those," Jadara added. "There's something glinting several yards behind those." Du'kai nodded in agreement.

"Could just be ice on the rocks," Annese said. "Look around. There's some amount of ice on just about everything."

"Bring the light back up, Jeremy," Grandfather suggested.

"Stay on your toes," Kenyer whispered, pulling out his sword. "I got a bad feeling about this."

"Ditto," Jordon replied, following his friend's lead. Du'kai and Kenyer looked at him with a questioning scowl.

Jordon sighed. "It means: me, too." Kenyer nodded and started out into the cavern, Jordon right on his heels.

"Spread out," Du'kai whispered, staying near the rear.

"Stay back, my dear." Grandfather waved to Annese from the opening. "If we need a healer, we'll need you unharmed."

The gnomes also stayed behind. Aiya and Jadara set themselves on either side of the tunnel and readied their bows. Odessa took her cue from them and set herself up between them.

As they moved further forward, the sight at the far end of the cavern made Jordon's blood run cold. Slowly the boulders in the rear moved, stretching out bigger and bigger. Soon three figures stood spread out and ready to fight.

"Those aren't rocks!" Jeremy trembled behind Jeremy. "Those are ice golems!"

A deep, evil laugh echoed through the cavern in a hideous, dangerous way. "Maw-ha-ha-ha-ha! I've got you now!"

18 – MIKKEL'S CONFRONTATION

JORDON

"Maw-ha-ha-ha-ha! I've got you now!" The laughter echoed off the rocks from every angle, making it virtually impossible to discern which direction it was coming from. It was the kind that sent an icy shiver up your spine.

Jordon noticed Fang sniffing at the golem nearest him. He backed away and growled at it, sniffed again, then jumped when the foot flicked his nose. The ortik bounced back and growled, growing a little larger.

"We're in trouble," Jordon nodded towards Fang.

"What was your first clue?" Jeremy asked sarcastically. He was looking at the ice golems.

"Trap!" Du'kai called back.

"Not quite," came a deep voice from the cavern. A tall, thin man with long, dark hair and a scraggly beard stepped out from behind the second boulder from the left. He wore dirty gray pants and a bluish tunic. His hands were behind him. Sharp blue eyes surveyed the group before him. "So, you are the ones I have spent the last year searching for. Hmmm. Not exactly the warriors I expected."

He stepped back behind the boulder. He showed up again from behind the boulder to the far right. "It appears you aren't as formidable as I presumed." He chuckled a bit. "Funny. I don't understand how you managed to get this far." He stepped back again behind the boulder.

Again, he stepped out, but this time from behind the next boulder to the left. "You have gathered some friends, I see. It will do you no good."

"We don't understand," Jordon called to him. "What have you got against us? We've done nothing to you."

"Nothing?" He leered, stepping back behind the boulder. He walked around the first boulder on the right. "Nothing? Really?" He chuckled again. "Do you know who I am?"

"No," Jeremy replied boldly. "And right now, I don't want to know. Let us pass."

The man let out a laugh; a loud, dark, evil laugh. "Let you pass?" He stepped back behind the boulder. He stepped out again, two boulders over.

"Never!" he spat. "I am Prince Mikkel! I am the future of Asteria! And I am through playing games with *little boys*!" He stepped back again.

Jordon noticed Fang grow again. Not a good sign.

Mikkel stepped out from behind the second boulder from the left. "I have tracked you two since you set foot on Asteria this time. You have evaded every ally I sent. But you'll not escape me now! Say your prayers, boys! You've met your match!"

As the man stepped back behind the boulder, the boulders stood up, showing massive, hard rock golems.

The ice golems in the back uniformly lifted their arms and swung. Ice shards flew through the cavern.

"Ahg!" Kenyer fell over, holding his shoulder as one of the knife-sharp shards embedded in his left shoulder.

"Kenyer!" Jordon yelled.

"Keep fighting!" he growled. "Grandfather! Keep the kids back!"

Du'kai yelped as he took a shard to the back while turning for the tunnel. Jordon looked back to see him fall on his face from the force, catch his breath quickly, and crawl to the tunnel. Annese helped him back towards a wall and began working on the wound.

Jordon wasn't sure what happened first, but everything burst into a flurry of activity. He bent down to Kenyer to help remove the shard. Kenyer pushed him away.

"What...?" Jordon questioned his friend.

"He's just declared war. Go! I'll join you in a few minutes," the Drelt instructed.

Jordon set his jaw, rose, and pulled a glowing Sharijol from its sheath. With determination, he turned and joyed the fray.

GRANDFATHER

"Ofkrat!" Grandfather yelled, waving his hand across the cavern. He didn't know how it would work on more than one golem. He'd never needed the spell walking through the islands before. Before the other night, he'd never needed the spell at all. To his surprise, it worked. To his disappointment, it only took out one of the stone golems. With his limited magical knowledge, he wouldn't be much help during the battle. There were only a few spells he could get off, and the spells required more energy here than he had to give.

Grandfather turned towards the tunnel with a gleam as he heard Seda issuing orders.

"Blul! Boom!" Seda demanded, taking a pan out of her pack. "Hurry! We guard." Rexa pulled a pot out of hers.

Blul nodded, dodged back to the tunnel wall, and sat down to scavenge through his pack. Both Seda and Rexa set themselves up around Blul. Grup began devising a plan as Blul worked frantically.

On either side of him, the girls had set up to dispatch arrows. Even Odessa joined them. Grandfather watched as the girls each got off a volley of arrows. Unfortunately, they just bounced off everything. The stone golems moved forward towards the party. The ice golems got another volley of shards off through the cavern. Jeremy got his shield up just in time for two of them to miss him and Aiya. Unfortunately, two of them hit Odessa squarely in the chest as she reloaded an arrow. She screamed and dropped to the floor. Du'kai and Grup quickly raced out and dragged her back into the tunnel for Annese to work on her.

DU'KAI

"Don't do complete heals," Du'kai warned to Annese. "You'll kill yourself, literally. Just heal us enough to keep us alive."

Annese looked up at Du'kai with wide, fearful eyes. She took in a deep breath as she heard the twang of bows setting off another volley of arrows. She nodded and began clearing the ice shards from Odessa with shaking hands.

"I... I... don't know if I can do this," she whispered.

Du'kai smiled reassuringly at the young girl. "You can do it! I have confidence in you. Your skills are amazing for someone of your age. We'll help as we can."

Annese nodded hesitantly and started healing the wound on Odessa.

JEREMY

Not sure what was going on, Jeremy cast freeze at the second stone golem that stood in front of him. A layer of ice formed over the golem, freezing the joints. He heard a grunt, followed by a crack, and the golem broke free. Ice sprinkled around them like rain.

He swallowed hard as another volley of arrows rained down from behind as four Mikkels stepped out from behind their respective golems. The first one, nearest Kenyer, got hit in the arm with one arrow. Another hit the Mikkel that stepped out next Jeremy. He hollered as it hit his shoulder. Growling, he pulled the arrow out again and eyed Jeremy with hatred. Jeremy backed away. The second set of arrows struck the Mikkel next to Fang. The man growled as he yanked the arrow out of his shoulder and threw it to the ground. He glared at the ortik in front of him. Using his might, he swung at the pup with the great hammer in his hands. Jeremy saw Fang dodged the hammer and came back, grasping the man's pants and tearing them from his leg. The sharp teeth sliced into that Mikkel's leg. With a sharp movement, Mikkel kicked Fang in the nose. Fang shook his head and dropped the cloth in his mouth. He growled at the man as he grew once again, almost doubling. Mikkel's eyes grew wide as he stepped back in surprise.

"Contego!" Jeremy shouted and pointed towards Jordon. A slight shimmer let Jeremy know the shield was in place. Not only was it in place, but it was covering everyone from Tyler across the cavern to Fang. Satisfied, he tried hard to figure his next move. Unfortunately, a volley of ice shards bouncing off the shield distracted him.

The Mikkel in front of Jordon raised his sword high in the air. He came down sharply on the shield, certain it would crack. He shook as his sword bounced off the shield, throwing him off balance. The Mikkel in front of him pointed at the shield. The stone golems in the back moved up towards it. In unison, they struck the shield. Jeremy's heart faltered as the shield failed from the strength of the hit. What now?

TYLER

Tyler moved his head back and forth, his axe held at the ready. He watched the golem move up towards him. "I don't think I'm ready for this!" he muttered shakily.

"You'll be fine. Try to anticipate their next move, then move away from it," Kenyer instructed. When the Drelt had gotten there, Tyler didn't know. "Let them move first, then you duck under and strike when they're following through. Just watch what they do and react faster. You'll be fine!"

"You'd better be fine!" He heard Jordon yell across to him. "If I don't bring you back alive, Mom's gonna kill me!"

"And that's a good incentive why?" Tyler threw back in the tease. The two cousins exchanged a quick, grinning glance. His mind got distracted as he looked to his left. He thought he saw something move, but when he looked towards it, nothing was there. The golem in front of him raised its arms and brought them crashing down. Tyler ducked out of its way just in time. Stone flew everywhere as the giant fists met the solid floor. Another Mikkel moved around past Tyler, his eyes on Jeremy. Something cold touched Tyler's shoulder. Tyler shook it off and focused on the stone golem in front of him.

DU'KAI

Du'kai watched from the entry of the tunnel. Everything was happening so fast it was hard to keep track of the events. Another volley of ice shards came flying at them. Jordon took one to the shoulder. Du'kai dodged from the tunnel as one flew past him. Aiya and Jadara ducked as the tinkling of breaking ice fell behind them when the shards shattered against the wall.

He watched Fang dodge left to avoid Mikkel's next swing. The stone golem next to him, however, was ready. With a swift swing of its large fist, the golem caught Fang in the ribs and tossed him towards the wall of the cavern. The pup yelped as he slid across the floor. Shaking off the dirt, Fang stood to face his opponent. Once again, the pup grew, shaking his head to clear his thoughts. Mikkel charged the pup with the hammer over his head. He swung down to crush the ortik, but the pup moved. The hammer crashed into the floor, causing a mini earthquake. Rocks spewed from the hole the hammer made. Several dropped from the ceiling of the cavern. Unstable waves shook the cavern, knocking several fighters off their feet. Mikkel backed up quickly, however, as he looked up at Fang's face. The Ortik's mouth was open. The eye teeth had grown into large fangs dripping with saliva. His nose was curled in a snarl. His eyes glinted with hatred as he crouched, prepared to strike again. He was a frightening sight.

Du'kai tore his gaze from Fang to survey the rest of the battle. He sidled up to Grandfather.

"What do you make of it?" he asked the elder man.

"One of them is the real one," Grandfather said, his eyes darting from one Mikkel to another. "I just can't figure out which one."

"I'll see what if I can help figure it out," Du'kai offered as Grandfather got off another mini fireball.

KENYER

Kenyer rose, grasped his sword, and prepared for the fight. He dodged up between Tyler and Jordon. He reassured Tyler and gave him a few quick pointers without taking his eyes off the golem. The stone golem in front of him swung his arm so fast it sent him off balance, missing Kenyer. Mikkel came around swinging dual axes. Kenyer eyed back and forth between the two axes, wondering which one was coming at him first. Mikkel faked the first strike, taking Kenyer off guard. As Kenyer moved to block the axe, the second axe struck him in his leg. Kenyer landed hard, the first axe digging into his hip. Mikkel laughed as Kenyer struggled against the pain.

"Kenyer!" Jordon's voice hollered as he pushed the Mikkel before him back. In a moment he raced to Kenyer and began assessing the wounds. Blood was pouring from the wounds. Without help, the Drelt would bleed to death in a few minutes.

"Congelo Somes," Kenyer heard Jeremy call at the same time. The Mikkel that was attacking him froze in a thin layer of ice with one axe raised.

Out of nowhere, Grup and Du'kai appeared next to Kenyer. "Go," Du'kai told Jordon. "We've got him."

Kenyer met Jordon's worried expression. Jordon whipped the medallion from around his neck. Kenyer had seen it several times during their trip and just assumed it was a decoration. His friend quickly pressed it to Kenyer's hip and put the Drelt's hand on it. "Here," he told him. "Hold this there. Don't let go."

Kenyer gripped the medallion to his hip with as much strength as he had. Strangely, it was heating up. The heat was going through his hip. He winced as Du'kai and Grup dragged him across the cavern floor to Annese; yet he was filling up with a strange, comforting strength.

GRANDFATHER
Grandfather looked around the cavern with concern. He had a hard time deciding who needed his help the most. One glance at Tyler told him the child was in over his head. Pointing his hand in that direction, Grandfather sent

several flaming spheres at the stone golem. The sphere whipped over Tyler's head and struck the stone golem on the left side. The explosion knocked Tyler to the floor. Grandfather shook his head at the results. The left side of the golem's torso was gone, leaving it with only one arm. Somehow, he was going to need to find out how to get more power.

He sent a small fireball in that direction. It struck the golem's right side causing the stone to meld together. The golem would have a harder time moving. That should give the boy an advantage.

Behind him, Aiya, Jadara, and Odessa let off another volley of arrows. One arrow struck the Mikkel coming up on Jeremy in the shoulder. It slowed him down a bit, but didn't seem to cause him any pain. Two more arrows struck the Mikkel with the great hammer in front of Fang. One struck him in the shoulder blade, the second in the back of his thigh. The man yelled in pain and struggling to remove the arrows while avoiding an angry Fang.

Imposters, but which one was the real enemy? If any of them.

GRUP

Grup came up next to Blul after he and Du'kai brought Kenyer to Annese. Blul was mixing chemicals carefully.

"Hurry! Friends hurt!" Grup complained.

Blul handed Grup three vials. "Go! Go!" he urged him to move out to help the party.

Taking the vials, Grup raced out into the cavern and looked about. Noticing another Mikkel with two axes coming towards Jeremy, Grup took off across the cavern. It would be tough to intercept, but he was one determined gnome.

JORDON

Jordon parried Mikkel as the two stared at each other. Their swords glinted in the dim light of the cavern. Mikkel struck, Jordon blocked. Sparks flew as the clang of metal echoed through the cavern. Gathering strength, Jordon blocked again as Mikkel swung at him again. Mikkel's sword bounced off Jordon's. The man spun around, swinging low to catch Jordon's legs. Jordon jumped to the side. As he did, he reached into his belt, pulled out his dagger, and buried it into Mikkel's arm. The man hollered as Jordon retreated, taking the dagger with him. The two glared at each other, continuing to circle.

GRUP

Grup moved up to the Mikkel with the two axes. He stopped momentarily to hold the vial in front of the man. "Oooh! Pretty!" the gnome murmured as Mikkel looked at the vial. Moving fast, Grup tossed the vial at Mikkel and took off running. Mikkel fumbled as he instinctively tried to catch the vial. The vial slipped between his fingers and landed at his feet. The explosion threw the man back half the length of the cavern and caused the stone golem next to him to fall, losing some of the rock that made him up.

JEREMY

Jeremy turned to his left as he thought something move again. He found himself staring into a gold-plated shield with a twisted serpent on it. The man behind it held an equally large sword and was moving towards him. Raising the shield in front of him, this Mikkel swung his sword towards Jeremy. Jeremy jumped back, narrowly avoiding the slicing blade. Mikkel advanced, hiding behind his shield. Thinking fast, Jeremy pushed his staff towards the man's arm and murmured, "Viscus..." To his dismay, Mikkel twirled around and knocked the staff off to the side. He struck with the shield, knocking Jeremy to the floor. Taking advantage of the position, Jeremy pushed the staff against the man's legs as he raised his sword. "Ut Calx" he whispered. The globe glowed for a second. As it went out, Jeremy rolled away as Mikkel's sword came crashing down onto the floor. The man tried to move but couldn't. Jeremy smiled as he rose. He watched the confused look on Mikkel's face turn to horror as he looked down at his legs turning to stone. The spell made its way up his body. The man screamed in rage, his echoing voice cut off as the spell took over his head. Jeremy nodded, satisfied that the statue remained in position.

Kenyer ran past the statue on his way back to the stone golem he was fighting. He nodded at Jeremy with a smile. Jeremy exchanged a happy nod with the Drelt, then looked around to see who needed help. He did a double take, looking around. He could have sworn he saw something moving out of the corner of his eye. Despite his belief, nothing was there.

A new volley of ice shards raced through the cavern. Getting use to them, the party ducked the shards, then continued with their battles. Only Grandfather encountered a problem, being interrupted as he prepared to cast another spell. Jeremy's heart went out to him. He didn't know many, but he was helping with what he remembered.

GRUP

Just in Grup's vision, Blul darted out of the tunnel they were hiding in. He held three vials in his hands as he quickly assessed the situations. He darted towards Jordon first. He wouldn't have much time. The distance was long, and Jordon was struggling to keep the great-sword-wielding Mikkel at bay and dodging the stone golem next to him. He'd meet Blul in the middle later.

Instead, Grup ran over towards Fang. He didn't wait to see what was happening. He rolled one vial under the stone golem attacking the poor pup. He turned and ran back as the vial exploded, reducing the golem to a pile of dust and knocking that Mikkel to his knees. Fang shook his head and sneezed from the debris left by the stone golem.

Heading towards the middle of the cavern, Grup took off again.

GRANDFATHER

Grandfather quickly caught his balance again by leaning on the stone behind him. That last explosion rocked everything! Glaring at the stone golems on Jordon, he once again commanded, "Ofkrat". Again, only one golem stopped in mid-stride and crumbled to the ground. The rock caused a dust cloud to rise; throwing off the combatants by making them cough and sneeze. OK, so he could take out the golems one at a time—for a while. It was a help.

BLUL

Blul helped his own way, running through the dust cloud to the other stone golem. Without missing a beat, he threw a vial at the stone monstrosity. It exploded as quickly as it landed, tossing the gnome into a forward roll. Jordon and his Mikkel were both knocked a few feet away by the force of the explosion. Without missing a beat, Blul ran towards another golem.

TYLER

Tyler struggled to avoid the stone golem in front of him. He was tiring and knew it. Twice the golem hit him to the side, causing scratches from the floor and bruises on his ribs. Tyler swung his axe again. The metal rang out as it struck, and the handle shook Tyler's arms. Not waiting, Tyler jumped back, expecting the golem to swing again. Instead, the golem brought down his remaining arm. The force knocked him into the fist as it slammed into the floor.

Ouch! A small hole appeared in the floor as the rock broke apart. Without missing a beat, the golem raised its arm and knocked Tyler across the cavern like a croquet ball. Tyler gritted his teeth as road rash filled his arms and back. Aiya helped him up.

"Try striking in his center," she suggested. "It looks like Grandfather left a weak spot there."

Tyler tried to ignore the pain as he turned to go back. The golem was heading towards him anyway. Taking a deep breath, Tyler set his eyes on his target and raced forward. He held the axe aloft, jumped to the side as the golem swung at him, dodged the second swing, and dug his axe deep into the center joint of the golem's torso. With a shake, the stone golem fell apart. It took Tyler a few minutes to dig out his axe from the pile of debris. He breathed in a few painful breaths, then jogged out to Annese. He definitely had some broken ribs.

JEREMY

Jeremy couldn't figure out what to do next. As he turned around and around to find out how everyone was doing, a sharp, cold pain struck his shoulder from behind. He bent forward in pain as icy shivers went through his body. He shook his head to clear away the sudden exhaustion. Twirling around, he tried to find the source. Nothing. The cold was gone, and there was nothing around him that could possibly have caused it. Maybe he was just reaching exhaustion.

GRUP

As if reading his friend's mind, Blul met Grup in the center of the cavern. Quickly he passed his last vial to Grup. Without a word, he raced back towards the tunnel. Grup poured on speed towards the outermost ice golem. Unfortunately, the next round of ice shards went sailing across the room before he could get there. No matter. He had his target.

FANG

Fang circled around the Mikkel with the great hammer in an attempt to catch the man off guard. Mikkel kept his eye on the ortik. Not finding an opening, he raised his great hammer and smashed it into the floor as hard as he could. Fang crouched as the hammer went up. Once again, the mini earthquake radiated across the cavern, causing varied effects and trip ups. The pup sneezed from the dust cloud the hammer caused.

Jordon gave Mikkel an advantage when he fell to the floor from the quake. Jadara knocked her head against the wall behind her as she went down. Du'kai lost his balance and knocked Grandfather over on his way down. The Mikkel with the two axes also fell to the ground as he tried to get back to Jordon. Several stalactites dropped from the ceiling, one of them taking out one of the central ice golems. The advantage this Mikkel wanted, however, backfired as Fang grew once again and launched himself at Mikkel. The pup was now almost up the Mikkel's shoulder. He dropped the hammer and dove to the side, just missing the massive beast's paws.

AIYA

Aiya mis-shot the arrow as a cold pain struck her arm. She stared around, trying to figure out what caused it. She grabbed her head as it spun. Slowly, she sank to her knees and dropped her bow, feeling extremely weak. Cold shivers went up her spine, bringing on a headache.

ODESSA

Odessa returned and quickly began shooting with Jadara. She struck the stone golem in front of Kenyer and nicked the Mikkel in front of Jordon. Albeit, most of her shots missed. She stamped her hooves in anger at her poor marksmanship.

"It's ok, Odessa," Jadara called, getting off another volley of arrows. "We're not all getting our targets. I've missed more than I've hit. Just keep trying."

"But I'm running out of arrows," Odessa frowned.

"So am I. Just keep going as long as you can."

Du'kai laid a gentle hand on the Centaus' shoulder. "You'll be fine. Just take your time aiming and don't forget to take into consideration which direction your target is moving."

Odessa smiled at the Drelt. She nodded and selected her next target.

ANNESE

Annese shivered as she lifted her hands from Tyler. "You should be alright for a bit," she said shakily.

"What's wrong?" Tyler asked, examining at the girl.
Even with her dark skin, Tyler could tell she looked pale.
Her lips were fading in color.

"I don't know. I'm cold," she said.

"Too tired?" he asked. "Are you over-doing it?"

"I don't think so," she replied.

Seda came over to join them. In her maternal way,
she put her hand on Annese's forehead. "Fever no," she
said. She looked into Annese's eyes. "Sight good." She took
Annese's hand and measured the girl's pulse. "Heartbeat!"

"I'm not dead or sick," Annese chuckled at the
gnome. "I'm just cold. It's probably just a draft."

"Could be," Tyler agreed. He shivered as well. The
cold pain was back at his shoulder. He shrugged as he felt
the energy being sucked out of him. Stepping back, the
cold stopped. "Move, Annese. It'll help," he suggested,
looking around. Strange. This wasn't a draft, but he
couldn't figure out what it was. Reluctantly, he returned to
the cavern.

FANG

Fang had enough of the great hammer-toting Mikkel.
He was now so large that he could look the man eye-to-eye.
He stalked his way around the man, looking for an
opening. Mikkel picked up the hammer and swung at the
pup. Fang turned sideways and brushed the hammer off.
He ducked next and grasped hold of the man's leg. Yanking
back, he tore a hole in the thigh and tossed it aside. Blood
spurt from the wound as Mikkel screamed and fell to the
floor. The man on the floor flung into his face. The huge

pup shook his head and pawed his face to get the dirt out of his eyes. He sneezed several times. It was enough of a break for Mikkel to grasp the hammer and limp towards the back of the cavern. An ice golem stepped between Fang and Mikkel to deter him from following.

Fang eyed the new enemy. With a growl, he grew yet again.

GRUP

Grup continued running as fast as his little legs could carry him. He raced up to the ice golem on the outside of the semi-circle. Not waiting, he tossed the vial at the golem with an upward swing, then changed directions back to the middle. The vial followed the golem's torso up before it turned and fell. It exploded before it ever hit the ground. Shattered pieces of ice darted across the chasm.

Swinging around wide, Grup dropped back to help Kenyer. While Kenyer focused on staying out of the way of the axes, Grup threw another vial at the stone golem. The vial missed the golem's back and tapped off its leg. Kenyer caught sight of the gnome's action and ducked back. As he heard the vial hit the golem, he dove backwards, out of harm's way. The vial exploded. It reduced the golem to a pile of stones. The force of the explosion knocked Mikkel head over heels. Grup didn't stick around. He turned his direction away from the explosion and aimed for another ice golem.

JORDON

Jordon swung back and forth, blocking Mikkel. The swords continued to clang. He had a hard time keeping up with the man. It amazed him that the older man showed no fatigue at all. Jordon had sustained a few cuts along the way. Luckily, nothing serious. It was a good thing since Kenyer still had his medallion. Jordon breathed hard as he circled Mikkel. The two swords pointed at each other. It didn't matter what he did; Mikkel bounced off his strike and blocked almost every move. Once again, Mikkel came in with a heavy onslaught. Jordon blocked him as much as he could. The dagger in his left hand suddenly gave Jordon an idea. He allowed Mikkel to disarm him. Quickly, he fell back into a backward roll, switching the dagger to his right hand. As he came back to his feet, Mikkel had his sword raised to slice through Jordon. Without wasting time, Jordon tossed the dagger at Mikkel. True to its mark, the dagger plunged into Mikkel's chest. The man stopped with a surprised look on his face. He stood only a second, then fell to the ground. Before Jordon's eyes, the man vanished, leaving the dagger on the ground. Jordon scowled. Where'd he go? No time to wonder. Jeremy's cry shook the thought from his head.

AIYA

Aiya tried to shake the cold. It was giving her a headache. She stood and aimed, mis-shot another arrow. The cold was getting stronger, radiating through her whole body. Collapsing to the floor, she let out a cry as she grasped her head.

"Aiya!" Jeremy called, and ran over to her.

Aiya looked up at Jeremy weakly, then closed her eyes. She was shivering.

Jordon and Jeremy rushed to her. Kneeling at her head, Jordon lifted it into his lap. Carefully, he brushed her hair back. She was clammy and cold. Her breathing was shallow. "Aiya? Are you ok?" He sounded worried.

Aiya shook her head. "C... c... c... cold," she murmured.

"I don't get it," Jeremy shook his head. "There's nothing here." A cold touch to his shoulder and a draining pain made Jeremy jump sideways. "There *is* something here!"

JEREMY

Grandfather met Jeremy's eyes from across the tunnel. He glanced over at the small group. He reached into his pocket and pulled out a small pouch. He poured a little of the glittering powder into his hand. Watching carefully, he tossed the glittering dust at the group. It outlined a humanoid form against the wall. "There's your culprit."

Jeremy raised his staff off the floor. "Sanctum fulsi de lumen," he cried in anger. The bright blue beam came again from the crystal globe of the staff. It seemed to sear right into the black shadow against the wall. An unearthly scream echoed through their bodies, but not their ears, as the shadow seeped into oblivion from the center out.

"It's alright," Jordon comforted Aiya. She glanced up at him with a weak smile as he brushed her hair aside again as Tyler came up towards them.

"Ahh!" Annese's cry came from the tunnel.

"Annese!" Tyler cried. Grandfather and Jeremy chased after Tyler as he darted back down the tunnel.

TYLER

Annese lay on the ground, totally unconscious. Like Aiya, her breathing was shallow and barely noticeable. She shivered with cold and was holding her head. Tyler skidded next to her head and tried to wake her. Grandfather threw a handful of glitter dust once more. Another humanoid figure came into view. Jeremy used the spell again to remove this creature from their presence. Rexa covered Annese with a blanket. Du'kai arrived with Aiya in his arms. He set her down carefully next to Annese. He and Grandfather set up a bunch of red crystals to give the girls some heat.

"Head back to the battle, Tyler," Du'Kai nodded towards the cavern. "Kenyer and Jordon can't do it all by themselves." Tyler glanced at Annese. "We've got her."

Jeremy had already touched his sister with his staff and was chanting the incantation for his minor wounds to heal her.

Back in the cavern, Tyler saw Fang get clipped with several ice shards. Angry at the gleaming creature in front of him, he launched himself into the air. His huge paws struck the golem in the chest, knocking it over. Landing on the golem, the ice golem shattered into tiny pieces and scattered across the floor. Fang stopped for a moment to figure out what happened. Instead, he caught the scent of Mikkel going towards the back of the cavern.

KENYER

Kenyer circled his Mikkel again. He had sustained a few more cuts, but Jordon's medallion kept his body from bleeding. It was a miracle! Mikkel continued to twirl the axes. Problem was that he could get three strikes to Kenyer's one. Once again, Mikkel rushed forward, swinging his axes. Kenyer blocked the first, twisted to block the second, and twirled around to block the third. He hooked his sword behind the axe and let the momentum of his body force the axe from Mikkel's hand. He used the momentum to put a little distance between them as the clang of the axe skittering across the floor echoed around the cavern.

On more even terms now, the two stared at each other. Mikkel motioned for Kenyer to come forward. Kenyer grinned wickedly in return. He'd wait. He was breathing too hard to take the initiative. At length, Mikkel tired of waiting and launched at Kenyer. The Drelt moved swiftly, dodging or blocking the axe again and again. At last, the opening came as Mikkel raised the axe to strike again. Kenyer gained the initiative as he dug his sword into Mikkel's stomach. Taken by surprise, Mikkel looked shocked, then disappeared. His axe fell, clanging on the hard floor. A third axe also lay on the ground. Kenyer stared at the space. What the.....?

Tyler ran up to retrieve his axe. "Yea," he said to Kenyer's confused face. "Weird, right?"

GRUP

Grup came flying around the cavern towards the ice golems. He quickly intercepted the one to Kenyer's right. Catching the golem's attention, he shook the last vial in his hand. He showed it to the golem, tossed it up, and took off. The golem followed the vial up towards the ceiling and tried to catch it on its way down. The vial hit the golem's hands and exploded, sending tiny shards of ice all over the cavern floor.

MIKKEL

"We're losing, you old bat!" Mikkel grumbled at the sorcerer in their tunnel. "You promised we'd win!"

"They've not won yet."

"Your creatures are all but gone!"

"I'm doing the best I can!"

"It's not good enough!"

"Stop being a spoiled brat and do something for yourself for a change!" the sorcerer snapped back at him. "I'm sick and tired of doing your dirty work. I wear myself thin for you, and you have no gratitude."

"I am king! I don't need gratitude."

"You are a lazy, self-centered brat! Now make yourself useful!"

Jujene looked out the tunnel he was hiding in. Mikkel was right. The battle that should have been a shoe-in was being lost. Only two ice golems remained. No, make that one. That blasted old man disintegrated another one. Worse, the over-sized puppy was coming towards them. Jujene needed a rest, but there was no time. Grasping his wand, he pointed it at the ortik.

A dark beam of shadow came from the wand and struck Fang in the chest. The pup shook his head and backed up a bit. The beam continued. The pup looked about confused. He sniffed about the ground again, trying to find the scent he was following.

JEREMY

Jeremy spotted Kenyer approaching one of the ice golems. Kenyer looked up at the huge ice golem in front of him. He heaved in air to catch his breath as he tried to dodge the golem's attack. Two ice shards embedded themselves in Kenyer's chest. Kenyer used his sword to defray the golem's arms. The sword only chipped off a few pieces of ice. The golem waited for the sword to go by, then jumped forward, slamming itself into Kenyer. The Drelt went flying backwards. The metal-on-stone sound echoed around the cavern when his sword clattered on the ground as it fell from his hands.

Jeremy stepped out of the tunnel and began his next spell.

"Congelo Somes," he whispered. The ice golem froze in mid-stride. The thin layer of ice that formed over it wouldn't thaw anytime soon since the ice golem was cold to begin with. The perfect reinforcement for that spell.

As Jeremy looked about, he met eyes with Jordon. Hoping his friend would understand, Jeremy looked at the ice golem he immobilized, then looked back. Jordon followed his gaze. Jeremy grinned as a slow, mischievous grin crossed Jordon's face.

Jordon took up the next move. Racing across the cavern, he barreled into the ice golem with his shoulder. The block of ice went flying across the open space from his weight. The golem hit the floor and shattered into hundreds of tiny pieces. Jordon just lay on the ground to catch his breath. Over.

Jeremy's expression fell as another mini-earthquake tremored through the cavern as the ringing of the huge great hammer struck the ground. Grup fell as he reached out for Fang. The pup crouched to maintain his balance. Blul also fell halfway across the cavern. He twisted into a skidding motion, probably to avoid shaking up the vial in his hand before he needed it.

JORDON

Jordon crawled back towards Kenyer. The Drelt stood up and helped the boy to his feet with a handshake. Jordon rose on shaky legs and balanced himself.

Suddenly, a dark beam came from the tunnel at the other end of the cavern. It struck Kenyer in the chest. The Drelt arched backwards in pain. He felt like his heart was being ripped from his body. He could hardly breathe. The beam stopped momentarily. Kenyer fell to the floor on his hands and knees. Jordon dropped to his side. Again, the beam came, grasping the Drelt. Kenyer struggled to shake away the feeling. He was getting weaker by the minute.

"Hold the medallion close to you!" Jordon whispered, grasping his friend's shoulders. Suddenly he, too, was overcome with exhaustion. A cold, energy-draining feeling was completely overpowering him.

Jeremy suddenly appeared. He had darted across the cavern as Kenyer and Jordon went down. Sliding up next to them, he pointed the staff. "Congelo!" he cried.

The barrier did the trick. It interrupted the beam from its targets. Instead, the dark beam bounced off and hit the wall on the far side of the cavern.

BLUL

Blul watched Grup grasped Fang's fur in an attempt to stop the pup. Unfortunately, the ortik had gotten so large, the gnome was more of an ornament against him. Du'kai and Tyler raced across just as quickly to help Grup. Jeremy's voice rang as he tried to call the pup. Du'kai tackled the ortik as Tyler wrapped himself around its neck. They tried with all their might to hold the thing back from the tunnel. Instead, Fang just continued to drag them along.

Blul burst past the pup, eyes set. Something bad was in the tunnel. Another set of tremors erupted from the tunnel as the metal echoed around. Stones began falling from the walls. More holes were opening in the ceiling. Cracks formed on the rock surfaces. Tiny darts of fire were shooting at Blul's feet as he sped across the floor. Blul quickly dodged them all. As he came closer to the tunnel, he began shaking the vials. Without missing a step, he tossed two of them into the tunnel entrance as he ran past.

"No!" Mikkel's shrill voice echoed from within just a second before the explosion blew Blul halfway back to his friends. Fang jumped back, taking everyone with him. The group watched as the walls and ceiling around the tunnel caved in, effectively blocking the tunnel.

JORDON

Jordon helped Kenyer to his feet. Jeremy dropped the shield. Jordon's gaze went across the cavern. Piles of rubble, melting ice, and a closed-up tunnel met his eyes. Behind him, Jadara, Odessa, and Aiya lowered their bows. Grandfather leaned weakly against the wall. Slowly, the party hobbled together near their entry point. The rag-tag group looked beaten up and worn out. They all glanced at each other to determine who needed the most help. The silence of the room was disconcerting. In fact, it hurt.

"I suggest we rest here for a while," Grandfather suggested quietly. "We could all use the sleep."

"But what if he comes back again?" Jeremy spoke what Jordon was thinking.

Grandfather shook his head. "You don't come back from that kind of cave in," the old man comforted the boy. "Let's get our things, have something to eat, and get some sleep. At least for a few hours."

"I'd have to agree with him," Kenyer replied, handing the medallion back to Jordon. "We didn't get much sleep before this battle, and personally, I'm don't think I could go on right now."

Jordon nodded. He was aching as well. "Agreed. We all need the rest."

Moving stiffly and with much effort, Grandfather helped set up camp just outside the tunnel. Tyler jumped to help the elderly man. Grandfather moved the set of red crystals into the campsite area and added a pot of water to boil. Seda began pulling out various foods while Rexa pulled out her healing herbs. Annese and Aiya were already asleep, wrapped in their blankets. Rexa added some water to her herbs, went over, forced the girls awake long enough to drink her concoction. Grandfather chuckled as both girls winced at the sour-tasting brew.

"Squint now, feel better in the morning," Rexa spoke wisely, walking back to her things.

Du'kai emerged from the tunnel, supporting Annese around her shoulders. The girl was incredibly weak, both from using her ability and the shade that threatened her life.

Jeremy was setting up his bedroll. Fang, much smaller now, was gnawing on a beef stick. Jordon noticed his friend shaking. They were all exhausted. It's been a rough couple of days. With a sigh, Jordon sat on the ground.

DU'KAI

"I'm sorry I didn't do more," Du'kai murmured to Kenyer as he dropped onto the ground next to his friend.

"What? Why?" Kenyer asked surprised.

"I... I feel bad about not fighting," Du'kai revealed. His head hung.

Kenyer smiled at his friend. "Du'kai, I've known you all your life. You are a peaceful person. That's why you're a tracker, not a hunter. I wouldn't expect you to get in the middle of a battle. You were a great help. You brought the broken back to the medic. That's a big job."

Du'kai smiled gratefully at his friend. "Thanks."

Kenyer held out a piece of meat jerky with a smirk. "Here. Eat up. And stop questioning your position in the party."

GRANDFATHER

Sitting around the red crystals, the battered group shared food and water. Grandfather heated some of the left-over stew. Fang was happy to get a bowlful. Grandfather smiled at the pup, now down to normal size, as he eagerly cleaned the bowl, then laid down on the bottom of Jeremy's bedroll. He looked like a cute, helpless puppy instead of the mean monstrosity that battled the golems.

One by one, each person crawled into the welcome warmth of their bedrolls. With Tyler's help, Grandfather finished cleaning up his things and added more crystals to the others to help with warming up the area. He looked around the room at the exhausted warriors. Nodding, he crawled into his own bedroll. Only a few snores interrupted the silence in the cavern. He thought about keeping watch, then dismissed it. The "fire" would keep the bugs, insects, and other animals away. And Fang would wake them all if something dangerous came into the cavern. No, he, too, would fall asleep. Who knew casting so many spells would completely drain a person?

19 – THE HIDEOUT

JEREMY

Jeremy awoke groggily. Something didn't feel right. He heard a shuffling sound nearby. Rolling over, he opened his eyes, expecting to see Grandfather shuffling by. Instead, a pair of toothpick thin legs clicked past, dragging a large cocoon of silk. Jeremy closed his eyes, then opened them again with a snap. He didn't hear Fang growling? In fact, he couldn't feel Fang at his feet.

Jeremy looked down towards his feet. Fear flew through him instantly. Fang wasn't there. He looked around the campsite. He wasn't anywhere else, either. Turning, he looked in the direction the cocoon went. A huge black and white spider was still dragging it across the floor. Behind it were two others dragging equally large cocoons.

Jeremy looked around. He began doing a head count. Five, six, seven, eight.... The gnomes! All four of the gnomes were missing! A clicking sound forced his head around. Four more spiders were coming towards the others. One each joined the other three and picked up the free end of the cocoons, helping to carry it off.

Struggling to get free of the bedroll, Jeremy tried to get up. "Jordon! Kenyer! Du'kai! Wake up!" he yelled.

The spiders at the other end of the cavern stopped and turned towards him. They clicked a little amongst themselves, then continued on.

Jeremy grasped his staff. He swiftly pointed it toward the spiders. "Congelo Somes!" he cried. The spider nearest him froze. The one it was helping continued to pull. It almost looked like a tug of war. Eventually, the cocoon ripped, revealing the black and gray fur so familiar to Jeremy.

"Fang!" Jeremy cried in horror.

The rest of the campsite stirred quickly at Jeremy's cry. Confused, they woke up and wriggle free of their covers.

"Jeremy," Jordon stretched. "What is it?"

Jeremy simply pointed. The rest of the group followed his arm. The spider was still trying to tug its prize free of the frozen one. The cocoon ripped further, letting a paw drop. It dawned on everyone the peril the pup was in.

"It's not just Fang. They've got the gnomes, too." Jeremy pointed to where the gnomes had bedded down for the night. The blankets were empty.

"Oh, no!" Jadara gasped, covering her mouth.

"We have to get them," Du'kai growled. He grasped a dagger.

"Whoa! Whoa!" Jordon grabbed his arm to hold the Drelt back. "We need a plan. Just rushing up to them is only going to get us killed!"

"We have to save them!" Du'kai pointed as he stared at Jordon with wide eyes.

"Have you seen the size of those things?" Jordon pointed after the spiders. "They're bigger than me!"

"Let's go! They've got Fang!" Jeremy urged.

Kenyer came up, strapping his sword to his hip. "Let's move. Every moment we wait puts them closer to death."

"Kenyer is right," Grandfather agreed. "Go! I'll stay here with the girls."

"The longairits!" Annese cried. "They're gone!" She was holding an empty basket. Strands of silk stuck to the edges.

"We'll get them!" Jeremy growled. He snatched his blanket and laid it out. "Congelo Somes," he pointed his staff at it. The blanket quickly froze. "Everybody on!"

"Great idea!" Du'kai smirked, sitting down. Kenyer, Aiya, Jordon, and Jadara joined him.

Jeremy climbed on the front of the blanket and laid his staff on it. Holding the side of it, he raised it with a levitation spell. Quickly he sped the blanket towards the spiders. The one unfrozen spider was trying to repair the damaged webbing on the pup.

Jordon pulled his dagger from his boot. He aimed carefully. Hopefully, he could throw the dagger accurately. He was still sore from yesterday's fight.

"Little more," he urged Jeremy. "Hold!" As the blanket stopped in the air, Jordon let his dagger fly. The group watched the dagger flip in the air over and over and over as if in slow motion until THAP! The dagger landed squarely in the creature's head. With a surprised squeak, the spider collapsed.

Jeremy brought the blanket in as close as possible. He landed it gently and ran to the webbed cocoon. Pulling out his dagger, he began cutting the webbing away from the creature inside it. Jordon retrieved his dagger and helped.

"His paws are cold," Du'kai said, grasping the paw that was dangling. "Hurry!"

Jeremy cut faster, trying hard not to cut the pup, but his hands were shaking. Jordon also cut faster. Eventually they found his head and cleared away the webbing. Without thinking, Jordon whipped off the medallion from his neck and pressed it to Fang. Jeremy rubbed the pup briskly.

"Come on, buddy!" Jeremy urged. "Come on!"

"The medallion's getting warm," Jordon reported. "It's a good sign."

"Come on, boy," Du'kai whispered. "You can do it!"

It took a while, but Fang eventually began stirring. With a heavy yawn, he blinked his eyes and looked up. The little party cheered him on. Jeremy wrapped his arms around the pup's neck.

"Atta boy!" he praised. "Good boy!" Fang leaned over and gave him a lick.

"Hey, Annese!" Jordon called back to the campsite. "Call Fang!"

KENYER

Kenyer swung angrily, knocking the head off the frozen spider. He had never been this angry! They had fought so many things to get this far; now half the party is missing. He whirled around towards his friend. "Du'kai, we need to know which way those other spiders went," Kenyer instructed firmly. "No time to waste!"

"I'm on it," Du'kai agreed, getting down on hands and knees. He began searching for clues.

JORDON

Annese's voice called the pup across the cavern. Fang's ears perked up as he looked in the voice's direction. "Come on, Fang! Breakfast! Come on, boy!"

"Jere," Jordon laid a hand on his friend's shoulder. Jeremy still hadn't let go of the pup. "The others?"

Jeremy nodded. "Go on, Fang! Go get Annese! Go on!" He pushed the ortik towards Annese. She was waving something in the air. It must have smelled good, because the pup went running sloppily across the cavern towards her. Apparently, he was still feeling whatever anesthesia the webbing inflicted.

Back on the blanket, the group followed Du'kai. He found several clues. It helped that they were dragging the gnomes along. The trail dead-ended at a wall. Du'kai continued to study the tracks. Jeremy brought the blanket in close.

"The trail goes up."

"We'd better hurry," Kenyer stated with determination.

"Why?" Jordon asked. "I mean, I agree, but why?"

"Fang wasn't dead," Kenyer pointed out. "He was unconscious, but not dead. That tells me these spiders are gathering meat for their young."

Jordon gulped. "As in, meat for their young when they hatch?" He'd learned of spiders and insects that did the same thing back home. The arachnids would wrap the meal in a webbing, then surround the egg sack with the webbing and meal so that the young would eat through the hapless victim while escaping the egg nest. Kenyer nodded.

JEREMY

Du'kai climbed onto the blanket. "Let's move. Straight up."

Jeremy directed the blanket up. He needed to refreeze it again. Du'kai continued to find tracks. Working quickly, they followed it up to a ledge that ran along the ceiling. Du'Kai studied it carefully and directed them towards the collapsed tunnel. As quickly as possible, they followed the trail along the ridge.

Just as he expected, an army of giant spiders met them, coming their way. Each one was the size of his little sister's ride-in coupe. Aiya and Jadara began the arduous task of picking them off one arrow at a time. Kenyer and Jordon began swatting those they could reach. One by one, they began clearing the way. Jeremy kept inching the blanket forward.

A tunnel opened up to the right. More spiders were coming out of it. Jeremy finally tired of the fight. Holding up his staff, he warned the others to watch their eyes.

"Solar lux lucis!" The bright glow of light burst into the tunnel. The spiders scattered with squeals of fear and pain.

Squinting against the light, Jeremy and Jordon looked down the tunnel. At the far end was a mass of webs. Huge egg sacks hung around the large silk cocoons that were neatly tucked into the webs.

"I'm going in," Kenyer announced, squeezing through the two boys.

"Right behind you," Du'kai volunteered. "Jeremy, keep the blanket steady. Girls, keep those eight-leggers away. Jordon, get ready to receive the cocoons."

Armed with blades, the Drelts crawled down the tunnel. Cutting the webbing as they went, they cut out the first cocoon. Quickly, they passed it back to the boys. Jordon and Jeremy began cutting away the webbing around Blul. He was in the same drowsy state Fang had been in. Soon, the Drelts passed out another cocoon; Seda. Two others came back the same way. With much difficulty, the group on the blanket aroused the gnomes.

"We're not all going to fit on the blanket," Jadara surmised. "We're going to need to walk back."

"No. We'll make it," Jeremy insisted. "It'll be really tight, but we'll make it."

"The longairits!" Jordon called to Du'kai.

"We're looking," he called back.

"I'm not sure which ones they are," Kenyer called back. "There's gotta be fifty cocoons the same size."

"Start cutting," Jordon demanded. "Annese is counting on us to save those things."

Side by side, Du'kai and Kenyer began cutting away webbing. Many of the cocoons were dead spiders. Some were lizards. A few were worms. At length they found seven of the eight longairits. Du'kai brought each one back to the blanket as they found them. Kenyer came out with the last one.

"There's only seven." Jeremy counted the fluff balls in his lap. "Where's....."

Kenyer closed his eyes and shook his head. "It was too late. That set of eggs had already hatched. I'm sorry."

With a sad sigh, the boys nodded. "Come on," Jordon said. "Climb on."

Kenyer looked at the crowded blanket. "I don't think we'll fit."

"Come on," Jordon teased with a mischievous grin. "Where's your sense of adventure?"

"Still in my blankets," Du'kai chuckled.

Slowly, the two climbed on the blanket. The transport made a sudden dip. Jeremy squinted with concentration to keep it up. Jordon's hand grabbed his friend's shoulder for added energy. Carefully, the gnomes crawled onto the laps of the Drelts. Shakily, Jeremy directed the blanket down the tunnel, but he lost control around the bend and crashed at the end.

"Ow!"

"Ooph!"

"Augh!"

"Ooo!"

"Eep!"

The grunts, groans, and exclamations resounded as the group tumbled off the blanket and over one another.

Jeremy saw one gnome bounce off Jordon's back on the floor.

"Sorry," Jeremy muttered embarrassed, holding his head. "It was too much for me to handle."

"Good try," Kenyer groaned, struggling to get up. "We'd best keep going. It's only a matter of time before those spiders come back after us."

"Especially after we destroyed their nest," Du'kai agreed, rising.

"Here," Jeremy suggested, setting up the blanket again. "Let me take the gnomes back to the campsite, and I'll come back for you guys."

"I'll ride backup," Aiya offered. Jeremy nodded.

In only a few moments, Jeremy and Aiya had the gnomes settled on the blanket. They were off, riding rapidly across the cavern floor.

The sight before them made the group panic. Many of the enormous spiders were attacking the group that remained behind. Odessa shot off as many arrows at a time as she could. Tyler was running about with his axe. Each swipe cut off more legs. Grandfather was setting some on fire with small fireballs.

Aiya began shooting the spiders from behind. The arrows did minor damage, but added up. Jeremy touched down a short distance away from the spiders. Since they didn't have any of their things with them, the gnomes quickly ran for cover. Jeremy let off a fireball.

"Drop!" Grandfather cried, seeing the ball. He quickly hit the ground. The others dropped in panic as the fireball hit.

The fireball flew into the spiders, knocking out four of them. The power of the ball flew over those on the ground.

"That's my hair!" Annese screamed at her brother.

Amazingly, the remaining spiders quickly retreated. Jeremy yelled back a warning to the others. The rapid clicking of the spindly legs against the rock echoed around the cavern. Soon, the yells of Kenyer and Jordon reverberated through the air. Tyler and Jeremy ran back to help, only to find the remaining party members walking towards them, smiling.

"What happened?" Jeremy asked.

"We yelled, and they took to the ceiling," Kenyer explained smugly.

"Ran like scared, little children," Jordon smirked. "I don't think they're used to things fighting back." Jeremy chuckled.

"They aren't going to stay that way when they discover we destroyed their nest," Du'kai reminded his friends. "Let's move!"

"They're still a bit disoriented," Grandfather informed Jeremy as they returned. He was watching over the gnomes back at the campsite. Jeremy folded up his blanket.

"Ya know," Du'kai began as he bent over to help. "I really like this little transport of yours, but does it have to freeze my behind?"

It started as a giggle. It moved up to a chuckle. It broke out into an out-and-out laugh as Jordon and Jeremy looked at each other. Kenyer couldn't help but join in. The rest of the campsite chuckled as well. It was a wonderful tension breaker.

ANNESE

Annese rushed up to Jadara with a squeal to scoop up her fluffy pets. The longairits were coming around, gleeping as they looked around.

"Wait!" she frowned, looking in her arms and quickly counting. "There's only seven. Where's Brownie?"

"You don't want to know," Du'kai muttered, gently laying a hand on her shoulder as he passed.

Annese turned to look at Jeremy. Her brother merely lowered his eyes. Fearing the answer, she hugged the other longairits closer. "Jeremy?" she asked worriedly.

Jeremy looked at his sister as Odessa came up with the longairits basket. He shook his head. Slowly Odessa took the longairits from her and put them in the basket. "We were too late," he whispered. "I'm sorry. We tried. Really."

Annese crumbled to the floor. Her lower lip bowed out as water filled her eyes. She sniffled, then the tears flowed down her cheeks and dripped onto her pants.

"Aw, come on!" Jeremy moaned.

"They... he... he," Annese sobbed.

Jeremy sighed. "Annese, knock it off! I know you're hurt, but there was nothing I could do! I can't resurrect something!"

Jadara came over and sat next to Annese. Annese leaned into her friend as the Drelt wrapped her arm around the child's shaking shoulders. Jeremy threw his hands up and moved away.

"Shhh!" Jadara tried to comfort the girl gently.

JEREMY

"We all pitched in and packed things," Grandfather told Jeremy. "We kinda figured we weren't getting any more sleep."

"You're probably right," Jeremy responded, kneeling down to hug Fang. The pup licked at Jeremy's face happily. "You alright, boy?" he asked, examining the pup closely.

"She'll be alright," Grandfather said softly as he looked at Jadara trying to comfort Annese.

"I know." Jeremy looked over his shoulder. "I lose patience with her. She cries at the drop of a hat over anything and everything!"

Grandfather chuckled. "My sister used to do the same thing. She's just being a girl." His eyes lit up with dawning. "I have a sister!" he exclaimed excitedly.

"Isn't there an easier way to be a girl?"

Grandfather chuckled again. "Son, there are two types of girls. There are those like your sister—high strung and emotional—and those who are fairly tough and keep it all bottled inside. Both kinds have their difficulties and their appeals."

Jeremy looked at Grandfather as if he were nuts. "I think you've been away from society too long. There's nothing appealing about *that!*" he nodded towards his sister.

"Give yourself a few years," Grandfather grinned. "You'll understand then. Come along, now. We'd best get moving."

Jeremy nodded and went over to the gnomes. "How is everyone?" he asked.

"They're doing well," Aiya replied. "Seda had some herbs to help with their healing, and your medallions helped quite a bit. They should be able to move along in a few moments."

"Would they rather ride? I can gather up the blanket again."

Aiya shook her head. "I think walking would be a better option. It'll get the blood flowing. Get them awake."

"Ok. Let's gather the team. We need to move on."

"All I want is a warm bed and a good night's sleep," Jordon muttered from the floor near Aiya. He was leaning back on his pack. "I don't think we've slept a full night in over a week."

"Have we been out here a week?" Jeremy smirked.

"I have no idea. I lost track of days and nights."

JORDON

Slowly, the party gathered together. They all shared a quick meal and took off towards the far end of the cavern. Jeremy kept the solar light up to scare off any would-be attackers.

"Which tunnel?" Jordon asked. The two options led in opposite directions.

"Let me see. If we go that way, we come to a transport pad that will take us back to the little men who dig for gems," Grandfather pointed to the one on the right as he examined Fuzz's maps.

"Yea, we don't want to go there," Kenyer said darkly. "They'll probably kill us on sight."

"That good, huh?" Grandfather raised his brows questioningly.

"Don't ask," Jordon replied.

"Then I guess we're going this way," Tyler said, pointing to the tunnel on the left.

"Guess so," Grandfather said. "Talley ho!"

Jordon looked at Grandfather strangely, shook his head, then started for the tunnel.

The tunnel widened and narrowed in various places. It twisted and turned as it went. Several times they had to squeeze through some outcroppings. They traveled for the better part of an hour before they came to a split in the tunnel.

"Which way?" Odessa asked.

"Don't know," Jordon shrugged.

Fang kept sniffing the ground. He followed the pathway to the right as he sniffed.

"What'd ya find? Huh, boy?" Jeremy questioned the pup. He started following the curious little guy. Jordon shrugged and followed.

The pathway was fairly narrow. Only one person at a time could fit through. A soft, warm breeze came through the archway. Jordon bumped into Jeremy's still form in an archway. He stared over Jeremy's shoulder in surprise, then jerked forward as Annese bumped into him from behind.

"What's all this?" Annese asked.

The little cave in front of them was made up as a bedroom. It held a bed and a dresser. A large chest sat at the foot of the bed. A small nightstand had a partially used candle on it. A table in the corner had a chair next to it and five very used books. A painting hung on the wall of a Rho'taak flying over the ocean with a fish in its claws. Opposite them was a small archway. A curtain hung as a door.

"It... it looks like a bedroom," Jordon said confused.

"Keep on moving!" Jadara pushed, looking over Annese.

Jeremy moved to look at the books. Jordon joined him while looking at the furniture. The books were old with fraying and faded covers. One was the history book about Asteria they had seen on the surface—the one that had Jordon's and Jeremy's picture in it. Another was a spell book. The other three looked to be fiction.

ANNESE

Annese slowly pulled back the curtain to look on the other side. She straightened as she opened it the rest of the way. A kitchen of sorts was in the next cave. A small table sat in the middle, bordered by two chairs. Several urns sat on one side of the room on a series of shelves. The other side had a shelf of plates, utensils, and goblets. Another large urn filled with water sat on the floor. Annese started looking through things.

"What are you doing?" Tyler asked.

"Finding a whole bunch of food," Annese replied. "Look at these."

Tyler's eyes widened. "Are those chocolate chip cookies?"

"I think so," Annese replied. "And they're fresh. So is the fish in this urn. It smells like tuna."

"And here?" Tyler asked, picking up the lid on one urn.

"Looks like string beans." Annese reached in and picked one out. She broke it in half. The snap echoed around the room. She looked at Tyler with raised brows. "*Fresh* string beans."

"How'd they get here?"

"I don't know."

"Don't know what?" Grandfather asked, coming in.

"This food. It's all fresh," Annese waved at the urns.

"Really?" Grandfather lifted the lid on one jar. Fruit. Grandfather picked one out and looked at the reddish peach-type fruit. "A Quonant. Hmmm." He sunk his teeth into the soft flesh of the fruit. Juice ran down his chin as he chewed. "Mmmmm," he moaned with closed eyes. "Delicious!"

"How?" Tyler asked.

"I wonder......" Grandfather murmured as he took another bite of the fruit. "Oh. Here. Have one. They're quite good." Grandfather tossed each of them a quonant. Annese looked at it, shrugged, and dug in. Just as Grandfather had done, her eyes closed in contentment.

TYLER

"What's beyond that curtain?" Jordon asked, coming into the room. He was looking at a curtain in the wall to the right. Jordon turned over his shoulder as Jeremy called to him.

The three turned in the direction he pointed. None of them had noticed the curtain, nor the archway it covered. Walking forward, Tyler pushed the curtain aside to reveal another bedroom in this chamber. This one had a bed, a trunk, and a nightstand like the other one. On the table in this room sat a large, round, clear ball on a tarnished silver stand. A shelf carved in the wall held several books.

"They're strange looking books," Tyler began reading the spines.

Grandfather peered over his shoulder at the runes engraven on the bindings. "I think they're spell books. Except for the purple one. That's a cookbook."

"I don't get it."

Jordon came in from the kitchen. "We think we do. Look what we found in the nightstand of the other bedroom?" He held up a small framed painting. It was Jamiss on the throne, dressed in an ancient black tux with a blue ascot. A golden crown sat on his head. A beautiful, thin woman with long black hair stood next to him. Her green lacy dress was absolutely beautiful. She wore a golden ringlet on her head. Tyler and Annese looked at the picture in confusion and shrugged.

"And...?" Tyler asked.

"Jamiss," Jordon said softly. "Sitting on the king's throne."

"You mean, that's the guy that caused the rebellion?" Tyler asked. Jordon nodded.

"So how does that tell us who was here?" Annese asked.

"Don't you remember what that Mikkel guy said? He was supposed to be king, but Jeremy and I halted the plan. I think this is where Mikkel and whoever was helping him lived."

"Which says this isn't far from the castle," Grandfather said with new dawning.

"That means they've been raiding the castle's stores for food," Kenyer added, coming in.

"Which means we're very close to getting to the surface!" Odessa's eyes lit up brightly as she poked her head in.

Jordon's eyes lit up as well. Tyler and Annese exchanged excited looks.

"Jordon! Come quick!" Jeremy called through the caves.

The four in the far bedroom quickly made their way through the kitchen into the first bedroom. Fang had made himself comfortable on the bed. Jeremy stood at the foot of the bed beside the open trunk. Something inside the finely crafted case cast a blue hue over him.

"Whatcha got?" Jordon asked. The rest of the group gathered around them.

"Take a look," Jeremy invited. "But I don't know how we're going to carry this one."

Jordon looked into the trunk. It was about half filled with blankets. Sitting on top of them was a large, blue, glowing crystal. The sides were smooth as glass. A sparkle glittered from the center. The top edge was jagged, like it had been broken. Jordon reached into Jeremy's pack and pulled out the bags he had. Only two didn't jingle with crystals.

"How many crystals you got in here?" Jordon asked with a scowl.

"I don't know. Fifty? Sixty?" Jeremy replied. "I didn't count them."

"Here," Jordon said, handing him the two sacks. He put the others back.

Jeremy opened the first bag. Jordon pulled the blue crystal piece out and tried to line it up with the one in the trunk. It was harder than he thought. Tyler leaned over to hold up the larger crystal for his cousin as he tried to figure out where it went.

Grandfather opened the other bag so Jeremy could pull that piece out. He shook his head as he looked at it. "Such as shame," he murmured. "It's such a beautiful crystal."

"So pretty!" Odessa replied

Jordon finally figured out where the piece went and put it in place. Annese reached over to hold it there. Jeremy passed over the second piece. It didn't take Jordon as long to figure out this one. As he slipped the piece in place, a warm, blinding light burst from the center of the crystal. Everyone closed their eyes in pain as it glowed brighter. At length it dimmed again. Opening their eyes, they looked at the crystal. It hovered above the trunk on its own.

"Look!" Odessa pointed at the top of the crystal.

Not a single crack showed on the crystal. There were no pieces missing. It looked as if it was brand new.

"Wow!" Aiya murmured in surprise. "Now that's magic!"

"That's awesome!" Annese whispered.

"That's beautiful!" Jadara added.

"I think we might be able to carry it in the trunk," Kenyer suggested.

"Yea," Du'kai agreed. "If we can get it in there." Jordon nodded with a smirk.

TYLER

The party picked their way out through the far bedroom into another tunnel. A series of rock slabs stood across the tunnel with six-foot runes carved into them. Runes and pictures also covered the walls of the tunnel.

"It looks like the ancient hieroglyphics," Tyler mumbled, lightly touching the paintings.

"Yea, but what do they say?" Annese wondered.

"Grandfather, do they look familiar?" Odessa asked.

Grandfather looked at them carefully. He struggled to remember his youthful days. Finally, he shook his head. "I'm sorry. They don't mean anything to me."

Tyler touched another of the stones. The raised knob on the rune depressed. The slab swung inward, opening the tunnel for them to pass.

"Excellent work, Tyler," Jordon smiled, patting his cousin on the shoulder. "All that studying paid off."

"Yea. Way to go!" Annese cheered.

"I don't know what I did," Tyler shrugged. Confused, he followed the others through the door.

JEREMY

"Are we there yet?" Annese whined.

"Not yet," Jeremy whined back. Tyler chuckled on the side.

The tunnel stone smoothed out as it went on. The walls became narrower, allowing only two people to walk through at a time. The air changed slightly, but enough for the Drelts to notice it. Almost imperceptibly at first, the tunnel turned upwards, twisting and turning until it finally dead-ended at a pile of rubble. Someone piled rocks of all sizes and mixed them with dirt.

"This is strange," Du'kai scowled. He began to climb the pile.

"What is it now?" Jadara's expression mirrored Jeremy's feelings.

"Someone placed this pile here on purpose," Du'kai announced, examining the pile. "It wasn't a cave-in."

"So, what are you saying?" Jeremy asked, leaning against the wall.

"I'm saying with a little muscle, we can move enough of these rocks to reveal the opening on the other side," Du'kai pointed.

"More muscle?" Annese whined. "I'm tired of using muscles. I'm tired of walking and tired of fighting. I just want to go to sleep!"

"O.K. You can stay here and get eaten by spiders," Jeremy teased, putting down his pack near the wall. He chuckled as Annese jumped and looked behind her. The others joined him, dropping their gear near the wall.

"Let's make a chain," Jordon's voice suggested.

"What is a chain?" Kenyer asked.

"It's when we make a line and pass one rock all the way down it. The last person makes a pile of the rocks," Jeremy explained simply. "We have enough of us to make two of them."

"Let's do it," Grandfather nodded excitedly.

For the next two hours, the party moved one rock after another. Several times Jeremy had to levitate one down the row, but mostly they could pass them down. Du'kai climbed up to the top and looked through the hole. Jeremy's eyes lit up with excitement as his friend announced he could see the other side, but the hole still wasn't large enough. They continued moving rocks, getting slower and slower and slower as the energy drained from each of them with all the work. Finally, Du'kai made the announcement they wanted to hear.

"We can get through!" he cried with excitement.

"What do you see?" Odessa asked with excitement.

"More tunnel," Du'kai groaned wearily.

"What?!" the three youngest party members cried. Jeremy chuckled to himself. Of course! What else would they find?

"More tunnel," Du'kai smiled. "And this one is going up and lined with torches!"

Slowly, the group made their way up the tunnel. Torches lit the walls. Only one every thirty or forty paces was lit. Archways angled off this main tunnel, many of them closed by bars. Inch by inch, the party trudged uphill.

"Hey, look!" Odessa pointed to one arch. The room beyond was small; maybe five-foot squared. A smooth, black stone glistened off the walls. Eight beams of bright blue light came from the corners and converged in the middle into a small burning ball. The comforting light reflected off the walls.

"Do you think...?" Jeremy asked.

"Probably," Kenyer replied.

"Should we put the crystal back?" Jadara asked uncertainly.

"No!" Annese, Tyler, and Odessa cried together, turning towards her.

Jadara jumped back and knocked into Kenyer. He caught her firmly. "Ok!" she replied with a start. "It was only a question!"

"If we put the crystal back, another cataclysm will happen," Tyler began.

"And the earth will open up and come crashing down," Annese added.

"And all those people that live down here are going to die!" Odessa exclaimed.

"I got it," Jadara said softly.

"Halt! Nobody move!" came a deep order.

The party turned to view two guards staring at them with spears. Their tunics wore the crest of King Narim. Their dark brown leggings were a little dirty. However, the fierce determination in their eyes made the group sag.

"I don't want to fight anymore," Annese whined.

"We're not," Grandfather said murmured. "Believe it or not, we're among friends." He walked through the party and approached the two guards. "Hello, gentlemen. How are you today?"

"I said halt!" one guard threatened him.

"Do you know who I am?" Grandfather bluffed sternly.

"No, sir," came the unsteady reply.

"Drats!" Grandfather snapped his fingers. "I was hoping you could tell me."

"Hands up, old man," one guard pushed the tip of his spear into Grandfather's stomach.

Jordon and Jeremy pushed forward until they were beside Grandfather. "Here. Let us handle this," Jordon smiled.

20 – THE BLUE CRYSTAL

NARIM

"Please! Please!" King Narim urged the angered Centaus. "I'm certain things are fine."

"Those rescuers have been gone more than a week! How long does it take to find a child in a hole?" Mauseleth roared. His front hooves stomped as his hindquarters rocked nervously.

"Mauseleth, please," a feminine voice urged. "We are all concerned." A tall, slender, Elthorian woman approached the Centaus. Her pale green gown brought out the startling green of her eyes. Her walk was as if she was walking on a cloud. Her features expressed her concern for the children in question.

"None of you has a child in that hole," Mauseleth pointed a finger in her face.

"No, we don't," she replied softly as she gently pushed his hand down. "However, we all have equal concern for the youths involved."

"You can say that again," Zelmar grumbled, staring out the window. "I should've been with them."

Mauseleth turned back to Narim. "I will hold you personally responsible for the death of my daughter!" he threatened the king.

"Death?" a high, fear-filled voice echoed. "Who died?"

"My daughter," Mauseleth growled, still staring at Narim.

"But... I'm your *only* daughter," the voice said confused.

"What?" The crowd twirled towards the doorway. Standing on either side of the archway were two worn out guards. In the doorway stood a young Centaus child, a dark-skinned mortal girl carrying a basket, another mortal child with sandy hair, Jordon, Jeremy, and an assortment of other beings. A black and gray puppy was sniffing around the floor at Mauseleth's feet. The group was dirty, ragged, and had blood-stained clothes. The pup looked to be in the best shape.

Mauseleth opened his mouth in stunned silence. The Centaus child galloped into the room and wrapped her arms around her father. "Daddy!" she cried as tears ran down her cheeks.

Chaos quickly erupted as people all around the room talked at once. Zelmar and King Narim quickly caught Jordon and Jeremy up in a big hug. The others gathered around quickly. Jeremy quickly pushed back as a low growl reverberated around the room.

"Fang! No!" he cried. Tearing himself away from Narim's grasp, he swooped down and grasped the pup. "No! It's ok! No one will hurt us!" he urged the pup, petting him gently. "See? Meet Narim!" Jeremy pushed the pup in Narim's face.

Narim backed instinctively and took the pup. "Well, now. Aren't you a cute, little thing!" He reached around and began stroking the Ortik's soft fur. Fang quickly rewarded him with a huge lick right up his face.

"We're so glad you're back," King Narim beamed, putting a wiggling Fang on the ground.

"Did I hear....." Thrundra burst into the room.

"If you were here," Durmond growled. "You wouldn't have had to hear. You would have seen! Never on time!"

Thrundra scooped the boys up in his arms. "We were so worried!"

"Why?" Jordon asked.

"We hadn't heard from you in days," Thrundra began.

"And we didn't know what we were sending you into," Narim added.

"We thought for certain you were dead," Mauseleth mumbled, still clutching Odessa.

"I must admit," Narim lowered his head. "It seemed hopeless. And look at the state of you! Does anyone need healing? Guard! Fetch the cleric!"

"Why didn't you just ask Tannis?" Jeremy asked with a smirk. "He could have told you where we were and what we were doing."

Narim exchanged a blank look with the rest of the adults in the room, then rolled his eyes. "I never even thought of Tannis."

"Nor I," Zelmar agreed.

"Nor I," Thrundra and Durmond nodded together.

"But I don't understand?" Aresa said, looking towards the door.

Jordon and Jeremy smiled at the party they had come to love. "What's not to understand?"

"We sent you after your sister, cousin, and a Centaus," Thrundra pointed out. "You came back with... with... an adventuring party."

The youths all chuckled. "You could say that," Jeremy laughed. "It didn't start out that way."

"Let me introduce you." Jordon pulled King Narim over. "You already know Annese."

"Welcome back, Annese," Narim smiled at the child. He ran a gentle hand along her cheek.

"Thank you, your majesty," Annese shied with a slight curtsy.

"And you now know Odessa," Jeremy pointed to the Centaus child.

"A pleasure, Odessa," the king grinned.

"Thank you, sire. Oh! Look, father!" she quickly pulled the bow off her back. "Look what the girls gave me! They taught me to shoot, too!"

Narim smiled as her father took the bow and examined it. "It's old," he observed, "but an excellent first bow. We'll have to see what we can do about training you." He handed the bow back to her with loving adoration. The king turned back to the group at the door.

"This is my cousin, Tyler," Jordon introduced. "Tyler, this is King Narim."

Tyler held out his hand. "It's a pleasure, sire," he responded, standing tall.

"You're supposed to bow," Kenyer whispered in the child's ear.

"Oh," Tyler winced. He bowed properly.

Narim laughed heartily. "It's a pleasure, Tyler. Don't worry about the bowing stuff. You're among friends." Tyler smiled appreciatively.

"These are our friends Kenyer, Aiya, Jadara, and Du'kai. They're Drelts. They've been a huge help." Jeremy smiled at them. Each bowed at the mention of his or her name.

"A pleasure to have you," Narim nodded at each.

"And these are Grup, Seda, Rexa, and Blul. They, too, were vital to our survival," Jordon introduced the gnomes. Again, Narim smiled and welcomed them.

Jeremy pulled the last of the group up front. He grinned as Narim and Grandfather looked at each other eye to eye. It was Durmond who actually introduced him.

"Barim?" Durmond asked, coming close. He eyed the old gentlemen closely.

Grandfather looked at the wizard, who approached him questioningly. His eyes squinted as he struggled to recognize the face. "Durmond?" he asked hesitantly.

"Narim!" Durmond reached out and hugged the man. "Where have you been? We searched everywhere for you!"

"It's rather a long story," the old man replied. "But it is so good to see you! Wait!" Grandfather's eyes grew wide. "I have a name!"

"Wait! Wait!" Thrundra interrupted. "Narim? Are you telling me this is...?"

Durmond nodded. "Yes! I told you we never found him. We just assumed his father sent him off to the mainland."

"So, this is..." King Narim began.

"This is Prince Narim. Your great, great, great, great, great, great, oh, however many greats, grandfather," Durmond replied to the king. "You'd know that if you ever read that history Thrundra gave you."

"I *did* read that history!" King Narim countered with his hands on his hips. "I just did not get *obsessed* with it!" The entire group laughed.

"Grandfather?" Grandfather asked, looking at the king. "That means my wife survived?"

"Yes," Durmond replied with a whimsical smile. "Devinia had a son. She named him after you."

"I had a son," Grandfather mused amazed. He turned and grasped Jeremy by the shoulders excitedly. "I had a son!"

"There is much to catch you up on," Durmond laid a calming hand on the old man's shoulder. "There will be plenty of time."

"I am so happy to see you, my friend," Grandfather smiled, turning to grasp Durmond's shoulders.

"Of course, you'll stay with us at the palace?" King Narim offered.

"Are you certain you want to be saddled with a doddering old man?" Grandfather asked sympathetically.

"Why not?" Jordon replied. "We have enough of them." He put his hands out. Jordon's smile became serious as he suddenly became acutely aware of several glares aimed at him. "Did I say something wrong?"

Mauseleth laughed heartily. "I suggest, young sir, you pick your words more carefully!"

"We have a gift for you, your majesty," Kenyer distracted the crowd. Jordon looked at him gratefully. He and Du'kai brought forward the chest they found in the underground bedroom.

"A gift?" Narim scowled. "You were trying to survive! Where did you find a gift?"

"Oh, here and there," Jeremy giggled.

Narim kneeled beside the chest and opened the lid. The blue crystal rose instantly and hovered over the chest. Everyone gasped as the magical blue glow spread about the room.

"Where did you *find* this?" Narim asked in awe. "It's beautiful!"

"It's the aged Crystal of Asteria. They found it!" Durmond whispered reverently. Durmond reached a hand out, but he didn't dare touch it.

"Perhaps we should return it....."

"NOOO!!!" The sudden cry from the party knocked Narim back on his rump.

"What? Why? It would return Asteria to one land mass." He looked up at everyone.

"When the crystal was removed from its bed," Jordon began the explanation.

"Asteria split apart and was pushed into this dimension," Odessa picked up.

"It caused the cataclysm," Jeremy explained.

"In the midst of the cataclysm, some of the inhabitants were thrust into the caverns that formed below," Kenyer added.

"Are you saying there are people who live below the surface?" Zelmar asked incredibly.

"Where do you think we picked them up?" Jeremy replied slightly sarcastically, pointing to the group with them. "We have met inhabitants on virtually every island."

"There were those snake people in the island we started on," Annese said.

"And the Kaptrix are a group of smaller people who are very much like the seers, only they don't see. They are in touch with the oracle." Tyler piped up.

"There are the Drelts underneath Elthoria. They, too, have a forest underground with flowers, trees, and animals," Jeremy smiled. "That's where we got Fang. He kind of adopted us."

"There's these fire people who live in the lava pits below Acentia. The dragons know about them. They go there for the heat," Jordon added.

"And the Miknars live below Kriltnar," Jeremy picked up again. "They look a lot like smaller Krilts, only they aren't as nice."

"That's why they're there," Zelmar growled. King Narim startled at the Krilt's aggressive reply. "They tried to overthrow the government and lost. Their punishment was being imprisoned in the caves under Kriltnar. The wizards cast a special spell to keep them there."

"*That* explains why they couldn't mine their way to the surface!" Tyler hit his forehead.

"And we found an old wizard city under what we think was The Keep," Jeremy exclaimed with excitement. "You should see it! There's fantastic ruins, a beautiful garden, and wizard vines!"

"And a poison trap that nearly killed you!" Jordon grumbled.

Jeremy pulled a face. "Yea. That, too."

"And the talking trees!" Annese added. "Although, they started a fight with us."

"And the peeks!" Odessa added excitedly, looking up at her father. "They look like ours, but they can fly! They're so cute!" Her voice rose as she sang the last line.

"And the crystal cave!" Jeremy cried, reaching into his pack. He pulled out a bag of crystals and dumped a few in his hand. Narim picked one up to examine it.

"Amazing!" he murmured.

"The red ones create heat like a fire," Tyler explained.

"Wait! Wait!" Thrundra held up his hands. "Are you telling us there's an entire world under the islands?"

The kids just looked at each other blankly. "Isn't that what we were just telling them about?" Annese asked.

"They're a little slow," Jordon replied to her. "You'll get used to it." He turned quickly and flashed Narim a smile.

"So, by putting the crystal back, we put an end to the inhabitants under Asteria," Narim said slowly from his position on the floor. His head was spinning. "I'm sorry, people, but that simply is not acceptable."

"May we make a suggestion, Sire?" Kenyer asked, offering Narim a hand to help him up. Narim nodded and grasped the offered hand. Kenyer helped him rise from the floor. "Perhaps it would be more ethical if you assign a contact party to go down to the caverns and invite the people to the surface."

"Sure!" Jeremy agreed. "I have copies of Fuzz's maps. We can probably fill in the missing destinations on the transport pads."

"Transport pads?" Thrundra asked.

"It's the way you get around from island to island down there," Grandfather explained. "Each pad comes in from one site and goes out to another."

"Captain Zelmar," King Narim called his friend.

"Yes, Sire!" Zelmar snapped to attention.

"Gather a search party and prepare to approach the people under Asteria about returning to the surface."

"Immediately, Sire."

"Well, you can wait until the boys go home," Narim smiled with a wink. "And, of course, we need to return these nice folks to their people." He motioned towards the Drelts and gnomes.

"Welllllllllll," Jeremy hunched his shoulders.

"Well?" Durmond demanded over Jeremy's shoulder.

"You needn't worry about us," Du'kai spoke up. "We... are not welcome home again."

"Long story," Jordon intercepted Narim's next question. "We'll fill you in later."

"Then we would be happy and proud to have our ancient allies come make their home on Elthoria," a tall and elegant woman moved forward. Her long, dark hair flowed with the grace of her gown. "Many generations have passed since your ancestors lived with us. Consider our home your home."

"It would be an honor," Kenyer bowed with a fist over his heart.

"This is Queen Aresa," King Narim introduced. "King Eliramond's daughter."

Jordon and Jeremy approached the woman. "We're sorry to hear about your father," Jordon said softly.

"Yea," Jeremy nodded. "He was a pretty cool guy."

"That's a compliment," King Narim mouthed behind them so Aresa would understand. She nodded.

"Thank you, young masters," she smiled, laying a gentle hand on each shoulder. "He was very happy and proud to assist you in your endeavors, and he was extremely pleased to hear you had won before he passed."

The boys squirmed, not knowing what to say next.

"And you, my friends?" King Narim asked the Gnomes.

"No home. No family." Grup responded. Seda smacked him in the back of the head.

"No family?" she questioned with her hands on her hips.

"You wife! Not family!" Grup grumbled, rubbing his head. Blul and Rexa giggled.

"We last gnomes," Blul explained. "No home."

"If I recall," Durmond began, "the gnomes used to live on Faeyruun. Perhaps they would like to re-establish a village there."

The four gnomes huddled together, mumbling amongst themselves. Several times heated words came out. Each one tried to make a point. After a few moments, they turned back to the King.

"Fayeruun," Blul agreed.

"Wonderful!" Narim smiled. "Now. Let me summon the maids and gather a feast for us!"

"Narim," Jeremy said with a yawn. "With all due respect, we'd really prefer some sleep."

Jordon stretched. "Yea. It's hard to sleep when you're what everything else has on the menu."

"What's your sister got in the basket?" Durmond asked Jeremy. "She's holding it pretty tight." Narim glanced over to Annese, who had settled against the wall and was slowly falling asleep with her arms securely around the basket.

"They're company for Quilly," Jeremy announced with a smirked.

"What? Quilly is one of a kind," Durmond huffed.

Jeremy reached into the basket and pulled out a white longairit with black spots. "Not anymore," he grinned as he held the longairit up. "We have seven of these babies."

"Seven?" Durmond asked warily.

"Seven."

"Narim, we're about to be overrun."

Narim laughed. "Wonderful!" he cried, taking the squeaky longairit. "They're such cute little guys. Thrundra, why don't you get these people settled where they can sleep, and arrange some clean clothing for them. We'll have our feast when they awaken."

"Right away, Sire," Thrundra laughed. "This way, folks. Come along, Annese," he chuckled, reaching down and picking up the sleeping child. Narim replaced the longairit into the basket.

"May we stay?" Odessa pleaded with her father. "Please? I've never been to a feast. Please?"

Mauseleth smiled at his daughter. "Yes, we may, if that is acceptable with King Narim?"

Narim smiled at the child. He gently stroked her cheek. "I would be honored to have you attend, young miss. And you as well, my friend."

King and Centaus clasped wrists in friendship. "Thank you, my friend. I should not have suspected you."

"Forget it," Narim waved him off. "Parents often jump to many conclusions and fears when worried about a child."

"I greatly appreciate your understanding."

Narim looked off after the group following Thrundra out the door. "They may not be mine biologically, but they're mine by heart," he whispered. Mauseleth nodded his understanding.

JEREMY

Several hours later, a servant awakened the boys. Stretching, they slowly got to their feet. Baths had been drawn for them and fresh clothing laid out on their beds. Jordon slipped into the silky clothing carefully.

"Wow!" he sifted the material through his hands. "This is a far cry from our tattered leathers."

"Yea," Jeremy agreed, smoothing the tunic. "It feels so good."

A knock came on the door. Annese poked her head in. She had glittering yellow ribbons braided through her hair.

"Good! You're up!" She smiled as she came into the room. She twirled in front of the guys. "Whatcha think?"

The royal blue gown shimmered and twirled about her as she spun. Pure white lace trimmed the neckline and the sleeves, creating an elegant contrast with her skin.

"You look beautiful!" Jordon grinned.

"That's really pretty." Jeremy smirked, knowing his sister was looking for compliments.

"Aiya and Jadara have new dresses, too. Queen Aresa designed them."

"Are you ready to go?" Jeremy asked his sister.

"Not yet! I want to go to the party!"

"That's what he's talking about," Jordon chuckled. "We're going to the party."

A guard knocked on the door. "His majesty is awaiting your arrival," he announced.

"We're on our way," Jeremy grinned. Jordon grabbed his camera from his pack and stuffed it into a pocket. Leave it to Thrundra to remember pockets!

The enormous feast was overwhelming. Dracaina and Gralena had accompanied Zelmar. Jordon had a great time catching up with them. Annese really got along wonderfully with Gralena. Kren had come in from Ascentia to represent the dragons. Master Wren had come in from Faeyruun. It delighted him to meet the gnomes and instantly began discussing where they'd like to settle. Lord Rauthdel and his wife were in attendance and eager to meet up with the young masters. Matikata sat majestically in a corner, maintaining conversation with those around her. She was especially happy to see the boys again. She had heard about Annese and Tyler's visit to the woods and was eager to meet them. Lord Eebron was pleased to catch up with the boys as well. Tannis was very pleased to see everyone was safe. Jordon snapped picture after picture, often having to explain his "painting box".

The boys were excited to meet all their old friends from their previous visit. They had left so quickly they didn't have a chance to thank everyone for all their help. The Drelts and Odessa seemed rather out of place, although the boys introduced them to as many people as they could. They didn't know anyone here except for Aresa, Narim, and Grandfather. She made certain to keep them in conversation and make them feel at home. Mauseleth also had found friends amongst the party.

King Narim finally tapped his goblet for everyone's attention. "First, I'd like to thank everyone for joining us this evening on such short notice. We are extremely pleased to have you all with us.

"Second, I'd like to welcome our new friends. We all hope you will find your new homes comfortable and to your liking. Our council is pleased to welcome you." A polite applause echoed his sentiments.

"And third, we raise our goblets to Masters Jordon and Jeremy once again. Not only have they rescued three children from the depths of Asteria, but they rescued entire civilizations. Thanks to them we have new friends and now have the Crystal of Asteria. Once again, they, and their friends, have rescued Asteria. To Jordon and Jeremy."

"To Jordon and Jeremy," the crowd repeated while raising their goblets to the boys.

JORDON

The feast went on for hours. Both boys noticed Narim hanging around a beautiful young woman in a striking red dress. Jordon nudged Jeremy and raised his eyebrows. The pair wandered over silently.

"Something you failed to tell us?" Jeremy whispered behind the king.

Narim turned and grinned. "Maybe," he teased.

"Well?" the boys asked together.

"You gonna introduce us?" Jordon asked, trying to peer around his friend.

Narim grinned as he stepped aside. "Malinda, may I present Masters Jordon Hallstead and Jeremy Blackhurst, Heroes of Asteria. Gentlemen, may I present Malinda, my fiancé."

"Fiancé?" the boys both exclaimed in unison.

Narim raised his brows, glanced at Malinda, then back at the boys.

"It's a pleasure," Jordon bowed to the young woman.

"I'm pleased to meet you," Jeremy also bowed.

"The pleasure is mine," Malinda replied in a soft, melodic voice. There was a hint of a giggle in her reply.

"So... when's the big day?" Jordon asked.

"Twenty-eight days from yesterday," Malinda replied.

"Congratulations," Jordon replied with a grin.

"You boys will be back for the wedding, won't you?" Narim asked worriedly. "I'm hoping you'll stand next to me."

The boys grinned wide. "Wouldn't miss it!"

As the night wore on, Thrundra helped them calculate when they'd need to return. Eventually, the boys found Annese and Tyler. It was time to go home. They began their rounds, saying good-bye to everyone. As they were talking with Mauseleth, a guard cleared his throat.

"Your majesty," the lanky, young man began tentatively. "We have sort of a situation. A rather *large* situation."

"What kind of situation?" King Narim turned in concern.

Fuzz peeked around the guard. "Hello, sirs," he smiled.

"Fuzz!" the five kids exclaimed together and ran for the door.

"Another friend of yours?" Narim asked knowingly.

"Fuzz was the whole reason we were able to get around!" Jeremy exclaimed.

"He was tracking where all the transports went to and came in from," Annese added. "We used his maps to figure out where to go next!"

"Well, more like we used his maps to figure out where he hadn't been yet," Jordon chuckled. "They helped a lot."

"We have used the same maps to gather the Kaptrix below this place," Fuzz said quietly. His hands wrung nervously. "A few friends and I traveled up the tunnel when this nice guard found us." Two other Kaptrix poked out from behind Fuzz. They smiled and waved.

"What about Riemer?" Tyler asked anxiously.

"He is traveling about the islands warning the other races," Fuzz informed them.

Tyler looked down. "I have something that belongs to him," he said sadly. "Would you return it to him?"

"I assume you are referring to his axe?" Fuzz asked with raised brows. Tyler nodded. Fuzz smiled. "Mr. Riemer has given strict instructions that you are to keep it in your possession. He is not expecting to use it any further."

"As Suji said," Annese looked at Tyler with concern. "Riemer declared you his next of kin."

"A huge honor, sir," Fuzz added.

Tyler smiled sadly. "Thank you."

"Well, now," Narim rubbed his chin. "Where are you from?"

"They live below Mystic Island," Jeremy replied.

"I thought the features looked familiar," Tannis came forward. "We had people such as these living on Mystic Island for centuries before the cataclysm. We'd be very happy to have them return there."

"I will discuss it with our people. I'm certain they will agree." Fuzz smiled nervously.

"Mauret," Narim addressed the guard. "Get some help and get provisions down into the tunnels for these people, then see about lodgings for the night."

"Immediately, sire," the guard snapped to attention, bowed, and moved in a different direction.

GRANDFATHER

"It appears the exodus has begun," Durmond mused to no one in particular.

"Bound to happen sooner or later," Grandfather agreed with a smile.

"Yes, indeed; but to what end?"

"Your guess is as good as mine," Grandfather replied. "If we as a people can maintain the inclusion of your heroes, we will be a prosperous nation."

"They are pretty special," Durmond grinned.

"More than that. They had no problems taking on an old man who slowed them down considerably. They continued to encourage me. Their acceptance of the Drelt, the Ortik, and the Kaptrix, despite racial divides, kept this group working together like a well-oiled machine. They are destined to be leaders in their own right."

Durmond nodded his agreement. "With some training and maturity."

Grandfather laughed. "Don't let their age fool you, Master. They may be young and they may be inexperienced, but they are capable of so many great things."

"So I'm learning."

21 – THE TRAVEL HOME

JORDON

Many hours later, after changing back into their normal, tattered clothes, two dragons once again dropped the mortal children off at the Aerie. Mauseleth and Odessa insisted on joining them, although Odessa needed some help along the way. Her wings, though they had grown a little on their excursion, simply weren't strong enough to carry her well.

"Thanks, guys!" Jeremy patted his dragon friend.

"A great pleasure, Master Jeremy," the green dragon replied. "May I have the pleasure again."

"Me, also," the other golden dragon replied.

"Us, too. You guys are sweet!" Jordon slid off his dragon.

"Sweet? We don't eat sugar." the green dragon questioned.

"It means you're great," Jeremy chuckled.

"Oh! Then thou art also sweet," the golden dragon smiled. The two took off with a brief bow.

The group turned to Odessa. "I guess this is the end," she mumbled. A tear threatened to fall from her eyelashes.

"Nah," Annese smiled and wiped the tear away. "We'll be back again. We can look you up."

"Look me up?" Odessa scowled.

"It means we'll come visit you," Jordon explained.

"Oh!"

"It will honor our herd to have you stay with us," Mauseleth said softly.

"We'll be honored to be there," Jordon nodded.

"Where's Fang?" Odessa asked, looking around.

"We left him with King Narim," Jeremy replied. "While he's a great pup, the people in our world wouldn't understand his growth spurts."

"Yea," Jordon agreed. "We don't have creatures that can do those kinds of things at home. We felt it safer for everyone to leave him here."

"And the longairits?" Mauseleth smiled.

"Well, Narim has most of them," Annese squirmed.

"*Most* of them?" Jeremy turned to his sister.

"I only brought two," she said, motioning to her pack. "The one I saved, and the calico."

"Somehow, I think we're going to regret this," Jeremy muttered. Jordon and Mauseleth chuckled.

"Aw, come on! They look like hamsters!" Jordon nudged his friend with his elbow. "Furry, round, squeaky hamsters. People will love them!"

"Probably. We'd better get going. We've been gone too long," Jeremy said unwillingly.

"Thank you for being our friend," Tyler said to Odessa. He reached out and gave her a hug.

"Thanks for being *my* friend," Odessa replied, looking at the ground. She swirled her hoof in the dirt. "I don't have too many playmates."

"You will now," Annese gave her friend a hug. "When word gets out about where you've been and what you've done, you're going to have more friends than you can handle."

Odessa laughed. "Maybe. And Father says he's going to continue my lessons with my bow and arrow."

"See, you've grown on this trip," Jordon smiled. "I'll bet you'll be the best marksman the Centaus has." Mauseleth cleared his throat. "Next to your father, I mean." Jordon gave Mauseleth an embarrassing smile. A merry laugh erupted from the rest of the group.

"I think you all have grown," Mauseleth smiled down at them. "On with you now. You have your timing correct for King Narim's wedding day, yes?"

"We think so," Jordon replied. "It took us long enough to figure out. We're planning to come over a few days before, just to be certain."

"Very good. In that case, safe trip home," Mauseleth nodded.

"Oooh! Wait! Group shot!" Jordon exclaimed, reaching for his camera.

"Excuse me?" Mauseleth reared.

"No, Father!" Odessa chuckled. "It's Jordon's picture box. He presses a little button on the box and it makes a tiny little painting inside. He says he can move it to a bigger canvas when he gets home. He's been making all kinds of little paintings, and the little box remembers them all!"

"I... see." Mauseleth looked at his daughter suspiciously.

"Here. Let me show you." Jordon smiled. He got everyone close together around Mauseleth and took the picture. "Smile!" Quickly he pushed a few buttons on the back and showed the image to Mauseleth. "See? Here's you and Odessa, Tyler, Annese, and Jeremy."

"Amazing! What type of magic is that?"

"In our world it's called electronics," Tyler explained. "It's kind of complicated."

"I see. Very well. Off with you now. You still have to explain all this to your parents."

"Oh, joy!" Tyler slumped. Jordon slapped his cousin's shoulder with a laugh.

TYLER

Annese and Tyler followed Jordon and Jeremy down the stairs to the cave. Once again, they looked out over the islands before going inside. Mauseleth and Odessa were flying off over Elthoria as a full moon shone on the water. The older boys pointed out which island was which to Tyler and Annese and which dignitary they had met came from there.

"I'm going to miss this place," Tyler mumbled. "It's been a fantastic adventure."

"The adventure has yet to begin." Jeremy smiled at him. "We have to make it past our Moms!"

After a final look, he turned and followed the tunnels into the cave. The lights from the tunnels still fascinated Tyler. He collected a few rock samples to examine at home.

Prepared, Jeremy pulled his flashlight from his pack. "I replaced the batteries," he announced as he flipped the light on. He secured his staff in his pack.

"Good thinking. Come on." Jordon agreed as he laced the straps of his pack around Sharijol.

Jeremy led the group through the portal and into Docker's Cave. He and Jordon picked up their normal clothes where they left them. It was harder struggling up the ruined pathway in the dark than it was in daylight. They all agreed they'd need to get down here to make a more defined path. They finally emerged from the pathway into the assembly lot for the tours. The moon was full and up. The boys looked up into the starry night sky.

"We'd better hurry," Jordon said, looking up.

"Why?" Annese asked, pushing the longairits back into her bag and tightening it more.

"Because if my estimations are correct, it's almost midnight."

"Oh, are we in trouble!" she sang.

The kids didn't waste time. They quickly got their bikes and pedaled off home. They dodged a police car along the way. The park was empty. It looked a little spooky as the playground equipment moved back and forth in the light breeze. The dim moonlight made the darker shadows look haunted. It didn't take too long for them to pull into their driveways and pedal back towards the garages.

"We'll see you guys tomorrow," Jordon whispered to Jeremy and Annese.

"Sure thing. Welcome home, Tyler," Jeremy smiled.

"This is definitely different than *anything* I've *ever* done," Tyler replied.

"The hard part is yet to come." Jordon laid a hand across his cousin's shoulder.

"What's that?"

"First, we need to explain to Mom why we're so late, and second, you can't tell anyone else about it."

"No one?"

"No one," Jeremy reiterated.

"Others might go in and contaminate the islands or capture the creatures there. We don't want them harmed," Annese explained. She lowered her head. "I really shouldn't have brought you there."

"It's over. Let's get some sleep—again," Jordon chuckled. "Come on." Tyler waved goodbye to his new friends.

JORDON

As their friends went into their house, Jordon could instantly hear Mrs. Blackhurst yelling at them about how late it was and where were they and how they were about to call the police. With a brave smile, he nodded to Tyler and opened the back door. The two walked into the kitchen.

Mrs. Hallstead came marching into the kitchen.

"Where were you? It's way too late for you to be out!"

After appeasing his mother by telling her they'd found the kids, played with them for a while, but fell asleep on the beach, Jordon brought Tyler upstairs.

"Great excuse," Tyler said. "You use it often?"

"No," Jordon whispered as he opened the door to his room. "I've been trying to think of an acceptable excuse all the way home." Tyler chuckled, following him in. "Here's hoping she doesn't compare notes with Mrs. Blackhurst."

"You'll be bunking with me," Jordon said to his cousin. "Tasha has the extra bedroom."

"Where are my things supposed to go?" Tyler scowled, looking around the room. It seemed too small for two people.

"You have the top bunk, that dresser, the right side of the closet, and that desk over there. Let me give you some advice," he told his cousin lowly. "Hide your axe in the back of the closet and put your Asterian clothes in the bottom drawer all the way to the back. Then Mom won't throw them out."

"Great idea!" Tyler began unloading his pack.

Jordon checked his computer. Sure enough, they had been gone only a day, albeit several hours longer than the first time. It was nearly midnight. He supposed they could've been home earlier if they didn't take a nap or stay for the feast, but that really would've been rude. And after all, his mother always taught him not to be rude! Carefully, he put his things away; once again musing over the adventure. He'd have to update his scrapbook and adventure journal. Next trip: wedding day!

EPILOG

The day finally arrived that Jordon and Jeremy needed to get back to Asteria for Narim's wedding. They had a hard time coming up with a wedding present the happy couple could use, considering they didn't have electricity, matches, or technology. They had a harder time convincing their parents to let them go exploring again. After promising to be back on time, they got permission to go.

Annese had been excited to be included. She had gathered copies of all Jordon's pictures and made a scrapbook for Odessa and another for Narim. She chose the wrapping paper carefully—not too flashy, not too plain.

Tyler wasn't sure he should go. It was only after all three of them insisted that he finally accepted.

They arrived two days prior to the wedding. Thrundra met them at the aerie.

"Good timing," he chuckled. "I've only been here a short time."

He ushered them to the palace right away for the clothier. She measured every direction possible, then released them. Thrundra helped them get over to Griffin

Woods. They found Mauseleth and the Centaus with little trouble. They totally surprised Odessa with the scrapbook.

"This is so... so..."

"Sick?" Tyler smirked, knowing Odessa had been catching on to their slang.

"Yeah!" Odessa smiled, clutching the book. "I'll cherish it always!"

"Don't let it get wet," Annese warned her friend. "The pictures will get ruined."

The wedding took an entire day. Jordon and Jeremy got to stand next to Narim as the bridal procession came into the room. Tyler helped usher people to seats. Malinda had Annese as one of her bridesmaids. She surprised the boys with how pretty she looked in the white silk dress with her hair styled and a little color on her face — and the bride was beautiful, too.

Narim started shaking. "Am I ready for this?" he whispered nervously.

"Ready or not, here she comes!" Jeremy teased.

The audience stood as the bride entered the chapel. As she passed, each row bowed to her.

The ceremony was nice, but long. There were several rituals they went through. The party afterwards, however, was so much fun! Everyone was there. Kren, and Eebron, and Rauthdel, and Aresa, and the gnomes, and the Kaptrix, and the Drelts, and Matikata, and Mauseleth, and everyone else who normally was there. Elves, fairies, Centaus, Krilts, wizards, clerics, mortals, and more filled the ballroom and spilled out into the courtyard. Grandfather sat back, smiling as he looked over what would have been his kingdom. He was so happy with the way things turned out.

During the festivities, a quick ceremony crowned Malinda as Queen of Asteria. The entire crowd bowed at once.

King Narim presented her to the crowd, then released her hand. "We have another ceremony today. Would Masters Jordon and Jeremy come forward, please?" Confused, the boys made their way to the dais. The king motioned them to kneel. Two pages came in carrying pillows. Laying a sword on each boy's shoulder he announced,

"Having the authority of this land, I, King Narim of Asteria, crown you, Jordon Hallstead, and you, Jeremy Blackhurst, princes of Asteria with all the rights thereof." He took a gold-leafed ring and placed one on Jordon's head and one on Jeremy's. He motioned them to rise and face the audience. "Their royal highnesses, Prince Jordon and Prince Jeremy!" The crowd once again bowed, but a cheer went up through the crowd as they rose. The boys blushed, speechless.

The four heroes were brought up to speed with the rescue efforts. With Kenyer's help, Zelmar had reached the Drelts. While quite a few of them chose to stay underground, knowing the risks, many of them came to the surface. The Elthorians quickly helped make housing for their new friends. The Kaptrix had been successfully settled on Mystic Island. The Miknars gave Zelmar quite a bit of trouble. He finally left them there. The wizards helped move the talking trees up to a comfortable area on The

Keep. They moved several of the ruins and the deadly
garden up there as well — *after* they deactivated the death
trap. Durmond and Thrundra placed a special spell on the
ruins to ensure they wouldn't be harmed if another
cataclysm occurred. The Peeks were gathered and brought
up to the surface to dwell in the trees at The Keep. They
quickly made friends with the other squirrel-like creatures
there. They put Grandfather in charge of the crystals. The
team had gathered as many of the crystals as they could
and moved them up to the caves on Faeyruun. Since the
fire elementals lived on lava, the team left them alone.
There would always be a lava cavern below Ascentia.

With everyone covered, Zelmar let the boys in on the
decision to replace the Crystal of Asteria. They all looked at
each other, knowing it would cause a total disruption on
the islands.

"What about the nursery?" Jeremy asked. "And the
dragon nurses?"

"The dragons will be fine," Kren reassured him.
"Magic itself holds Ascentia together. It will not change,
even if the islands come together and another cataclysm
occurs. In fact, we're so certain of that fact that the royal
families of each island are being moved there during the
replacement for protection."

"What will this do to the portal?" Jordon asked
worriedly.

"We don't know," Thrundra came up behind them
solemnly. "Perhaps nothing, perhaps something. For that
reason, you are to return to your own world *before* we
return the crystal to its nest." He smiled at the boys. "While

we'd love to keep you here, your families would be terribly worried. We wouldn't want to upset them."

For several months, Jordon or Jeremy stayed near home. Even though they had arrived home on time, even a little early, their mothers were hesitant to let them travel farther than the park. The boys simply had to be content with reading the adventures of Steven Devereaux in the secret room. Since Tyler now knew about Asteria and the portal, Jordon let him in on the secret of the lab.

It was a hot Saturday morning when Jordon and Jeremy went back to Asteria. They wanted to visit Asteria one more time before school started. They carefully made their way to the caves, ducking out of sight when the tour went into the upper cave. Enjoying the romp, they slid down the pathway before Donny could finish his spiel about stalactites and stalagmites.

As they had in the past, they pulled flashlights out, and they made their way to the back of the cave. They found the engravings in the wall and prepared to go through the portal.

Jordon reached the portal first, went to walk through, and promptly smacked his head on the rock. "Ow!" he cried, rubbing his forehead. "What happened?"

Jeremy pushed on the rock, expecting his hand to go through. "I don't know. Do we have the right place?"

He went back to their names. He turned and started counting. Ten, eleven, twelve. Once more, he pushed on the stone. Nothing. It didn't move.

Jordon went up and down the wall. Everything was solid. The portal was gone.

"Why?" Jeremy asked as they sadly started back towards home.

"I don't know," Jordon replied. "It should be there."

"Do you think replacing the crystal destroyed the portal?" Jeremy asked.

"It's possible, I guess, but how would that close the portal?"

"I don't know." He kicked a rock across the cave floor. "Boy, that rots!"

"Sure does."

With heavy hearts, the boys carefully made their way home. Jordon stopped to look at the castle in the park. He'd never again be able to play there without remembering Narim and the rest of his friends in Asteria. He looked down at the ground to get a grip. The ache around his heart made him feel as if someone had ripped it out of his chest. He looked up when Jeremy touched his arm.

"Come on," he said sadly. "Maybe there's something in the lab that will tell us what to do."

"Yea. Sure. Maybe." Jordon followed his best friend home, but didn't feel any better. His favorite world was gone to him now. They had just happened upon the portal. They didn't have what they needed to build another one, nor did they really know how. Oh well. Asteria would live on in his memories. He'd have to continue working on the scrapbook he was making. It included all his adventures in Asteria and pictures of the friends they'd made. At least he still had Sharijol, a golden leafed crown, and a drawer full of Asterian clothing as proof.

APPENDIX I

<u>Spell Translations</u>

Incantation	Translation
Solar lux lucis	Solar Light
Sanctum fulsi de lumen	Holy Burst of Light
Vicis Subsisto	Time Halt
Viscus ut Calx	Flesh to Stone
Lux Lucis de Poena	Light of Pain
Contego	Shield
Congelo Somes	Freeze
Divello	Untie
Ortus	Levitate
Od	Off
Incendia Telum	Fireball

Sharijol (Jordon's Sword) – Battle Light, a spell that protects against evil.

ASTERIA 3

RESCUING DEVEREAUX

CHAPTER 1

JORDON

"Are you kidding me?" Jeremy exclaimed, dropping his game controller. "You have to move! But what about the lab?"

"I don't know," Jordon replied worriedly, pausing the game. "I figured we can pack it up and take it with us, but it seems a shame to have to leave it behind."

"Where are you going to go?" Jeremy nodded towards the TV screen. They could play and talk at the same time.

"Don't know. Dad just came home with the news last night." Jordon resumed the game.

"Aunt Jean sent me for the newspaper this morning," Tyler said, turning his attention back to the TV to continue their game. "She's probably looking for someplace now."

"From what I understood," Jordon added. "We have 60 days to find someplace, and the college is willing to pay for the move."

"That rots!" Jeremy griped. "Actually, I'm surprised your folks told you all this."

Jordon and Tyler exchanged a glance. "They didn't," Tyler admitted.

"Then how do you know about it?"

"They were in the kitchen talking when Tyler and I were coming up the stairs. We just didn't go all the way up."

"You were eavesdropping?" Jeremy asked incredulously.

"How else do you find out information you need to know but no one will tell you?" Jordon asked.

"So, what do we do?" Jeremy asked.

"We wait, get a bunch of boxes to pack up the lab, and hope they pick someplace close."

"Why do you have to move anyway?" Jeremy asked. He sat up, suddenly worried. "Your dad didn't lose his job, did he?"

"No. The way I understand it, Devereaux, the guy who owned the house, worked as a research scientist for the college. He taught Geological Physics. When he would go on an exploration to do research, he left the college in charge of taking care of the house. I think there was an account or something that the college could pay the bills from. Anyway, when he disappeared, the college continued to care for the house, renting it out to help offset the costs. Well..."

"They ran out of money," Tyler explained bluntly. "And with that guy not around for a really long time, they've decided to sell the house."

"So why don't your folks buy it?" Jeremy asked.

"They can't afford the down payment. Dad said he'd look into a few other options, like seeing if the college would hold the mortgage or something, but it really looked like we'd have to move."

"Dang!"

The boys sat in silence for a few moments as they continued their game.

"I suppose the good news is that you really can't move that far. I mean, your dad is still working around here. And the island isn't that big." Jeremy tried to find a bright side.

"It's big enough," Tyler grumbled.

Jordon smirked at his cousin. The boy had grown quite a bit since his experience in Asteria last fall. While Jordon wished he'd find some friends of his own once in a while, he understood what it was like to feel like the outcast. In reality, Tyler wasn't so bad.

Something stumbled down the last couple of steps behind them.

"Annese, stop trying to sneak up!" Jeremy accused without looking. "We're only playing a game."

No one answered, and there was no sound from behind. Tyler glanced over at the stairs and froze.

"Who's that!" he exclaimed, wide-eyed.

Jordon and Jeremy turned to look at the stairs. Both froze in surprise. A tall, thin youth with pale blue skin was staring back at them in horror from the floor. His dark eyes complimented his hair. Tiny antennae stuck out of the messy jet-black hair. His shirt was a thin weave, not unlike the Elvin cloths of Asteria. His pants were a type of tweed; brown, old, and full of holes. His feet were bare.

Since no one moved, the boy set his lips together and darted across the room. Simultaneously, Jordon and Jeremy jumped over the back of the couch and ran to tackle him. Jordon toppled the boy with a grunt.

"Who are you?" Jordon wrestled the struggling boy to the ground.

"Leave me!" the boy ordered. He wriggled and fought back as much as he could.

"You're trespassing, buster!" Jeremy threatened, kneeling next to him. "That's against the law."

"My father owns this house. Leave me be!"

Jordon and Jeremy instantly held still as Tyler joined them.

"What do you mean, your father owns this place?" Jordon squinted.

"This house belongs to my father, Steven Devereaux! I need to get some things for him."

"Who are you?" Tyler demanded, squatting down to look at the boy.

"I mean you no harm. Please, this is vital to the safety of my family."

"Who are you?" he repeated.

"My name is Maliik. Maliik Devereaux."

A stunned silence filled the room as the three looked at each other in surprise. Jordon's mother's voice came down the stairs.

"Are you boys alright? I heard something fall."

"We're fine, Mom!" Jordon called back. "Just goofing around."

"Ex...." Maliik began his objection, but didn't get far. Jordon's hand wrapped around his face and covered his mouth.

"Well, be careful!" his mother warned. "I don't want anyone or anything hurt."

"We will!"

The boys all waited as they listened to Mrs. Hallstead cross the room above them. Finally, Jordon nodded. Jeremy motioned towards the laundry room. Jordon agreed. He pulled Maliik to his feet.

Tyler put his finger to his mouth to indicate silence, then waved as he led the way behind the laundry room. The four made their way through to the storage part of the basement. Jeremy reached up over the concrete wall and tugged on the large nail sticking out of the wooden beam. Jordon barely heard the dim click as a concrete slab door opened soundlessly. Maliik jumped back in surprise.

"It's just as Father said!" he whispered in awe.

Jordon guided him gently into the room. Carefully, he closed the door until it almost shut completely. Jeremy lit the battery-powered lantern on the table.

"My parents don't know about this room. If you really are Devereaux's son, then you already knew about it."

"Yes, but there is another room that wasn't in Father's descriptions."

"The laundry room. I guess it must have been added since your father was here," Jeremy said.

"Fellas, how do we know he's Devereaux's kid?" Tyler asked suspiciously.

"Look. I'm not from your world."

"No kidding," Jeremy retorted. "For starters, you're blue, and you have antennae!"

"How could I know the name of the man who owns this home if I'm not his son?" Maliik reasoned.

"Makes sense," Jordon replied.

"Unless he's a thief trying to steal something from Devereaux and posing as his son," Tyler suggested, crossing his arms. "I don't believe him."

"Tyler, I think you're reading too many mysteries," Jeremy smirked.

"My name is Maliik Devereaux. I am the eldest son of Steven and Bea Devereaux of Wild Lakes Village. I have two sisters and a brother."

The boy was getting frustrated. Jordon figured he didn't understand why they were suspicious of him. He looked to be around 12; slightly older than Tyler, but younger than he and Jeremy. His slight build indicated a lack of nourishment, or at least low-fat foods.

"How'd you get here?" Jordon asked.

"Through the invisible door. My father told me where it is."

"Another portal?" the three earthlings exclaimed together in excitement. "Where?"

Maliik stepped back and looked at the three rather strangely. "Portal? That's the term my father used. It... It's in the pond."

"The one behind my house?" Jordon asked with raised brows. Various flowers surrounded the garden pond in his yard. His mother loved the fairy look of the area and planted flowers to enhance it. Maliik nodded. "Yes!" Jordon exclaimed, pulling in one fist to his side.

"We never thought about there!" Jeremy smiled.

"I didn't think it would be deep enough for a portal!" Jordon exclaimed.

"Why did your father send you here?" Tyler brought the conversation back to Maliik.

"My father has been taken prisoner by the presiding powers. They have accused him of being a magician, and are trying to convince him of aiding their cause. Father sent me for some items he said he needs, but I don't know why."

"What items do you need?" Jordon asked, looking around the old laboratory.

"We can find them, then help you get your dad," Jeremy suggested.

Tyler stared at his friend incredulously. "Are you suggesting we go with him?"

Jordon looked his cousin in the eyes and gave him a slight smile. "We save people. That's what we do."

"Oh, no!" Maliik declared emphatically. "It is much too dangerous in my world."

"And you can handle this by yourself?" Jeremy asked with a knowing tone.

"I... I have to," Maliik stood bravely, but the fear in his eyes betrayed his tone. "My family depends on it. My village depends on it."

"He needs help," Jordon acknowledged.

"And how can you help?" Maliik challenged. "You know nothing of my world. I don't even know who you are!"

"We knew nothing about the other world we went to, but managed to do fine there," Jeremy explained. "I'm Jeremy, this is Tyler, and he's Jordon."

Jordon placed a friendly hand on Maliik's shoulder. "Tell ya what," Jordon suggested. "Let us go with you to deliver these things to your father. Let us talk to him. After we've spoken with him, we'll all figure out if we're going to stay, or if we're coming home. Deal?"

About The Author

Jan is the mother of four, a lovable cat, and a cuddly dog. Five grandchildren call her "Nana." She has a vivid imagination and loves to weave adventures. The more outlandish the adventure, the better she likes it. Much of her story creating has been put to good use setting up Dungeons and Dragons quests for her children and their friends.

Jan started writing at thirteen as a way to cope with life's stress. Over the years, she has continued to learn about writing and has honed her skills. She enjoys encouraging young writers to continue writing and explore their imaginations.

Jan loves to read with favorite genres being fantasy (go figure) and sci-fi. She dabbles in art and computers, enjoys cake decorating, and collects vinyl and porcelain dolls.

Watch for the third book in the Asteria series, coming in 2022. Visit Jan's website at janmhill.com and sign up for her newsletter to stay up to date on all things Asteria.

CPSIA information can be obtained
at www.ICGtesting.com
Printed in the USA
LVHW020045121021
700156LV00002B/17